HAMBURG'S HYBRIDS

Hamburg's Hybrids

S. "FLIT" THOMAS

To order additional copies of this book, contact:
Xlibris
1-888-795-4274
www.Xlibris.com
Orders@Xlibris.com
727812

CONTENTS

I am the seed of the Nile
Planted on this green earth by Alpha and Omega
Infiltrated with His amazing spirit overflowing with His
Will, intellect, wisdom, knowledge, and understanding,
touching cultures from my birth land of Africa
To the vacant lands of Australia
I was here before you beheld His great creations
His voice brought land, moon, stars, and planets into existence
His hand clapping created plants, animals, and all that dwell
His breath invigorated life into all Homo sapiens' cultures
Many have tried to eliminate my influences
Eradicate my presence in personalities and characteristics
Downplay my intellect, wisdom, knowledge,
abilities, and understanding
Never, for Alpha and Omega is ingrained in my entire existence
No Homo sapiens has the tools to sever or cut the umbilical cord
Cut me into pieces, and I generate and I multiply
My regenerated life grows stronger and reaches deeper into all lands
Mightily overflowing with additional intellect, wisdom,
knowledge, abilities, and understanding
The evidence of my presence is apparent in
The North and the South
The East and the West
The good and the bad
In the just and the unjust
In the biased and the unbiased
In hatred and in love
Neither my presence nor my influences will ever dissipate!
For I am the seed of the Nile!

This novel is dedicated to the most wonderful parents in the universe: the charismatic, dynamic, caring, giving, and loveable father and mother, the late Col. Alfred and Lena (Barkley) Thomas. Thanks for guiding me in the right directions and providing a solid foundation for me to build upon. Thank you for using more words and less spanking to direct my path so I could become a productive adult. No, you did not spare the rod, but one of the best punishments was reading a book and either writing a brief synopsis of the lesson learned or orally answering questions about the novel. This type of behavior modification and correction opened up my desires to become an avid reader, gave me the opportunity to learn more about other countries and various cultures, as well as introduced me to a plethora of authors of written prose and novels. Yes, my range of reading ranges from nonfiction, historical data, self-help, biographies, inspirational, and fictional. Although you are not physically here to read the contents, I know heaven has made you aware of my accomplishments. All of my achievements and my accomplishments have been realized because of you instilling in me the knowledge of the will of God and how his love for his children will help them realize their dreams and visions. Thank you for pushing all six of your children to get excellent education, become productive citizens, and make sure you are active participants in some type of outreach or humanitarian project in your community. Thank you for implanting these aspects of life in my siblings and me. I try hard to ensure that my life is reflective of what you have taught me.

ROSITA SMYTH

I never thought an ancestor would open the door to reveal the parts of the puzzle missing from my mother's many conversations, but my position at the Langleys' estate began my journey down legacy row.

My name is Rosita Elena Hamburg-Petersen-Smyth. My mother is Helga Imelda DuPont Hamburg Petersen-Smyth, my brother (now deceased) is James Leon Hamburg Petersen-Smyth, and my sister is Helga Adolphus Hamburg Petersen-Smyth. Even as a little tot, my thoughts daily were wondering about my existence and whose DNA shaped me physically and psychologically. My mother had given each of us a string of surnames and would not give a logical reason for this action. My mind, spirit, and heart wanted desperately to fit into my existing culture and environment, but the longing in my heart told me there was more to me than what was reflected in my naked eyes.

When inquiring about the many surnames, my mother would say, "We are not a product of our environment, but of the spirit and chemical makeup of our ancestors. Each of these names provided us with a unique characteristic and personality that will guide and direct each of us into the destination carefully planned for our lives. We (meaning my mother, my sister, and my brother) are not like anyone else because of our existence and chemical makeup. We are uniquely designed to be place in the Hamburg dynasty. The creator understood this specification because he allowed your ancestors to make you unique."

From our many conversations about my ancestors and our lineage, I believed that my mother had been married twice. She knew the surname Petersen came from her mother, Lillian Anne. The Smyth surname was that of my father's; however, she could not remember nor did she want to remember the origin of the other names. At different times of our conversations, I would hear her distinctly whisper as though she was talking to her ancestors, "One day the Nile River will wash up the bones of not only my ancestors but those of your father's, and you will come to understand how unique you are."

It appears that my father was a dreamer. He had visions of owning his own business. When it did not materialize, he disappeared into the night, never looking back and never returning home.

On days when I was not working and my mother drifted in and out of time zones, I would quietly go into the attic and look at some of the old photographs of her family. Many of the antiques were locked up and I did not have access, but those I could retrieve told me I came from a long line of people whose DNA and ethnicity blend was so tight that I was not sure of any specific ethnicity I could officially claim.

I would listen to every word uttered by my mother during our sometimes sane conversations. She would always end her conversation with, "My life began and ended in Hamburg, South Carolina, a city that no longer exists, but if the grounds surrounding this area could talk, it would reveal a plethora of deep, dark secrets about the DuPont-Hamburg family."

My curiosity had me completing some research on the city since one of my surnames mirrored its name. Hamburg had once been a productive little place using the waterways between it and Augusta, Georgia. Most of the inhabitants of the city had vacated it by 1929; therefore, many historical facts related to my family had disappeared into never-never land.

There was a short historical trail where a few of the citizens, especially those with the last name of Hamburg, stayed until 1942 and either died on the land or migrated to other cities and states.

At times, I would cover my head and ears to block out the babbling of my mother regarding her make-believe life or real life in Hamburg, South Carolina. Her eyes would seem to lock in a certain position as though she was locked in space and time, dreaming of her past-life journey.

In my teens, bravery surfaced enough to ask the question, "Are your children freaks of nature, or did someone mess with our DNA and genetic makeup?"

She smiled, looked at the sky, and stated, "Only the one who is greater than us knows the real truth."

During those moments of bravery, my discussion with my mother would hinge upon my feelings regarding my chemical and physical makeup. She would look at me with those funny colored eyes that went from hazel to gray to blue, laugh, and say, "Rosa (my nickname), you are quite an inquisitive person. I see characteristics of your father, grandfather, and great-grandfather in you. Each of them had big ideas when it came to wealth, culture, environment, and their offspring."

She would look at me with a forlorn demeanor, throw her head back, and begin talking to maybe a spirit in the room. "If my grandfather were alive, he would be heralded as the one who had the hybrid breakthrough with animals, plants, and people. His study shaped the foundations for the study of the physical development and psychological behavior of animals, plants, and people. Many of his innovative ideas and inventions are the basis for continued research and development in those areas."

After her long and descriptive speech on our ancestors, she would drop into a deep sleep, mouth moving as though she were communicating with the past and head bobbing, responding to unheard questions. Never would she reveal what she saw, but she would turn around, look at the front door, and say, "One day soon, the ancestors will come through this very door and reveal the secrets that have been hidden in my grandmother's, mother's, and my heart. I have the proof locked away in my attic, and soon you will be able to understand our ancestry makeup."

While matriculating at Paine College in Augusta, Georgia, my inner restlessness and my longing to know more about myself kept me from finishing my degree in sociology/anthropology. After completing two years of academic training, my departure was plagued with ancestry questions and a child growing in my stomach. The answer to the puzzle still baffles me to this day—who are you?

Today is the day that my employer's, the late William Langley Sr., granddaughter is getting married. My mother is probably sitting somewhere in heaven or hell laughing, knowing that the ties between Mr. Langley and me are greater than employer and employee. What is so ironic, he never revealed the secret to his only surviving son, William Langley III.

The door did open, and I am sure it is going to be a cultural and social shock when the Langley offspring know how deep my relationship with them is ingrained into the facets of their life.

HETTIE IMELDA

After living in Augusta, Georgia, for about seven years, my mother quit her teaching position as a chemistry teacher and moved to Charleston, South Carolina, to continue her profession as a chemistry teacher.

Mother began her initial stages of dementia shortly after she was retired as the biology and chemistry teacher in one of the high schools in Charleston, South Carolina. It is as though it happened yesterday.

She was teaching her class and began lecturing her students more on anthropology than biology: "All of us have the same blood running through our veins and arteries, each of us has been blessed with the many nutrients from the seed of the Nile, and all of us are related regardless of culture, heritage, and ancestry. We all began on the continent of Africa, the cradle of civilization, the place where the spirit of all of us still linger and still hold hostage our ability to rid ourselves of the seed of the Nile's influences. Look at me, don't my features look like your sister, your cousin, your twin, or your aunt? Our DNA and genetic helix module are the same. Just like we make hybrids in plant and animals, we do the same with people."

My mother was removed from her classroom, questioned by many doctors regarding her comments, sent to the mental ward of the hospital for additional testing; however, she never changed her answers to the questions regarding heritage, DNA, blood, and the seed of the Nile. Eventually the school board put her on a disability retirement status at the age of fifty-eight.

During our dinner table discussions, my mother often talked about her four children: "Three beautiful daughters and a son," she would say. "Each had the eyes of the sky, hair as soft as cotton as silky as fine linens, flawless skin fair to dark, immeasurable intellect and love for all humanity.

Soon each of them will come together on common grounds, not knowing they are flesh of my flesh and bone of my bones. They will experience the love that my ancestors put into their inner soul. They will understand why the separation was necessary to establish our dynasty again." Then she would close her hazel eyes, and tears would stain her beautiful fair skin, skin that knew pain, but not age.

It appeared that her skin cells stopped aging when she turned fifty; gray hair only knew her temples, and aging spots were afraid to live on her flawless skin.

Where was this third daughter my mother would often speak of: "The wind carrying her in another direction to fulfill the legacy of our ancestors." The conclusion drawn from this statement was she lost the third one in childbirth and never came to grips with this loss. It was not clear if she was older or younger since it was only two daughters and a son that were raised together in Charleston, South Carolina. There was only a span of two to three years between each of us.

I gave my mother a party on her ninety-seventh birthday. No one at the party believed that my mother had reached her ninety-seventh birthday for she could have easily passed for the age of seventy-eight or seventy-nine.

On this day, however, the wings of dementia completely infiltrated her mind, body, and soul, never to escape again. Dementia began its visit before the age of fifty-eight, but on this day it decided to take permanent residence.

My mother had her good days and bad days, thus the reason a number of my friends didn't believe me that she was in the early stages of dementia, soon-to-be Alzheimer's.

Hettie could hold everyone's attention, by intelligently discussing the events of the era, whether political, social, technical, or religious. She would often speak of her grandfather, whose love for life and living things made him a genius in the area of crossbreeding and hybrids. She would also speak of how he had lectured on his hybrid projects in some of the most prestigious schools in America and abroad. She often spoke endlessly about the many books he had written. She would babble on how these documents were once in the library of the most prestigious schools; however, they were removed due to ignorance and jealousy.

She would look through me and state, "I have the proof of his work, locked not only in my heart and head but in a safe place where doubters cannot destroy. Soon one of the ancestors will deliver proof into the hands of those who doubt."

A smile would grace her beautiful face. "Oh, if my grandfather were alive, he would be the father of technology and innovation, the one who would find the formula to reduce the evils and ills of this world, justify the reasons for varied cultures, and show that all life has value." As though her body had used up all of its energy at that moment, she would drop her head and go into a world of either sleep or meditation.

My mother passed on without the ancestors ever coming through her front door, but the restlessness of knowing who my paternal and maternal lineages plagued me daily.

My oldest brother had attended West Point, majoring in electrical engineering. We were not sure what strings Mom pulled to get him into that prestigious school, but he did attend and graduate. When asked, her answer was, "Because of your ancestors."

My brother James died in the Vietnam War at the young age of twenty-eight. My mother cried and mourned privately about this loss for more than five years. She would often say the war and this society attempted to destroy my connection to the Nile, but my daughters will continue to pass on the seed of the Nile.

My youngest sister, Helga, was more than ready to leave this madhouse, so at the age of seventeen, the day after she received her high school diploma, she packed her bags, emptied her bank account, legally changed her name to Helen Adele Smith (Smyth), moved to Augusta, Georgia, and eventually to Baltimore, Maryland. As the years increased, we heard less and less from Helga (Helen) until there was no connection and no contact.

Even though my mother received a small pension from her years of teaching to help pay for her in home nursing care, it was not enough to maintain everyday living expenses and the care for my son.

Due to pregnancy, bewilderment, and confusion, my academic degree was not obtained until later on in life; therefore, with my limited education and professional skills, the only business available to me was a cleaning service.

How little did I know that this business would open the front door to my ancestral past.

JENNIFER DUSETT-LANGLEY

Jennifer Dusett-Langley sat on the side of her Thomasville king-sized bed, gazing out of the bay window of her master bedroom. Her eyes scanned the beautiful gardens, the tennis court, the Olympic-size pool, and the several cabanas on the grounds. As tears slowly developed in the corners of her eyes, a single drop bounced from her silk bathrobe onto the satin sheets. Was she dreaming, or had life indeed been this real for her—a little girl from a small town in Barbour County, Alabama?

Another tear slowly dropped. She wiped the wetness from her eyes with the sleeve of her silk robe. *Yes, this was real. I own all of this with my husband of twenty-nine years, William Edwin Langley III.* A smile developed on her beautiful face, and her blue eyes became clouded with several more tears as she whispered, "This is for you, Mom and Dad."

According to my aunt Onnie, who raised me, my parents, Lawrence and Suzanne Barclay-Dusett, were killed in an automobile accident when I was four years old.

Yes, I had read about my parents over and over in the little town newspaper. Dr. and Mrs. Dusett were leaving a medical conference in Montgomery, Alabama, returning to their home. The article revealed that Dr. Dusett was probably tired and fell asleep at the wheel, hitting an oncoming 18-wheeler on Highway 431. Each of them was killed instantly.

Another tear dropped on her silk gown. Yes, she had missed growing up with parents, knowing the warmth of their love, smile, and embrace. *However, my aunt Onnie had made sure I had more than enough to go around.*

What was puzzling her this day was not so much her ancestral background and who loved her but the package she was holding in her hand. The day of her daughter Bria's wedding, the late William Sr.'s personal lawyer delivered a package to her. According to the lawyer, the package was to be delivered on the day of his firstborn granddaughter's wedding day and only to his daughter-in-law, Jennifer Dusett Langley.

Jennifer turned the package over. She was afraid to open it since it may contain information that would impede the beautiful wedding she had planned for her beloved Bria.

The lawyer had assured her that the late William Sr. had confided in him that the information would be more of a revealing and a cleansing for him than an opposition to his granddaughter's marriage. Yes, my beloved Bria's marriage vows would be with one whose ethnicity was different from hers; however, the family had come to love and respect the family of Marcus H. Jennings II. The only person who had a problem was William Sr.'s widow, Tessa.

As she removed the handwritten document from the leather-bound case, several documents fell out. Some were ledgers written in Old English style. A quick glance revealed it contained maybe names of people who may have some connection with the Langley family. Beside each of these names were some codes that Jennifer had no knowledge of as to their purpose. These ledgers were very old, some of them dating back to the early 1700.

As she flipped through these documents, some very old photographs dropped to the floor. As she bent down to retrieve them, she stopped. The young lady or young girl in the picture looked so familiar. Why would William Sr. give her an early photo of Rosa? What would Rosa have to do with the Langley family?

She did not want to let the contents of this package put a damper on today's joyous occasion; therefore she would just place it in the safe until she had the opportunity to read it.

In fact, today was all about family. The good times the Dusett and Langley families had experience and the joy of joining with the family of Dr. and Mrs. Marcus H. Jennings of Maryland.

She was focus on making sure her daughter Bria's wedding day was inundated with love, affection, joy, peace, excitement, blissfulness, harmony, and enthusiasm. Whatever was William Sr.'s reason for choosing this day is beyond her reasoning. Any other day would have been better than this day.

As she reached down to retrieve the photographs, she observed her limousine pull up to the front door. Yes, this was the day for family to rally around her precious daughter, Bria. Not a day of confusion and chaos. In fact, there would be enough drama, since Tessa and her aunt Onnie were always on opposite ends of the spectrum when it came to family.

ONNIE DUSETT

Another smile formed on Jennifer's face as she watched her aunt and her aunt's personal assistant, Florence, slowly get out of the car. She was dressed impeccably as always, and her gait, her physical condition, her flawless skin, nor her wit and direct responses would reveal that she was in her eighties.

My aunt Onnie, what a character she was! It would take Charles Dickens, James Patterson, Danielle Steele, and James Grisham to write an account of her lifestyle. It was not commonly known where my aunt had acquired many of her personal possessions, but she owned a large parcel of land and a number of businesses in Barbour County, Alabama.

My aunt Onnie often spoke fondly of her mother and implied there was a wealthy man (her father, the resident doctor in the county) in her mother's life. This man had moved my grandmother from Columbia, South Carolina, to be close to her and her two children, my dad, and my aunt Onnie. No, they were not married, but my dad and aunt were his biological children.

In fact my grandfather had an established family in Eufaula, Alabama. He was one of the practicing doctors in the city, owned the only hospital that would admit people of all ethnicities and several businesses. From all indications, I know he was the one who established the many businesses for my grandmother and my aunt.

When my aunt was in a melancholy and talkative mood, we would sit in the large living room where the walls were adorned with two large oil paintings of her mother and father. It appeared that my grandmother was probably about fifty and my grandfather was fifty-five in these pictures. As a child, my mind would mentally paint a picture of the love triangle of my grandmother and my biological grandfather.

Aunt Onnie, who raised me after the death of my parents, had been classically trained at Julliard and Boston Conservatory of Music. I was aware that she had begun her professional career as an opera singer with the New York Opera House. She had been the understudy for a number of famous opera singers, and she performed several times at Carnegie Hall.

Even after the death of my parents, she continued performing as a guest singer at different opera venues throughout the country.

I can never remember her being bitter regarding her inability to fulfill her dream as an opera singer. Several years after performing in New York, she had to return to Alabama to be the caregiver for her mother.

Upon returning to Alabama from New York, she began running the businesses that had been established by my grandmother. She was the person that notarized a number of documents for many of the farmers and domestic workers in the area regardless of their culture. She also owned the nearest independent grocery store, a pecan orchard, and several pieces of rental property.

Her home and the home my parents once occupied were the largest two in the area. At an early age prior to me going to private school in another state, a male friend of my aunt would come and visit. She would often say he was a friend she met while performing in New York. He and his chauffeur would stay in the home owned by my parents.

I later found out that he was also a close friend of her half brother.

Sitting on the side of my bed reminiscing about my formative years, my thoughts were on my parents and how they would feel about their oldest granddaughter's wedding day. My only daughter, Bria, is getting married today, and I would love to provide my family with an insight of their family tree; however, with my aunt Onnie deep into the beginning stages of dementia, this may never happen.

I closed my eyes reminiscing about my formative years with my aunt Onnie; I physically looked more like her than my parents. I had her pale skin, her hazel/blue eyes, her long face, brunette hair with blonde streaks, and a small mole on the lower left side of my nose. Well, anyway, from these descriptions, I knew I was a Dusett.

Was something in William's package that would shatter my knowledge of who I really am? I know my aunt Onnie would have disclosed this to me for she never kept secrets from me. In fact, she often said to me, "I often tell you about my formative years for I want you to know everything about the Dusett family. I will not hold anything back from you."

How often I had expressed to Aunt Onnie how much I loved her and adored her for clothing me in the spiritual, moral, ethical, and educational fabrics of her inheritance to make me what I am today. As a single woman she had used her tenacity, wit, charm, and intellect to mold and shape me into what I had become—a very successful wife, mother, and civil rights attorney.

To no one in particular since I was the only one in the room, I heard my inner voice saying I wished my parents were here to see their beautiful granddaughter, Bria, on her wedding day or that my aunt's mind was void of dementia to really know that what is happening, for today is a true testimony of her love for my family and me.

A smile again formed on her face, for no one knew her aunt Onnie like she did. It would be fun for all to see her in action without dementia. They would be in awe seeing her barking out orders and directions to the wedding planner, the chef, the lawn service, the florist, and anyone else who would be involved in this great occasion. I can imagine the stern look on her face—"What part of 'do this' don't you understand?" If she did not have the onset of dementia, I know she would have placed herself on the wedding reception program in order to toast her beloved great-niece, Bria.

I must remind Florence and Rosa to keep an eye on Tessa and Onnie, for we do not need any drama on this beautiful day.

Jennifer placed the package and pictures on her dressing table. She must remember to place them in a safe place prior to the wedding. She was still captivated by the picture of Rosa, but when she turned it over, it had the name Katerina at the age of thirteen and it was addressed to Maman Hettie.

Why does this lady resemble Rosa? Well, it is said that everyone has a twin.

THE SPA TREATMENT

As Jennifer continued to stare out of the window, her thoughts were interrupted with a knock on the bedroom door. She gained her composure, wiped her tears and nose with her silk robe, and answered, "Yes, who is it?"

"It's me, madam, Rosa. I brought up some coffee, pastries, and fruit for you. I thought you might want a light breakfast before the wedding festivities."

Jennifer moved toward the door. "Come in, Rosa, and place the tray on the table in the sitting room."

Jennifer watched Rosa as she stepped down into the sitting room. She had been with the Langley family for over forty years, probably knew a number of the secrets hidden in the walls and grounds of this enormous place.

"Rosa, do you know if Edwin has had breakfast? If not, let him know you have prepared a tray for us in the sitting room."

"Yes, Mrs. Langley. Mr. Langley and your sons just finished eating. In fact Edwin—I mean Mr. Langley—is on his way to Bria's room. It must be the wedding jitters, because Bria did not want any breakfast and only asked for orange juice and tea. I am sure he is there in her room calming her nerves and trying to influence her to eat something."

As Rosa ascended the steps into the bedroom, she stated, "Don't worry, Mrs. Langley, I am sure she'll be OK. All brides have jitters on this special day. I can remember you and your reaction, but what I remember most was your aunt Onnie. She really had control of the situation on that day. Everyone who was assisting—and I do mean everyone—did not want to cross your aunt or make a mistake. The small string orchestra sat in the corner fearing the worst from your aunt. The caterer continued to ask me to sample the food, and the coordinator was a nervous wreck. In the end, it all came together beautifully, and you were such a graceful and beautiful bride. Just look at you, after twenty-nine years, your beauty is still shining through."

Rosa walked closer to the dressing table and placed her hand on Mrs. Langley's shoulder. All the years she had worked for the family, she could sense the mood of each member. Mrs. Langley's eyes and nose were red; therefore, Rosa's sixth sense told her something was eating away at her.

Mrs. Langley was always very poised and graceful, even when she was handling a difficult professional or personal problem. Today it appeared she was not handling an activity or a situation very well since her poise and her demeanor were so not her.

Jennifer felt Rosa's arm around her, and she looked up at her. "Rosa, don't worry about me, I'll be just fine. It must be Mother's jitters. I would appreciate if you start preparing my bath. Include some bath salts and oil in the Jacuzzi tub."

Rosa had been with them for a long time, and she felt almost like family, but her gut feeling knew Jennifer was not her usual self. As she began to walk toward the bathroom, her eyes focused on the package that was on the dressing table, especially the picture. It almost put her in a state of shock for the lady on the photograph could have been her mother's twin.

Rosa could feel her body turn hot, then cold, and her hands began to shake. She wanted to ask Jennifer about the picture but decided to hold off because of the event of the day. However, she placed the information in her photographic memory for her intentions were to broach the subject with Jennifer later on in the week.

Jennifer must have felt the tremble in Rosa's body.

Jennifer patted Rosa's hand and stated, "I am just in a melancholic mood thinking about the Dusett side of the family, especially my aunt Onnie. I am going to be fine. Today is just an emotional day for me."

Rosa quickly exited to the bathroom. She knew if she had stayed there a minute longer, not only would she have picked up the photo, but she would have also asked why she had it on her dressing table.

Jennifer looked down at the dressing table. Her heart skipped a beat. Why didn't she put that up before she invited Rosa into her bedroom suite? In her mind she was hoping that Rosa had not seen the picture, but who was she fooling?

Yes, she saw it, and like Rosa always did when she learned more of the Langleys' secrets, she kept her mouth closed.

I will discreetly ask her questions to see if she had honed in on the picture.

WILLIAM LANGLEY SR.

As Rosa entered the bath/dressing area, she began to remember her first encounter with Jennifer's father-in-law, Mr. William Edwin Langley Sr. She did not meet his second wife, Mrs. Tessa Adkins-Langley, until months later.

One Friday afternoon, while working late in his main office building, the door of his office was ajar, and I noticed he was just looking intensely at the Charleston Harbor.

I walked into his office. "Working late tonight, Mr. Langley? You know it's after 10:00 PM."

"Hi, Rosa, is it that late? I had so much on my to-do list, the time just slipped away. I guess I need to get up and leave so you can finish your tasks."

"Don't mind me, Mr. Langley, I can clean the offices across the hall and then come back to your office. My team and I usually complete our tasks around 11:30 PM, so I have plenty of time."

"Rosa, I keep looking at your features, and you remind me so much of someone I once knew. Did you grow up around here, or is your family from another city in South Carolina?"

"Mr. Langley, with the number of diverse workers you have in your plants from different parts of the country, I am sure among them, there is someone who may look like me and have features and skin tone the same as me."

"No, Rosa, there is something about your personality and your entire demeanor that reminds me of my friend."

"Well, let me see. My mother, whose name was Hettie Imelda DuPont Hamburg Petersen-Smyth, was very vague about her ancestors. However, she did provide as much information as possible to my siblings and me. My brother James Leon Hamburg Petersen-Smyth died in the Vietnam conflict. My sister Helen (Helga) Smith (Smyth), with whom we lost contact almost twenty years ago, lived in a number of cities, and the last one was Baltimore, Maryland.

"When we were young, Mom would say we came from a nowhere land, a city in South Carolina named Hamburg. After the turn of the twentieth century, the city no longer existed.

"It appears that a German or Polish man—or he could have been from some other country—named Henry Schultz founded the town in 1821. He named the town after his good friend and business partner William Hamburg. I remember the names of the persons my mother discussed, but I do not remember much about them.

"She often talked of a Lillian Malveaux, a Helga Malveaux DuPont, a Lillian Anne DuPont-Hamburg-Petersen, and a Mary Elizabeth DuPont. My mother, Hettie Imelda DuPont Hamburg Petersen-Smyth, worked for some time in Augusta, Georgia, and then she migrated to Charleston, South Carolina, where she worked as a biology and chemistry teacher in the school system.

"I don't know much about my father. She just said he disappeared somewhere in Augusta, Georgia. I am not sure if a real husband or father was in the picture. I can say though all three of her children looked like the man in the picture she claimed was our father.

"Her mother's name was Lillian Anne Hamburg. She thinks she left Hamburg and settled in New York at the age of sixteen or seventeen. Lillian Anne returned to Hamburg at the age of twenty-one to deliver her firstborn, my mother. From listening to my mother's account of the situation, somewhere between the ages of sixteen and twenty-one, my grandmother had married someone by the name of Charles Henry Petersen, a musician.

"My grandmother returned to New York after the birth of my mother, Hettie Imelda Hamburg-Petersen. Neither my grandmother nor the father of the child ever contacted my great-grandparents. My great-grandparents raised my mother.

"According to my mother's storytelling, her grandmother Helga also had two older sons from her relationship with the plantation owner, Adolph Hamburg. Both of her uncles attended the Naval Academy and were given instructions to never to return home or contact their family, but blend into the fabric of America.

"There was a younger sister or daughter in the family whose name she was forbidden to mention in her grandmother's home. This sister or daughter was taken away at an early age and given to the father's sister in Charleston.

"From my limited knowledge and if I remember the story, the father of this child was of French descent, who eventually went back to France. After placing the child in his sister's home in Charleston, he never tried to contact my mother's grandmother. I may have some distant relatives such as cousins or maybe an aunt somewhere in France or the United States of America."

"Rosa, what an interesting story. You do remind me of someone I know. It escapes me right now, but I will remember later on. I will gather my business information and leave you to cleaning my office."

As William Sr. exited the office, he looked back at Rosa. *How interesting*, he thought, *because my first wife, whose name was Katerina Amelia Hamburg Petersen-DeBeaux, before her death told me a little about her ancestry, and it appears her family also migrated from Hamburg to Charleston. Rosa does have some of her features and some of her qualities.*

He paused at the door of his office, looked at Rosa, and asked, "How do you spell the Petersen in your last name? Is it with a 'sen' or a 'son'?"

"It's funny you would ask that, Mr. Langley. My mother would often state that one culture of the people on the Hamburg-Petersen farm when born usually bore the name of Petersen with the 'sen' or the 'son.' She did not understand the reason, but her grandmother often told her it had something to do with a special code and the *Seed of the Nile*."

Rosa remembered how he looked at her, opened the door of his office to exit, and stated, "This has been more than interesting, and I would like to hear more, but I need to get home to get me some rest and let you continue your tasks."

He put out his hand and shook mine, smiled, and said, "We will continue this discussion soon, but I also have another matter to discuss with you. Have a good evening, Rosa, and I will speak to you soon."

My thoughts began to wander back to some of the conversations my mother and I would have. There was no way this man's first wife could have been related to our family.

My ancestors may have been born and reared in the same city of South Carolina, but knowing my mom, she probably changed her name from Peterson to "sen." For some odd reason, the spelling of the surnames was significant to your environment, your culture, and your acceptance in the community. It also afforded you opportunities that others could not fathom.

Little did I know that from that day forward, I would be hired as the chief engineer of Mr. Langley's estate, household operations. I took over this position after the death of the senior Mr. Langley's first wife, Katerina Hamburg Petersen DeBeaux Langley, and his daughter Ophelia.

THE JOB PROPOSAL

H is current wife, Tessa Adkins-Langley, and he had only been married about three years before I assumed this position. His son by his first marriage, W. Edwin III, was about ten or eleven years old. I was twenty-two years old when I began my position in the Langley household.

My primary source of income was from a small cleaning service that had contracts with several of Mr. Langley's office buildings. In fact, I am sure he was not aware that his HR staff had interviewed me and he had signed off on their recommendation.

After my initial face-to-face meeting with him, and my sketchy description of my ancestors to him, Mr. Langley took an interest in my small business. He allowed his lawyers to help me organize my cleaning business and acquire some additional contracts within the city.

The day he presented this information to me, I thought this was the end of my source of income, some rich man trying to take over my lucrative cleaning services. How did I know it was the beginning of something wonderful and unimaginable? The statement from my mother flashed before my eyes: "Ancestors walking through the front door."

Maybe a month or two after our original conversation, Mr. Langley called me into his office.

"Have a seat, Rosa. My lawyer and I reviewed your business plan and your current business operations. We were able to improve upon your current business plan and organize your current operational plans to help you develop this small business into a more profitable one. In addition, we were able to acquire you several large accounts in the city. My accounting staff will help you with your payroll and your responsibilities with the state and federal governments."

"Mr. Langley, I don't know what to say. I do appreciate you taking an interest in my cleaning services, but I don't understand why you are taking such an interest in me."

"Rosa, I have watched you over the years, and I have noticed what a good relationship you have with your work team. Your employees value you as their boss. You have a certain way when you speak to your workers, and they respect you for that. Since you took over the cleaning service operation in two of my businesses, I have never had any complaints. I am sure you are aware of the prior cleaning service and the problems we had with them before we terminated their contract."

"Yes, but all this for me, I will never be able to repay you, and I am truly grateful. As a single mother with two children, I could use the additional funds. My future plan is to ensure that each of my children would earn a college degree and an advanced degree. The additional funds will help me realize my dreams for my sons. Thank-you is not enough for what you are doing for me."

"Don't get hasty. I need you to read over this business plan and the business operations. I have scheduled a meeting between you and my legal staff. Read the document carefully for the meeting is scheduled within the next two weeks. If you have any questions, we can discuss them prior to the scheduled meeting."

"Mr. Langley, I am really puzzled. Why are you taking such an interest in me? I hope there's nothing in this plan that will cause me to have to forfeit my business to your conglomerate. I have worked too hard in establishing this business."

"Rosa, I assure you that is not the case. If you wish, you can always engage the services of another lawyer to review the plans with you. My father was always helping others to establish themselves, and yes, he sometimes lost a lot of investment monies on companies that failed. I promised myself that I, too, would do some outreach to help others who are trying to establish a lucrative business. I have seen you and your business savvy, and I like what I see. I am only trying to enhance what you have already established."

I stood up and shook Mr. Langley's hand, took the folder he had prepared for me, and walked out of his office. In my mind I thought I will make sure he is not trying to sabotage my business. I will have another lawyer review these documents before I made a decision.

"Rosa, have you completed your MBA? I overheard you talking about it to one of your workers."

"No, I had to put it on hold because of my business and my three sons. I was determined to complete my BS since I dropped out with my oldest son. I plan to go back, but must be able to take care of my parental responsibilities."

"Just was wondering, Rosa, maybe with the new business plan you may not have to put it on hold."

"Thanks, Mr. Langley, and I will get back to you regarding the proposed business plan."

Later as our relationship grew, Mr. Langley (William) expressed that he took an interest in me because of my personality; he felt that I could be trusted to see and hear intricate matters within the Langley household.

He often said to me, "It was something about you that I really liked, and I knew you would hear and see all, but keep it to yourself. What has really intrigued me the most was your close resemblance to my deceased wife and the strange string of surnames, especially the surnames of Malveaux, DuPont, Hamburg, and Petersen. I have several genealogists looking into these names and will discuss their findings with you later."

I looked at Mr. Langley, smiled, and said, "It's OK for you to do research, but remember the culture of my ancestors and our existence are based upon another man's culture, research, and documentation. Our ancestry history is usually based upon oral history and not written history."

He smiles and stated, "We'll see."

During one of our conversations, I had once mentioned to Mr. Langley that my grandmother, whose name was Lillian Anne DuPont-Hamburg-Petersen, lived in a city whose spelling was similar to her middle surname. It was some type of family tradition to affix these strings of names to ensure the future ancestors would be knowledgeable of their legacy.

I do believe this reference piqued Mr. Langley's curiosity. I am not sure, but I do believe this information helped Mr. Langley make the decision to hire me as the chief of staff for his household operations.

At first when he asked me, I had said no to his proposal. I felt uneasy about this proposal. He reassured me that my employment with the Langley family would be an asset to both families. Of course I was a little leery—why would this man want to help me?

Now I know the ancestors that my mother often spoke of had surely opened the doors and the windows.

As our relationship grew, William (what I called him in private, but Mr. Langley around Ms. Tessa and the staff) talked more and more about his deceased wife's ancestry, his current wife's deceit and secrets, and how he was in love with his mistress. I knew quite well how to keep my mouth shut because the monetary salary he was paying was much more than I had ever thought I would make. This salary would definitely help me send my two children to college and help me pay for my MBA.

Oh by the way, it must have been in my DNA—three children, no spouse, and no prospect. Was there another dark secret to this madness of my life that I did not understand?

Within twelve months after my initial meeting with Mr. Langley, I had become the chief engineer in charge of the daily operations of the Langley household.

Mr. Langley's legal staff had also helped me acquire several contracts with a number of the small businesses and office buildings within the city. My oldest son, who was now in elementary school, was able to attend one of the preparatory schools in the area.

TESSA ADKINS LANGLEY

When I took the position as the chief engineer in charge of daily operations, the new Mrs. Langley (Tessa) had only been a member of the family a little more than three years. She was once the full-time head nurse of the children's department at Memorial Hospital. William Sr. had been introduced to Tessa by the wife of one of his partners in his law firm, Jonathan Mandalay. His wife, Annie Mandalay, a pediatrician working out of Memorial Hospital, was a colleague of Tessa. She had invited William Sr. and Tessa to a formal dinner at their home.

William confided in me that he was drawn to this beautiful small-framed woman who was passionate about her work, loved to help others, was well-educated, and especially showed she had enough love for all of the children in her department. He and Tessa had dated for a little over two years when he decided she would be the ideal person to provide maternal guidance to his young son.

As he stated to me almost with a slight smirk, "I was not in love with her. I loved her grace, her charm, and her ability to interact with others regardless of culture and wealth. Her smile and her laugh had won me over."

Even though William Sr. had only been in the company of her parents three or four times, he was sure they would embrace their relationship.

Who wouldn't? This eligible rich bachelor, known throughout the South and southeastern areas for his many businesses and his business savvy. However, when he would frequent the Adkins' home to pick Tessa up for a date or just to visit, he would often see signs of worry and reservation on Tessa's mother's face.

I became aware that Tessa's father (who died while they were dating) was a man of few words and only spoke or responded when necessary. He had worked in one of the Langleys' textile factories, where he had been employed as the manager of the quality assurance operations. Mrs. Adkins had been a housewife.

To him they seemed more reserved than happy to have their daughter date such a high-profile bachelor in the city, but for the need of maternal guidance for his son, he ignored the signs.

I remember him telling me that "Tessa's parents were invited to the Thanksgiving dinner in November of 1967, the day he proposed, but was declined due to her father's failing health."

He stated, "I had discussed my marriage intentions with the parents prior to the invitation. They both seemed pleased and stated they were happy for their daughter. However, the mother did ask if her daughter had discussed her family with him."

William thought maybe she had been married prior to this and just went back to her maiden name. Her parents assured him that she had not been married before and did not have any children.

William advised me that he asked pointed questions about her medical conditions. Again he was reassured that she was in great physical health. The Adkins made sure William was aware of their Irish bloodline and how it would blend well with the Langleys' English bloodline.

Again, William could not put his finger on it, but Tessa's mother did not show the kind of enthusiasm a mother of the bride would; however, he attributed it to the age of the daughter. Tessa was in her middle thirties and had never been married. This was unusual for a young professional woman in the 1960s. Therefore, he went ahead with his plan because he felt of all the women he had dated, Tessa would be a good maternal influence on his son.

I listened intently as he continued with his conversation.

"After the death of my first wife, there had been several women suitors, but none I thought would be a good fit for my son like Tessa. Tessa's charming personality and her commitment to her position at Memorial Hospital and the care she provided for her aging parents were turning points for me. I liked the way her face would glow when she talked about the infants or the children under her care. She especially paid close attention to the children with rare diseases and those needing constant medical attention.

"I had discussed with her about my daughter and wife's rare blood disease, but for some reason, never told her the name of the disease or what the doctor stated about this disease being more in people of another culture."

This was the first time I had heard him discuss the cause of deaths of his first wife, Katerina, and his daughter, Ophelia.

"It amazed me that as a highly skilled nurse, she never asked me any questions about the disease that destroyed the lives of two people that I dearly loved, my first wife and daughter."

Then he looked at me and began to tear up. I could not imagine what he would disclose next.

"Later on in our initial relationship, we had discussed the possibility of having a child of our own. Edwin was an only child, and the idea of a younger brother or sister brought sparkles to Edwin's eyes. She agreed with me and even stated, 'I am sure my Irish bloodline will mix well with your English bloodline.'"

He put his hands on my shoulder, using the other to wipe away the one tear that lingered in his eye.

"I never expected a woman who seemed to love children as much as Tessa would find ways not to let her pregnancy go full term. I am still not sure if all three of them were natural miscarriages."

He sighed again but continued his conversation.

"We often talked about her parents' reservations, and she would say, 'Oh, don't pay them any attention. It has something to do with an ancestor on my father's side that was either a thief or a robber.' She would smile and say, 'With my knowledge of genetics, this behavior is not genetically transferrable.'"

As Mr. Langley continued to relay this story to me, tears would develop in his eyes.

"How could I have known she was really harboring a secret about her family genealogy? She just did not appear to be that type of person. I wonder if she had initially told me the truth, would I have gone through with the marriage. When you think you know someone and have met the one you can count upon to be your companion and helpmate for life, why do they change after the marriage?"

I looked him in the eye and place my hand upon his hand that was still on my shoulder.

"William, the signs were there. You just didn't read them correctly."

I bet any amount of money that Tessa was very excited about her pending marriage to William, a man of great status and wealth in the

Charleston community. I could tell from reading the *Charleston Gazette* social pages that she had assumed the role of wife and stepmom to Edwin with the greatest of ease and portrayed herself as the esteemed wife of the Mr. William Langley Sr.

Her pictures in all of the articles showed her as a loving and faithful wife and mother. No one could tell from the many pictures that this woman, Tessa Adkins Langley, was harboring a secret—her family genealogy.

What always puzzled me was why she did not quit her position at the hospital. She was now married to one of the wealthiest men in the Charleston area; therefore, money could not have been her motive.

SECRETS, DECEPTIONS, AND HEARTACHES

I could tell from my many conversations with William he had wanted Tessa to quit the position at the hospital, but he felt she had a passion for her work and the children under her care. William would often state that she used her wit and her charm before and after the marriage to convince him. Her primary goal was to show she could be dynamic in both roles.

Not just being the wife of Mr. William Langley Sr. but as a confident director and head nurse and businesswoman who had worked hard to make the children's section of the hospital was known throughout this country and other countries. Indeed, she had accomplished this! Many interns from several prestigious medical schools did their pediatric internship and specialization studies at this hospital.

Tessa had convinced William that even with that position, she could run the household, be a good wife to him, accompany him on his business trips, and be a good stepmother to Edwin III.

As I continued to prepare Jennifer's—I mean Mrs. Langley's bath, my mind wandered to the year that William had been diagnosed with prostate cancer. I had worked with his assigned nurse and others to ensure he would be comfortable upon his return from the hospital.

Prior to the nurse entering the room, he looked at me and said, "Rose, we have had a number of conversations, but today I want you to know that I wish that I had introduced my mistress to Edwin. I never imagined myself having a mistress all these years. However, it was the most gratifying experience I have ever had."

I really did not understand that statement until years later during his years of debilitating illness and after his death. What I saw and what I heard made his statement a much more vivid reason for his infidelity.

As I began to put a little more salts and bath oils in the tub, I smiled for people on the outside looking in would never agree with me. We are so externally moral when it comes to others looking at our lives and with us assessing someone else's life; however, most of us could not begin to write a book on morals based on our own personal behaviors.

My mind went back to the conversation between William and me the day he returned home from the hospital following his cancer treatment.

I looked him straight in the eye as I adjusted the pillows under his head.

"If you were so unhappy and had to acquire a mistress to fulfill your needs, why did you stay with her?"

William stated, "I stayed with Tessa because I had grown very fond of her and her ability to take on the role of Mrs. William Langley. She was very successful as chairperson for several charitable organizations, improving the medical facilities for the children's portion of the hospital, but I loathed her deception and lies about who lived inside her."

"If you could turn back the hands of time, would you do things a little differently?"

"I am not sure, for initially she was a good wife for me and a good stepmom to my son. I admired her for these traits, her strength, her tenacity, her ability to interact well with others within the business and social world, her finesse as a great hostess, and how much she had accomplished personally and professionally by the age of thirty."

With his head bowed and hands folded across his chest, his response to me was, "After the two miscarriages, she changed drastically. She became a different woman, one that seemed to surface out of nowhere. In other words, she took on the persona of her father, and it has stayed with her all of these years."

William placed his hand oddly against his heart and stated, "Now that I look back on the situation, I guess we used each other. It was more of a marriage of convenience. I could not put my finger on it until the day you . . ." His voice trailed off.

He never finished the sentence because he heard Tessa and the home nurse coming down the hallway to his room.

Tessa entered the room and introduced the home nurse to William and me.

She looked at me and stated, "Rosa, if you have other tasks to complete, I can discuss the home care procedures with the home nurse.

As a previous nurse, I am very familiar with the medical procedures. If your assistance is needed later, I will let you know."

I watched her as she walked close to William's bed.

In her role as a pretend caring wife, she leaned over and kissed William's forehead and asked him how he felt.

As I started toward the door, William stated, "Since Rosa will be assisting the home nurse with my care, I prefer she stays in the room to hear your instructions."

I could tell from the look on Tessa's face she did not like his statement, but she formed a false smile on her face and looked at me with a lot of distain and said, "It's OK if you want her to stay, dear."

I looked away for there was not only distain but also fire and venom flowing from her nose and mouth. I watched as she lovingly rubbed his shoulders and back as she provided the medical procedures and directions to the home nurse. Not only was she a skillful nurse, but her acting skills that day outweighed her nursing skills. I thoroughly enjoyed the performance she was putting on for her audience, the home nurse.

As she and the nurse prepared to exit the room, she again leaned over and kissed William. Then she looked through me, focusing on the window that overlooked the beautiful grounds that Jacob had landscaped.

"Rosa, the home nurse will start tomorrow at 8:00 AM. Make sure he takes his afternoon medicines, and I can provide medical assistance throughout the night."

During her tenure as the director of the children's hospital and a seasoned nurse, several articles had been written about Tessa's skill as a director and a stellar nurse as well as the exceptional job she had done to improve the conditions and medical acumen in the children's portion of the hospital. Many of the pediatric doctors looked up to her and sought her opinion regarding some of the complicated children's illnesses.

Once William was aware that Tessa and the nurse had departed, he continued his conversation with me. "I would be so angry sometimes when she was more involved in the operations of the hospital and would not participate in some of Edwin's school activities. I guess that was the reason I put him in a private school out of state, so when I visited, I did not have to give him an excuse why Tessa wasn't there. I think she often felt bad when she declined to participate, but she still did not show signs of giving up her status or her position."

"William, maybe she had something to prove to herself and others."

"I know why I like you, Rosa, because you are so insightful."

"Not sure about that, but I believe that many of us live in a semifairyland. We try to make whole those areas of life that was broken during our adolescence and young adult years."

"What you are trying to say is Tessa knew about her internal struggles and wanted her external aura to look different."

"Yeah, but I am not a psychologist and do not have a degree in this area unless my MBA makes me an expert."

He smiled and said OK. "Dr. Smyth, give me your professional opinion."

"I think people like Tessa try to overshadow their childhood hurts and abuse whether physical or mental by helping whom they perceive as the ones who have experienced misfortunes, illnesses, mistreatment, and loneliness. In her mind, you and the children in her department were in such a place, and she felt she had the formula to remove those experiences and feelings. Remember you had recently lost your wife and your child. Her caring and outreach behaviors were ways to mask her own hurts and to prove her worthiness to those who had thought she was unworthy— especially her father, the one she loved and adored."

"I never thought about it that way."

"William, you were in all of those places when you met her, and I am certain she sensed your vulnerability and used it to her advantage."

"Rosa, I guess you may have a point. She did have something to prove, and I clearly understood that once you provided those documents about her and her family.

"Do you think she knows it was you that made copies for me?"

I looked at him and shook my head no. "Remember those papers surfaced when she was experiencing a mini meltdown after you questioned her about her female problems and why she kept keeping them a secret. Therefore I am not sure if she remembered which one of us really saw the documents."

"Prior to having that information, I would often ask Tessa if the prenuptial agreement had any bearing on her decisions, but she would look at me, smile, and say, 'No, William, my parents left me a small inheritance, I've made some investments, so if you decide to leave, I can take care of myself.'

"She would never give me a solid answer as to why she could not carry our child full term. I suggested us visiting a fertility specialist in New

York, but she refused. I now understand what she was trying to conceal. Her birth certificate information made me aware of her personal secret."

"Well, William, I guess she had a point. She had a career, an inheritance, a prenuptial agreement, and a BIG *secret*." We both laughed at the statement.

MORE LIES AND DECEPTIONS

Rosa continued with the preparation of Jennifer's bath, but it seemed like only yesterday when she and William had another conversation regarding Tessa's instant personality change. She had become more demanding, sometimes rude to the housing staff, and would pout when William would not change his business meetings and schedules to fit her plans.

One Friday afternoon upon his return from a business trip to New York, he noticed how stressed Tessa was and again expressed his desire for her to quit the position at the hospital.

William was not aware that she was pregnant with their second child and was threatening another miscarriage. Therefore, when her OB/GYN physician called him to come to the hospital, he was stunned, livid, and angry.

After leaving the hospital visiting Tessa, William asked me to join him in his study. I knew something was bothering him, since William seldom drank alone. He was more of a social drinker trying hard to break the bond of his alcoholic grandfather. He never looked up at me. He just began speaking.

"I should have suspected something and been more aware of her condition when she slept a lot, went to work late, and exhibited bouts of irrational behavior. I was livid when I found out she had another miscarriage. The doctor called me at work to ask me if I could come to the hospital. He had something very important to discuss with me. I walked into her room, Tessa was lying in the bed staring at the ceiling, and tears were staining her swollen and stressed face. I attempted to kiss her, but she turned away and went into a fetal position."

He let out a long breath of air from his lungs. "I have made arrangements for her to get therapy after the miscarriage. However, she is refusing to go. One good action that has resulted from this tragedy is Tessa has arranged to be absent from her job for the next six months. I am still puzzled though why she refuses to seek medical help from a specialist in that field. I even discussed it with her attending physician."

It was after this second miscarriage that William insisted on hiring someone to oversee the household and grounds staff since Tessa's job was so demanding and she had refused to work part-time. This is about the time that he offered me the job as his chief of household operations. Little did I know that the ancestors were in the mix and was opening the door to my heritage puzzle.

It was still mystifying to William why Tessa had failed to mention these pregnancies.

William spoke to Tessa's mother concerning Tessa's health and her refusal to give up her nursing position. Tessa's mother only reassured William that Tessa was strong and sometimes women who were thirty or older experienced several miscarriages with their first pregnancies.

She also reminded William that Tessa loved him and his son and wanted to make a loving home for the two of them. That did not make it easy for William, because he was looking for another Katerina Hamburg Petersen Langley to fill the hole or void in his heart, and no one could fill those shoes.

In walked Onnie Dusett, the sister of his college friend and business partner, G. Papas of Eufaula, Alabama.

I remember William looking directly at me with a smirk and a smile, stating, "The more I interact with my mistress, the more she is becoming more like the first love of my life, Katerina Hamburg Petersen Langley."

William and Tessa had been married about ten or twelve years when she had her first breakdown. This was also during the time when I discovered the revised birth certificate documents. After William received the documents that clearly negated the pure Irish background of Tessa, it became clearer to him why she did not want to have any children.

I wish she had been honest with him. I believe he would have accepted her lineage information and worked hard to make the marriage work. Instead, he gravitated more and more toward his mistress.

Many times, I asked him why he didn't divorce her privately. He would look at me and say, "It was a business decision I had to make, because the fallback from the decision would have greatly affected my business operations and my standing in this community."

In my job as the chief of household operations, after William learned of the revised birth certificate, he worked late at least two days a week and would dine alone. During those times when he dined with Tessa and Edwin, Tessa would often remind him that she had changed her work schedule to accommodate his business hours. She felt he should do the same so the family could dine together. William mostly ignored her comments and would engage in conversations with the dinner staff, his son, or with me.

When Edwin became a teenager, he was sent away to boarding school in Massachusetts. On his visits from school, he often ate dinner in silence. This was due to an inappropriate statement he once blurted out, and his father nicely put him in check. On this day, Tessa was addressing the fact that all members of the family should be timely for dinner. The planned dinners were served at 6:00 PM, not 7:00 or 8:00.

Without thinking, young Edwin looked at Tessa and stated, "If you are so unhappy, Tessa, why don't you just leave."

His father looked at him and stated, "This is an adult situation, and you're years too young to understand. Please refrain from making such statements at the dinner table." From that day forward, when he was home and ate with the family, it was in silence.

Five years after the second miscarriage and several months of pretending to go to counseling, Tessa quit her job at the hospital and saturated herself with social activities and fund-raisings for the hospital and other charitable organizations. William was unaware that she was not attending the counseling session but often complained to me that she never included him in the sessions. He felt that his presence at the sessions would bring more light and healing to the situation.

Rosa rubbed her chin as she adjusted the jets in the Jacuzzi. In a loud voice and to no one in particular, she stated, "I wonder if William had gone to the counseling sessions and had known about the revised birth certificates, would he have broached the subject during the counseling sessions?"

As she entered the linen closet to retrieve the essentials for Jennifer's bath, in her mind she continued her thoughts of previous actions and activities.

I would often read about her community fund-raising successes in different magazines and newspapers. Tessa often chaired two to three fund-raising galas during the year. As William spent less time at home and more attending business meetings and visiting his son at boarding school, Tessa spent more time at committee meetings than she did at home. She only relinquished those outreach activities after her second stroke.

I often wondered if she had an extramarital affair. Her constant consultant and analyst for her fund-raising activities was a James McCall, the owner of a midsize business consulting firm. The talk from some of the household staff led me to believe it was more than a business relationship.

James was always available as her escort when William was not available. Rosa smiled; it is clear why the staff made this assumption.

THE PROPOSAL

As Rosa placed the bath essentials on the dressing table, she remembered her first day as chief of operations for the Langley household.

Even on my first day on the job, I could sense there was a lot of tension in the household between Mr. and Mrs. Langley; therefore I quietly went about completing the tasks of my new position and keeping my observations to myself. Yes, I have seen and heard a lot during my more than forty years with the Langley family. I have watched W. Edwin III grow up, enter college and law school, become a partner in his father's law firm, and control the Langleys' business interests.

Rosa finished preparing Jennifer's bath, but her mind drifted back to the day Edwin III brought Jennifer to officially meet his family. The two of them had met at Brown University in Providence, Rhode Island, and continued their relationship at the University of South Carolina's School of Law. How well she remembers that day, August 1, 1982.

The family was aware of their friendship, and they knew of Jennifer's desire to become a civil rights attorney, working for the needs and rights of America's unforgotten citizens. Mr. William had no objections to their relationship or courtship, but Ms. Tessa would not hear of it. She felt that Jennifer was an outsider to the aristocratic South Carolinian ways, had not been brought up with the same culture as the debutantes in South Carolina. If it were left up to her, no outsider would destroy her plans for this family and what she had worked so hard to maintain. She did not care that Jennifer had finished second in her class. She still was not the right choice for Edwin.

Tessa knew that after graduating from law school, Edwin's primary functions were to ensure the entire Langley-owned industries were legally and financially sound. The Langleys' fortune and industries had grown tremendously since Edwin's grandfather started his textile and canning business. Now he would become one of the primary corporate lawyers for the Langleys' conglomerate corporations, which included coffee, textile, canning, rental properties, a small wine company, and a financial investment company. She also knew he would soon assume the CEO position of the conglomerations. Therefore she felt it was her duty to find the perfect mate for him.

Tessa had done research on the Barclay and Dusett families of Barbour County, Alabama, and could not find any connections between the Barclays in Massachusetts or the Dusetts in Biloxi, Mississippi. Even though Jennifer had a stellar education, many social graces, ethical training, belonged to the Presbyterian religious denomination, and maintained other amenities, Jennifer only partially met the criteria Tessa had in mind for Edwin's wife. There was something about her entire persona that had Tessa puzzled.

On the other hand, Mr. William was not concerned. He knew firsthand about Ms. Jennifer Suzanne Barclay-Dusett. He had a personal connection with her aunt Onnie and had influenced Onnie to send her precious niece to Brown and the University of South Carolina. Not known to Tessa, Mr. William was also aware of his handsome son, Edwin, influencing Jennifer to join him at the University of South Carolina's Law School.

Jennifer did not know that Mr. William and her aunt Onnie had made sure this was her law school of choice. Each of them was aware of her relationship with Edwin, but Jennifer was not aware of William and Onnie's plans and schemes to ensure Edwin and Jennifer were together not only in law school but also after law school. Even if she had such an idea, Jennifer would not have complained since she was madly in love with William Edwin Langley III. He had her heart, her soul, her love; his touch and intimacy was only for her, and deep inside she knew Edwin had the same feelings for her.

It was sort of a celebration dinner for the two graduates. Both had finished the required courses needed to earn their law degrees, and each had completed the bar examination. They were anxiously awaiting the results of this examination. The Langleys had planned a dinner party with many of their closest friends to congratulate Edwin on his accomplishments; however, who would have guessed that Edwin had an announcement of his own.

Tessa had taken it upon herself to invite several of the young ladies Edwin had taken out on dates during his high school and college years. Although Edwin had never really shown a romantic interest, Tessa felt their status of being a psychologist (Jacqueline Moore), editor of a magazine (Sylvia Kennedy), and a neurologist (Wylinda Upshaw) would help steer him toward one of them. Tessa was aware that Edwin was bringing Jennifer to the dinner party, but Tessa had assured all of her friends and invited guests that Edwin was only intrigued with her. It was nothing serious, and after tonight, Jennifer Suzanne Barclay-Dusett would be a memory of the past.

One couple in attendance was the Greys, a partner in the Langleys' law firm. The Greys had tried on numerous occasions to get Edwin interested in their daughter Marcia. Marcia was a graduate of the University of South Carolina and the principal of one of the elementary schools in the area. When she heard Edwin was bringing Jennifer to the dinner party, Marcia had declined the invitation. However, her parents had not given up on their dream of having Edwin III as their son-in-law.

Tessa intentionally did not extend an invitation to Jennifer's aunt Onnie because she did not want to be in her presence or have her around her carefully chosen guests. She was not aware that Mr. William had personally invited Onnie until Tessa saw Onnie walk through the doors of their home. Rosa laughed out loud, remembering the incident like it happened yesterday, the look on Tessa's face and her motioning to William to step into the foyer.

"I don't believe that you invited that woman to our home. How could you?"

"Yes, I did because her niece is here visiting with my son, Edwin."

"Let this be known this day! If I have something to do with it, this will be her last visit."

William looked at Tessa with a smirk and kept his voice as softly as possible: "Tessa, now is not the time to discuss this matter. We have guests, and if you don't feel comfortable, fake a headache and excuse yourself, but you will not spoil Edwin and Jennifer's celebration dinner party."

He carefully placed his arms around Tessa's shoulder and pulled her closer to his chest.

"Yes, I invited Onnie and that's that! No matter how upset you are, there's not a damn thing you can do. Now let's get back to our guests.

Oh, and by the way, not only did I invite Onnie, but I sent Jacob to pick her up from the airport, and I reserved a suite at the Charleston Hilton Hotel for her."

With a smile on William's face, he sweetly took hold of Tessa's hand, and the two of them walked into the formal dining area. They looked like the most loving couple you had ever seen.

Ms. Onnie Barclay Dusett walked into the Langleys' home dressed immaculately and glowing like a proud peacock. The queen Onnie could make a statement anytime she entered a room. She was at least five feet eight inches in height, weight in proportion for a woman of her age, beautiful external features, and a glow that said, "Watch me."

Many of the guests were so intrigued with this lioness as she entered the Langleys' home that most of them were focused on her and never heard Tessa as she sighed in disgust.

Even though the guests had noticed Tessa's angry and bitter disposition while she and Mr. William were discussing something in the foyer, Onnie's entrance had overshadowed the Langleys' dispute and brought in a totally different atmosphere.

As the dinner party progressed and each in attendance had been introduced to Jennifer Suzanne Barclay-Dusett and her aunt Onnie, the attendees began to inquire about Jennifer's parents, grandparents, her future career goals, and other topics of discussion.

Jennifer had been well schooled by her aunt Onnie, and she only provided a skeleton of information that would keep inquisitive minds wondering.

While speaking to each of them, Jennifer made sure her eye contact mirrored her aunt Onnie's. Each of the guests was very impressed with her ability to express herself and her knowledge of political, financial, and social topics of the day.

Although she impressed the guests, you could still see they were apprehensive about her acceptance into their South Carolinian lifestyle.

Tessa was livid about Onnie's attendance, but as usual, Ms. Onnie was able to play the game and had the guests mesmerized with her conversation about her niece and her social, educational, and political experiences and exposures.

"My niece Jennifer has been my sun, moon, and sky. After her parents' death, I gave up my career as an opera singer to ensure her upbringing was filled with experiences that would provide the skills needed to become a successful civil rights attorney."

She put a broad smile on her face. "My niece Jennifer speaks three foreign languages, plays the violin and the piano, and she loves to read. She has traveled extensively in the United Stated and abroad. She was an exchange student in England during her high school junior and senior years and has worked as an intern in the White House during her freshman and sophomore years at college. I know you will enjoy her piano skills. I am going to volunteer Jennifer to play a classical piece for you after dinner."

The smirk on Mr. William's face was large enough to start a barn fire.

Rosa smiled as she continued with the preparation of Jennifer's bath. In fact, she laughed out loudly and looked around to ensure Jennifer had not walked into the bathroom. Her smile grew wider as she remembered the falseness and the tension around the table, especially the three young ladies Tessa had invited to help break up Edwin and Jennifer's relationship.

However, Jennifer's training had been stellar, and she knew how to control her emotions, actions, and her facial expressions. Her aunt Onnie had taught her well. You could see from the expression on her aunt's face that this dinner party was progressing as she had planned.

Jennifer looked at her aunt Onnie and said, "I would love to play a piece for the guests after dinner, and I may include a love song I wrote especially for Edwin."

Rosa laughed out loud again; she continued to reminisce about that night and how the atmosphere changed so many times, especially when Onnie controlled the conversation. Tessa's silence that night made a number of her guests uneasy. The serving of the dessert and the coffee was the most surreal part of the night.

Especially when Edwin stood, clicked his wineglass, and stated, "I have an announcement to make about my future plans."

All in attendance knew he would be taking a job within his father's many businesses, but never in their wildest imagination were they prepared for Edwin's surprised meteor shower.

He began his statement with, "Each of you know that Jennifer and I have been friends for the past four or five years. We both have successfully finished law school and are awaiting the bar results, so tonight I am pleased to introduce to each of you the future Mrs. W. Edwin Langley III. I asked her last night, and she graciously accepted."

He reached into his coat pocket, pulled out a 10-carat pear-shaped diamond ring, and placed it on Jennifer's ring finger and then leaned down and kissed her in his guests' presence.

The congratulations came slowly. Several of the women guests excused themselves from the table, and Tessa Lorraine Adkins-Langley turned stark white as she walked around the table to plant a kiss on Jennifer's cheek.

She reluctantly hugged her stepson Edwin III and begrudgingly shook Aunt Onnie's hand. As I turned to look at Mr. William and Ms. Onnie, both had that special twinkle in their eyes.

Mr. William grabbed his son's hand, pulled him close, and gave him a loving father's hug. To this day I can see his lips moving and stating, "Good choice, my son, I wish each of you the best and much happiness throughout your married life."

Then he turned to the guests, who looked stunned and had questioning looks on each of their faces.

"Let's all raise our wineglasses and give congratulations to Jennifer and Edwin on their recent nuptial announcement. To the future Mr. and Mrs. William Edwin Langley III. I would also like to officially welcome Ms. Onnie Barclay-Dusett to the family."

Although glasses were raised and words of cheers went out to the newly engaged couple, if there had been some type of radar detector in the room, you could have seen the anger and disgust seething from Tessa's pores into the atmosphere. She raised her glass but never drank a sip of the wine.

Rosa bent down to adjust the jets in the Jacuzzi tub. A thought of wow went through her mind. Over the years she had expertly and quietly performed her duties with opened eyes and ears. Although she had heard and seen a lot, no one could say she had exposed the secrets within the Langleys' household. She had held long and private conversations with the senior Mr. William, especially during the time of his illness.

In fact, during the time of his illness he had insisted that I stay in the room with the medical assistant or home nurse and not Tessa. However, Tessa would use her title as Mrs. Langley and her nursing skills to make sure I only observed and not assist.

The laughter, the secrets, and the long conversations would continue when the room was void of extra ears. The secrets and conversations that had been exchanged between the two of us during this time remained confidential and unspoken. The secrets and lies of the Langley family would never—no, never—come from my lips.

Rosa stepped out of the bath/dressing area into the bedroom. Looking in the direction of Jennifer, she noticed Jennifer was still preoccupied with her thoughts.

Rosa cleared her throat and stated, "Mrs. Langley, I have finished preparing your bath, but I need to know what bath salts and oil I should put in the tub? There are so many in your linen closet, and I was unsure of the one you wanted to use today."

Jennifer waved her hand and stated, "It doesn't matter as long as it has a soft fragrance—in fact, why don't you use the ones shipped from London last week. I believe it's from Viktor & Rolf. I haven't tried it yet, but I love their products."

"I surely will," said Rosa as she walked back into the bath area.

Rosa felt a wave of cold air and saw a shadow hovering over her. She knew immediately it was Mr. William's presence. He was here to ensure his favorite granddaughter's wedding day would be special and nothing out of the ordinary would happen.

Yes, I could write a book about this family, from the sudden accidental death of Mr. William's mother, Jacqueline Olivia; to the unknown disease that killed Mr. William's first wife, Katerina Hamburg Petersen DeBeaux, and his daughter, Ophelia; to his dysfunctional marriage to Tessa Adkins; the engagement and marriage of Edwin and Jennifer; and the frequent trips with his unnamed mistress. I know many, many secrets about this family but would keep them safely in my heart and my mind.

As my mother used to say, "Why bring the skeletons out of the closet?" Rosa laughed as she continued preparing the bathwater for Jennifer; then she carefully laid out the lingerie, the silk bathrobe, and the house slippers on the dressing table. She entered the linen closet and took out two sets of monogrammed towels and laid them on the bench next to the tub. Then she walked back into the bedroom and stated, "Mrs. Langley, everything is ready for you."

SECURING PIECES OF THE PUZZLE

J ennifer turned and looked at Rosa; the faraway look was still present in her eyes.

"Thanks, Rosa. If I need your assistance again, I will call you. Before you check on Bria, please see that Ms. Tessa is up and Florence and the home nurse are helping her get prepared for the wedding. I know my aunt Onnie has arrived for I saw her as the car service let her out by the beautiful gardens. For my sanity, please check to see that both Tessa and Aunt Onnie are in a good mood for this great day."

"Mrs. Langley, I know Florence and the home nurse can handle both Mrs. Tessa and your aunt Onnie, but I will check on them for you."

Rosa smiled, and in her mind, she thought, but was not aware she was speaking her thoughts loudly, "Now I know why you have shown up today, Mr. William. You are concerned about the behavior of both women in your life, your wife and your mistress. I will keep them in order and as far away from each other as I can.

"Tessa can be a handful, and so can Onnie, but Tessa is in a wheelchair with limited speech and mobility, and Onnie is in the beginning stages of dementia. Yes, your spirit is much needed to control both of them, Mr. William, but don't worry, Florence and I will keep them comfortable before and after the wedding."

"Rosa, were you speaking to me?"

"No, Mrs. Langley, I was just talking to myself."

"Before you leave, I know you and Mr. William spent some quality time with each other during his illness. Do you think he would object to the mate that Bria has chosen to marry? He comes from a very good family."

Rosa did not audibly answer, for she was in awe that she had spoken aloud to William Sr., hoping Jennifer did not think she was deranged.

"Rosa, you know his father, Dr. Marcus H. Jennings Sr., is a well-known orthopedic surgeon and is known throughout the country for his medical assistance and consultation for the NFL and NBA. He has offices in Columbia, Maryland, one in Chicago, Illinois, and one in Santa Ana, California. My future son-in-law, Marcus Jr., is going to work out of the office in Maryland, and Bria is going to do cancer research out of the Cancer Center in the Columbia area. I am very proud of each of them, and I know in my heart she has chosen a wonderful person to be her soul mate."

"As far as I know, Mrs. Langley, Mr. William would not only be pleased, he would be scheming to keep Bria and her husband here in South Carolina. Don't you dare fret over the way Ms. Tessa has acted toward Marcus! She is still holding on to past beliefs that people should marry within their own culture and ethnicity. Today is not a day for you to upset yourself about small thinking and small-minded people."

"Thanks, Rosa."

As Jennifer began pulling her robe closer to her body, she stated, "Someone must have adjusted the air in here. All of a sudden I feel a chill."

"Mrs. Langley, that's just your nerves. It's better to be cool rather than having those awesome hot flashes."

Jennifer laughed and stated, "You are absolutely correct. Rosa, I know you need to go check on Bria, Tessa, and Aunt Onnie, but I am sitting here in a daze and a little puzzled about a package I received today. This package was delivered by William Sr.'s attorney, and it was addressed to just me. Maybe you can help me since I know you and Mr. William had a good relationship and he often confided in you."

"Jennifer, yes, Mr. William and I had a good relationship, but I have no knowledge of any package he would have prepared for you."

"William often stated, 'I know I can trust Rosa and Jacob if I can't trust anyone else.'"

"Yes, we had a special bond and relationship, but a package for you was not one of our discussions."

Jennifer walked over to the window with the package in her hand.

"I do not understand why today of all days, Mr. Lambert, one of the attorneys in the corporation, hand-delivered me a package that had been prepared by Mr. William. Mr. Lambert advised me that Mr. William insisted that I was the only one to receive it on Bria's wedding day. Would you have any knowledge of what could possibly be in this package?"

Rosa's heart began to beat faster under her dress. Yes, she did have a good relationship with Mr. William. Sometimes Mr. William would talk for hours about his family, his mistress, his wife, and other situations that were troubling to him. Rosa smiled for she knew during those times she was not just a listening ear but a sounding board to help him clear his conscience and to help him repent before his demise.

What he had placed in that package was one of the things he did not share with her.

Rose looked at Jennifer and shrugged her shoulders. "Mrs. Langley, Mr. William and I did do a lot of talking and laughing, especially during the time of his lengthy illness, but I assure you I don't have any knowledge of what could be in that package. Didn't Mr. Lambert give you any hints as to the content of the package?"

Jennifer continued to look out of the bay window onto the beautifully manicured lawn. She did not turn around but spoke a soft troubling no.

Rosa walked over to Jennifer, placing a hand in the small of her back.

"You also know Mr. William spent a lot of time with Jacob, especially when he was driving him to Alabama, Georgia, and North Carolina. Since Mr. William was not very fond of flying and when there was no need, he would often ask Jacob to drive him to a number of states in close proximity to South Carolina. I am sure during those times they discussed a lot of items. One may have been the package he prepared for you. Maybe you should broach the subject with Jacob. He may have some idea."

Rosa chuckled and looked at Jennifer. "Even though he did not like to fly, he did frequent Hawaii a lot. I am sure whoever was his flying companion could possibly give you some good hints about the content of that package."

Both Jennifer and Rosa laughed out loudly for each was very aware of his unnamed mistress.

Rosa hugged Jennifer and headed toward the door. When she turned around and looked at Jennifer, she noticed that Jennifer had moved from the window and was sitting on the bed, staring at the package.

She could feel the stress in the room and knew that Jennifer felt today's package might bring chaos to this beautiful event, her daughter Bria's wedding day.

Rosa walked back over to Jennifer. She attempted to remove the package from Jennifer's grip, but she could not.

"Mrs. Langley, if I were you, I would wait until after the wedding to read the information in this package. Today is too important for you to become stressed out over the contents of this package. In fact, I know Mr. William would not have provided you any information that he felt would upstage his granddaughter's wedding day."

"In my heart I know he would not for he loved his grandchildren and did all he could to shield them from harm."

"Since you are aware of his nature, I would suggest that you place the package in a safe place and retrieve it after today's event. Mr. William stipulated you should be the first to read the package and do what you think is necessary to disseminate the contents to your family. The package might contain some assets he did not disclose in his original will and wanted to do it after Bria's wedding. If I were you, I would just put the package in a safe place until after the wedding."

"You make a good point, Rosa. I will put it away until after the wedding."

"I am on my way to check on Bria, Ms. Tessa, and Ms. Onnie. Your bathwater is ready, and you should relax in the Jacuzzi before the water gets cold."

Rosa looked back at Jennifer as she remained sitting on the bed.

"Don't forget to eat your breakfast. If you need me later on this morning, let me know. I'll be in the other wing helping Florence with Ms. Tessa and your aunt Onnie."

Rosa exited Jennifer's bedroom and noticed Mr. Edwin coming toward the door.

She stopped him and asked loudly, "Mr. Edwin, have you calmed down Bria, and are Ms. Tessa and Ms. Onnie exhibiting lady qualities? I can just feel it in my spirit this is going to be a wonderful day. God has already blessed us with a beautiful and sunny day. I left some fruit, pastries, and juice in the sitting room of your bedroom. Make sure Ms. Jennifer eats some. See you later."

Jennifer sat for a few more minutes, turning the package over in her hand. She felt the same way as Rosa. It didn't matter if it was good, bad, or indifferent information. She should wait until after the wedding festivities.

Still holding the package close to her heart, Jennifer quickly got off the bed after hearing Rosa talking to Edwin in the hallway. She needed to hide the package before he entered their bedroom. She looked around;

there was not enough time to place it in her private wall safe, but she could place it in her lingerie drawer. She ran to the dresser and placed the package under her lingerie. Her thinking was to transfer it to her wall safe after the wedding.

As Edwin entered the bedroom, Jennifer moved toward him. In her mind he was still as handsome as the day she met him. Jennifer could not believe it had been more than thirty years ago.

In her mind she thought, *My love for him is as strong today as it was then. I will never grow tired of him and will always need him by my side.*

Her thoughts gravitated to William and Tessa; it's strange how it was just the opposite with William and Tessa. They had not slept in the same room at least twenty of the twenty-nine years since she had become a member of the Langley family.

ETERNAL FLAME OF LOVE

Jennifer was aware of William's mistress, whom he kept for at least twenty-two of those years. She had never seen his mistress, nor had William ever spoken her name. It was obvious that some of the staff were aware of her, especially Rosa and Jacob. She also knew Tessa was quite aware of his infidelity, for their heated discussions around the dinner table often centered on William's mistress.

Edwin would often become silent on the issue whenever she broached the subject.

One day he did say, "Jennifer, it is best that you do not know the details, because it may shatter your image of one very dear to you."

She often thought his response was in regard to William since she was very fond of him. In fact she regarded William as the father she never had.

Jennifer placed her hand on Edwin's back and placed a kiss on his forehead. "Hi, sweetheart, it appears that Ms. Marsha Kennedy, the wedding consultant, has done a terrific job of orchestrating this occasion."

"Yes, she has, but what about the garden landscape?"

"Jacob and sons have done an exquisite job landscaping the grounds. The landscaping he created for this day is just breathtaking. The intricate details of making many of the shrubs look like wedding bells, the way he has interwoven the different floral arrangements and colors of calla lilies, the ivory roses, the star of Bethlehem, and the Queen Anne's lace throughout the gardens. All of his little details and creations remind me of paradise, a place I could lose myself in and never think about the evils of this world."

"I bet the aroma in the garden smells heavenly."

"My mind can't fathom or imagine how it will all look once Bria's wedding begins."

Edwin pulled Jennifer closer to him and planted a kiss on her forehead and lips.

"Nothing can be as gorgeous and exquisite as the woman I am holding in my arms. You were beautiful the first time I met you, and it has not faded over the thirty-plus years I have known you. My love for you grows deeper and deeper each and every day. Too bad today is our daughter's wedding day, for I would not let you out of this room. It would be my day to show you how deep my love for you still runs."

He pulled her even closer, and the kiss they both experienced began to stir up emotions that would be very difficult to contain. Jennifer did not want to let go, but she knew if she didn't, she would be late for her own daughter's wedding. As the kiss lingered in her mind, she felt her husband's manhood swelling against her body, and she could not control the kindling of fire that began to arise in her groins and her entire body.

Jennifer restrained herself and pulled back from Edwin.

"Have you calmed down your daughter? Rosa stated she was a little agitated when she took her some light breakfast."

"Don't worry, sweetheart, Bria is fine, just bridal jitters. Bria is much like you, nervous energy on a big event. She has not touched her breakfast tray, but I did get her to drink a cup of tea. She will be fine. Now, Ms. Jen (Edwin's nickname for his wife), I understand your bathwater has been prepared, and I don't want the water to get any colder, or we might have to go to the wedding a little dirty."

A smirk formed on Edwin's face. "In fact I have a better idea. Why don't we both use the prepared bath? I will perform my special massage for relieving you of stress, the deep tissue type massage I often give you."

Jennifer loved this man with all of her heart, and if his hands could help alleviate the stress she was experiencing at this moment, she was all for it.

"Nothing would suit me better than to have my lovely and handsome husband of twenty-nine use his magical fingers to calm my nervous energy."

Jennifer took his hand in hers and lightly kissed each of his fingers. "I don't believe I will need the jets. I'll just let your healing hands do the job." With a big smile on her face, hand in hand, she and Edwin walked toward the bathroom, and with each step, the two of them began to rid themselves of their garments. As they faced each other naked, Edwin placed his foot on the bathroom door and closed it.

The steam in that bathroom helped increase the temperature of the water in the Jacuzzi. There was no need to add any warm water to the contents.

DISCOVERING AN UNKNOWN NEPHEW

As Rosa made her way to Tessa's room, she saw Jacob in the foyer arranging a large bouquet of flowers. The flowers were simply magnificent. Jacob had them flown in from the floral markets in some cities in California, New York, and other countries.

Rosa thought, "Yes, Jacob's business had really flourished under the watchful eyes and guidance of Mr. William." He now owned one of the largest lawn services and floral warehouse businesses in the area. He and his sons have a monopoly on the landscaping and floral business in the area. He is one of the most sought-after minority businesses that have contracts with the state government, city government, and many of the large corporations in the area. I know Mr. William would be proud as a peacock knowing that he had a hand in all of this success.

Rosa's mind wandered back to the day William Sr. engaged Jacob's services as the lawn service provider for his estate and some of his other real estate properties in the city. I had been employed with the Langleys a little more than twenty years. When I laid eyes on this young man who had recently received his degree in horticulture from Hampton University in Hampton, Virginia, something magical happened in my spirit.

His name was Jacob Smith (not Smyth), born in Augusta, Georgia, and raised in Baltimore, Maryland. He had been hired by the Department of Agriculture for the state of South Carolina, but he had also opened a small business of his own. He had been in South Carolina about three years. There was something familiar yet daunting about his physical features. He could have been mistaken for my deceased brother, and my oldest son's facial features mirrored Jacob's.

I had to look away to catch my breath. Was this a reincarnation? Did the ancestors open the door of life for my brother? Had my mother been correct all these years regarding the ancestors coming through the door? It was just not the door attached to my mother's home.

Was he a lost son of my brother that no one knew about? Even his mannerisms and the use of his left hand while completing his gardening tasks were all like my brother's. I had to find out more about this young man.

Had the ancestors decided it was time I knew more about who I was and how the seed of the Nile was an intricate part of my entire being? This was such a frightening feeling. I did not want to begin taking on the mystical ways of my mother, but today, I felt like the ancestors were pulling me more toward Hettie Hamburg Petersen Smyth's behavior. As I engaged in conversation with the young man, and watched his behavior, I knew the ancestors were having a field day with my emotions and my nerves. Little did I know that the front door had truly opened and now my ancestral history would begin to unfold slowly in this lifetime.

My heart began to beat faster and my breathing was very intense as I came closer to the area where Jacob was working. Little did I know that nearly twenty years ago, the ancestors would place in my path an unknown family member, my long-lost nephew.

"Jacob, you and your business associates are just too much. You have outdone yourselves on the grounds and the floral arrangements throughout the home. This floral arrangement in the foyer is just perfect. Do I see blossoms associated with calla lilies, bird of paradise, gladiolus, lavender, white and yellow roses, decorating fern, baby's breaths, star of Bethlehem, and Queen Anne's lace? I know I am missing a few, but the aroma that is oozing from this arrangement is breathtaking."

Rosa touched her nephew's hand. "I also saw the bouquets for the bride and the bridesmaid, the boutonnieres and the wrist corsages for the other family members—each of the floral arrangements has a mixture of star of Bethlehem, Queen Anne's lace, and baby's breath."

Jacob laughed but quietly answered, "Aunt Rosa, you have an eye for floral varieties. You captured the names of most of them."

"Thank you, my nephew, you and your staff have a wonderful eye for mixing colors and blending them in with the bride's color scheme."

Pointing to the gardens and the different shrubbery designs, her heart only felt love and pride for the skills of her nephew.

"Jacob, you need to take this talent to the floral magazines or some of the *Good Housekeeping* magazines. Ms. Kennedy loves your special touch and vowed since working with you, she would not use any other florist in her event-planning business. You are just too much."

Rosa looked around to ensure no one was in close proximity. "Jacob, do you have a minute? I need to ask you something very important. Walk with me over by the door."

Rosa and Jacob exited the foyer and walked onto the circular porch of the home.

"I just left Jennifer's room. She is concerned about a package given to her by Mr. Lambert that was prepared by Mr. Langley prior to his death. A package only addressed to her. According to Mr. Lambert, William was adamant that the package should be delivered to Jennifer the day of his granddaughter's wedding. She asked me about it, and I said I was not aware of what could possibly be in the package. I sort of mentioned that you and Mr. Langley spent some quality time together. He may have discussed the contents of the package with you. I know she is concerned, and she may come to you about it after the wedding. This is just a heads-up."

Jacob looked down at his boots and removed several pieces of decorative fern.

"Thanks, Rosa, but like you, I, too, am in the dark. Yes, sometimes Mr. Langley confided in me but not about a package. You know in private he insisted that I called him by his first name. I only referred to him as Mr. Langley around his associates and the other staff members."

"Jacob, he did me the same way. He always said I would feel more comfortable if I called him William when we were alone."

Jacob moved closer to Rosa and looked around to ensure none of the wedding planning staff was in close proximity. A helper carrying tablecloths and chair covers passed by; both Rosa and Jacob nodded and said hello to the worker.

Jacob continued with his conversation. "I often drove him to Alabama to visit his friend from college, Douglas Cromwell Pappas, and his secret mistress."

They both looked at each other and laughed out loud, and together they said, "Ms. Onnie."

"I also went on weekend fishing and hunting trips with him from time to time, but we never talked about a package. Even when he was getting really ill and called for me to come and visit, he confided in me regarding some skeletons in the family lineage, but I was sworn to secrecy not to divulge it to anyone."

Rosa patted her nephew on the back. "After the wedding we may need to compare notes, because Mr. Langley did the same with me. I thought he was incoherent and was out of his mind when he said certain things to me, like 'I have been carrying these secrets for a long time, and it's time for me to let go of this burden and let my family know our real lineage.' He said he loved his family and wanted the truth to come from him and not from some outside source or the news media. Sometimes his eyes would fill up with tears at the mention of his father, his mother, his first wife Katerina, or he would have that faraway look as though he was replaying all the past and present scenes in his mind."

Jacob looked away for a minute and looked at Rosa.

"If I had any knowledge of the real contents of the package and if it's what I think it may contain, I would suggest to Jennifer to wait until after the wedding to read the contents. This information could cause a real uproar if it is pertaining to what William spoke to me about."

Jacob played with the work gloves on his hand before he continued. "Sometimes I would ask him if he really wanted to discuss this with me, and he would look at me and smile and say, 'Yes, you are the right person.' Maybe we should get together to ensure our answers to Ms. Jennifer are identical in the event she speaks to each of us alone."

"I would suggest the same."

"It's odd that you mentioned this to me because all day, it appears that William—I mean Mr. Langley has been with me in spirit. I have had such an eerie feeling all morning. I know we have been sworn to secrecy about his family, but I hope the package doesn't affect us since no one, not even Edwin, knows that we are related. I mean blood relatives, same genetic makeup."

"When William broached the subject with the two of us, I really thought his medication had him talking out of his head, but when he shared the pictures, I was convinced."

"It was truly a day of discovery. I never knew my mother had other relatives for she seldom spoke of them. Can you believe he went through all the investigation to bring us together? That's why I know I feel William's presence all over this place today."

"Jacob, I know what you are saying. I, too, have felt the same way. I have to say Mr. Langley was special. Even though he lied when he told me I was the only one of his staff that could call him William when we were alone. He told you the exact same thing. I know now why he chose us to talk about these family secrets. I was just wondering, do you think Tessa knows, and that's why he never divorced her? He had to maintain his image to keep her quiet."

"Even if she did, she had her own skeletons and probably did not want the door to open on her family."

"Were you aware that Tessa did a background check on Jennifer and Onnie? She did not find much, so I wonder if she did the same for Mr. William."

Rosa and Jacob walked back toward the foyer. She looked up at her nephew with a worried look on her face.

"The contents of the package now have me wondering. Just what is he going to reveal to Jennifer?"

"Rosa, we could talk about this all day, but I have a few more tasks to finish before I go home and change for the wedding. Don't forget, Tessa has a shaky past also. She stayed with William so her family secrets would stay in the closets. I know you remember the falsified birth certificates you found and gave copies to William. He was livid that day. I have never seen him so angry."

Jacob clipped the end of a flower and placed it into the large vase in the foyer. He stepped back to observe his creation.

"Enough of this, Aunt Rosa. We are making an assumption about what is in the package, and it could just be deeds to pieces of land for his granddaughter and her soon-to-be husband."

"Yes, we are probably letting our imagination run wild."

"Do you know Jennifer invited my entire family to the wedding? I know Ms. Tessa would be unhappy to know they invited some of the staff and their family to this special occasion. She is probably going to get up and walk out—I mean wheel herself out—when she sees us seated in the chairs on the bride's side. In fact, Jennifer asked me to arrive early so my family and I may be seated in close proximity to the family."

"Well, Jacob, it's going to be a double whammy because my family and I were also invited. Jennifer provided me with the same instructions. Well, let me go finish up with Ms. Tessa and Ms. Onnie, so all of us will be on time for Bria's wedding."

"Jacob, it is a good thing we both will be present because Florence may not be able to control both of those biddies, especially Ms. Tessa.

You know she is not pleased with Bria's choice, and it has shown in her disposition from the moment she met Marcus. I know because William confided in me that most of the time when Bria and Marcus came to visit, Ms. Tessa would not come downstairs to greet them, nor would she eat dinner with them."

"On the other hand for all of their visits, Ms. Onnie insisted on being brought over to see her great-niece and her soon-to-be great-nephew. Ms. Tessa can be a piece of work, and we may be needed to assist her if she becomes enraged."

Rosa hugged her nephew and started toward the west wing of the estate. She stopped and looked at Jacob, then walked back toward him.

"I do have to say Ms. Tessa is a little afraid of you and Ms. Jennifer. Both of you know how to handle her. She was never comfortable with the relationship you and Mr. William had. In fact, one day prior to her second stroke, she asked me why I thought the two of you were so close since the two of you came from different worlds and cultures. I said to her, Ms. Tessa, you will need to ask Mr. William, because I don't have a clue. She gave me that strange look and wheeled herself back into her sitting room."

Jacob touched Rosa on the arm. "Rosa, don't fret over Ms. Tessa. With the last stroke affecting her mobility and her speech, all she can do is look mean or use her wheelchair to run over us."

"Ms. Tessa may be unable to talk and walk today, but I am sure she clearly remembers the loud discussion she and Mr. William had regarding you and his friendship. The trees, the flowers, and the birds can remember that heated and loud conversation she had with Mr. William about funding your new business and getting clients for you. She intentionally brought it up while you were pruning the hedges near the breakfast nook.

"She wanted you to hear the conversation. She even stated with utter distain, 'Is there some sort of secret relationship between you and the gardener, the reason you are doing so much to help him establish a solid horticultural and landscaping business? Does he know something about you that I don't?'

"Rosa, you were not close enough to see the rage in Mr. William's eyes when he stated, 'First of all, this is my money that I am using to finance Jacob's business. You married into this family, which was long established prior to our meeting. You may not like it, but you can sit there and fume because you have no authority to change any of my business decisions. This is just another business deal. That's what I do, negotiate business deals daily.'

"He began tapping his spoon on the breakfast nook's table, almost knocking over some of the food substances. He continued his conversation looking directly in her eyes.

"'Why are you so bent out of shape regarding this deal? Did you question me when I assisted your friend Vivian's vision of opening her personal chef business? She did not have any business savvy, and if it had not been for me, she would not have maintained her business venture this long. A few of the clients she has only patronize her because of my involvement.'

"Tessa started to move away from the table, and William spoke with so much authority in his voice and told her to sit down, he was not finished with the conversation.

"When she remained at the table, he continued by saying, 'At least Jacob is able to communicate professionally and provide excellent service to his clients. I have heard nothing but good things about the Jacob and Sons Horticulture and Landscaping business. I can't say the same for your friend, Vivian. Listen, I am not going to discuss my involvement with Jacob's business with you again. What is done is done. At least Jacob's business has remained solvent. He makes a profit every year. I cannot say the same for your friend, Vivian. In fact if I had not allowed her to open up a small deli and café in two of my buildings, she would probably be out of business today.'

"He picked up his coffee cup looked down at me and smiled, before taking a sip.

"'Tessa, understand clearly this subject regarding Jacob's business is not up for discussion with you again.' Then he looked down at me winked and said, 'Good morning, Jacob. I like the way you have shaped those hedges.'

"Aunt Rosa, don't worry about Ms. Tessa. From that day forward she has been really cordial toward me. I know you remembered her sixtieth birthday party. She hired me to make the special floral arrangements for her guests' tables."

"Yes, from that day forward she was silent on the subject of Jacob Smith's business ventures."

Both Rosa and Jacob let out a loud laugh and continued in the direction of their next task.

They looked back at each other several times until all each could see was the shadow of the other. However, the laughter from this conversation followed each of them to their next task.

REMINISCING AND BONDING

J ennifer felt so vigorous and rejuvenated after the bath. These were the special moments she missed with her husband of twenty-nine years. With his schedule and hers, those special moments seemed to be getting fewer and fewer. She had to put that on her personal agenda to find more time to spend with her husband. Maybe she would plan a sensuous vacation to their estate in Maui. No servants, no children, just her and Edwin.

She had not prepared him a meal in years. He always complimented her not only on the taste but also her presentation of the meal. This was one of the teachings of Aunt Onnie—her ability to plan meals for dinner parties and to show the chef and staff how to present each fascinating dish.

Jennifer looked over her shoulder at this wonderful man; yes, her next project would be a getaway with her husband. She would plan it so the two of them would only leave the bed for food, baths, and massages.

Jennifer smiled as Edwin walked into his closet in his briefs and T-shirt. Her eyes scanned his handsome body, and her desires for more of him were more than a fantasy—it was a reality.

She blinked twice, fanned herself, and in her mind she thought, *I will make my fantasy a reality right after the wedding. How I have missed making love with and to my husband. I must and will figure out a time for just the two of us.*

She walked into his closet and began kissing him so passionately that Edwin had to restrain himself.

He pulled back and looked at her with a smile. "We need to plan a vacation just for us."

"It's on my to-do list. I was thinking about the home in Hawaii or in Florida and sometime right after the wedding." Then she walked out of his closet to her dressing table.

Sitting on her dressing table was a medium-size black velvet box. How well she remembered this box. It was given to her by her aunt Onnie the day of her wedding. She could hear her aunt telling her how beautiful and special she was and no one was more deserving of her fine qualities, except the man she had chosen, William Edwin Langley III.

She told me how proud she was of me and how I had adhered to all of her training and teachings to become the woman she knew was within.

My aunt Onnie came into my bedroom with this special black jewelry box. As she sat there holding my hand, I will never forget her special words to me prior to the wedding.

"On your special day, your marriage to William Edwin Langley III, I am presenting you with this diamond necklace, bracelet, and earring set that your father gave to your mother the day you were born. When you wear it, a spirit of love and peace will illuminate from within, showing your true beauty and grace."

She opened up the box and placed the necklace around my neck, the earrings on my ears, and the bracelet on my wrist.

"If I am not around on your oldest daughter's wedding day, present this set to her as I have done with you this day. I love you, and may you always experience joy, peace, and happiness in your marriage as well as your personal and professional endeavors."

Then she planted one of her sloppy kisses on my forehead and my cheeks. It was a good thing I did not have on makeup because the tears that flowed from both of our eyes would have gravely messed it up.

My wedding day was truly grand. My aunt Onnie spent a fortune on it, although both Edwin and I asked her not to. Instead of having the wedding in Barbour County, she rented the Renaissance Hotel and Spa in downtown Montgomery, Alabama, for the grand occasion.

Over one thousand guests were in attendance from Alabama, Georgia, South Carolina, Florida, California, Canada, and other cities and states that I cannot remember. Many of the people I knew, and many I did not know.

My gown, the bridesmaids' dresses, and the flower girls' dresses were made here in Charleston by a boutique owner that Mr. William knew. It didn't seem odd then, but I don't know why she didn't use the boutique owners we knew from New Orleans and Atlanta. All I could do was laugh, because this was my aunt Onnie. Everything she did had to be grand and perfect.

A large number of the staff and workers of my aunt Onnie were invited. Not only did she invite them, but she had arranged for several of them to stay overnight in a hotel in Montgomery.

I have to give it to her; my aunt Onnie is something else. I sure wish her mind was as sharp today as it was the day of my wedding. Oh well, at least she can see her oldest great-niece get married.

As Jennifer picked up the box and headed out toward Bria's room, she felt the same chill she had felt earlier in the day. She hoped she was not coming down with a summer cold because she had several court cases for her civil rights law practice. She also needed to begin planning her most needed getaway with her husband, Edwin.

Jennifer lightly tapped on her daughter's door. "Bria, may I come in?"

"Of course, Mother, in fact I was going to come down to your room to speak to you. Dad has already calmed me down, but I need a special hug from my sweet and loving mother. I know that some young women my age would say they have never experienced the love and caring of a perfect mom, but you are the most perfect and loving mother any growing child, now adult, could have."

Bria leaned over and kissed her mother on the cheek. The tears that flowed from both of their eyes bonded together in droplets on each of their silk robes.

"You have been there for me through all of my formative years. You have provided sound directions and guidance ... Some I took and others I avoided and had to come back to get directions on how to amend my actions. You always had my best interest at heart even when I was unsure of my directions in life."

Jennifer walked over to the dress and retrieved several tissues. The amount of tears flowing from each of their eyes could fill a juice glass. Jennifer gently wiped the tears from Bria's eyes and then hers.

"I was torn between going into the business since my great-grandfather had started it or doing what I loved, being a doctor or being in medical research. You sat me down and said, 'Follow your dream and your heart. I am sure your two brothers will end up in some areas of the business.'"

Bria reached over and pulled her mother close to her; the tears and the sobs from each of them were overwhelming. The continuous flow of tears formed an enormous amount of wet spots on Bria's and her mother's silk robes.

Jennifer lightly touched her daughter's cheek.

"You have also been a very good daughter, and sometimes in life's journey, the human mother learns from the mother eagle. She drops the young eaglet from the nest even though she knows he/she is not physically and mentally ready to soar. She allows her young to experience the air flow and the elements against their wings, thus training and teaching them the mechanics of flying and soaring. Upon his/her return to the nest, each has learned a valuable lesson, ready to conquer the mechanics of flying and the art of hunting prey."

"Mom, you always have a way of clarifying life and its many challenges and obstacles one may have to experience."

Jennifer held Bria's face between her two hands. "The journey of life will throw you curves, trials, tribulations, and even may be paved with stones of despair, hatred, and distain. The mother eagle has experienced many of these feats along her journey and could provide valuable teachings to her little ones. However, she allows them to learn the lesson on their own."

She removed her had from Bria's face and brushed a single strand of hair back. "It is the same for us humans. Once we have taught and laid the foundations, it is up to our children to put them into practice.

"Dear, I was no different than you. I wanted my own experiences. Therefore, I attempted to carve out my own niche, neglecting the training of my aunt Onnie. I soon found out I had to rethink my pathway and add some trails that had already been trodden and described to me."

"Mom, did you really make mistakes along the way? You always seem like you had the right hold on life."

"Bria, no one, not ever your aunt Onnie's or mother Tessa's life story, is without mistakes. Although we make them, someone in our life provided the training and the foundations needed to help us resolve the mistake and continue the path we choose.

"I am no different from the mother eagle. I felt I should give you lessons of life whereby you will be able to make some sound and good decisions as you travel your life's journey of maturity. I knew you would not use all of my suggestions, but at least you would have a foundation built upon sound principles, guidance, and directions to help you understand how you could overcome the many obstacles along your pathway. Just like you had to return to me to resolve issues you attempted to challenge on your own, I did the same and had to go running to Aunt Onnie with tearstains on my face and my pride in my hand."

"Wow, Mom, I never would have thought that. Did Dad make mistakes also?"

"Most adults have, and I expect you will make some also. However, I am proud of many of the decisions you have made during your teen, adolescent, and young adult years. You have done a stellar job and look at you today, all grown up and ready to make that next step on life's pathway."

"Today I am beaming with joy, not only for your professional decisions, but for the personal one. You have chosen to marry your best friend, companion, confidant, and lover."

"Mom, how did you know Marcus was my best friend?"

"I could see the confidence each of you had in the decisions you were making about your life and your careers, plus each of you had the best models, your mother and father."

Bria smiled and gave her mother a big hug.

"However, as a mother with a keen sense of insight, I just know things about you that you would never realize. Today I am transferring this same keen insight to you to pass on to your future children. Use it wisely, and you will be making the same speech to your daughter on her wedding day." Jennifer leaned over and gave her daughter a kiss and a big hug.

Bria smiled and gave her mother another big hug.

"You and Dad are the best parents in my world and outside my world."

"The instant I met Marcus, I knew that he and I would become best friends. We have the same interest, our formative foundations were the same, and he often discussed his parents' expectations of him. It was ironic that our rearing was similar. I would discuss my formative years of training with him and beamed as I spoke highly of our family bond and love. He often said we must have had the same parents because there was not much I could do without my parents knowing about the incident. He and his sister Michelle are very tight and often got into mischief together. They are only eighteen months apart."

Bria took a breath. "Mom, he is my best friend and we can discuss almost anything. He respects my ideas, and I respect his."

"My dear, I hope that the two of you will always be best of friends. When there are difficulties, discuss them openly, try to resolve them that day, never keep secrets from each other, and always go to bed as best friends and lovers."

"Thanks, Mom, that is some good advice."

"Listen, Bria, I could sit here and talk to you for hours, but this is your wedding day, and we must begin to prepare ourselves for the festivities. I brought you something that was given to me by Aunt Onnie on my wedding day. I would be honored if you would wear it today."

Jennifer opened the black velvet jewelry box and showed Bria the contents.

"Aunt Onnie stated it was a present my dad gave to my mom the day I was born, so this day, your wedding day, I am giving it to you so you may pass it on to your oldest daughter on her wedding day."

Jennifer removed the diamond necklace, earrings, and bracelet. She placed the necklace on her daughter's neck, the earrings on her ears, and the bracelet on her wrist.

"My aunt Onnie had a long speech for me when she adorned me with this jewelry, but I will say to you today and forever, I love you and I know you have chosen your soul mate for life. Edwin and I can't wait for our first grandchild to spoil, so make this happen on your honeymoon night."

Bria looked at her mom with a questioning face. "Are you sure you are ready for grandchildren? You and Dad live such a fast-paced life, grandchildren might slow you down."

"Yes, speaking for Edwin and me, we can't wait.

"OK, enough of this, we both need to get dressed. I know the stylists and the makeup artists were in the large cabana assisting your bridesmaids. I'll call Florence to ensure they are ready for the two of us."

As Jennifer was beginning to exit the room, she stopped.

"Oh, I almost forgot to give you this lace handkerchief from your grandmother Tessa. She used it the day she married your grandfather. When she handed it to me, I saw a tear form in her eyes. She loves you and also wants the best for you. I am sure her initial reaction to Marcus has changed. She has had numerous opportunities to see how happy the two of you are together."

Bria did not want to think about her stepgrandmother's reaction to Marcus's introduction. It was as though she saw a ghost in the past when I brought him home for a visit. On subsequent visits, she often pretended she was not feeling well and did not dine with us. The day of my engagement celebration, she came, but her interaction with Marcus's parents and grandparents was laced more with vinegar instead of honey. On the other hand, my aunt Onnie had a finesse about her that drew strangers and friends to her. She made up for the distance and distain that Grandmother Tessa exhibited.

No, he was not from South Carolina and did have parents whose culture and lineage did not mirror Bria's; however, Bria was not concerned with status, culture, and lineage. She was in love, and so was Marcus. The ancient thoughts of Mama Tessa or her friends would not deter her from loving and marrying the man who has stolen her heart.

Bria smiled; she and her friends were not concerned with the way society put a negative spin on specific cultures and lineage. If her parents had taught them to hate those who do not look like them, then she would have never known how love truly feels. Today she is marrying her best friend, her confident, her companion, and her lover. Nothing else mattered to her.

As she looked out of her window at the beautiful landscape designs fashioned by Jacob, her heart skipped a beat. *What if Granddad had never hired Jacob to be our landscape technician? I do not believe there is anyone else in this community that could have done a better job. I must let Jacob know how beautiful the grounds look.*

As she adorned herself with a new silk robe, she thought, *These are different times. The culture and fabric of the United States of America are changing. It doesn't matter how the older generation of my culture and some of the younger generation think they can hold on to past behavior and thoughts against others. The more forward thinkers are moving on to embrace all people regardless of culture, lineage, and ethnicity. Their refusal to accept the changing times will not have any bearing upon the thinking and the desires of many of the millennial generation.*

Bria laughed and thought, *Let them live in the past, but my friends and I are ready for the future.* Bria looked around her room. *Today is my wedding day, and Mama Tessa will have to live with my choice of a mate.*

Upon returning to her bedroom, Jennifer went to her lingerie drawer to exchange her bra. Rosa had set out the one with the original design of Dolce & Gabbana, but Jennifer had decided to wear the other original dress made by an unknown designer, Mykal. When she opened the lingerie drawer, the package slid to the front. She looked around to ensure Edwin was not within eyesight. She picked it up slowly, still wondering about the contents and why was it addressed only to her. Yes, she and Mr.

William had a very good relationship. Sometimes they would talk about political and social issues until the wee hours of the morning. This often occurred when Edwin was out of town on business.

She heard a stir behind her and quickly placed the package back into the drawer. In her mind, she thought, *I have to remember to place this in my personal wall safe.*

"Jennifer, you need to drink a cup tea and eat a piece of pastry before the wedding. We will not be eating at the reception until five thirty or six."

"I'm OK, but because you are concerned, I will eat a little before I go to the powder room down the hall where the hairstylist and the makeup artist are waiting for Bria and me."

"Both of my girls are beautiful without those services, but for today I will concede and let the professionals showcase their skills. Thirty-three years ago when I first met you, you were beautiful, and today you still emit that same beauty. Don't let the makeup artist put too much of her products on you. You are flawless and beautiful without it. I'll be here waiting for your return, my gorgeous Jen."

ONNIE'S SECRETS

O nnie was restless as she sat in the sitting area of the guest room. In her thoughts, "Maybe I should have accepted William's proposal of divorcing Tessa so he could marry me. William had suggested to me several times that he would just buy Tessa out of the marriage so that we could be together until death do us part."

A tear dropped on her cheek, and she gently wiped it. "Today is not the day for me to be reminiscing about my relationship with William. It is surprising though, I know for a fact that Tessa was aware of our relationship, but she never told anyone else. I wonder why!"

She looked out of the window and took in the beautiful garden scene. She would tell Jacob after the wedding what a magnificent job he had done. She looked down at the diamond and emerald ring William had given her almost twenty years ago. She brought the ring up to her lips and kissed it. Her thoughts focused again on her beloved William.

"Anyway, my marriage to William would not have been an appropriate position to be in since I was more focused on Jennifer meeting Edwin and the two of them becoming one. I enjoyed my relationship with William, and I knew it was wrong, but for once in my life someone other than Jennifer has made my life worth living. There were also some secrets I had not divulged to William about the Barclay-Dusett family, but I know he would have still loved me even if he knew."

She looked around at the guest room and a tear dropped down her cheek.

"Yes, I had plenty of material possessions and status in my hometown, but before William came into my life, it was dull and lonesome. I had a pretty steady friendship and relationship with my half brother Douglas Cromwell, William's friend and college roommate. Many people in my hometown did not know that Cromwell was my half brother, and that was why we were so tight.

"Since there was no romantic involvement, Cromwell easily gave his blessings to my and William's romantic relationship. Like me, my mother had been Cromwell's father's, Douglas Cromwell Pappas III, mistress for many years. My brother and I were the products of their love connection. Although his surname was Pappas, he used his mother's maiden name, Dusett, for our surname. My mother hyphenated our name to Barclay-Dusett.

"When I was three, my father moved my mother from South Carolina to Barbour County. Douglas Cromwell Pappas III was well-established in his town of Eufaula, Alabama, and his many businesses and holdings made him very rich. In fact, he bought the land I currently own and created business connections for my mother. He never neglected his parental responsibilities for my brother and me."

As she reached over to grab a tissue, she felt a cool breeze move across her face. She smiled, for she knew it was William's spirit letting her know everything would be OK.

Onnie laughed out loudly and long. Yes, she had them all tiptoeing around her thinking she was in the beginning stages of dementia. Her mind was just as clear as the day she was born.

She can recount all of her life experiences from childhood to now.

"It's funny how your mind can sometimes take you back to times and places you do not want to remember. You think these events and situations have been totally erased from the memory chip in your brain. However, it surfaces at the most inopportune time. No, today is not the day or the time to remember how Crowell came to my aid while I was living in New York."

"It must be a part of my DNA or my formative training, because I seem to gravitate to married men. Yes, I wanted badly to be married and have a family of my own, but the single men did not and could not steal my heart. There was something magical about the married men I met. Especially the senator from New York.

"From the onset of our relationship, I felt comfortable, secure, loved, captivated, and charmed by him. I had this torrid love affair with a well-known senator from New York. He was very attentive to me and always came to the New York Opera House to see me perform. It was as though he was not married, for I spent most of my free time with him either in New York or Washington DC.

"One night during our lovemaking, I advised him that I was pregnant with his child and I was going to keep it. Our love affair had lasted four years, and I knew he was not going to divorce his wife and marry me. Therefore, I needed a child of my own to maintain the love bond between us.

"How vividly I remember that night, a different personality was revealed in my lover when I broached the subject of my pregnancy. This personality had been kept hidden from me for the past four years. He was filled with rage and hate. He called me names that hurt me to my soul. I was accused of trying to sabotage his political aspirations. I was aware that he had his eye on the presidency, and no one, not even Ms. Opera Singer (what he called me that night), would bring damage to his political career. I could fell his rage and hurt penetrating through my very soul. I totally felt like a worn-out dish towel that was now being discarded and never to be used again. How dare he insinuate that I was attempting to destroy his political aspirations!

"All my life my model and my environment revealed to me that love did not hurt, had no obstacles to prevent it from going forth, and it had no boundaries. My father loved my mother, and although he never divorced his wife, I could tell in his touch, his kiss, his devotion to her and to us that the love for his second family was as great and as real as the love for his legal family. He would often say to my mother, 'I have enough love to embrace my legal family and my specially loved family.'

"How often had my lover told me how special I was to him! Although he was legally married, I was the one that truly had his heart. Now he wanted me to rid myself of our love child, a part of him and me. Our love child growing inside me. Had I mistakenly thought this man mirrored the personality and characteristics of my real father? Did he really think I would use our love child to block his political aspirations and opportunities?

"This was not in my DNA, nor was it a part of my model. You accepted what is/was and learn to love and live within your situations and circumstances. Wasn't this the behavior the Dusett women exhibited, the role of the mistress, the true commitment as the other woman? What do I do now? I had no song, no script, or model to handle this situation.

"My mother's situation was different. There was need for her to worry about the next move to make. My father never made her cry. I never saw her sad, only happy and much in love when my father made his weekly visits. My model never provided the formula on how to handle the situation I was now facing. My mother was always smiling and walked around with an aura of happiness. There was no reason for me to second-guess her reactions on how to handle my father's legal wife or legal family. Even when my father had to cut his visits short or could not stay long during special celebrations, my mother kept her emotions intact and her smile bright.

"The situation with my lover was clouding my judgment. At that moment, I knew I was not as strong as my mother. I was devastated. All I could think of was taking my life, leaving my career, but never would I rid myself of this love child. When my lover threw money on the bed and stated, 'Handle it,' and walked out of the door, a new Onnie developed in my soul and my spirit."

Wiping the tears from her eyes, Onnie began to smile, but these thoughts of suicide were only for a fading moment. "I was Onnie Barclay-Dusett, a woman who had been trained to be emotionless, to exhibit strength, and to overcome whatever obstacles life may scatter along my pathway. My mother had definitely modeled that behavior in my innermost soul. I was too strong and too independent for any man, no matter how much I loved him, to alter my career goals and aspirations. No, he would never be able to penetrate my inner soul to challenge me or dictate the choices for my life.

"I had been schooled well by my mother not to show emotions openly, to be strong through all and in all situations, not to let any man see you sweat and to be independent financially yet dependent on love. My lover would not leave this situation without me letting him know he was not in charge of my destiny. I was my mother's daughter, but I had my father's independent and get-even nature. He would pay for the hurt that Onnie Barclay-Dusett was experiencing.

"I knew I had to rewrite the script, score a different song, and dance to a different rhythm. It was not going to be easy, but strength and tenacity were ingrained in me from birth. I knew what others in my hometown said about my mother and her living arrangements, but it did not deter her one inch. She knew her role as the other woman, and those who criticized her were jealous that their lives were not as rich and fulfilling as hers.

"My mother had it all, just not a piece of paper to denote a legal bonding to the one she loved. Yes, I was sure I would be victorious in this situation. I was a Barkley-Dusett. No one would upstage my dreams. No one would or could change the script. No one would be able to replace me as the lead in this operatic drama. Yes, I knew the senator would pay, and the damage would be for a lifetime."

Onnie's smile widened when she thought about her brother Crowell. Yes, he came to her rescue. Her senator lover was not aware of the relationship between her and Former Senator Pappas, now Governor of Alabama Pappas. "With all of the contacts my brother had politically and professionally, my senator lover would soon feel the wrath of my brother's contacts. As soon as I made that phone call, he immediately came to New York.

"I am not sure what was discussed with my senator lover. However, his political career and aspirations for the presidency were no longer an option for him. In fact, during our last conversation, he was more concerned about my health, about my career as an opera singer, and the financial obligations for his unborn child."

Onnie looked around the guest room to ensure no one was there as she wiped the tears from her eyes. She had made a promise to herself after the affair with the senator that she would change her affinity for married lovers, but when William Edwin Langley Sr. walked into her life, the eagle departed and the dove entered. He softened her heart and her newly found outlook on love. "What a beautiful love affair it was, and I have never regretted the times I spent with him!

"Yes, my life has been overflowing with a number of waterfalls, pitfalls, raging rivers, and gentle streams, but my ocean of love for William Langley II (Sr.) no one would be able to fathom. He was more than my moon, sun, and planets. He was my other universe where only the two of us existed."

Onnie walked over to the bay window of the sitting room, taking in the beautifully landscaped garden created by Jacob. She smiled for she was aware of the bond and relationship William had with Jacob. She had often counseled him to tell his son, before his demise, but William was afraid that it would bring a wedge between father and son. Her thoughts went back to the day Jennifer insisted that she move from Alabama to South Carolina.

"When I began to pretend I was in the beginning stages of dementia, I did not believe that my beautiful niece would uproot me from Alabama and move me to South Carolina. I was concerned about how I would handle being that close to my lover William and his wife Tessa, but remember I am Onnie Barclay-Dusett. I had a good role model and teacher, my mother. Here I am today, a true living testimony of tenacity, endurance, and strength. Thanks, Mother.

"I had tried every trick I could to stay in Barbour County. I even convinced my primary doctors to suggest to Jennifer that I may be in the beginning stages of dementia and should not be moved because I was still able to care for myself. One even suggested that the move may trigger a faster progression of the disease.

"All of my carefully planned schemes backfired on me, and here I am back in my mother's home state. I should have come up with another scheme since Jennifer was a replica of me and would not budge from her decision of moving me to South Carolina.

"She was determined to have me close to her. Can you imagine she wanted to move me into this estate with Tessa, my lover's wife! What a disaster that would have been. I laugh now just thinking about that suggestion. It was a good thing that during this transition, William was very ill and needed constant medical attention. Otherwise I would have been adamant about not moving to South Carolina."

A tear formed on Onnie's cheek. "I was sad the whole time William was ill, my beloved William not knowing who I was most times whenever I would visit him secretly in his living quarters. My heart would be filled with much joy when he would reach over and touch my face and run his fingers across my lips. How I longed to get in the bed with him and hold the man that stole my heart almost thirty-plus years ago. Every so often he would be able to slowly say, 'I love you.' Then tears would form in both of our eyes.

"I knew I could not coexist in the same house with Tessa. It would be total chaos each and every day. Although there were three wings to the house, I could not bear to see the face of the one who brought so much pain and unhappiness to my beloved William.

"Well, you know me having to be in control, so I suggested an assisted living facility or a condo in a retirement facility instead of moving into the BIG HOUSE. My niece made my suggestion a reality. I ended up moving into a very exquisite over-fifty-five living facility with my own unattached three-bedroom condo. These facilities were developed and designed for the powerful and rich. They have all the amenities anyone could have imagined.

"How I wished that William had not been ill when I moved here, for the facilities were just far away enough so we could continue our love relationship. Tessa's second would have kept her from traveling here to confront us.

"Now I know it was not meant to be. I have my memories, and I cherish every minute and hour I spent in the arms of my beloved William."

ONNIE'S SPECIAL PRESENTATION

Onnie moved over to the table and picked up several sheets of paper. She had to get this to the wedding coordinator and the orchestra's leader. This was going to be her surprise to her favorite great-niece and the family. She moved closer to the door, papers in hand, and called out to Florence. "Florence, would you please come here? I need your assistance."

Florence entered the door. She was used to Ms. Onnie barking out orders, but this request did not have any malice attached to it.

"Yes, Ms. Onnie, is something wrong?"

"No, Florence, I need your assistance to get me to the wedding coordinator and the orchestra's leader. I have a special surprise for my niece I would like to provide during the wedding reception."

"Ms. Onnie, is Ms. Jennifer aware of this surprise?"

With attitude in her voice, she stated, "No, Jennifer and no one else are aware of this special presentation, that's why it's special and it is a surprise. Florence, do not hassle me today over this matter, just take care of my request. If you don't, we both know I could inform Jennifer about our secret regarding your son's misfortune? Yes, I can remember what happened today and yesterday, and if you don't assist me, I will have a private audience with my niece."

"Ms. Onnie, you know I will assist you. I just don't want you to get in trouble with Ms. Jennifer. Today is so special for her and her family, and I would hate for you to do something to upset the day."

Onnie looked directly at Florence with a condescending smile.

"Florence, you are quite aware of my capabilities. Let me see, you have been my personal assistant—or should I use the word maid?—for the past four years. If anyone besides my personal physician knows my mental capacities, it is you."

Looking directly into Florence's eyes, she asked, "Did you hesitate to get my assistance when your son was about to get expelled from the University of Alabama? Of course not, you knew I had contacts and would use them to save you and your son from the wrath of your husband. Just because he is one of their prize football players, he has to remember it is still the South. Need I say more? Now if you want the old Onnie to surface today, it only takes a minute. I do not have time to quiver with you over this matter. Just escort me to see the wedding coordinator, and I will take care of the rest."

Florence walked Ms. Onnie out to the gardens and located the wedding coordinator.

Ms. Onnie turned to Florence and stated, "Come back to get me in the next thirty minutes."

"Ms. Onnie, I do not want to get in any trouble leaving you here alone."

"Florence, I will be OK, and if I get out of hand, I am sure Ms. Kennedy will put me in my place. All I need is thirty minutes with Ms. Kennedy."

Marsha Smith-Kennedy had been coordinating weddings and other social events for the upscale Charleston communities for the past twenty-five years. She was very capable of dealing with the snooty and the hard-to-please clients. She had also been instrumental in coordinating birthday parties and dinner parties for members of the who's who list in states such as Florida, California, Nevada, New York, Texas, and Washington.

She had heard about Ms. Onnie but had never had any dealings with her. This was not the day or the time for Ms. Onnie to upstage all of her planning for this wedding. The guest list consisted of the famous, the wealthy, the well-known politically and socially, as well as those who were climbing and clawing their way up.

Marsha knew she had at least two hours before the guests begin to arrive and didn't have time to listen to this old lady's tirades; this lady was not going to alter her plans.

She had made sure this wedding would have no mishaps, and Ms. Onnie would not put a damper on her plans today.

From the steps of the veranda, Florence could see Ms. Onnie speaking to Ms. Kennedy, showing her the papers she had in her hands. It appeared that Ms. Kennedy was in agreement with her special surprise and walked her over to the orchestra's leader. She handed the band leader the papers, and he shook Ms. Onnie's hand. Then he gave a sheet of the paper to each of the members of the orchestra. As they began to play some melody, Florence heard Rosa called her name. She turned into the direction of Rosa's voice.

"Florence, have you lost your mind? Why is Ms. Onnie over there with Ms. Kennedy and the bandleader?"

"Rosa, I don't believe we have anything to worry about. Ms. Kennedy has done too many of these types of events to let one old demential woman counteract her plans. She said she had a special presentation for her great-niece during the reception. My knowledge of her professional endeavors, she was once a great classical pianist and opera singer during her youth and most of her young adult years. I have heard her sing and play portions of several classical, religious, and pop pieces. For the past two months, I have seen her writing some notes on paper and playing it to make some adjustments or changes to the melody. She even had some musical professor from the college to come over and help her with the piece. I wonder if that is the song she has shared with the musicians."

Florence smiled and shook her head. "You know what, most of you think she is in the beginning stages of dementia, but I am with her every day, and I have not really seen her in a bad way. She still knows how to bark out orders and directions and how to keep me in check. She is a stellar actress when she is around her family."

"OK, Florence, it's your job if she does anything out of the ordinary, something that may be embarrassing to her family. Listen to that melody, it is beautiful. If she wrote that, then the family and guests will be amazed. Let's hope that's what she wanted with Ms. Kennedy and the bandleader."

Rosa pointed toward the stage on the large cabana. "Look, Florence. She is waving her hand at you, time for you to go get the queen." Both of the women laughed, and Florence walked toward the stage to get Ms. Onnie.

As Florence walked closer to Ms. Onnie and Ms. Kennedy, she heard Ms. Onnie thank Ms. Kennedy for accommodating her.

Florence knew it would take some time for Ms. Onnie to get dressed for the occasion, because she was an immaculate and stylish dresser and no one would believe that this diva was seventy-eight years old. She still had a head full of hair, her skin was still smooth and soft, and no age spots could be noticed on any parts of her body. Every day at 7:30 AM you could find her on the treadmill in her bonus room. Was she vain, for a woman of her age? No, she just remembered the way she was and wanted that image to stay on everyone's mind. Therefore she hurried their steps toward the east wing of the estate.

Onnie stopped in front of a beautiful punch and wine fountain decorated stately with beautiful flowers and a bride-and-groom ice sculpture. She looked around at the estate grounds and smiled.

"Florence, isn't Jacob's landscaping services the best? Just look at these grounds, ready for any magazine pertaining to gardening and landscaping. I remember Jacob when he first started as the groundskeeper for the Langley estate. He was not only the groundskeeper but also Mr. William's chauffer and companion on short business trips. There were times when Mr. William did not want to fly. Therefore, Jacob would drive him to Barbour County and other cities in Alabama to check on his textile factories. I don't know when I first met him, but I knew he had talent, because he helped my groundskeeper design my floral gardens. William had already bragged to me about his skills, talents, and work ethics, many of the reasons William helped him establish his business. Yes, Mr. William was a pioneer in helping others become established. I can remember . . ."

She stopped in the middle of her sentence; she did not want to reveal too much to Florence, she already knew too much, but there were several pieces missing to the puzzle, and she would not be the one who would supply them.

Florence looked at her, and in her mind, she thought, *You almost gave away your darkest kept secret, but all of us except Ms. Jennifer and possibly Mr. Edwin knew you were the reason Mr. William made all of those trips to Alabama, the reason he purchased the condo in Maui and the one in Destin, Florida. Yes, those were the lovers' getaway places for you and Mr. William.* Then Florence reached out for Ms. Onnie's hand and gently guided her into foyer of the estate toward the east wing of the estate.

"Come on, Florence, just looking at these grounds and how beautiful the day is going to be is causing me to be sentimental, and you know that is not a part of my demeanor. I often hear you and Rosa refer to me as a tough old cookie. That I am! I do have another side, you should know that, especially when I made an effort to resolve your son's issue at the University of Alabama. You know I can beg, plead, and cry when needed."

Florence placed her arm under Ms. Onnie's arm and began walking her toward her room in the east wing of the estate.

"Ms. Onnie, it is almost time for the family to gather in the downstairs theater. I know you may want to make sure your makeup and attire is just right so let's hurry to your room.

When they passed the door of Tessa's room, Florence was shocked to see it ajar and even noticed some items on the floor. She wondered why the nurse had not dressed her for the occasion.

Not to alarm Ms. Onnie, she made sure she would walk her to her room and then go back and check on Ms. Tessa.

Tessa could be a handful even in her current state, so Florence did not want to make any sudden moves to stir up the storm that could be raging inside Tessa. She let go of Ms. Onnie's arm and advised her she would be back in less than fifteen minutes.

TESSA'S INTERNAL RAGE

Florence, not Rosa or Ms. Onnie, was aware that Tessa had been watching the whole incident from her bedroom window. However, she was not knowledgeable of the interaction, but she was sure it was some presentation that Onnie was planning for her granddaughter. She heard the orchestra playing a beautiful melody but was not sure if it was one to be heard at the wedding.

In her mind, she thought, *She will not outdo me. I am the only grandmother Bria knows, and if something fabulous is to be presented, it will come from a collection of jewelry that William gave me. This presentation has to be something grand and more momentous than hers.*

While Tessa was pondering her next move, she looked at the pale silver-colored dress hanging in the closet that Bria had designed for this wedding. Although hers was not made like Onnie's, she did not want on the same color as that bitch. She rolled her wheelchair over to her dress and pulled out a pair of scissors from her wheelchair the nurse used to sometimes change bandages and dressings.

She looked around to see if the nurse had returned. She had sent her on an errand to the kitchen to fix her a light lunch and to summon her grandson Michael.

She carefully placed the scissors in her unaffected right hand and began cutting the sleeves, the blouse, and the hem of the dress. She carefully placed the scissors back in the side of the wheelchair, and then she wheeled herself to the dressing table and picked up the hairbrush and began to undo the style the stylist had completed hours ago.

A smirk graced her face as she took her tissues and began clearing the makeup from her face. She looked at the clock on her nightstand, and it was 2:30 PM. She had ample time to get changed into her new gown and to prepare her presentation for her granddaughter. Then she rolled herself out into the hallway. She knew that Florence, Rose, or the nurse would be checking on her soon.

As soon as Florence reached the lower end of the east wing, she saw Ms. Tessa in the middle of the hallway, hair in disarray and tears streaming from her face. She was wondering why she was there and why she was crying. Florence looked back and saw Ms. Onnie walking toward them from the designated guest room.

Florence hurried to Ms. Onnie and stated, "Do you mind if I see to Ms. Tessa? I am not sure why she is out in the hallway without the assistance of her nurse. I must see what is wrong. I know you are capable of getting back to your sitting area without my assistance."

Florence released Ms. Onnie's hand and walked swiftly toward Ms. Tessa. As she got closer to Ms. Tessa's wheelchair, she saw the disaster that Ms. Tessa had performed on her hair and her makeup.

She quickly pushed her into the room and asked her, "Ms. Tessa, what happened, why is your hair and makeup in disarray. Are you OK?"

Florence scanned the room. "Do I need to call the nurse? Where is she, where did you send her? Why don't you have on your dress for the wedding?"

As Florence walked into the large closet, she saw pieces of Tessa's dress lying on the floor of the closet.

In Tessa's lap was a whiteboard she often used to communicate with Florence or her private nurse. The words on the board were "need changing now." Florence was distraught—should she call Rosa or just wait for the nurse? This was Bria's wedding day, and she did not need any drama from this woman.

"Would you like for me to find you another gown to wear to the wedding?"

Tessa nodded her head in an affirmative way.

"Let me push you into the walk-in closet, and you can pick another one. I hope Ms. Jennifer will understand that you had soiled this one and we had to change it."

Tessa looked up at her and mouthed yes. On her whiteboard she wrote, "The one I wore to William's sixty-fifth birthday party."

Florence did not know the significance of this dress, but she did not need any more drama. So she allowed Ms. Tessa to point to the gown she wanted to wear.

Tessa smiled, because she knew this was the dress that she had designed for William's birthday party, and many of the female guests were so amazed at the color and the style that Ms. Onnie's presence at this affair was vaguely noticed. Yes, she knew what she was doing and why she did it. She smiled and almost laughed out loud as Florence carefully removed the dress from the closet's bar.

On her whiteboard she wrote, "Jewelry." As Florence began to walk toward her dressing table, the nurse and Michael walked into the room. Tessa wheeled the chair around and spoke slowly, trying to enunciate each word, "Leave. William—I mean Michael stays."

Tessa looked at Michael; he was so much like his granddaddy in statute, personality, and in looks. He had his family fooled—they thought he was the son who had it all together; however, she knew the other side of Michael. That was the reason she summoned him for this task.

"Sure, Ms. Tessa, as soon as I dress you in the other gown, then we can find the jewelry to match, and I can get the stylist and makeup artist to come back and redo your hair and makeup."

Tessa looked at Florence and then the nurse and began to slowly speak, "Nooo, juust the dress. I need Michael! Leave! Hair, face done later!"

Florence and the nurse asked Michael to step outside while they dressed his Mama Tessa.

Tessa and Michael had a special relationship that most of the family did not know about. Yes, he exhibited the model professional and business side to his parents, siblings, and aunt, but she knew the foolish and wild side of Michael. She had helped him out of several scrapes with his bookie, his gambling troubles in Las Vegas and Atlantic City, as well his numerous troubles with wayward women. In fact, he was the one that gave her the sordid truth about his grandfather's affair with his aunt Onnie.

She received this information at the time when she had stated enough was enough and she would not give him any more money for his gambling and womanizing troubles. She smiled as she remembers him saying, "I have some news about Granddad that may be of valuable interest to you and help you win back his affection. I know who has been his mistress for years. In fact I have seen them in Maui, New York, and Destin, Florida, but they never saw me. They were busy being lovers. I know you are concerned about the large credit card bill at the Ritz in Maui, but there is a perfectly good reason for this bill. I will pay you back as soon as my buddies send me their part."

Tessa lifted her arms with the help of the nurse so Florence could slip the gown over her head. In her head she continued to reminisce about her relationship with Michael.

Michael went on to tell me how he had made plans a number of times to use the various houses in each of these cities but noted they were being occupied by his grandfather and a woman friend. At first he thought that it was a coincidence, but after seeing them several times at the same locations, he knew what was for real—they were lovers!

When he finally figured out the truth one spring break weekend, some of his previous MBA buddies from Wharton School of Business (University of Pennsylvania) and he had planned a grand weekend celebration in Maui. When he arrived at the airport, he saw his granddad and aunt Onnie getting into a limo. He hailed a cab and had the cab follow them to the Maui condo. From his view from the cab's window, they looked like any loving and married couple. He left without them noticing and checked into the Ritz Carlton. He had to use my American Express credit card to rent a suite at the Ritz Carlton for his weekend party.

During his moment of confession, he also informed me that this was not the first time he had seen them together. He had seen them often in New York, Alabama, Maui, and Destin, Florida.

I knew William had another love interest when he moved out of our bedroom years ago. This action took place when he discovered some fake documents of mine, but why Onnie? When I gained knowledge of this relationship, it made perfect sense why he was so enthralled with the courtship and marriage of Edwin to Jennifer. As the two of them would look at each other, smile, and say, "Keeping it in the family . . ."

Tessa was glad when Florence and the nurse had finished dressing her in the new gown, because now she and Michael could work on her surprise presentation to her granddaughter, Bria. Within less time than Florence thought had expended, she and the nurse had changed Ms. Tessa and advised her they would return within thirty minutes with the stylist and the makeup artist.

Once the ladies exited the room, Michael entered with a worried look on his face. Tessa signaled to him to lock the door. On her whiteboard, she wrote, "Open the Safe for me."

Michael did not question her but wheeled her into the large walk-in closet toward the location of the safe. Again she spoke slowly, "Opeen!" Michael looked at her, with a frown on his face. He knew she had helped pay off his last gambling debt, so what did she need from the safe? She looked at him again and on her whiteboard wrote, "Open Safe."

"I need the combination of the safe, Mother Tessa, I do not know it, and you have never given it to me."

She wrote on the whiteboard, "BONNIE."

"That's a strange combination or password. What does it stand for?" Tessa smiled as she wrote, "Bitch ONNIE, can always remember!"

Both Michael and Tessa laughed out loudly.

Once Michael opened the safe, she had him retrieve an emerald and diamond necklace, bracelet, and earrings from her wall safe. He also removed a beautiful velvet jewelry box and bag. From the pocket on her wheelchair she gave him a monogrammed note card.

On the whiteboard, she instructed him to write a prose to his sister from her. Each of them knew how gifted he was with words and how some of his special notes to his special women had gotten him into plenty of trouble.

Once the tasks had been completed, she hid both the jewelry and the note card in the pocket of her wheelchair. She then instructed him to advise the wedding coordinator, Ms. Kennedy, of her presentation. William would read the prose due to Tessa's stroke; Tessa would present the package to Bria.

It was all settled, and Tessa felt the internal anger and rage subside. She laughed for in her mind she thought that her presentation would more than outshine Onnie's.

Michael was delighted to run this errand, because he wanted to check out Ms. Kennedy to see if she had a sexual appetite like he did. He was already plotting how he would see what other types of skills she had besides coordinating weddings. He was planning to check this out in the cabana during the reception while everyone else was enjoying the concert and dancing.

As he opened the door, he saw Florence and the nurse coming down the hall with the stylist. Their timing was just right.

While descending the stairs of the third-floor east wing toward the gardens, Michael thought he saw his aunt Onnie slip out of the room next to Mother Tessa's, but his mind was so focused on the wedding coordinator, Ms. Kennedy, that he did not turn around to make sure it was her.

Yes, she was at least ten years his senior, but he preferred older women, and her wandering eyes this morning as he and his brother walked through the gardens after their tennis match revealed she liked them young. To him, this was more important than worrying about Aunt Onnie.

THE SNITCH REVEALED

O nnie was very familiar with the layout of this house, especially the third-floor east wing. William Sr. had confided in Onnie that the walls in the room next to Tessa were very thin, and not only could you hear the conversation through those walls, but if you opened the fireplace grate, the conversation was very coherent even if the inhabitants were in the closet. That was the reason he had chosen the larger room three doors down and on the west side of the hall.

Onnie's blood began to boil in her veins. She knew there was a special closeness between Tessa and Michael, but she could not put her finger on it. Now she knew why he was so loyal to Tessa. She had been paying off his gambling debts and womanizing activities in exchange for his information on his grandfather and his lover. She was not concerned about Tessa knowing about the relationship; for years she had wanted William to tell her, but he refused. He still felt some type of obligation to her since he was legally married to her on paper but not in his heart.

Onnie's real concern was the reputation of the Langley family. Her lover William, his son, and her niece Jennifer had worked hard to maintain their dignity and reputation, and Michael and Tessa would not be the ones to tarnish their hard work. She thought how long can his wayward actions escape the news?

His family was well-known in the Charleston area, and any amount of gossip about the Langley family would be news for the various business competitors and his enemies. She needed to approach Michael on this subject because she did not want any unnecessary gossip to surface on this family.

She and William had been careful to protect their affair, and she had been an ideal role model for her niece and great-niece. She was not going to let anyone, including her great-nephew, paint another picture.

She was very familiar with the paparazzi and wondered how he had avoided them all these years. She would have to get to the bottom of this. However, today was not the time to discuss it, but she would find the right moment and the right time.

Onnie knew she would also have to clip his wings, since he was the one who revealed her and William's secret to Tessa. *We thought we were so careful with our rendezvous. I just can't imagine my own great-nephew would be the one to find out our little secret and use this knowledge to help him out of his sordid affairs with women and his obsession with gambling.*

She walked into her assigned room with a smile, and speaking to no one in particular, "If Tessa thinks she can outdo *Bitch* ONNIE, she is gravely mistaken. I always travel with the jewels that my beloved William gave me. On one of our many trips to New York, William had bought me a beautiful diamond and sapphire bracelet and ring. He had a matching tiepin and lapel pin made for him. I will present these items to Bria and Marcus after I serenade Bria.

"No, Ms. Tessa, you cannot outscheme the true schemer. You would be surprised if you knew the personal information William had discussed with me. You hurt him to his soul, and I am the only one that will see to it that you pay for all the pain you brought to my beloved William."

Onnie's smile turned into a big grin; yes, she would devise a plan that would trap Michael in revealing his wayward side to his family and one that will ensure Tessa would be eternally grateful to her for not telling the secrets of her heritage. After the wedding, these two will be sorry they ever tangled with her.

When Florence and the nurse entered Ms. Tessa's room, she could tell that her entire demeanor had changed. She was glowing and smiling, and she had on a single strand of black pearls, with matching earrings and bracelet. They matched perfectly with the black and white pearls inset on the pale yellow gown she was now wearing. Although it was a far cry from silver, she was sure that neither Jennifer nor Bria would object.

In fact, Florence and the nurse looked at each other, for it appeared there was a certain glow emitting from Ms. Tessa. Even her eyes had a certain twinkle. After the stylist and the makeup specialist completed the tasks of redoing Ms. Tessa's hair and face, the nurse turned to her and stated, "Ms. Tessa, you look beautiful today. It's time for me to take you to the theater room on the second floor. All of the wedding members will be in this room. I'll stay close by you in the event you may need some assistance."

Once Florence could tell that Ms. Tessa's entire demeanor had changed and she appeared stable and ready for the wedding, she started toward the guest room to take Ms. Onnie to the second-floor theater room.

Before departing Tessa's room, Florence carefully walked the nurse to the door.

"Today is a special day for the Langley family. Let's make sure that the two old biddies are nowhere near each other in the theater room. We do not need any type of drama or chaos today."

TESSA'S FAMILY SECRETS

T he nurse knew Ms. Onnie would be in the same room, and today was not the day for two old biddies to cause chaos.

As the nurse wheeled Ms. Tessa to the elevator to descend to the second floor, Tessa's mind began to think about her life as Tessa Adkins. If her mother could see her in action today and if her father were alive, she would tell him a thing or two about his actions toward her mother.

Most people who observed her behavior did not realize that she loved William until the day he died, but it appeared that her father's evil and malicious ways had infiltrated her body, mind, and soul, and this same inherited behavior transcended to her actions toward the man she loved. Since she did not have a good model of marital love, it was obvious she did not know how it looked and felt and how it should have been given.

Tessa remembers very clearly the day her father took his last breath. Her mother had done a good job of comforting him during his illness. He never stopped smoking even when the doctor and the family asked him; therefore, his death was a result of lung and throat cancer.

As he laid there suffering from the treatment and the pains of the cancer, his evil and deceitful actions toward my mother were quite evident in his reactions to her touch. Sometimes he would refuse to open his eyes or turn his head toward her when she entered the room.

I sometimes wondered what was going on in his head—was it disgust with my mother or with himself? This day as his breathing became short and shallow, he looked around the room for my mother, his wife, Cora Anne Massie (Massey). Whatever he whispered in her ear that day brought a big smile to her face. To this day, my mother had not revealed the last words he spoke.

In her mind, Tessa thought, I loved my father, but there were no tears for his dying. I just stood there looking at him, realizing that now my mother and I could relax and not feel so stressed in his presence.

In fact, I can remember a smile formed on my face, the tension melted away from my body, and I had to hold back the laughter. Was this right for a daughter to feel this way?

I am not sure but as soon as I had these thoughts it felt like a blanket of despair was carefully removed along with the anger and disgust I had harbored for years. My body instantly became hot and then cooled down. I could actually see the perspirations forming on my torso.

Subconsciously, I told myself that I would not be my father's daughter, but reflecting upon my actions to William, I was my father's daughter. I kept secrets from him and I did things to upstage his relationship with his grandson Michael.

This day made her think more and more about her family and she began to reminisce about her family life. My mother was so passive toward the actions of my father. It appeared that the two of them grew up in the same community of Hamburg, South Carolina.

Although it was not understood until she was a young adult, how her father's bragging nature of his family's descendants were pure and the A on the census report so noted, which made him more acceptable in their community as opposed to my mother's family descendants, the Massie's who were recorded in the census as a R.

Sometimes he would say, I married you because you were pretty and could blend into any culture, you were smart, a hard worker, knew how to be an obedient wife and mother and not make waves.

Yes, I chose the right one even if your ancestors were dubbed as an R during the 1800 census report of Hamburg, South Carolina. During my young adult period, I began questioning my mother about the statements my father would make. Oftentimes she would answer, "Do not listen to your father. It is a combination of his knowledge of his mother's promiscuous nature with different men and him really denying his own bloodline."

After much prodding and research about some of the inhabitants of the Hamburg community especially the farmland belonging to the Hamburg Plantation, I understood why my father degraded my mother and was not very lovable and fond of me.

I made up in my mind then and there I would not be passive to any man like my mother. I would be an independent, successful woman who would carve out my own niche with or without a man.

My ancestral or descendant background would not hinder me from blending into the right cultural, because the woven fabrics of most nations were changing and it was becoming more difficult to determine the ancestral background of many of the inhabitants.

My father was a tyrant and ruled his house as though he was king. He became worse once he earned a degree in business and a MBA. My mother, although according to my father was of the wrong culture, had a BS in elementary education prior to their marriage, but he refused to let her work outside of the home. He often said, "I am the man of this household. I bring in the money and tell you how to manage it."

His degrees and his obsession of being successful in his profession helped him obtain one of the executive positions at the Langley's textile industry. Once he gained this notoriety, his playing field for numerous extramarital affairs increased and his cruelty toward us escalated.

I would watch my mother stay up half the night waiting on him to come home. Sometimes he would come in, see her asleep on the living room coach, laugh and leave her there.

In public, you would think they were the most loving couple; he was always embracing her or kissing her and expressing what a wonderful wife and mother she was. No one could see the bruises on her upper arms and her thighs where he had pinched her throughout the night.

I am sure those bruised transcended from her body parts to her heart.

God knows I tried hard not to be anything like him, but the more I fought the urge, the more his behavior penetrated my being. I would sometimes go into my office and cry especially when I had spoken offensive or harsh words to my subordinates or those I deem as not as successful as I was.

My mother's passive nature was nowhere to be found in my spirit, it consisted only of my father's egotistical and haughty nature. I knew I was a gold digger like my father and it showed in my desire to become more than a nurse in the pediatric unit of the hospital. I was determined to become the director of the children's wing of the hospital as well as the one everyone came to for directions and solutions. I was driven like my father to become successful and dared my maternal ancestral and cultural to hamper my success.

During my times of deceiving William and speaking harsh to him, I would confide in my mother about my actions. Her response was always you are your father's child and you must work hard to relieve his spirit from you, if not it will destroy you and your marriage.

Don't wait until it is too late to reverse your actions.

After my second miscarriage or abortion, whichever you prefer, she said to me, "Your father's spirit stems from him observing his mother's behavior with men. Even though there were only two living children, according to the talk in the community, the midwife helped stop the birth of several others.

"According to community talk, your paternal grandmother is believed to have died from a sexually transmitted disease that was not treated. Prior to her death she went blind and lost her ability to think or talk. After your father and I married, I would suggest that he visited her at the nursing home, but he never did. He even refused to attend her funeral.

"One of the things he instructed me on the day of his death was 'Pray for Tessa to not carry the seed of my mother into her marriage.'"

Tears begin to fill Tessa's eyes, and she reached into the pocket of the wheelchair and retrieved a tissue. The nurse watched her as she dabbed away the teardrops but did not respond.

With her head bowed, Tessa continued to remember her formative years as an Adkins.

Yes, I looked more like his mother than him. I know this is why his actions toward me were so horrible. He saw his mother each time he looked at me.

I could see the tears in my mother's eyes when she said, "There were other things he spoke, but I will keep them only in my heart and carry them to my grave, but he had a good reason for choosing me as his mate. I understood his reasoning. Therefore his verbal abuse did not penetrate my soul. He really wanted to say those things to his mother."

Prior to my father's demise, I decided that the altering or the correcting of the mistakes on my mother's and my birth certificate would bring him around. It was easy to do since the Birth and Death Certification Department for the state of South Carolina did not become effective until January 1, 1915. My father, Joseph Phillip Adkins, was born in 1912, and my mother, Cora Anne Massie, was born in 1914.

Cora Anne was an only child, but my father had one brother. During the early 1900s, the birthday records were either recorded in the Bible or on a sheet of paper by the midwife or the doctor.

Both of my parents' birthdates were recorded in the family Bible and on a strange ledger denoting an R or an A beside each of their descendants' names.

As the director of the pediatric unit, I could easily send in a correction to the birth certificates with or without supporting documents or a declaration from the parents.

I altered the certificates for my mother and me to show my father we were now of equal status. In fact it was very simple since there was no notation on the race line of the original birth certificates for my mother or for me. I assumed this would change his disgust for the two of us and would view us as his equal. To my dismay, he laughed in my face and stated, "This doesn't change a thing, and the two of you could never measure up to my culture and status. The seed of the Nile was permanently removed from my ancestors and the documentation in the ledger proves that. You two are still beneath my family and me, no piece of paper will change that." Then he took the new birth certificates and threw them at me and with an evil smirk, he turned over in his sick bed and grunted, "You are still nothing."

This was the day I lost it, and for the life of me I don't remember my reactions to his words, but the next thing I knew I was acting like a madwoman. How I drove myself back to the Langleys' mansion, I can't remember. All I can remember is my father throwing the documents back at me and saying something about the seed of the Nile removed from his ancestors but not from your mother's. Rosa must have observed my behavior and heard my screams, because she immediately came to me as I began tearing my clothes off me. Once Rosa calmed me down, she called my personal physician. He gave me a sedative and instructions to stay in bed for at least three days.

A vision of my mother as I stood in her home having a short-lived psychological breakdown flashed clearly into my mind. She began to cry and said, "I was passive with him, because I knew he viewed me as his mother on some days, as the woman he truly loved on other days and as the one culture he was trying to remove from his being. I did not help the situation being passive and your view of our unhappy marital bliss has scared your ability to give love and accept love."

A tear formed on Tessa's face, and she immediately wiped it away. Today was the day to show strength and not weakness. Her presentation to Bria had to be far better than Bitch ONNIE's. Her dreary demeanor blossomed into a happier one for she was sure the look on Onnie's face would be one of disgust after her special presentation.

As the nurse settled Tess into the theater room closest to the window overlooking the garden, she noticed Michael speaking to the wedding coordinator, Ms. Kennedy. She smiled, and in her mind, she thought, *I hope it's about my presentation and nothing else.*

While turning away from the window, she noticed Onnie walking into the room. Evilness filled her heart. *This woman who took my William from me for almost forty years can just casually walk into my home and disrespect me.* The rage in her seemed to cool down when a sudden breeze crossed her face and a calming hand brushed across her back. She turned her head to see if Michael had made it back from the gardens, but there was no one behind her. She knew it could only be her mother's or William's spirit letting her know today is not the day to show dissention.

THE ELEPHANT IN THE ROOM

Onnie looked around the room at the wedding party and the family members of the bride and the groom. She strolled over to Marcus's family and greeted each one with a hug and a kiss. She worked the room with her grace and her charm. She made each person feel that they were welcome and that the Langley/Dusett families welcomed them.

In fact she ushered Marcus's parents and grandparents over to chat with Tessa. Although Tessa could not speak clearly, she would often nod her head toward the one speaking. She had her whiteboard on her lap but refused to use it. She did manage to say, "Welcome to the Langley family."

Of course Onnie was very observant. She noticed that Tessa was not wearing the dress Bria specially made for this occasion, nor was it the same color.

Then she realized this was the dress Tessa had made for William's sixty-fifth birthday party. A Calvin Klein original made only for her. It was a beautiful dress, but it did nothing for her at the party and will not stand out at the wedding. *I wonder if she did this to make me jealous, or did she soil the other one. It doesn't matter, because after I do my presentations, that dress may be soiled with tears of pain, sorrow, and hatred.*

An idea formed in Onnie's head. She had to get to the coordinator about her presentation. Instead of going first, she would ask her to let Tessa be the first one to present special gifts to the bride and the groom since Tessa is the only grandmother Bria knew.

This seemed like a logical reason for her grandmother to go first and then her great-aunt. *Yes, that is what I will do as soon as the coordinator comes into the room to get us lined up for the processional. This will surely make Tessa angry, and due to the lateness of the hour, she would not be able to summon Michael to embellish her presentation.*

Onnie covered her mouth because her own thoughts almost made her laugh out loudly. Yes, she was good at what she did!

As she sat down in one of the theater chairs, she could not wait until her beloved Jennifer and her husband, Edwin, arrived.

Again her grace and charm would be a scene out of the best Broadway play.

THE LOVE OF A MOTHER

J ennifer took another look outside at the grounds. This was a very happy moment for her and her family. She had dreamed of this day. Each of her children had done well with her and Edwin's guidance and teachings.

Yes, sometimes they had voiced their objections to their parents' interference, but never to the point of being defiant. Bria had been amenable to most of her parents' suggestions regarding her life choices. *And look at her today, my little girl or young adult is making her first step toward being a responsible wife and mother.*

Jennifer laughed how different it will be with her two sons, Michael and Edwin IV (Will as his nickname). Michael had a disposition like her aunt Onnie and his grandfather William, and of all the children he is closest to Tessa. In fact it is amazing how he often spends quality time with her during some of his not-so-busy weekends, pushing her through the gardens and often taking her to dinner at her favorite restaurant.

Will on the other hand has that giving or humanitarian spirit, more like me. He is cordial to both Tessa and Aunt Onnie but prefers spending time with his best friend, Warren. I think it is because Warren has a sister who is a year younger than Will.

I must remember to discuss with Will about inviting her over for dinner so the family may meet her.

Jennifer continues with her mental thoughts. Both of them have been good sons, and each is working in the family business. Michael has completed his MBA and is currently working on a law degree. Will is not too keen on school but would soon finish a degree in computer engineering and might work on completing an MBA. Both Edwin and I are just praying for him to complete the computer engineering degree and hope maturity will set in soon.

Yes, this was her family, and she loved each one of them no matter how different the personalities they displayed. Edwin had been an excellent role model for them as well as a very good father. Although they came from wealth, Edwin often reminded them that no matter how much we may have, we need to stay focused and work hard to maintain it.

Our children were frequently instructed by their father that nothing could be obtained without working hard or putting forth your best effort. There are prices each of us has to pay to be successful, there will be numerous obstacles to deter us from our successes, but the four Ps will keep us on the right road: preparation, persistence, prayer (unceasing), and continued preparation.

She smiled as she fondly thought of the dinner table discussions between Edwin and his father, William. They often discussed the business ideals of hiring one for the skills the prospective new employee could bring to the table to benefit the goals, objectives, products, and processes of the business.

She would often hear William say, "A business does not thrive on hiring underskilled or underprepared employees. Cultural differences should not hinder the selecting of the right employee who will and can perform the tasks of the position. In the company's management training sessions, the training guide put much emphasis on the following: the self-starter, the communicator, the out-of-the-box thinker, and the one who values the suggestions and ideas of the employee."

Edwin would agree with his father on many of his business practices and philosophy. He continues to maintain the business integrity his father established in all facets of his business ventures.

Another lesson from William was to ensure that each of the children understood the business and would be able to maintain it if something happened to one of them. Therefore during the summers, all of the children had small jobs not only to help them learn the dynamics of the business but also to earn funds to help them with any material items they desired.

Edwin also taught them about saving and investing; therefore, before monies could be spent on recreational activities, each had to invest a certain amount for the future.

Jennifer moved toward the dressing table to take a last look at her hair and her makeup. She looked stunning and was ready for this great day. She heard Edwin's steps in the hallway, but she had to hold the package in her hand one last time. She slowly opened the chest of drawers, picked up the package, and said loudly, "God, whatever is in this package, let it not negatively affect the stamina and bond of this great family."

Edwin walked in without her noticing, because her mind was on the package.

"Why are you praying? I am sure God is aware of the many prayers you have prayed for this family, and today is evidence."

Jennifer quickly threw the package in the drawer and closed it. "Oh, one more prayer to him would not hurt. I know he has heard them and has shown much favor. Just look at our wonderful family and the aura of excitement and enthusiasm on this great day."

"Even your sons have been in their best behavior and have not teased their big sister. In fact did you see the silver charm bracelet the boys bought her to wear? The charm consists of many artifacts from our international summer vacations, for all of our birthdays, and a heart that has been divided into three pieces."

"Yes, Edwin, this family had been truly blessed, and this day is a wonderful day for the Langley and Dusett families."

Edwin walked over to his wife, placed a quick kiss on her lips. "You are the love of my life, and no other woman could have given me the joy, contentment, peace, and love I have happily experienced during our twenty-nine years of marriage. I was thinking, after this wedding, the two of us should go somewhere quiet. We haven't done this in a long time, and from the short time with you in the Jacuzzi, we both need some alone and quality time together."

Then he kissed her again. "Come, my love, let's make this moment happen for our daughter."

Hand in hand they both descended the stairs to the theater room on the second level, the room that was being used as the holding area for the wedding party.

The theater room was filled with much joy and laughter, and why shouldn't it? This was a joyous occasion when two young people would declare their love for each other and become one. Edwin and Jennifer were just ecstatic as they saw both sides of the family as well as the members of the wedding party interacting. She saw her son Will, but Michael had not made it to the room. She looked around to see if she had missed him, but then she saw him entering with the wedding coordinator, Ms. Kennedy.

She made a mental note to express her gratitude to Ms. Kennedy for the exceptional job she had done coordinating her daughter's wedding.

Jennifer's eyes were looking at Tessa, who was facing the outside gardens and not interacting with anyone.

She leaned over to her husband and whispered, "Do you think I should see if Tessa is OK? She is sitting over by the window alone. I am going to ask her nurse to bring her over here by the family."

"Leave her alone. There may be a reason she wants to be alone. I noticed she is wearing the gown she wore at Dad's sixty-fifth birthday party. Do you know why?"

"She may have had an accident in the other gown. I see her smiling with Florence and the nurse, so I will leave her alone."

THE WEDDING PREPARATION

M s. Kennedy took control of the moment and began lining up the family members for the processional. Jennifer looked again at the gown worn by Tessa. It was not the one Bria had specially made for her, but she distinctly remembered the dress as the one made for her father-in law's sixty-fifth birthday. It appeared that Florence must have noticed the look on her face for they both made eye contact, yet they remained quiet.

The cool breeze she felt this morning in her room had passed over her body again. She softly said, "OK, William, I will not inquire until after the ceremony." She winked at Florence; each of them silently laughed. The nurse saw the silent interchange and joined in with the silent laughter.

As Ms. Kennedy continued to provide instructions for the processional, the wedding, and the reception, she heard her aunt Onnie interrupt her instructions regarding special presentations at the reception.

"Ms. Kennedy, I think that since Ms. Tessa is Bria's grandmother, she should make her presentation before me at the reception. This would be more in line with protocol."

Ms. Kennedy looked at Ms. Onnie and stated, "You are absolutely correct. Let me make that correction on my notepad this instant. Thank you for bringing that to my attention."

The smile that engulfed Onnie's face was out of the world; yes, she changed it with little effort and in the presence of all of the wedding party. In her mind she thought, *Now I know I have the upper hand on this matter.*

Onnie refused to look at Tessa, for she knew she was steaming from the inside out.

Ms. Kennedy took one more look around the room to ensure the lineup was correct.

"I believe we are ready for the grand occasion, Mr. Langley. I will escort you to your daughter, Bria, and the rest of the party will be escorted by my assistants to the designated garden entrance.

"The minister, the groom, and the best man will enter from the southeast entrance to the gardens. Please proceed to that entrance now.

"Michael and Will, the doves are in the cages to the right of the bridal arch. Once the minister has officially announced Bria and Marcus as husband and wife, Bria wants her brothers to release the doves.

"Upon my arrival at the garden south entrance, the orchestra will begin the song for the processional. Each of you looks beautiful, handsome, and radiant. It is time for us to let these young people say, 'I do.'"

As each of the members made their way to the south entrance of the garden, Tessa looked into the eyes of Onnie as if to say, "You have won this small battle, but not the entire war."

Onnie leaned over to Tessa and placed her hand on top of Tessa's hand, and then she quietly whispered, "I know Bria is going to be ecstatic over each of our presentations."

The only thing Tessa could do was grunt loudly.

Florence, Rosa, Jennifer, and Nurse Brown all held their breaths hoping nothing chaotic would happen between Onnie and Tessa.

Tessa looked up at her nurse and slowly stated, "Puuush me!"

Onnie walked over to Jennifer, softly kissed her.

"I plan to be in my best behavior for my great-niece's wedding."

Jennifer kissed her back and walked up to her son Michael and took his arm.

THE WEDDING

At exactly 3:30 PM on June 22, 2013, the string orchestra began the processional music for the entrance of the minister, the groom, and the best man. The groom's smile was so bright you felt as though the sun had landed on his shoulder to reveal to all in attendance how bright and solid his love was for the women he was to make his wife.

Jennifer's smile as she saw the minister touch him to help calm down his anxiousness to marry the woman of his dreams. As Jennifer looked around the grounds, her eyes began to tear up; she knew this day was coming, the day she delivered Bria and the day Bria brought Marcus home to meet the family. Her little sweet and precious girl had now become a woman, and soon she and her mate, Marcus, will begin their own family.

She looked up toward the beautiful sky and whispered to William Sr., "I know you are somewhere on these grounds, for not only do I feel your breeze, but I sense your spirit and presence. I am not losing a daughter, but gaining a wonderful son-in-law. I wish you were here to meet this lovely family, but I know in my heart you are smiling down on this occasion. I sensed it in Edwin, and I see it all on Marcus's face.

"My concern for this day is the package that was delivered on her wedding day. I pray it holds information that will continue to bond and strengthen this family and not separate us. However, knowing how much you cherish family, I am sure the contents will draw us closer."

The processional had not begun; she guessed they were waiting for her to come back to earth. She was not aware that her eldest son, Michael, had his arms around her shoulder and was softly wiping tears from her eyes.

Michael looked at her and stated, "Mom, this is a big day for you and Dad, and I can't imagine what is going on in your head, but believe me, Bria will always be your little girl. You can look for a phone call from her every day to check on you and Dad. I can't wait to be an uncle, and then I will have spoiling rights for my niece and/or nephew."

Michael pulled his mother close to him and planted a soft kiss on her cheek.

"Come, it's that time that I walk the most gorgeous woman I know down the aisle."

Jennifer replaced her arm into her eldest son's arm and stepped back into the processional line. It was that time to release her daughter to her soon-to-be husband.

Michael did not see the look that Tessa had shown while he was consoling his mother. Tessa was wondering why he was so attached to her feelings today. She was jealous for she felt that Michael's affection had been bought by her. Prior to her stroke, she had confided in Michael about a lot of personal information, and she hoped he would keep it to himself and not divulge it to his mom. Yes, she knew that he loved and cherished his mother and would do anything for her, but if he broke his promise to her, she would sing like a canary to his mother and father.

Ms. Kennedy gave the signal for the orchestra to begin the processional score for the seating of the family members.

The groom's family proceeded down the aisle: Dr. and Mrs. Marcus H. (Elaine) Jennings Sr., paternal grandmother Mrs. Gwendolyn Jennings, and maternal grandparents Mr. and Mrs. James O. (Jolene) Beasley.

Now it was time for the bride's family. Jennifer looked around to see if Florence and the nurse had both Tessa and her aunt Onnie under control. She knew both can be cantankerous, but each of them loved her daughter, Bria.

Jennifer, arm in arm with Michael, took two steps back to place a kiss on Tessa's and Aunt Onnie's cheeks prior to proceeding down the aisle. Tessa was stoic there in her wheelchair, holding a beautiful monogrammed handkerchief, and Aunt Onnie was standing tall and proud, holding on to the arm of her great-nephew Edwin IV; each had an unusual smile on their faces.

Jennifer was satisfied with what she had observed, replacing her arm in her eldest son arm, Michael, and slowly walked down the aisle. Her youngest son, Edwin IV, was pushing Tessa down the aisle, and Michael returned to the holding area to walk Aunt Onnie down the aisle.

The space next to Jennifer was measured out so Tessa's wheelchair could fit. But when Aunt Onnie was escorted to sit next to Tessa, Jennifer's heart began to beat fast; in her mind she thought, *I hope each can remain civil during the ceremony. I know how much each of them loves drama, and we do not need any this day.*

To keep her mind off Tessa and Aunt Onnie, she looked around at the grounds. She thought, *I must make it a point to let Jacob know what a magnificent job he had done with the grounds.*

As the music began for the bridal party, Jennifer looked in awe as the bridesmaids, groomsmen, flower girls, and ring bearer proceeded toward the bridal arch. Jennifer took a deep breath and stood with the invited guests; she looked back and saw her handsome husband and her beautiful daughter waiting to proceed toward the bridal arch.

Not one but several tears began to roll down her face. Out of the corner of her eye she saw both Tessa and Aunt Onnie wiping their eyes and noses. For some odd reason the chill she felt in her bedroom had returned. She smiled and knew it was William Sr.'s spirit.

As her handsome husband and beautiful daughter proceeded to the bridal arch, Jennifer whispered, "You would be as happy as a peacock today," grinning from ear to ear. "In fact, you probably would have helped Edwin walk her down the aisle. She was the apple of your eye, and you openly expressed it to her and to me. You often stated she looked just like your Katerina and had the same mannerism and drive as your precious Katerina.

"I know you would also approve of her mate. He is such a model young man, and his parents have provided him with the foundations needed to be a good husband to our beloved Bria.

"However, I still need some answers from you. What's in that package, and why did you address it only to me?"

As Edwin and Bria stopped before entering the bridal arch, the minister again had to hold Marcus back from grabbing his beloved Bria. The guests began to smile and laugh for they knew how anxious Marcus was to make Bria his wife.

When the minister asked the question, "Who gives this woman to be wedded to this man," Jennifer walked on the other side of her daughter.

And together she and Edwin stated, "We do."

The minister then directed Marcus to walk down to his bride and slowly guide her to the right spot under the bridal arch.

As Bria and Marcus began repeating their wedding vows, Edwin grabbed Jennifer's hand and placed an endearing kiss on her knuckles.

Then he gave her that erotic smile that sent all kinds of sensations through her body. She squeezed his hand and whispered, "I will always love you, and I hope Bria can experience the same kind of love and bond we have had for the past twenty-nine years."

Jennifer thought, *Yes, I have to plan that special time with my husband to bring back many of the bells and whistles we've often set aside for the children and our professions. Yes, I am going to plan a romantic getaway for us that will keep a smile on Edwin's face eternally!*

Edwin nudged Jennifer. "It's time for the parents to light the unity candle." The bride's and the groom's parents proceeded to the bridal arch to light the unity candle.

Each returned to their prospective seat, and Jennifer went back into her mode of reminiscing about her wedding day and how she was going to plan for a special getaway with her husband.

When she heard the minister announce, "I now present to each of you Doctor and Mrs. Marcus H. Jennings II. You may now kiss your bride," Jennifer could not believe she had missed the whole ceremony.

The newlyweds began walking down the petal-covered runner smiling and waving. As they neared each of their parents, they stopped, provided kisses, and invited the parents to join them on the runner.

Mr. and Mrs. William Edwin Langley III and Dr. and Mrs. Marcus H. Jennings Sr. followed behind the newlyweds. The gesture revealed a show of solidarity between both families.

Once the parents had exited with the bride and the groom, the wedding party and the other family members began to exit.

The nurse wheeled Tessa out since Will was a groomsman, and Florence walked Onnie out. Each had been on their best behavior for they knew this was a special day for the Langley family.

While the guests meandered on the garden grounds for refreshments prior to the reception, the family and wedding party gathered on the beautiful grounds to take wedding pictures.

Everyone seemed to be in a happy and jovial mood. Each one was hugging, kissing, and expressing how beautiful the wedding ceremony was. Even the bride and the groom joined the family and bridal party in this celebration.

Edwin and Jennifer were holding hands and greeting all the family and the wedding party while the photographer were assembling the bride and the groom for different poses for their wedding album and DVD.

Jennifer noticed that Tessa had rolled her wheelchair off to the side and was looking forlorn. She nudged Edwin and pointed out the dejected disposition of Tessa's entire demeanor.

"Let's go over and bring her back into the crowd. She is probably just wishing that Dad was here with her to witness such a beautiful occasion."

Edwin and Jennifer walked over to Tessa and realized that she was crying. Edwin and Jennifer put their arms around her, and each kissed her cheek lightly.

Jenifer looked at her and stated, "You look absolutely beautiful in that dress, and the color complements your skin tone. You were stunning in it on William's sixty-fifth birthday, and I am glad you wore it for this joyous occasion. Come, we all are getting ready for the photographs, and I want a special picture of you with Bria and Marcus. I have picked out the very section of the garden for this photograph as well as the wall in the foyer to display it."

The beam and glow from Tessa's body was ecstatic. She felt more inclusion than exclusion on this day. She took out her makeup case from the pocket of her wheelchair and gave it to Jennifer.

Jennifer reached down and sweetly kissed her. "The tearstains give your cheeks a special glow."

With much love in her touch, Jennifer refreshed her makeup to eradicate the tearstains from her face.

"Tessa, you are going to look so beautiful in all of the pictures. The photographer and the videographer are here, so let's go and have a good time taking pictures."

Jennifer wheeled her toward the other members. From the corner of her eyes she could see her aunt Onnie and the worried look on her face as though she had replaced her with Tessa.

Tessa's smile was so bright, it appeared that the sun had turned on a couple of its spare electrons. The sunspots began to do a fan dance across the sky, and with each combustion it appeared as though the heavens was having its own July Fourth celebration. That was the magnitude of Tessa's smile.

This interaction of Jennifer with Tessa did not go unnoticed. Both Onnie and Michael were watching carefully, questioning Tessa's intent.

As Jennifer and Edwin neared the two of them, she smiled. "How are my beautiful aunt and my handsome son? Tessa was feeling a little melancholy about this day, her first grandchild leaving the nest. I have assured her it's OK. She and Marcus will visit us often.

"Maryland is not that far from South Carolina. We can always travel to see them."

Jennifer looked at her oldest son and smiled. "Michael, we are waiting on meeting that special person in your life. Don't wait too long. Your father and I would like to see a house full of grandchildren before we age too much."

Edwin patted his son on the back. "That's right. I would like to have a little life in me so I can play with my grandchildren."

The tenseness seemed to melt away from Michael. His eyes focused on Tessa, and he saw a serious smirk pass across her lips.

"Mother, now is not the time. Let's celebrate Bria's day." He looked at Tessa and gave her a wink.

Michael did not want any of his secrets to come out on this special day, and he promised this day that he was going to get counseling and help for both of his addictions. Never would he want to place any shame on his family for his sins.

Onnie smiled internally. Tessa's false pretense of being caught up in the moment would not deter her from being the belle of the reception for her beautiful great-niece, Bria.

She thought, *I know this is what William would want me to do on his behalf.*

Out loud and to no one in particular as Michael wheeled Tessa toward the photographer, she stated, "Tessa, watch a pro in action."

As the photographer took the Langleys' family picture, you would have thought that Tessa and Onnie were the best of friends as Onnie put her arms around Tessa in one shot and held her hand in another one. The picture of the two of them with Bria showed each one of them placing a kiss on the bride's cheek as she stood between each of them.

Another set of pictures showing all of the Langley children, including Marcus and Bria, with his mother and father, Aunt Onnie, and Mama Tessa, could fool the sharpest eye of an observer that this was the most happiest and loving family in all of America.

As the photographer and videographer completed their processes, Ms. Kennedy arranged the family and wedding party accordingly for the receiving line. Again, both Tessa and Onnie cooperated and blended into the process without any altercations.

Florence, Rosa, and the nurse all looked at each other and laughed.

"I wonder when the fireworks are going to begin."

Florence looked at Rosa and said, "I was wondering the same thing."

Nurse Bell said, "Let's keep our eyes on them for I would not be surprised if it doesn't happen soon."

THE RECEPTION

T he chef, Pierre DeLouch, was still providing directions to his staff of twenty-three as the guests moved from the wedding scene to the reception scene. Among the guests, you could hear the oohs and aahs as their eyes feasted on the breathtaking centerpieces on the reception tables.

Again, Jacob's landscaping company had done a spectacular job of creating the centerpieces, which blended in with the bride's color scheme of pale pink, white, pale lavender, and greenery. As the hostesses directed the guests toward the receiving line and to their assigned tables, each guest was provided a glass of wine or sparkling cider and their choice of hors d'oeuvres of crab tartlets, stuffed mushroom, cranberry barbecue meatballs, vegetable bruschetta, and various chocolate-covered fruits.

After each guest was seated, Ms. Marsha Kennedy set the atmosphere for the presentation of the family members and the wedding party.

This introduction included the parents and grandparents of the bride and the groom, any special family members, and any special dignitaries. When each of them was introduced and seated accordingly, she completed the introductions with the names of the bridesmaids, grooms, matron of honor, maid of honor, flower girls, ring bearer, and of course the bride and the groom, Dr. and Mrs. Marcus H. Jennings Jr.

All eyes were on the newlyweds as they walked into the reception area with smiles and an aura of loving surrounding each of them.

The serving of the food was also a grand occasion; the cadence was similar to the serving of the dinner on a luxury ocean liner. The servers stepped to the music of a lively jazz tune as they served each of the guests the dinner feast for this grand occasion.

As the orchestra began to play a favorite jazz tune, the wedding coordinator, Ms. Kennedy, placed a beautifully decorated chair in the center of the dance floor and asked the groom to escort his lovely bride to the chair. All eyes were on the bride and the groom as Ms. Kennedy announced special presentations for the bride by her grandmother, Tessa, and her great-aunt, Ms. Onnie Dusett.

Jennifer looked at Edwin and then at Rosa, Nurse Belle, and Florence. She was not aware of any special presentations from Tessa or her aunt Onnie. This had not been discussed with her or Bria. As she began to feel anxiety build up inside, the same cool breeze that she felt in her bedroom was felt again. She knew it was William's spirit saying it's OK.

Michael pushed Mama Tessa to the dance floor and placed her wheelchair as close as possible to the chair of his sister. Tessa reached into the pocket of her wheelchair and took out a beautiful black velvet box. She laid the box in her lap. Michael retrieved the microphone from Ms. Kennedy along with the monogrammed note card.

He began to read from the monogrammed note card, "Bria, this is a very special day for you and a special day for the Langley family. Mama Tessa along with the spirit of your deceased grandfather would like to present you with a special token to say how much you are loved and admired for your strength, your tenacity, and your dedication to becoming the research doctor you always talked about. We welcome Marcus into this family for now we have all gained either a son, a grandson, or an older brother.

"The words written on this note card are words of love from the heart and soul of Mama Tessa. She will also present you with a very special piece of jewelry that she hopes one day you will present to your daughter on her wedding day."

Once Michael completed the reading of the prose and Tessa presented the diamond and emerald necklace, bracelet, and earrings, there were more oohs and aahs and flowing tears.

Onnie could not be outdone. When Ms. Kennedy introduced her as the next presenter, and before she could come and escort Onnie to the dance floor, Onnie grabbed her youngest great-nephew Will's arm for him to escort her to the floor.

Once Will placed her beside the bride and the groom and stepped back, Ms. Kennedy smiled and placed the microphone in her hand. The band began to play, and Ms. Onnie stated, "I wrote this melody especially for my great-niece, whom I love and adore and hope that her life with her new spouse would be a lifetime of joy, peace, patience, intimacy, and love."

As she began to sing, it appeared that the heavens opened up and the sun was shining directly over the newlyweds. Jennifer leaned over toward her husband. "I had forgotten how beautiful Aunt Onnie could sing. She is more than outstanding. I hope she remembers all of the words."

Jennifer looked around the garden; there was not a dry eye among the guests or the family. Everyone was in awe as Aunt Onnie in her mezzo soprano voice belted out the sweet melodious song to her niece. Even Tessa's eyes were red and puffy from the tears that still stained her face.

As Onnie finished her song, she walked over to her great-nephew Will and retrieved a wooden jewelry box. Walking toward the newlyweds, she stated, "The song was for my niece, but I have a special gift to welcome Marcus into the Dusett and the Langley families."

In the wooden jewelry box were two beautiful black velvet boxes, and she presented one to Bria and the other to Marcus.

"Open them up," she stated.

Bria's package consisted of a diamond and sapphire bracelet and ring, and Marcus's package consisted of a matching tiepin and cufflinks.

"Wear them on your first anniversary and the day of your firstborn's birth. I pray that each of you will wear them with much love and in doing so, each day the bond of oneness will become more apparent to you and to others. Cherish each moment that is given to you, walk in faith, love, and freshness. Laugh hard, embrace the love of God and your spouse, be joyful and happy. Always admit our human shortcomings and never go to sleep angry. When doing so, each day of your lives will be filled with sunshine and goodness. Remember, I love you!"

Onnie placed a kiss on Bria's cheek and one on Marcus's cheek.

The audience again clapped, and you could hear rumblings of oohs and aahs; several guests and family members dabbed at the tears flowing from their eyes.

Onnie grabbed Will's arm and walked very distinctly and dignified to her assigned seat.

Florence looked at Tessa, and she wondered, are the tears related to the song and the presentation or to the fact that her husband's mistress stole the show at age seventy-eight and she is bound to a wheelchair unable to counteract. In her mind she wondered if the presentation was one of the many gifts that Mr. William had given Onnie.

Florence and Rosa knew that only Tessa knew why the tears stained her cheeks this day. A secret she may never be able to reveal, but they were positive she will soon have some form of retaliation.

Tessa was not to be outdone; after all, this was her deceased husband's oldest grandchild. She may not be able to deliver today, but she had purchased a beautiful condominium in Miami that no one had knowledge about. During the family breakfast, she would present it to Bria and Marcus and have the deeds transferred to their names. *I bet Ms. Onnie can't top that. She may have been considered wealthy in her place in Barbour County, Alabama, but I am sure her wealth cannot touch the Langleys' assets.*

No, I shall put the finishing touches on this. She has not seen the last of what Tessa Adkins Langley can do even from a wheelchair.

Menu for the Reception

SOUP
Carrot Ginger Soup
SALAD
Triple Berry Mixed Greens Served with Raspberry Vinaigrette
ENTRÉE (choice of)
Macadamia Crusted Salmon with Mango/Papaya Raisin Chutney
Grilled Chicken Breast with Blackberry Sauce
Beef Tenderloin with Pear and Watermelon Rind Relish
VEGETABLES
Vegetable Medley with Glazed Baby Carrots
Garlic Mashed Potatoes
BREAD
Basket of Sweet Potato, Molasses, and Whole Wheat Rolls
BEVERAGE
Orange Spice Tea
Raspberry Lemonade
Coffee/Tea
DESSERT
Wedding Cake

Words to Auntie Onnie's Song
My Precious Niece

You are Auntie's special niece,
loaned to me from heaven above,
to hold, to mold, and to love.
My breath of sunshine, my sweet bundle of joy,
your joy gives me joy,
your smile brightens my day,
your rare fragrance fills the very air that I breathe.

Today, I release you, my precious niece,
for the angels told me so.
You have become a woman to soar on your very own,
to fulfill the role God has ordained:
of wife, friend, and lover,
and what God has joined together,
no earthly obstacles can put asunder.
So this day I release my hand, but never, never my heart!

Mama Tessa's Tribute

Papa Will and Mama Tessa's bundle of joy,
our prayers were answered on the day you were born.
Special memories of you running through the beautiful gardens,
playing hide-and-seek with your Papa Will,
sitting upon his knees as he read your favorite poem.
Papa William and Mama Tessa loved to hear your echo in the gardens,
as you called out to each of us,
"Come and find me, come and find me, if you can."
Bria, today is your special day,
and I can feel Papa Will's presence, and his big smile.
He often nodded and blew you a kiss, a gesture he would exhibit today,
on this your wedding day.
In his physical absence but spiritual presence,
I would like to give you a piece of jewelry
your Papa William gave to me on the island of Maui,
during a celebration of love on our fifth wedding anniversary.
Today I give to you a symbol of his precious love for me
and his devoted love to his precious granddaughter.

THOUGHTS AND SCHEMES
AFTER THE FESTIVITIES

Jennifer and Edwin along with Tessa and Aunt Onnie stood at the opening of the garden saying good-bye to their guests. In her mind she was singing the lyrics. "What a day this has been, what a rare mood I'm in, it's almost like being in love. There's a smile on my face for the whole human race, why it's almost like being in love . . ."

She immediately drew closer to Edwin and held on to him as if her life depended upon it. Yes, she loved her family, and today had been a marvelous day, but why was her soul restless. Then she thought about the package in her chest or drawer. Would this package haunt her and her family for the years to come, and why did he choose her?

As soon as the uneasiness came, the calmness appeared in the form of a cool breeze. She whispered to the wind, "Why are you here today? I hope it is more to enjoy the festivities and not to bring some chaos and turmoil in our lives."

Edwin leaned over and stated, "If you are speaking to me, remember I am fifty-six years old and may need you to speak just a little louder." Then he winked. "Whispering in the bedroom is OK, because I am all focused on you, my love, but out here, you need to speak louder due to the noise and laughter."

"I was just commenting what a grand day this has been, and the atmosphere is laced with so much love."

As the last guests walked through the garden opening, Edwin pulled her close to him and planted a sexy long kiss on her lips. "I think it's time we finish what we started this morning. It appears this wedding has rekindled some memories of what was and what should continue since our three beautiful children may be embarking upon their own lives of marital bliss and family."

"Don't make a promise you can't keep. You know women's libido intensifies in their fifties, and since the fifties are the new forties in the twenty-first century, I am ready for whatever your heart desires."

Hand in hand Edwin and Jennifer walked over to Tessa, Aunt Onnie, and Florence.

"Ladies, I know each of you must be tired from this lengthy day of activities." She looked over at Florence and Nurse Brown. "Would the two of you make sure that each of them gets to their rooms to rest, and we will see all of you in the morning for breakfast.

"Aunt Onnie, instead of going back to your condominium, why don't you rest here, and the driver will take you back tomorrow."

Florence placed her hand gently on Onnie's shoulder, but this gesture did not stop Onnie from speaking her mind.

"Jennifer, my beloved, you know I would love to stay the night, but I prefer sleeping in my own bed. You can have the driver or Jacob take me home tonight. I will come back tomorrow for family breakfast and lunch. Now don't argue with me, Jennifer, my mind is made up on this one."

Onnie had thought of another presentation scheme during the family breakfast. She had trusts for Jennifer's children that were not known; thus, this was a good time to present it to Bria and her husband. She had outdone Tessa at the reception and was sure Tessa would strike again at the family breakfast.

Onnie had been in communication with her lawyer and was sure he had completed the required legal actions for her presentation tomorrow. She was feeling victorious about her surprise presentation; therefore she did need to go home, get a good night's rest in her bed. A needed boost to her energy and her internal fighting spirit.

Jennifer was too tired to argue with her aunt; she turned to Florence. "Florence, please ask the driver to take my aunt back to her home. Aunt Onnie, I will see you in the morning."

Jennifer looked down at her feet. Those stilettos were beautiful, but right now they were rubbing against every muscle in her foot and affecting ever muscle in her legs and thighs. She carefully pulled them off, threw them over her shoulder, and walked gracefully into the foyer of her home.

The aromatic smell of the floral arrangement still lingered in the air. It was breathtaking to the point of helping her glide up the long winding staircase to her bedroom on the third level of the estate.

As she entered the bedroom suite, she saw her handsome husband, Edwin, removing his tuxedo. She threw her stilettos on the floor and seductively walked closer to her husband. She wrapped her arms around his neck and brushed her lips across his.

In his ears she whispered, "Let's finish what we started this morning. Right now I need my loving husband to touch me in places that only he knows. This has been a long weekend, and right now, we need some us time to rekindle our intimacy, and tonight is going to be the beginning."

She slowly turned her back to her husband, lifted her hair up, and immediately he began to unzip the exquisite gown she was wearing, allowing it to slither to the floor. Then he removed her bra, and he took in the wonders of this amazing woman, the one he has loved for almost twenty-nine years. Even at the age of fifty-five, she could still arouse every feeling in his body and cause him to think he was twenty-five years old again. Her size 10 body with little or no fat aroused his manhood, and he could not contain himself. There she stood in front of him with just nylons; his hands gently released her hips and thighs from them to explore the body of his friend, his lover, his wife, and the mother of his children.

How he got out of his clothes so quickly and when they made it to the bed was a little fuzzy, but what he saw lying next to him was not a dream. He explored every part of her body with his hands and his tongue. He nibbled at her ears, slid his tongue down to her breast, and tasted the sweetness of both of them. Then his tongue began to examine her body below the navel and to the innermost part of her thighs. During the exploration of her body, he thought, *This is what I have missed with my long office hours. This is just what I needed this day to realize intimacy and time spent with my wife and family is more gratifying than working long business hours.* He heard his wife's moans and groans approving of his erotic moves and thought this was more rewarding than looking at balance sheets and deciding on new managers and corporate mergers.

Jennifer gently rubbed her husband back, and as he lifted his head, she began kissing him on his eyes, his nose, and his mouth. Her tongue traced his muscles down to his manhood, and she began to place sweet kisses in places that was so familiar to her tongue. Then their bodies met, and with each rhythmic movement she reached a higher level of ecstasy. Higher and higher she reached until both she and Edwin reached that climax so intense that even the table lamps approved.

As she laid her head on Edwin's cheek, she could feel and hear his heartbeat. This was the man she loved, and he had taken her to a place she never wanted to leave. She wanted to return to it now and forever and ever.

To keep this moment of intimacy lingering in their lives forever and ever and to keep the lightning and thunder fresh in their minds, she had to plan a two-week trip to their home in Maui.

There was always some type of charitable event, dinner party, or conference each of them had to attend, which oftentimes worked its way into their personal and private times.

After today, Jennifer was going to make sure she and Edwin always had time each month to explore the intimacy of their love.

Her two court cases were not scheduled until January. Almost seven months from now. She could use this time to relight and rekindle some of the flames that were smothering her personal life, snatched away as she diligently worked on her civil rights caseload. She needed time from the office, and so did Edwin.

As she pushed her naked body closer to her husband's, she felt his sweet breath against her neck, and then the cool breeze reappeared. She looked around the room; in her mind she stated, *William, I have not forgotten the package, and the two weeks in Maui will give me the opportunity to review without interruption.*

Jennifer placed her hand on Edwin's midsection and smiled. Although he had not gained a lot of weight, she would have to work on him changing his diet and visiting the trainer more often. She wanted her man in shape so they could physically enjoy these times. She closed her eyes and thought, *I must get some rest, because I am sure breakfast in the morning is going to be quite interesting with the Langley, the Dusett, and the Jennings families.*

But before I close my eyes, I need to experience the love that only Edwin can provide.

She pulled her beloved husband close to her and began to explore the wonders of his special places. She touched him lovelily and softly. She explored all parts of him and tasted the sweetness of his love.

Edwin moaned, and he enjoyed the erotic touches of his wife.

Yes, he definitely missed these moments with her, and tonight he would enjoy every second.

As he covered her body with his, he felt her rhythmic movement and fell in synch with her. As he entered deeply into her, Jennifer made sounds that he had forgotten she knew.

Jennifer was rising to another level of ecstasy, and she loved how it felt.

As each of them reached the point of rapturous delight and a state of overwhelming fulfillment, they knew the time spent away from each other had to cease so nights and days like this could still exist.

As they climaxed simultaneously, it appeared that the flares from the Fourth of July had invaded every inch of their bedroom suite.

Edwin rolled over on his back, pulled Jennifer close to him, kissed her softly on her forehead, and they fell asleep holding each other.

CONVERSATION AT THE BREAKFAST TABLE

The morning breakfast went off very smoothly. There were no out-of-place comments from her aunt Onnie since Tessa announced she did not feel well and would have her breakfast in her room.

The newlyweds were very excited about their honeymoon trip to several counties in Europe like Sweden, Switzerland, and the Mediterranean, and if time permitted, Scotland.

Bria talked excitedly about the wedding, her gifts from both her grandmother Tessa and her aunt Onnie.

She looked at her aunt Onnie. "Aunt O, you still can blow. You need to go back and finish your operatic career."

"Darling at my age, I probably would forget the words to the Aria and stand there waiting for my queue card. In my youth, I often made up lyrics when I did not remember the exact ones. No one but the director and the orchestra knew. Today if that happen, I probably would just hum."

Everyone at the breakfast table laughed.

Michael stood with his orange juice glass in his hand. "I would like to make a toast to my aunt Onnie, who still has the gift of song and can probably outcompose some of the newer artists. To you, Aunt Onnie, for the use of your magnificent gift."

Everyone lifted their juice glasses and drank.

Marcus's father, Marcus Jennings Sr., looked at Onnie and winked. "If I had any knowledge of the music industry, I would sign you up today as one of my clients. Your voice, depth, and clarity is just marvelous. I know you were a great opera singer."

Onnie was feeling ecstatic with all of the complements. This was her moment to shine so she decided not to present the gift to the newlyweds but apprise them of it. She wanted Tessa to be at the breakfast table during

this time. Since she wasn't, the mention of it would surely get back to her
by her great-nephew Michael.

"Since we are giving out compliments and gesture of good will, I do
have another gift for Bria and Marcus, but it will be presented when the
two of you present me my first great-grandniece or nephew."

She smiled and winked at Michael. He was taken aback, but Onnie
knew he would take the message back to Tessa.

Everyone at the table smiled and began to hold individual conversation
while continuing to enjoy the breakfast.

Rosa stood over in the corner observing all that was being said and
done at the breakfast time. How she wished that William Sr. could have
been present to enjoy this entire weekend. Even though she knew he was
absent physically, she could feel his spirit throughout the room.

Jennifer was also saddened that William Sr. was not physically present,
but from the cool breezes she had experience during the weekend, she
knew his spirit was among them.

She was glad the weekend festivities were over and she could
concentrate on the package in her Chester of drawers. Although she had
enjoyed each moment of the weekend, her tenseness was easing because
the Jennings were flying back to Maryland that evening, Bria and Marcus
would leave at midnight for Switzerland and Aunt Onnie would return to
her senior citizen condo after breakfast.

The evening would belong to her and Edwin. She could now relax and
enjoy this time with the man she fell in love with over thirty years ago.
She was glad there had not been any drama at breakfast. However, she
should not speak up too soon; her aunt Onnie always had the last word
or a trick up her sleeve.

Jennifer smiled and sipped some of her coffee. She was sure Tessa
was still brooding in her room over Bria's choice of a husband and Aunt
Onnie's unexpected gifts.

She looked across the breakfast table at her two sons who were
engaged in a deep conversation with Bria and her husband. Michael and
Will, they were good sons and she was glad that neither of them had
caused problems to the family during their formative years. Her next
project was to get Will out of school, find a suitable mate for Michael and
enjoy the time she had left with her wonderful husband Edwin.

Deep in thought, she did not hear her son Will call her name three
times.

Edwin, reach over, lightly touching her. "Will has been trying to get your attention."

"Yes, Will, I must have been in deep thought about this weekend festivities. Someone please remind me to give my thanks and compliments to Jacob for his artistic display in the gardens. They were simply beautiful."

"Mom did you see Michael leaving the cabaña with the wedding coordinator? He said he was helping her find some planning documents she had left there. I think it was more to the search than that."

Michael hit Will on his forearm. "Baby brother, you are always tripping on something, my explanation is on point, I was helping her to find her wedding documents. How would you know since I saw you sniffing around one of Bria's bridesmaids? I think her name was Michelle. She was sort of cute, but when I spoke to her, she is already engaged, just has not received the ring."

Bria looked at both of her brothers and shook her head. "Both of you need to stop it. The wedding coordinator, Ms. Kennedy, is much too old for Michael."

"I would not be too sure of that," stated Aunt Onnie. "He has a very special relationship with a seventy-four-year-old woman. That is much puzzling to me."

Michael looked at her with a smirk expression like do you really want me to go there?

Bria turned her attention to her great-aunt.

"Aunt Onnie, we all know each of us have special places in our heart for you and Mama Tessa, but didn't we just have your eighty-first birthday party?"

"It might not be me. You need to ask Michael about this relationship. And yes, I did turn eighty-one, and I look very good for my age."

She focused on Michael and gave him a broad grin.

Jennifer placed her coffee cup in the saucer and the napkin in the breakfast plate.

"Michael, if older women are your preference, then I give you my blessings. It's been a long weekend, but I need to get some rest. Rosa, would you summon Florence to ask the driver to take Aunt Onnie back to her Condo, Dr. and Mrs. Jennings, once the driver returns, he will take you to the airport and the newlyweds are leaving late tonight."

As Michael excused himself from the breakfast table, he walked over to his aunt Onnie, planted a kiss on her cheek, and whispered in her ear, "I have a lot of you in me and you are treading on thin ice."

Onnie's face was expressionless as she picked up her coffee cup to take a sip, but her sharp mind was on her next action to take against Michael and Tessa. Neither one of them had seen or heard the last of her. Michael was not aware that she also knew a lot about his fraternizing and the monies Tessa had spent to keep his name out of the papers.

Jennifer and the others swiftly excused themselves from the table. The newlyweds kissed the family members and headed up to their room on the third level. The Jennings said their good-byes, and Aunt Onnie and Will waited hand in hand for Florence to take her to limo.

Will loved his aunt Onnie and could not believe the rift between her and Michael. He would discuss this later on with his brother, because they were all family and the love for family was so important.

As he walked his aunt to the waiting limousine, he could feel her shaking. He hoped it was her age and not her anger with his brother Michael.

Jennifer pulled Edwin close to her as she watched all of the people leave to go their separate way. In a way she was sad, but she was also grateful to have a less chaotic and noisy house. She and her husband could curl up on the lounge chair in the sitting room of their bedroom and enjoy the peace and comfort of each other's arm.

As she slowing began to caress his arm and his back, she knew it would be more than cuddling, this wedding had ignited a fire in her that did not want to die and from the look in her husband's eyes he was ready to take the plunge.

The walk from the foyer to their bedroom suite calmed her overactive body and hormones. She thought back to her wedding night. The night she knew that only Edwin could satisfy the fire that was burning deep inside her special place. She could not wait for Edwin to explore the special places of her body.

Entering the suit her eyes went directly to the dresser where she had placed the package from William Sr. No way would that package interrupt the feeling she had at this moment. It would just have to wait until the morning for her to place it in her wall safe.

She smiled and began to remove her "mother of the bride" wedding gown. Tonight belongs to me and Edwin. Jennifer laid naked on her bed as she watched excitingly as her husband exited his closet robed in his birthday suit.

THE PLANNED VACATION

J ennifer had arranged her scheduled for her much needed vacation to their home on Maui. She laid the two briefs on her desk and the completed investigation package. Her last tasks on these two items were to write up her final decisions and request additional information from her staff.

She had at least another Seven to eight weeks before she had to present the cases before a judge; therefore she had time to enjoy her two weeks' vacation with her husband in Maui. Her calendar had been cleared; however, if needed, all the convenience of modern technology was at her disposal in Maui.

Jennifer wrote several messages to her assistance regarding the two cases and the two recent cases she had received for investigation. She was proud of her new assistance, Nila Johnston, a graduate of University of Alabama and Vanderbilt School of Law. She was very sharp and very intense when it came to the law and her research methods.

Jennifer placed in her subconscious mind how Nila would make a perfect match for her son, Michael. At his age, Jennifer felt Michael needed to focus on his personal life and stop spending so much time at work and with his college buddies. I wonder how Tessa would react if I brought her to dinner. Would she give her instant approval or her noticeable absence when Bria would bring Marcus to dinner?

Jennifer just smiled and continued to make notes on the briefs as well as on the instructions to her new legal assistance, Nila Patrice Johnston.

She could not imagine in the year of 2013, there was still so much greed, conflict, and hatred among the cultures and ethnicities in these United States of America.

One of her cases consisted of 220 acres of land in a prime location in Alabama where the original owner had given to his out of wedlock son born to his mistress of color. The records clearly showed that for over 150 years this land had been deem as his son's and his son had paid the property taxes and all other expenses on the land. Even though it had not been officially recorded in the state of Alabama, the descendants of John Clarke Bullock III had retained a document signed by their great-great-great-grandfather dividing up his land and giving these acres to his son born to Anna Maria Bullock.

The son, Warren Benjamin Bullock had been an excellent business man, using the land to build farm processing units for the poor and tenant farmers in the area. He had a grist mill to make corn meal and flour, a smoke house and cold storage to store the meat after processing, a device used to turn sugar cane into syrup and other farm related processes. Those farmers who were unable to pay for the services rendered usually paid using some of their harvest of vegetables or fruit or different farm animals. The owner of the land would usually sell the processed merchandise to the local corporate or independent markets.

The descendant of his father's legal family is attempting to sue for the rights of the land that he willfully gave to his out of wedlock son.

The second case is a suit brought by a ten-year-old male child born to a married couple of different cultures and ethnicity. His suit is related to the United States making a decision about how to label him. He has determined that no court of law should be imposed upon him or any other mixed culture child to declare his cultural and ethnicity. Just because his father is of a culture different from his mothers, he may want to be classified as his mother's culture instead of his father's. In fact the premise for his suit is for him to make a decision about his label, his culture and his ethnicity. He wants to be referred to as a male child of mixed origin.

In addition to his suit to determine his culture and his ethnicity, he is suing so the father of his mother will acknowledge him as his legal grandson and spend some quality time with him and his sister, as well as once in a while hug or touch him and his sister.

In fact as Jennifer thought about this case, her eyes began to become teary, especially when she read the part of the deposition where the young man stated, "My parents could not help whom they fell in love with, it just happened, and they are so happy and so in love. My parents, my brother and sisters, and I have loads of fun together."

Jennifer thought, have we not noticed the new melting pot or the fabric pieces of the United Stated of America? There is no true culture or ethnicity, we are a mixture of several ethnicities and cannot claim one specifically as our origin.

This is just another ploy of those who have ruled this nation for so long to ostracize those who they deem as undeserving to finally fit into the formula of the haves, the fortunate and the acceptable. We continue to make laws and pass laws to adversely affect those who should have a voice but have been silent by the lack of leadership who believe in them and the lack of funds to work for their own cause.

Jennifer leaned back in her chair that is why I have such a passion for the many people who are locked into this group. Not because they do not want to improve, but because others who have the assets have bought the systems needed to help improve the playing field for all citizens of the United States of America. Now that they have acquired the American dream whether legally or illegally, no one else matters, it all about them!

We can identify the type of governmental control with the terms like capitalism, socialism, communism, etc. It's just plain hatred and evilness on the part of those who make the rules because one does not look or think in line with their political and social logic.

There will always be individuals who are unable to amass wealth, but it does not mean they have no desire to better themselves or to acquire some of the American dream. Many who have a piece of the American dream have used the very systems they are now trying to dissolve or reduce to ensure others are not given the resources or opportunities.

Somewhere Jennifer had read that "bias and unequal laws grow up like weeds chocking out the good in all of us, spraying the air we breathe with evilness, hatred, disgust, greed, jealousy, and blocking the unfortunate from realizing a small portion of the American dream." Jennifer felt she needed to research that quote to use in her next court case.

Whatever happened to Christianity and love thy neighbor? It's all just a sham, too many of the megachurches preying upon the lost and the downtrodden, the poor, the forgotten, the confused, the depressed, and the oppressed. What is that verse? Something about many are called but few are chosen. Not all of God's disciples are false prophets, but many are in the profession, not to build God's kingdom on earth, but to gain status and wealth using half biblical truths and scare tactics.

Jennifer looked around her office and a forlorn feeling filled her weary soul.

Growing up she had many material items; however, her aunt Onnie taught her responsibility, love, kindness, respect, and to use good and solid financial practices. One of the strengths that she admired in her aunt was the ability to treat all people with respect.

Yes, Aunt Onnie had been a phenomenal and tough business woman; she knew how to manage the assets left to her by her mother and father. All of the people that depended on my aunt for their livelihood and survival, she never made them feel less than human.

Those human qualities of hers charted my professional course of becoming a lawyer for those who may not have been given the same opportunities and playing field I came to know.

Jennifer put her hands on the two briefs and the written instructions for her new assistant; these were two cases she must win. Instead of turning the hands of advancement back another fifty years, we need to forge ahead with new and stronger laws, procedures, rulings to continue to make this the land of the free and the brave, huddle masses yearning to be free—this ideal American that our forefathers had pondered in their hearts and minds.

Although America is composed of people of many cultures and ethnicities, it is very clear that even our highest court has overturned or interrupted laws to benefit only one culture. Can we as the most powerful country in the world continue to walk down the path of destruction of our inhabitants or is there someone who will stand up and say enough is enough.

She pushed her chair back and rose from her chair, why was she having such a melancholic day?

This is a time for her to be in a very good mood. Two romantics weeks with the man I have loved for over thirty years, a loving family that loves me back, a number of friends and acquaintances that have helped fill my life with constant fun, adventure, and inspiration. So why am I leaning toward the humanitarian side of me today?

Jennifer opened up her attaché case and lying on top was the package from William Sr. Why did she bring it in the office this day? She had too much on her agenda and her mind to even begin to review the contents of this package. I should have left it at home and let Rosa pack it with my play clothes for my trip to Maui.

A thought came into her: "This may be the ideal time to take Rosa with me. She was very close to William Sr. and some of the information in this package I am sure she is more than aware of it. William had often told me during our quiet and alone time that Rosa knew a lot about the Langley family, but in his heart he knew she would not divulge it to anyone."

Out loud, "Yes, I am going to ask Rosa to go with me. She can stay in the small cabana on the grounds while Edwin and I occupy the larger house. I need to plan for this new thought and run it pass Edwin. He has always admired Rosa. This will also be an opportunity to bring her two younger children along for a true vacation. I know they would just love being on the island of Maui."

Walking out of her office, she saw her assistant, Nila coming toward her.

"Good morning Jennifer, such a bright grin on your face, I can bet it's because of your pending two week vacation on Maui. I was on my way to your office to discuss a new case we received yesterday. I believe we can quickly resolve this one after you return from your vacation."

"Good morning Nila, I was on my way to your office to discuss the two briefs and the additional research we may need prior to going to court. After we conclude the discussion, we can talk about the new case and the directions to take."

Nila and Jennifer expended about forty-five minutes to an hour going over the two briefs and the additional information. Nila opened up the new case she received and provided a copy to Jennifer.

Nila begin to give Jennifer an overview of the case.

"This case involves an employee in a very large Health Conglomeration that was denied a promotion even though all of the paperwork and the supporting documents show that he has the skills, aptitude, knowledge and the experience to assume the new position. In fact he had been detailed to the position for more than two years and six months. During his tenure in the department he had made some significant changes inclusive of the tenor and climate of the department. It has also been noted that this department since his leadership had been the one that increased the flow of revenue to the corporation. I am not sure if one of the interviewers intended to write these notes on the HR papers, but it clearly shows that he was the best candidate. However, the corporation had their minority quota in the executive ranks of the company and needed to fill the position with someone different. This statement shows blatant discrimination."

"Nila, you have been here a little over a year and have done some very good research. However, sometimes a clear shot is not always a clear shot. There may be more to this situation than the surface information we have. During my absence from the office, I will need you and John, the legal aide to begin completing some in depth research. I will review this case today and provide you with specific directions and research we will need to represent this client. Prior to this, I need you to complete the final research on these two briefs. I may have some additional instructions for you before the end of the week, because Friday is my last day."

Nila picked up the two briefs and began to leave Jennifer's office.

"Nila, I know you are returning to the state of Carolina after matriculating in Alabama and Tennessee. I am not trying to pry, but have you met some acquaintances or friends your own age?"

"Some, but their interests are usually not the same as mine. John and I have gone to the movies and dinner, but I just consider him a colleague and friend."

She smiled and Jennifer understood her smile. John was not interested in her gender.

"I know this is sudden, but I would like to invite you to dine with my family on Thursday Night. I have a son Michal or Delbert Michael Langley, that is about your age and I would love for him to meet you. He is currently completing his MBA and has been working exclusively in the Langleys' business. I believe that you and he would have a lot in common. He is a workaholic just like you."

"If it pleases you Jennifer, I would be honored to dine with you and your family on Thursday night. Just let me know the time and address and I'll be there."

"Thanks, Nila. However, I will send either my son Michael or the driver to pick you up around five thirty on Thursday night."

"Sounds good to me, Mrs. Langley."

"My family and I will see you on Thursday night unless you have some questions about my instruction on these briefs"

Jennifer began whistling a tune that she had so often heard her aunt Onnie sing around their home, "The Impossible Dream." Not impossible, she had married off her daughter Bria to a wonder man, and now she thinks she has found the ideal mate for her son Michael. She has had twenty-nine years of wonderful bliss with her husband, Edwin, and she wanted the same for all of her children. Another thought came into her head. I should also ask Will's friend and his sister to attend dinner on Thursday.

"I'll talk to him about my idea tonight."

"I am doing something I love to do and have not done in a long time, planning a dinner party."

She picked up the package, and turned it over in her hand.

"William, is this the hold the contents of this package will have over me? To start back doing the things I love doing for my family and to ensure they always come first? Well you really have my attention and I can't wait to read the contents of the package. It is really thick. You must have a lot to say.

"I saw several ledgers in the appendage part of the package, they look very old. I hope this doesn't have to do with a case you want me to represent for the Langley or Adkins family. It may be too close to home if it is. If it is, I may want to act as a consultant and train my new assistant to actually try the case in court. Whatever it is, I can't wait to get settled in Maui to begin reading the contents."

Jennifer picked up the phone; she needed to call Edwin, something she seldom did to let him know about her brainstorming ideas for the dinner party and the trip to Maui. She was getting so excited, she could not contain herself.

As she placed the package back into her attaché case, she smile and stated, "This may be happy, intriguing, exciting, or sad reading. Whatever is the tenor of the content, I am ready for the challenge."

Instead of flying on a commercial jet, Edwin, Jennifer, Rosa and her two sons were enjoying the luxury of the Langley Corporations company jet. Jennifer looked at Rosa's two sons—Curtis Smythe, age nineteen, had finished one year of college at Hampton University and the other George Smythe, age seventeen, had been promoted to twelfth grade; both young men were really excited about their vacation to Maui.

Rosa had a third son, Charles Edwin Smythe who was finishing up his PhD in computer engineering at Tuskegee University. This son was much older than the younger two sons and was married with twin daughters. Rosa had never been married; therefore she used her surname for each of her sons.

Her two younger sons were playing an internet games via their personal tablets and observing the landscape of the world from thirty three thousand feet in the air.

Edwin had his eyes closed and Rosa was reading a book via her e-reader. Every once in a while I could hear her laugh or say wow; therefore it must have been an enjoyable and exciting read. I looked around for my attaché case to begin my initial reading of the package from William Sr. When I did not see it directly in front of me I panic thinking I must have left it back in South Carolina. Then I remembered, Rosa and the attendant had placed it in the overhead bin with some other items of Edwin's and mine.

I quickly moved out of my seat and reached in the overhead to retrieve the attaché case. This was one case I needed to keep close to me and make sure no one else took it off the plane except me.

Standing on the plane, I thought how many times I had been on the company's private plane to attend different functions, events and conventions with Edwin and William Sr. In the early years of our marriage, Tessa would accompany William Sr. and we would have wonderful experiences.

I was surprised when her attendance was selective and then she very seldom attended any of the business meeting gatherings.

Her excuse to me was she was very involved with her outreach activities. I do remember on one trip to China, I thought I saw or I imagined I saw another woman in the same hotel where we were staying who seemed to be very familiar with William Sr.

When I mentioned it to Edwin, he just looked at me and smiled. "Probably one of his associates from another office of ours. We do not know all of our employees we have a vast number in the state and in other countries."

I was nosey so I snooped a little. Yes she was one of their employees, working out of an office in the mid-west. When inquired about her position, she was the director of the computer data input department. She looked younger than Edwin and I. However, when I saw William going to meeting she was accompanying him. He never asked her to dine with us. I thought it was a little strange, but did not inquire.

Jennifer felt a breeze flow over her face. William's presence was everywhere. "I hope this package is not going to reveal you have a long-lost daughter. If so, I can't imagine how the family, especially Tessa will react to this news."

The breeze got colder and Jennifer began to shiver. "OK, I am a little off base."

Jennifer did not realize she had spoken out loudly when Edwin looked at her, "Did you say something, Jen? I guess I needed this vacation. I have slept the entire trip, and now we are descending. You should get in your seat and fastening your seat belt."

"I just need to get the attaché case out before we land there is something in it I need."

"Whatever it is, you can get after we land."

Jennifer reluctantly closed the overhead compartment and took a seat next to her husband. She looked out the window and saw the beautiful Pacific Ocean coming into view. A feeling of relief clouded her soul and spirit and she knew this was going to be an eventful vacation not just for her and Edwin, but the entire Langley and Dusett families.

As soon as they landed, Jenifer made sure the attached case was the first bag she retrieved.

Once they deplaned and entered the airport, the limo driver was there to take them directly to their home on Maui. Rosa's two boys were just too excited, so was Rosa.

Edwin took her hand squeezed it. "I hope we have nothing planned for this day, because I want to get reacquainted with my wonderful wife's body, mind and soul. The sleep on the plane must have aroused and awaken all of my sexual desires. Whatever is in that attaché case that you are guarding with your life, it can wait until tomorrow, for today is mine." Then he kissed her lips, cheeks and her hand.

She saw the smiles on the two boys' faces as they quickly took a sneak peep.

The grounds of the home were just beautiful; she could smell the fragrances of the flowers unique to the island: the heart-shaped anthurium, bird of paradise, various colors of calathea, white gardenia with their intoxicating aroma, various colors of hibiscus, the state flower, an abundance of ohia trees, palm trees, and many others she could not name.

Why had she stayed away from this place it was a paradise in its own right, built upon a hilly terrain on the ocean enclosed with its own private beach. She stood on the deck of the Master Bedroom and breathed in the smell of the ocean and the sand. From this view you could view the surrounding terrain, smell the fragrances of the many floras, look down at the various beaches and see the outstretched Pacific Ocean. Taking in all the scenery and the flora aromas made her feel like that sophomore student meeting Edwin for the first time. She had seen him in several of her classes and once she noticed him looking at her, she lowered her eyes projecting that shy girlish look. Her aunt Onnie always cautioned her to not be so forward with men. A first approach by them is more welcoming than a come-on by some busy body female.

He was the most handsome man I had ever seen. Even with all of the boyfriends I had growing up, there was something special about Edwin. He always carried himself in a respectful and polite manner, he knew how to charm you but it was not in an overly frivolous way. Sometimes when he would make comments or discuss specific points in our class, I would dream he was only speaking to me. I would always sit in the middle row of the class so I could focus in on him. One day he walked up to me took my hand and led me to the seat next to him.

"I think this is where you belong, you probably have a lot to contribute to the class, but sitting in the back, the professor cannot see your hand or your expressions."

From that day forward, we were inseparable and I knew I had lost my heart to this man.

Jennifer chuckled, she felt like some little teenager being love struck for the first time. No the initial flame for Edwin still burns as high and hot as it did when he took her in her arms and planted a kiss on her that was to die for. She has tasted tongued before but his had sweetness like no other.

Sitting in the beautiful bedroom suit that overlooked the Pacific Ocean, Jennifer felt heat at her back and as she turned she saw her husband looking at her with a definite want and desire in his eyes. She ran to him like the schoolgirl she was feeling wrapped her arms around his neck and kissed him with a kiss that said right now I am all yours do what you will.

Waking up in the arms of her beloved Edwin, her smile was broader than sunshine for he had taken her to a height where she soared more than thirty-three thousand feet. Her whole body knew she was loved and what an enjoyment when he caressed her breast, massaged her back and buttock, kissed her sweetly from breast to navel to her womanhood. When he entered her he took her to a height of ecstasy where she wanted to stay forever and ever. Of her twenty-nine years with Edwin this day found her climaxing more than she could ever remember. Yes, she had had several orgasms with him but this day, was a pivotal moment in their loving making process. She felt Edwin stir in his sleep and she moved her body close to him and inhaled his manhood and the love that surrounded the two of them.

"Yes life is good!" Jennifer declared, "I have really missed this and I am going to make every moment count while I am here."

As they took a quick shower and changed for dinner, Jennifer knew her rekindle efforts with her beloved Edwin had just begun. He had suggested a walk on the beach after dinner. She wanted more of what had transpired prior to dinner.

Jennifer smiled for she knew she had to wait until the housekeeper had unpacked their suitcases and placed them in the walk-in closet; therefore she had to make the most of her romantic evening on the beach prior to returning to their bedroom suit.

Jennifer loved the bedroom suit overlooking the ocean. It had a sitting room, a fireplace, and a wet bar. The housekeeper had included several snacks, her favorite teas, and flavored coffees.

As she walked down the beach hand in hand with Edwin, she smiled. *Maybe I will seduce him in the sitting room and give him dessert in the bedroom suite.*

Edwin looked at her. "You seem to be deep in thought. I hope it's not that darn package for I do not want it to interrupt our romantic time together."

"If I told you what was on my mind, we may not make it back to the estate."

"If it's what I think, then we should walk a little faster or maybe we should run."

"I think walking is better, running may cause our romantic bubble to burst."

Edwin pulled her close to him. "You are right, my love, we have two weeks to explore the terrain and to rekindle flame of our love."

THE PACKAGE

E dwin had arranged for a golf match with two business associates he knew on the island and Rosa and her sons had arrange an island tour to the pineapple farms and other wonderful attractions on the island of Maui.

After breakfast, this would be the right time and moment for her to begin reading the package from William Sr. His lawyer had called several times to see if I had perused the contents of the package. When he calls again, I can definitely say yes.

As she kissed her husband good-bye, her mind was more on the package than on him leaving. She did hear him say, "I should be back around 2:00 PM. We have a dinner engagement at the Ritz Carlton at 6:30 PM. We should be able to get a massage and go into the sauna before going to dinner."

"OK, I will make the arrangements. Have a good golf game."

Jennifer took two steps at a time as she rang up the stairs to finally begin reading the package William Sr. left for her. There was no one around to distract her. She had the morning and the afternoon all to herself.

As she pulled the package from the attaché case, the cool breeze she had experience during Bria's wedding had passed over her complete body again. However, this time it brought a sense of peace and contentment, not anxiety.

As she turned it over in her hand, there was nothing extraordinary about it, except the entire content had been written in William's handwriting. She had wondered why he had not asked one of the secretaries in his corporate office to transcribe it for him.

It was a personal document, but how many documents had his secretary completed for him not just for business but on a personal level?

Jennifer decided that she would ask the housekeeper to bring some mint/spice ice tea, cucumber sandwiches and some sugar cookies to the lanai for her. This would be an ideal place to begin this journey especially with the smell of the ocean and the flowers, a cool breeze across her face and a picture perfect exhibition of nature's handiworks.

Dressed in a beautiful floral pink, green, orange and blue over blouse and black leggings, Jennifer walked onto the lanai with the package hugging her bosom.

She saw the housekeeper placing her requested snacks on the table. She felt emptiness in her stomach even though it had been a little more than an hour when she and Edwin finished their breakfast.

Jennifer breathed deeply as she finally got a change to open the package, a document she knew would consume her. Slowly she opened back the first pack and again wondered why it was all in William's handwriting.

As though he could read her thoughts, the first page began thusly.

Jennifer, I can image you are thinking and wondering why William prepared this package for me and why it was delivered on the wedding day of his beautiful granddaughter. You probably noticed that all of the contents are written in my handwriting. This was done specifically because I did not want anyone's eyes to see the contents until after you had read them.

As I laid in my bed during the final stage of cancer, knowing these were the final hours on earth for me, I felt it was necessary for me to clear my conscience of my personal life and to become honest with the ancestral background of my family. I am the only one who knows it and too often we let those we love remain unaware of the past. I feel that knowing your ancestral beginnings helps shape one's future—mentally, physically, and psychologically—and keeps you from falling into society traps of inequality toward those they feel are inferior. Oftentimes we do not understand why we possess certain habits, have a pronounce personality as well as the interest, intellect and abilities we possess. We look at the physical characteristics and behaviors of our first or second generations and claim we have acquired specific amenities from them. This may be true, but all of us need to understand that our genetic characteristics and behaviors span beyond the first and second generation. Some of these genetic traits can go back at least five generations and surface into the next generation. Psychologist and genetic specialist will advise you that many of these characteristics may remain dormant and may not become observant until the fifth of sixth generation.

You or the family did not know this and it was hard for me to fathom, but I saw my beloved Katerina in Bria. Her smile, her kindness, and her concern for others. You never knew my beloved Katerina, but look closely at her picture in the library. There you will notice how much Bria looks like her. Bria has her eyes, her nose, the shape of hands and her oblong face. When Bria would play the piano, I would imagine my beautiful Katerina sitting there playing instead of Bria. She was a wonderful pianist and loved to play for me most evening.

Jennifer, I chose you because you have always had a special place in my heart and I knew that you would use your intelligence, wit and integrity to determine if and when you should discuss this information with the Langley family.

You were also chosen because I know that you can make a sound decision about this information since most of the information mirrors the type of cases you often defend as a civil rights attorney. You have shown me that you can be a tough but thoughtful and fair attorney when dealing with individual people's hurt, disgust, pride and emotions. You have been able to win civil right cases that I did not believe legally you would be able to show just cause for the compliant.

Your concern, care and passion for assisting many people of varied ethnicity and cultures who are not provided a fair chance for a piece of the American dream is what I admired most about you. On every case that you have represented, I have seen and sensed your passion and thus my reason for sharing this information about the DeBeaux/Langley family.

I may ramble as I write this, but I want you to know the background of each family but specifically my first wife, Katerina DeBeaux-Langley.

Jennifer, I wish you had known my father. He had the same care and concern you have for other cultures. He was a good business man and he made sure that all of the people that worked for him were treated equally and fairly. Sometimes he had to make tough decision, but these decisions were based on solid facts and truths.

Although I do not know much about his ancestors, since many of them came from Ireland and his mother was a teenage when she had him. He wasn't reared in the best of conditions. However, I do know that his grandfather owed a mercantile store and the members of the family lived on the second floor and each one grew up working in the store.

My father's mother, Elizabeth Anne Langley (never married), was adamant that he would receive a good formal education and did not allow her father to dictate otherwise. His entrepreneurship drive evidently came from his grandfather and his mother.

Jennifer, I know you are wondering, why is this important? The Langley family has done well in their business dealing and if they came from humble beginnings, this is the norm for most Americans.

You are absolutely right in your thinking. However, the contents and the information contained in this package has little to do with the Langley heritage, but more with my first wife, Katerina Hamburg Petersen DeBeaux. I do feel it is important that you are acquainted with both sides of the family history and our humble beginnings. Sociologists believe that our environment and rearing shapes each of us for our future life journey.

During my conversations with Edwin, you and my grandkids, I only provided skeleton information regarding my wife and Edwin's sister, Olivia. Each of you is aware that Olivia as well as Katerina died of a rare blood disease. It is true that my beloved Katerina died at a youthful age of thirty-four years old, but there were other quietly kept secrets regarding her family, especially on the maternal side. Before her death, she promised that I would tell Edwin about his heritage before he became a man. I failed to do this, especially since the mood of the United States would not have accepted him as an equal knowing his entire ethnic makeup.

You probably do not know that I had declared myself a bachelor forever. Even though my father told me an amazing story about the death of my mother, I was a young adult when I became aware that she committed suicide and during this act took the life of my baby sister Olivia. This knowledge in your young adult ages has a profound impact on your life and behavior as an adult.

After my mother's suicide, I observe my father keeping company with a plethora of woman and never being committed. His attitude toward women fashioned my desire to remain a bachelor forever. This attitude stayed fresh in my mind until I met my beloved Katerina. I was twenty six years old and she was twenty-one.

Prior to my courtship with Katerina, I had met her aunt, Ms. Gabrielle DeBeaux. Ms. DeBeaux owned a millinery, a dress shop, and a tearoom. In her spare time, she often taught piano lessons to young girls of varied ethnicity and cultures.

Attached to her millinery and dress shop was a tearoom where she served a variety of teas and French pastries. I would frequent the shop during my lunch time or right after work because I loved the aromas of the tea and had a fierce sweet tooth.

One evening while visiting the tearoom, I noticed a beautiful lady who was helping the customers with selecting various pastries. I inquired of Ms. DeBeaux about the young lady and discovered it was her niece. Her niece Katerina had come back to the states from France where she had been learning the crafts of her aunt's business. This trip to France also gave her the opportunity to visit her father and his family.

I was so enamored with not only her beauty but also her personality and intellect, her ability to hold a logical and thought-provoking conversation on the aspects of business and actions to take to make businesses prosper and expand. She was not shy in voicing her opinion about world conditions and the industrial growth in America. She was also very refined in presenting herself as a lady. She was charming and had much dignity, self-confidence, self-assurance and grace. I know I fell in love with her the first day I met her.

We dated for two years and became husband and wife on my twenty-eighth birthday. Katerina had just turned twenty-three two days before our wedding.

Her aunt, Gabrielle often talked to me about Katerina's father, but never shared very much about her mother. Katerina was born to a young girl (age fourteen or fifteen) in another city in South Carolina. At the age of ten, Katerina was taken from the young girl's home by her father, brought to Charleston for his sister, Gabrielle DeBeaux to rear her. The father went back to France and promised he would supply funds to her, but he never returned to the states. Katerina visited him at least three or four times before his death.

I know that I am digressing, but I have to write it as it comes to my remembrance. I am determined that I provide you a clear picture of the information about my offspring heritage. It is valuable and important information that will shape each of their lives for years to come.

Jennifer during many of conversations, you were aware that there were only two women in my non parental life that I truly loved dearly and deeply, Katerina and my mistress. Both of these women filled me with an essence that is not very easy to explain. When I was away from either of them, I felt empty and part of me had a hole or void until I could see or hold them again.

My mistress helped fill this void after the death of my beloved Katerina. I often asked God why he took Katerina from me at such an early age and why I did not meet my mistress until after I met Tessa. But God never answered me! He probably was disgusted with me having a mistress and a wife. I tried to be happy with Tessa, but she was deceitful and her entire disposition changed after she married me. At first I thought it was the two or three miscarriages (somewhere I stopped counting), but I found out it was something deeper, secrets she failed to advise me of related to her mother and father.

Please don't think I am an evil man and that I did not appreciate Tessa for helping me during some of my difficult times after the passing of Katerina, but deep down I knew she could never, never filled the void that I experienced after Katerina's death. Tessa added another dimension to my life, I loved her for helping me through those times, but I was never in love with her. A convenience marriage does not help you to come with the perils of life. I learned that the hard way.

Jennifer looked out over the ocean and she could feel tears gathering in her eyes. She knew William was miserable, that deep it ran was not apparent to her.

The housekeeper walked onto the lanai. "Excuse me, Mrs. Langley, there is phone call for you from your office. Would you like me to take a message or would you like to take it now?"

"Thanks Amelia, I can take it now"

"Hello, this is Mrs. Langley, Nila is there something wrong with the instructions that I left for you? If so please e-mail or fax them to me with your questions or notes."

"No, Mrs. Langley, I have almost completed the work on one of the briefs and will start on the next set of research instructions by this afternoon. I am sorry to disturb you on your vacation, but wanted to thank you for the dinner invitation."

"There is no bother, my husband is on the golf course and I am enjoying the scenery from the lanai. I welcome your phone call."

"I was calling, because I did not formally thank you for inviting me to dinner and meeting your wonderful family. I had a wonderful time and your chef is superb. A formal thank you will be waiting for you and your family when your return, but I wanted to personally thank you."

"You know that my invitation had a dual purpose: I wanted you to meet my son Michael and to provide thanks to you for all you do in my office. Your passion and love for the job you do for others mirror my passion and love. I have grown to respect you for that, because it is still very few people who have a humanitarian side for the right reasons."

"Thanks, Mrs. Langley, you know I was a little reluctant about meeting your family, but from what I observed you all are some kind of special."

"Well what is your opinion of my son Michael?"

"Michael and I seemed to have hit it off and we are going out to dinner on this Friday. I will provide you with an update on our first dinner date. I am really looking forward to our first outing. However, we need to grow our friendship and learn each other before we explore another party on the journey."

"That's why I chose you for your level head. Edwin and I became good friends before we decided we have a love interest. This is our secret, but please let me know the results of your dinner date. You are a special young lady and I would love for you and my son to have a good friendship relationship. You never know what friendship can bring."

"Again thanks for the invitation and I will give you an update regarding our dinner date. You and Mr. Langley enjoy your vacation and I promise I will not bother you again"

"Good-bye, Nila, and you can call me anytime on a professional or personal aspect. Have a good day."

Jennifer leaned back in her chair, she felt good about the relationship between Nila and Michael. She would try very hard to stay out of its development, but every once in a while it might need the Jennifer touch.

She smiled I might have to give nature a little nudge with this relationship. On the other hand Will seems to be doing OK with his female friend. However, she was really quiet and did not add too much to the conversation. Her brother is a little more outgoing than she. Next time I will only invite her and not her brother. You know mothers want the best for their sons.

Jennifer looked at the package as it lay nondescript on the table. This must have been very painful for William to pen, but I am sure he was determined to get it done.

Carefully she picked up the package and her eyes focused upon the paragraph she was reading prior to the phone call.

In my heart I believe I attempted to create an environment and an atmosphere where my like and admiration for Tessa would eventual grow into love, but it never materialized. Once I found out about her deep dark secrets, my respect and love for her dissipated and I became more involved with my mistress.

Even though she had inquired on many occasions regarding my mistress's name, I never told her. Somehow I knew Tessa was aware of her as well as her name. By this time I did not inquire as to how she acquire them, for my whole life was on "I did not care" button. Why? Because at this point in my life I knew I would not relinquish my mistress since she provided the support I needed to keep going.

Yes, Jennifer, Tessa knew about my mistress and oftentimes in the confinements of our bedroom we would have heated discussions, about my affair. I had offered to quietly buy her out of the marriage, but she refused and several times threaten to expose the hidden secrets of our relationship to the public.

Again, Jennifer, the writing of this document was also a cleansing for me. I needed to release some of the deep, deep feelings, and hurt I had built up over the years in relation to myself and my relationship with the women in my life.

Before our marriage and relationship went sour, Tessa had all of the charm and the beauty I needed when hosting dinner parties and attending business meetings—the perfect public appearance. This was a perfectly stage play that each of us performed daily to appease our audience and the media. We both had become the perfect actor/actress who could play any part and make it believable to the world. Our intimacy was a make believe and we both knew it, that's why I decided to move out of the bedroom since it was already defiled with the love I held for my mistress.

Even on my death bed, my prayer was for God to look down upon my mistress and keep her safe and then the afterthought was about Tessa. I know this was wrong, but those were my true feelings. I hope that none of my grandchildren will look at my life-style and adopt it as being good. That is why it is important that I provide them with information about their heritage that helped shape who they are for the present and future life journey.

I have sort of gotten off the pathway for this package, but it is a little difficult to continue with the information about Katerina without expressing to you about the broken relationship between Tessa and me.

I know the family was aware of the tension between us, but none of you ever broached the subject with me. Each of you just treaded lightly around us.

Believe me, this package is not about Tessa and me, but to provide you and the family with the truth about the ancestral background of the DeBeaux family and how sometimes outward appearances may not be the exact scientific truth we place our faith upon.

It is also a testimony of how one not knowing the other ancestral or ethnical background can learn to love each other and live harmoniously together. Katerina and I went against the grain and ideologies of the land and ignored the undertones of those who felt that we should not be together. Our love for each other was strong and we knew that regardless of our different cultures our marriage would survive. While we were newlywed, she attempted to apprise me of her ethnic and cultural background. I often kiss her tenderly and let her know it did not matter, for I loved her and not her ancestors.

I learned from my relationship with Katerina that individuals possessing two or more cultures or ethnicities can learn to block out the negativity of the world and live harmoniously with each other. This is what I had with my beloved Katerina.

You know I was not that keen on established religion, but I do believe there is a spirit who looks over all of us and helped us to discern good vs. evil, right vs. wrong and love vs. hatred. I believe in mankind and each of us has something to contribute to the progressiveness of this land. My philosophy was to treat each culture fair and equitable, for you never know which one may be able to propel you to another level in life, personally or professionally.

I believe these values and many others have helped my family and I build a very solid business enterprise. My father had these same values and principles and instilled them into me. One's character and principles follows them forever and when your aura, your speech and your actions emanates these characteristics, these behaviors transfer to others who interact with you daily.

You are probably thinking, but you had a mistress and a wife. That was one of my human shortcomings. I knew it was wrong, and I could not shake it, so I just continued on the forked road that I knew was not right. However, my shortcomings, especially with my love life, did not supersede my principles of treating others fairly in the areas of my business endeavors. I can see you shaking your head at me as you often did, thinking, *William, your relationships and extramarital affair are laced with hypocrisy, insincerity, and falseness.* We model our lives after our environment. I know better, but I go back to my father and his many escapades with women. There was one lady whom I admired and thought that my father would eventually marry, but when she began to speak the words related to becoming his wife, he retreated and found a new love interest. I think I was in my early teen when this transpired.

As I lay here knowing that my life span is short, I often think that maybe I should have been like my father. He never remarried after my mother's death, had plenty of women in and out of his life and never gave a second thought to marriage. A governess raised me until I went to boarding school in Virginia. After boarding school, I attended Brown University and received my law degree from Yale. When he visited me at each of these educational facilities, a different gorgeous woman was always on his arm.

Sorry that I am rambling, but as I think about it, I write it down. There is so much I should have discussed with you and Edwin, but was afraid how the two of you would accept the truth. My main concern was would you diminish the love and respect each of you had for me. I never wanted to lose my son not your love and respect.

Jennifer I had a good relationship with my father. He would often visit me at boarding school and we went on vacations every summer. He never spoiled me with material things. I had to show I was deserving of them. Most of the time, I would work in the business to help pay for those material things. This was the same training I gave to Edwin.

The compassionate side of me that Edwin observed was an asset given to me by my father. He loved me and I knew it, but his life style had a psychological effect on me.

When Edwin turned eight, Katerina began to experience the side effects of her blood disease. Katerina would attempt to work part-time at her shops; however, her energy level was beginning to wan. After school he would often sit in his mother's room and hold her hand. This scene was constant during the several months of her illness. He told her he would become a doctor so no other person would have to suffer with her illness. I really thought he would become that doctor, but my precious Bria has fulfilled her father's dream by becoming a part of the medical research profession. Edwin was only ten when his mother passed, but he was aware of her love for him and me because she confessed it to us daily.

Jennifer looked up toward the sky and blinked twice, she was not aware that her face was filled with the tears she was shedding. She took one of the napkins and wiped her face. Mentally and physically she could not read any more of this package. She needed a little reprieve from it, but what could she do to pass the time away.

She placed a bookmarker at the point where she ended, picked up the package and started toward the sunroom. Through the windows of the sunroom she saw Rosa and her two sons walking on the beach. Placing the package on the small accent table, she opened the glass door and began descending the steps to the private beach.

Rosa looked up and saw her. Simultaneously they both began to wave.

"The beach is so beautiful, so clean, crisp, and serene. I see your sons are having a fun time. Did they enjoy the tour of the pineapple farm?"

"They really did and we all are excited about the Polynesian Luau at the Western Hotel tonight. I will probably have to keep an eye on both of my sons as they ogle at those women Polynesian dancers."

They looked at each other winked and then laughed. Rosa's sons did not seem amused.

"Rosa, I know you are not in the mood to discuss the package from William and I really had to put it down because it was making me sentimental. Did William ever discuss his first wife Katerina with you?"

A surprised look appeared on Rosa's face; she looked away toward the ocean and began to walk toward the ocean. Jennifer followed her.

"Is there something wrong, Rosa? I don't mean to upset you about the information in the package."

"Mr. Langley did discuss his first wife with me occasionally. He was definitely in love with her and from our conversation his love for her never waned. She was his first and only love. In our conversation he would talk about her and her daughter's blood disease and the reason for him dedicating several wings to the Memorial Hospital. I can't remember if he ever told me the name of it. But he did say that his daughter had other complications from birth along with the blood disease."

"I know you did not begin working for him until after his first wife's death, but had you ever seen her? The portrait of her over the fireplace in his library is very stunning. She was a beautiful woman."

"Not only was she stunning, but the small Millinery business that is a part of the Langley Corporation was her initial business. From the newspaper articles, she was a good business woman and had built the business from one small shop in Charleston to several factories, on the east coast and one distributor in France. Many of the high end stores have several of her designs."

"She was amazing. I know William would never allow her picture to be moved from his library."

Rosa walked a little closer to the water and threw a small stone into it. "Is the package about her?"

"Some of it is, but I have not gotten to the crux of it yet. I think William just wanted to cleanse his soul of certain actions he had taken over the years, because the entire document is in his handwriting. What is so puzzling is that he chose me and not Edwin to read the contents."

"It is a possibility, that Mr. Langley—I mean Edwin may need your strength and tenacity when you decide to discuss the contents with him."

Jennifer laughed. "Addressing him as Edwin and me as Jennifer is OK, Rosa. I hope this is not asking you too much, but if there is a point in the reading of the package I need to discuss some situations with you, would you be amenable?"

"If I can be of any help or may be able to clarify some of the information, I will not have a problem discussing it with you."

"Oh, I see Edwin standing on the balcony. We have an appointment with the masseur at 3:00 PM today. Hope you and the boys enjoy the Polynesian Luau tonight. Why don't you and the boys join us for breakfast at 9:00 tomorrow?"

"Thanks, Mrs. Langley I mean Jennifer, we will because we have Deep Sea fishing tomorrow at 11:00 and a tour to see an active volcano in Kilauea. You and Edwin enjoy your massages."

Jennifer removed her sandals, letting the beautiful white sand move effortless between her toes. The touch of the warm sand on her feet and toes eased the stress and the strain she was feeling at this moment.

She wanted so much to miss the dinner at the Ritz Carlton to continue reading the package from William but she knew that was not possible. If she did that she would have to explain the reason to Edwin and she was not quite sure if this was the right time or moment. She also felt Rosa knew a lot more than she led her to believe. In her spirit, she felt that William Sr. relationship and fellowship with Rosa and Jacob was more than business and employee, there was something different about this friendship but she could not put her finger on it.

She and Edwin thought it was strange that William Sr. wanted to talk to Rosa and Jacob alone several days before his death. It also took the family aback at the reading of his Will when the lawyer revealed a trust had been set up by William Sr. for Rosa's three sons and Jacob's two sons and daughter. Yes, employers do leave something in their will for employees that they felt close to, but a trust for each of their children. William Sr. was an amazing wealthy philanthropic and corporate owner and he was good to many of his workers, but why these two?

Jennifer waved to her husband and blew him a kiss.

"How was your golf game?"

"Let's talk about it after the massage. I need to start taking more time to improve upon my game. Did not realize how rusty I have become. It was not awful, but it was not as good as my past games."

Jennifer smiled at her husband and he winked at her. "The ocean air is breathing some peculiar odor toward me. I think we may need to shower before our scheduled massage."

"Why did you put 'we' in the mix? I have not been on the golf course."

"There may be more than showering on the menus! Let's see if we can replay the scenes before and after Bria's wedding."

"Do you really think we have enough time?"

"Yes, if you stop talking and just follow me into shower."

Jennifer felt just like a schoolgirl and skipped gladly into the shower. The hot water not only opened her pores but also rejuvenated every erotic spot on her body. She knew she would enjoy this shower.

At breakfast the next morning, Rosa's sons were so excited about their deep sea diving quest and going to see an active volcano. On the other hand, Rosa seemed a little preoccupied. She rarely touched her breakfast, but drank at least three cups of coffee. Her eyes looked sad and Jennifer wondered if it was due to their discussion on yesterday.

Edwin looked at the two young men. "Don't tire your mom out today, she still looks a little tired from your tours on yesterday. Do either of you know how to play tennis?"

Jamal the second oldest looked at his mom and then at Edwin. "Only a little Mr. Langley, sometimes Curtis and I play on the courts in our neighborhood. Neither of us can play that well."

"Tomorrow, I will make arrangements for the two of you to take some professional tennis lessons during the morning so your mom can get some rest. What about around ten?" He looked at Rosa who seemed a little preoccupied.

"Rosa, do you and the boys have anything scheduled for ten tomorrow?"

"No we were planning on going on an unscheduled cruise to see some of the smaller islands or just do the helicopter tour. We can always pick another day for the cruise or the helicopter tour. So it is OK to schedule the tennis lessons."

"Thanks for breakfast, Mr. and Mrs. Langley, we need to catch the tour bus outside. It should be here in about fifteen minutes. Have a good day."

"Rosa you and the boys have a wonderful day."

"Well Mrs. Langley, what are your plans for this beautiful day? We are not here to work, so you need to put your work briefs away. I found this on the accent table in the Sun Room. Be careful with sensitive information lying around one of the workers or visitors. Even me could have easily picked it up. I did not peep, but the handwriting on the outside of the folder looks just like Dad's. Are you working on a special case he gave you before his death?"

"Edwin, thank you so much for bringing that out of the Sun Room. I want be so careless the next time. This is a special personal case for me and I was making some notes for my assistant Nila. Isn't she a wonderful young lady?"

"Yes, she is"

"I hope she and Michael can hit it off. A little bird told me that they have a dinner date for this Friday night. She is so energetic when it comes to doing the legal research and she is very knowledgeable about civil rights laws. It won't be long until she will be trying her own cases."

"OK, little Ms. Matchmaker, you have done your part stay out of it. Let nature take its course. I am sure it will. Look how happy we are after twenty-nine years of marriage. You know we are a statistics because the average tenure of most marriages is about five years."

Jennifer walker over to Edwin kissed him gently on the top of his head and retrieved the package from his hand. How could she have been so careless? She must make sure she puts it in a safe place away from

Edwin's reach, because I am sure he is now curious about this package and its contents.

"Once I put this away, let's take a leisurely walk along the beach. Upon our return we can decide our schedule for the rest of the day."

"Jen, don't be angry with me but I have accepted another dinner date with some of my business colleagues tonight at 6:00 PM and I have to be at the satellite office at 1:00 PM for an important conference call with some of our employees in the Japan market."

The butterflies in her stomach began to dissipated, she would not be angry at all, it saved her from faking a headache or a stomachache so she could continue her reading and this was working out in her favor.

"No problem, Edwin, I can continue to read my brief and make notes for my assistant Nila. We have plenty of days to enjoy each other and this island. As soon as I secure this brief in the bedroom, I will be ready for our walk."

Upon her return from the walk with Edwin, she could not wait to continue reading the package. It had really piqued her interest. She also felt that Rosa knew much more than she had led her to believe. Since Edwin had a conference call at the satellite office this would give her plenty of time to focus on the package.

On his way out, Edwin stated, "We are also scheduled for a dinner party on Thursday at the home of the vice president of operations for the pineapple canning division. You may want to go shopping for a gown for the affair. I know you understand."

"No problem, I may have packed an appropriate gown. I will look in the closet. If not, I will go shopping. Today is Tuesday. I can go shopping tomorrow if I did not bring anything suitable to wear."

Jennifer felt she could look for an appropriate attire after she had read several pages of this package. She walked over to her attaché case and removed the package. She looked out toward the ocean. Speaking to no one in particular she stated, "I hope this package doesn't bring undue chaos to the Langley family."

THE BROACH

Before heading to the lanai, Jennifer decided to go into the closet to review if Rosa or one of her house staff had packed any gowns or social attires for such an occasion. The housekeeper had unpacked her and Edwin's cases; therefore she was really not aware of his or her attire.

When she walked into the large walk in closet, instead of looking up, her eyes noticed a black felt jewelry box on the floor in between the shoe racks and the dress racks. Jennifer did not remember bringing any of her jewelry pieces with her, but she really didn't pack her clothes. The housekeeper must have accidently dropped it while putting away her clothes, since there was a small chest of drawers right under the shoe racks.

She immediately picked it up and opened the box. This was not one of her pieces, but she knew the piece very well. It belonged to her grandmother Dusett. It was a broach that her aunt Onnie loved and wore often. Come to think of it her aunt Onnie had mentioned that she had misplaced the broach somewhere in either her home in Barbour County or in the retirement home in South Carolina.

Jennifer looked at the broach and turned it over several times in her hand. How could it have gotten here in the Langleys' home in Maui? She had never mentioned visiting this home or either coming to Maui. I knew she had been to the Big Island Honolulu, never Maui.

It was strange that when she had chosen one of the other master bedrooms, the housekeeper stated that Mr. Langley had already given her instructions for this one. Why would he choose this one? I can guess that it was William Sr.'s favorite, and maybe Edwin wanted to feel his father's spirit and presence in this place. Edwin was aware that of all of the places his father could visit, he came here more. He would always say, "It makes me feel free, it open up my mind to think about personal and business possibilities and when I stand on the balcony and look at the ocean, the beach and the beautiful terrains of this island, the breeze and the smell of the waters comfort me."

Even the remembrance of William's word did not ease her spirit. It was still puzzling, how could her grandmother's broach be on the floor of this master bedroom in the Langleys' home in Maui? Should she approach the subject gingerly with Edwin tonight or just forget and return the broach to her aunt. What else was puzzling was this was not the usual bedroom suite she and Edwin often chose. She also wanted to know why he changed bedroom suites and chose William's favorite.

Out loud, she said, "Why am I tripping on this item? I'll just take the broach back to Aunt Onnie. William Sr. is no longer with us so Edwin is taking his rightful place as the head of the Langley family. We should stay in this bedroom suits."

Perusing through the clothes in the closet, she did not see a suitable attire for the dinner party. She would go shopping tomorrow to get her one. As she began to exit the closet, a very familiar perfume fragrance drifted into her nostrils. It was not the one Tessa often wore, but appeared to be the fragrance of her aunt Onnie. Something is really strange about these combinations: the broach and now the fragrance. She would get to the bottom of this, but right now the package was calling her and she needed to have a clear and uncluttered mind.

As she continued her directions toward the lanai, she thought, from time to time, Bria would borrow some of Aunt Onnie's jewelry for a special occasion and I know she loved the fragrance Aunt Onnie wears. It could just be a coincidence and with Aunt Onnie's dementia, she doesn't remember loaning it to Bria. I am sure Bria and Marcus might have spent a weekend here prior to their wedding. She smiled a great big grin.

The thought of Bria and Marcus slipping off here brought a special memory to her forefront. "I did the same, but no one ever knew about Edwin and my weekend getaway. We were so careful about framing the perfect cover-up about our weekend fun time with our friends. Well, I guess I have the answer. I'll just put it in my attaché case and return it to Aunt Onnie as if nothing happened."

I was young once and I remember taking chances and going against the grain of my aunt Onnie's teaching. I did not stray far, because I was much aware of my consequences.

Again, a smile came over her face, she can remember when she and Edwin were juniors in college and he came to visit her during the winter break. My aunt had all types of rules about place we could go and the times we should return to her home. Edwin stayed in our home, but knowing my aunt, she did not sleep but kept her eyes glued to my bedroom. In fact, I can remember her saying to me one night, "Jennifer, remember when you slept in my room so we could discuss the events of the evening? You often did this when you were in preparatory school and your first two years in college. I miss those talks and maybe we should do it again sometime."

I knew this was her way of getting me out of my bedroom to ensure that Edwin and I did not take advantage of the beauty of the night and the time in her home. What she did not realize was I respected her and her home and would not have done anything to upstage her teachings. As Edwin and I became more than friends and he visited me many times at my home, the subject was never broached again.

THE PACKAGE REVEALS

J ennifer took her favorite seat on the lanai and opened the package to the page where she had place the bookmarker. The housekeep had already prepared a small lunch for her along with her favorite green tea.

She began reading...

After Katerina and Olivia's death, Edwin asked me to start a foundation to assist people with rare blood diseases as well as those persons who were unable to pay for medical treatment. That is why several wings in the Memorial Hospital are name for me and my father. You also remember that Tessa chaired this charitable fund-raising event for many years. I never really had the chance to thank you and Bria for taking over after Tessa could no longer perform the duties associate with this worthwhile event.

During the days of Katerina's illness, she would often call me into the room to tell me how much she loved me and Edwin and wish she could turn the clock back on her short time with the two of us. She would apologize for being the donor of the two blood deficiencies to our only daughter and how she had prayed that Olivia would grow out of the deficiency. Both of the deficiencies were associated with a specific ethnicity and culture. However, you know that Olivia only lived to become three years old.

Katerina had the traits for both of these illnesses and the doctors advised me that the hemophilia type disorder was also the cause of her illness.

Jennifer's heart began to beat fast and she thought for a minute she might not be able to breathe. Is William really trying to tell her something that he never shared with Edwin? Does Edwin have any of these traits, and has he passed them on to our children? Now she was growing fearful of her offspring. Her mind wandered back to Bria, she must make sure she is tested for the traits prior to her having any children. She looked around the grounds of her home in Maui and tears began to fall. To no one in particular, she stated," How can this be happening to our family, this hereditary condition should have been revealed to us sooner. I am confused should I tell Edwin now or after I complete the contents of this package?"

She looked around to see if the housekeeper was in close proximity. She looked up toward the sky. "William, am I reading too much into this? Will you clear up my confusion later on? I really hope so."

As she looked back on the pages, she began to read the contents again. A tear fell on the exact word where she needed to begin.

While Katerina and I were dating, I often conversed with her aunt, Gabrielle Noelle DeBeaux with whom she had resided since she was ten years old. We often talked about Katerina and her aunt's millinery and piano training in France. Her aunt Gabrielle came from a poor family, but was given the opportunity to learn a skill and a craft by her father's employer. She and her brother, Raimond (Katerina's father) traveled to the Unites states as a servant/companion for the employer's children. She was a young lady of age eighteen, fell in love with the country, and did not want to go back to France. She used her skills as a hat maker and her classical pianist skills to build her business.

Her brother Raimond had read much about the hybrid research of an Adolph Hamburg. He also had attended a seminar at the Agricultural Department of the Sorbonne where Adolph Hamburg was the guest lecturer on plant and animal hybrids. He wanted to meet him in person to observe some of his research on hybrids. He convinced his employer to allow him to take agricultural classes at some school in Louisiana. This would allow him to meet Adolph Hamburg in person and to visit his research farm. His employer consented, but would only allow him to stay in the Americas for two years. After the two years he had to return to France as his employee.

Raimond's second year of study, he was personally introduced to Adolph Hybrid and the research extended an invitation to him to visit the farm. During his visit to the farm, his heart and soul fell for a young girl who followed them around and was very knowledgeable about the hybrid work. He soon learned this was Adolph's granddaughter. Hettie DuPont Hamburg Petersen was the daughter of his daughter Lillian

DuPont Hamburg Petersen, whose mother was his constant companion Helga DuPont.

. Sometimes during his visit at the farm and his return to France, he and the young lady Hettie fell in love. In his first letter from the granddaughter of Adolph, he learned that their love for each other had resulted in the young lady Hettie becoming pregnant. In his response to her letter he had vowed that upon his return to the states, he would bring his child and Hettie back to France. Of course this never occurred.

According to her aunt Gabrielle, Katerina was brought to her at the age of nine almost ten, where it was noted she had been given much formal educational training as well as violin and piano lessons. Her aunt Gabrielle continued the formal educational training and even had her to travel to France to learn more about the Millinery business. Her aunt seldom talked about her other relatives her mother, siblings or grandparents. We only extensively discussed the DeBeaux side of the family.

It appears from the little she told me about the DuPont/Hamburg side was that Katerina's mother was about fourteen or fifteen when she had her. She was very beautiful and had been trained in the sciences like her father. Since the mother was finishing up her educational training, the baby was taken from her and raised by the great-grandmother. The mother was sent back to finish school in Atlanta, Georgia.

Raimond was very much in love with Katerina's mother, but her grandmother would not give him permission to take her and the baby back to France.

When Gabriel's brother Raimond Pierre DeBeaux learn that Katerina's mother had finish her schooling and was now teaching in August, Georgia. He returned to the states and attempted to reach out to her but to no avail. Prior to returning to France, Raimond was determined that his child would learn about his cultural; thus he negotiated with Helga to allow his daughter to be raised by his sister, Gabrielle DeBeaux, who resided in the Charleston area.

Although her aunt allowed her to visit her maman, she was not allowed to stay any more than a week. From our brief discussions it appeared that Katerina was devastated when she realized that the person she called her maman was really her grand mama. Somewhere between her visits with her Maman and before she died, the grandmother revealed to her that her sister, Hettie was really her mother. She also advised her to never try to contact her for they now belong to two different worlds and two different cultures.

On one of her last brief trips to see her maman, her maman gave her a small trunk with some family artifacts and very old documents. She instructed her to read them to learn more about her rich and interesting heritage on the Hamburg side. Katerina was totally unaware of her lineage on her mother's side but had been schooled extensively regarding her rich French lineage and it was instilled in her that the French heritage would allow her to greatly achieve a preferred status that the American heritage. This was drilled into her daily by her aunt and the many letters she received from her father, who chose to return to France and live. Her father had become a shipping magistrate, exporting hybrid vegetation to different parts of the world. He was very well established and sent her aunt funds monthly to impact their business and living expenses.

Katerina was aware that her life would be short lived on God's green earth therefore she desperately wanted Edwin and me to know all she knew about her mother's ancestors, lineage, heritage and her early childhood. She wanted me to know about the Hamburg's side of her lineage and how some of these traits and skills could and would pass from one generation to the next.

In her room, there was an old trunk given to her by her great-grandmother. One of the items she made sure was transported to the Langleys' estate was this trunk. She felt it contained the documents that would reveal who she was and what unique behaviors, characteristics and traits she had passed on to her son, Edwin. These documents according to her great-grandmother would open up the door to her Hamburg lineage.

She had made me aware of some of them, but it appeared that she had some that had never been shared with me. Each of these documents had been professionally preserved and she would use each one to enlighten me about her heritage. All of the preserved documents not contained in this package are safe and secure with my attorney. When you are ready to discuss the contents of the package with our family, you may secure them from him.

Between her pain of telling the story and the pain of her illness, she would often state, "I can no longer hold this information inside. It is only right that you and Edwin are aware of who I am, the seed that currently runs through his physical makeup and those physical and humanistic qualities and characteristics that will soon be passed on to our offspring.

I was not being deceitful, but my life had been filled with a new culture, new exposures and experiences that my great-grandmother, grandmother or mother could not provide. Like many of us who migrated from one country, city or state to begin our life journey we can only relate to what was in our formative years since the past was rarely discussed. It was as though no one wanted to stir the ashes of the past for it may retard or stall the successes of the future. I truly believe that knowing the past helps us to shape the future and makes each of us better individuals for the future. Who I am and what I hope my future seeds become is totally dependent upon the strength of the past seeds that grow within us. This seed is the crux of our cultivation, our strength, our longevity, our beauty, our stability, our desires, our successes and our humanitarian approach to life."

Jennifer, this story may be a little unbelievable, but I need to begin with the years prior to the end of slavery in America for you to get the full picture of my love for Katerina and our son's, your husband, William Edwin Langley III, ancestral background.

There was town and plantation west of Augusta, Georgia known as Hamburg, South Carolina. I did research and could only find a small amount of information related to this town, its agricultural and industrial makeup as well as the outstanding farms and plantation owners. Katerina had a workers ledger that her great-grandmother, Helga Malveaux DuPont (surname of all her children was Hamburg, Wolfgang Adolph Hamburg Sr.'s son's companion), which showed that this place once existed. Sometimes she would add the surname Petersen, but never gave an explanation. The owner of the plantation, Wolfgang Adolph Hamburg Sr., of German descent, was very innovative, and besides growing the crops unique to the South Carolina area, he had also produced alcohols and beers unique to his native country. He had become wealthy in his own way and was well respected in the area. Many of the plantation owners came to him for assistance and loans. When they were unable to repay him, they usually had to forfeit their land and their slaves. Therefore, he had accumulated many acres of land that he rented back to the farmers in the area. Many of the old culture farmers were sharecroppers on the Hamburg's land. This land was very fertile for the crops of the time since it was very close to the state of Georgia's border. In fact there was a river, the Savannah River that separated Hamburg from Augusta, Georgia. This river was instrumental in being a causeway to transport goods to the

Southern and Midwest parts of the United States. It also helped establish the lifeline of this community, thus helping to create the wealth of the Hamburg family and others in that city.

He and his wife Wilhelmina had two sons, the eldest, Seifert Roderick Hamburg and the youngest son, Wolfgang Adolph Hamburg Jr. There was a four years age difference between their sons. The information about Edwin's ancestral lineage on his mother's side will concentrate on the youngest son Adolph who is an intricate part of Katerina's heritage. His parents as well as the neighbors often called him Adolph.

Adolph did not care much for the daily operations of the farm nor was he a lover of the institution of slavery, but he was more intrigued with the growth and reproductive phases of the plants, trees and animals. He read all types of scientific books his father had brought him back from Germany and England. He was what you may refer to today as a Geek or scientific genius. Prior to completing his formal education or attending college he had begun his own crossbreeding experiments with fruits and vegetables and animals unique to the South Carolina's area. Some of his ideas and hybrids were even introduced to the old culture farmers in the area.

He convinced his father that if he was given the opportunity to attend college that the knowledge gained would make them even richer and allow them to increase their holdings and business ventures. Since his father was overwhelmed with material possessions, he agreed to send his youngest son to college.

After completing his formative education, Adolph was sent off to a school in Georgia, the University of Georgia, where he matriculated at the School of Agriculture and Environmental Science. This school is located in Athens Georgia. Adolph's father was interested in sending his son to Yale, one of the oldest universities in the new America, but the son was thirsty for more knowledge of any subjects associated with the study of plants (botany) and new ideas on old culture farming techniques; thus he chose the University of Georgia.

Adolph was so obsessed with his studies that he seldom visited his family. His experiments with crossbreeding and the research he did on hybrid plants and animals brought him much success in this field of crossbreeding. Some of his studies were published by the university and these studies may still be a part of university's archives.

During the summer of his third year at the University, he noticed a beautiful female colleague in several of his science classes. This student was in a wheelchair and was often accompany by another female student, about her age and whose facial features were identical. He watched them intently during the summer session and often noticed the other lady who resembled the lady in the wheelchair did most of the note taking in the class, but the lady in the wheelchair asked all of the questions. Adolph formative years were inundated with his obsession with his experiments that he had little time to court the females in his communities. In fact his parents were afraid that he would never find a suitable wife to give them grandchildren.

However, he was drawn to both of these females and particular the one who assisted the young lady in the wheelchair. He was also puzzled about the female attending classes at the university, the school was established in 1785, and women were not allowed to attend until 1903. He wondered how she was able to attend classes since she and her companion were the only two on campus.

Adolph vowed he would befriend the young lady in the wheelchair in order to become acquainted with her companion. It was strange to him that her companion had no Negroid features and looked so much like her mistress that he came to the conclusion that she could not have been her slave. Her skin was as pale as the lady she was assisting, her hair the same golden brown/blond and her eyes were more emerald than the lady in the wheelchair. For some reason, he was drawn more to the companion than to the young lady in the wheelchair.

Sometime between the summer session and his fourth year of study, he had befriended the young lady. During their many encounters he discovered her name was Mary Elizabeth Anne DuPont from Biloxi, MS often referred to by her name Elizabeth. Her father was a rich and wealthy businessman who had matriculated at the University of Georgia and now contributed handsomely to the school. She was able to attend classes because of her father's monetary contribution to the school. Although she would not receive a certification or certificate, she would receive the knowledge.

Her companion was her half sister conceived by a Creole/mulatto woman Lillian and her father. In fact there were two older brothers belonging to the Creole/Mulatto woman, that her father had provided their freedom papers. She clarified by stating they were also her half brothers. He learned that her companion's name was Helga Imelda DuPont and had been her constant companion prior to and after she was afflicted with the crippling disease. It was at the age of five that several doctors had diagnosis her with the disease. Helga was three years older than she. Elizabeth father married her mother, Amelia Suzanne Bedford when Helga was two. His legal marriage to Amelia Bedford produced three children, two sons, John and Nathaniel and one a daughter, Mary Elizabeth.

Adolph had learned that Helga's mother Lillian was initially married to a freeman name Venezuela Peterson. No children were born to this marriage. It is not clear if he died of natural causes or his owner willed him dead, but once Lillian was bought by Elizabeth's father, she became the constant mistress of Mr. John Harvey DuPont until her death.

Elizabeth had two younger brothers by her mother and father that would eventually inherit her father's many businesses. Her father had decided to provide her with academic training since he was sure she would never marry or bear him any grandchildren, thus her presence at the University of Georgia. This training would help her become a teacher for other young girls in the Biloxi area.

Helga had been assigned to her to assist with her mobility issues; however, as her companion, she had also been trained academically and musically. Elizabeth confided in Adolph that Helga was a much better student than she and understood the math and science better than she. It was also noted that Helga was a great essay writer and composed all of the papers Elizabeth had to submit in her English and literature classes. In the end, Adolph began to rely heavily upon Helga for her exceptional writing skills.

Adolph was enamored and intrigued with Helga's coloration, hair texture, eye color, facial features and her ability to articulate and explain scientific principles sometimes better than his professors. He was determined to get to know Helga better especially since his interest was mainly in animal and plant hybrids but her blended nature was of much interest to him. He often wondered if he could create a hybrid new culture. In his hometown he was aware of the babies conceived by many of the plantation owners, but they did not have the same features as Helga. Anyway most of the workers on his father's plantation in no way mirrored that of Helga.

By the end of the fourth year, Elizabeth, Adolph and Helga were a threesome. When you saw one you saw the other two. Elizabeth was growing fond of Adolph and thought that Adolph was fond of her, but he had not made any advances. She confided in him that she did not want to go home but would love to be a part of his scientific developments with the hybrids. She wanted to go to Hamburg, South Carolina, with him to assist him with his hybrid research and maybe open a school for the children in that area.

Adolph knew that if Elizabeth came, Helga would have to also come. Therefore he consented to talk to her father to see if Elizabeth and Helga could visit his experimental farm for at least a month. The father was most agreeable since he thought that Adolph had a love interest in his daughter.

A month turned into one year and then into three years. Within those three years, his name had become a household one among the agricultural arena and even in some European countries. Elizabeth and Helga had accompanied him to France, Germany and England while he discussed his work with others related to the hybrid plants and animals.

During their second visit to France, Helga was pregnant with her first child for Adolph. She gave birth to a beautiful baby boy and named him Josef DuPont Hamburg. This young child looked so much like Adolph. He could not believe it. Again he saw no Negroid features on his son, thus he was sure his idea of creating a new culture by reducing the strength of the Seed of the Nile could be inevitable.

Naturally Adolph and Helga had kept their relationship a secret from Elizabeth; therefore Elizabeth thought the father of Helga's child was one of the workers on Adolph's farming business. However, when Helga gave birth to her second son, Leonard DuPont Hamburg and this son mirrored the first. She knew both children belonged to Adolph. This was not unusual for the times they lived in, when the owner of the plantation always had children by some of the women workers. Her father had three by Helga's mother Lillian.

Adolph continued to work on his hybrid animals and plants, but his thoughts were saturated with his idea of trying to create a new culture of people. Whenever he played with his two sons he knew that his idea would eventually become a reality, therefore he had to immediately start his experiment.

His father had already provided him with at least two hundred acres to use for his scientific developments so it was easy to convince his father he needed additional help in the fields for the hybrid plants and animals. In his requests for new help, he informed his father that there were very strong and capable boys, men and women in the states of Mississippi and Louisiana that would be most beneficial to his research. The father had no problem since his son's scientific interests and research had helped make him a very wealthy businessman.

On his trip to acquire his new workers, Helga and Elizabeth accompanied him. They would be able to offer him assistance in the selection of cultures not primary seen on his father's plantation. This would also give Elizabeth the opportunity to see her family and was hopeful that Adolph even though she knew of his two sons by Helga would ask for her hand in marriage. She had grown very fond of him, but a lady never approached a man in those days, so she kept her feelings to herself.

Since her familiarity with her father's other children by workers on his plantation was taken as a given, she also did the same for Helga's two sons, She also felt that Adolph was so into his research he had very little time for romantic interludes. What she was not aware of was the times that Helga and Adolph spent when she was sleeping or too sick to dine with them. In fact Helga has been his sole helper in the documenting of his research and results as well as writing the speech papers he shared with colleges and Universities over the South and parts of the Midwest.

Elizabeth was not aware of the reason for Adolph's sudden interest in quadroons, mulatto, and Creoles, but he had discussed it extensively with Helga. She knew he was possessed with a passion to see if he would be able to minimize or delete the seed of the Nile from specific cultures that were of African descent but did not totally comprehend this was his reason for obtaining the new workers. Elizabeth, felt that since these individuals were chosen for their ability to learn easily to read and write quickly and to acquire specific skills in a short period of time, they would be beneficial to Adolph's research. These abilities would help Adolph enlarge his research possibilities and in his ability to increase production in his agriculture business.

Helga knew the reason for his acquiring the workers who were classified as quadroon, mulatto, or Creole. When discussing with Katerina, she often stated how excitement filled his voice when he describe how his experiments would change the face and the fabric of the world, not just with hybrids of Animals and Plants, but with people. Helga told Katerina that she had listened attentively and often wanted to talk him out of this experiment, but she knew because of her status she could only listen and not provide her opinion, especially on the seed of the Nile idea.

Upon their return to South Carolina, Adolph had acquired at least thirty new workers—several men, boys, girls, and women. Before leaving South Carolina he had instructed his current workers to build several new homes for his new workers. This was no problem since he had workers who were skilled in building, canning, milking, preparation of meats, shearing and weaving as well as other crafts that made this farm different from others in Hamburg area. However, these new workers had no knowledge of the real reason for them being brought to Hamburg, South Carolina.

Helga was not in agreement with Adolph's new hybrid project and often discussed it with him during their nightly debriefing of the farms activity. One night, Adolph presented her with a three page document clarifying his positing in the new hybrid research.

Jennifer, I have attached this document for your perusal. You will notice that it has been preserved like the other documents I mentioned earlier.

Jennifer opened up the document and noticed it had been carefully penned by Adolph. He had penmanship reminding you of the old English or European style of writing. He began the document thusly:

My dear and beloved Helga,

There is no way I can continue my study and research if you are not in agreement. I need your support, your love and your scientific knowledge in order for me to be successful in my endeavors.

I know you think my research is being completed for the wrong reason, but let me clarify my thinking. As you know I am not at all in favor of the institution of slavery. I believe that all creatures that are made have a unique reason for being on this earth. If you will observe the workers on my plantation compared to the workers on the surrounding plantations, they are able to be trained and taught to do a plethora of tasks. Even though many have not been to a school of higher learning like you and I, there is more potential and skills, wisdom and knowledge in each of them than just being a field hand or a maid. Look at the many agricultural products we have been able to produce on this farm. It is more from their innovative ideas than from yours and mine.

Please have an open mind regarding my research. It is for humanitarian purposes. Not only will my hybrids have the academic skills to assimilate into the world as it is, but their behavior of love, kindness, forgiveness, understanding, justice, caring, concern, etc., would penetrate the fabric of injustice and hatred of many of the inhabitants of this land. I know it is a far reaching thought, but when I first saw you and realized that even though you are considered as unequal to me and to Elizabeth, you were the one who possessed the abilities to clearly decipher some of the most complicated aspects of the scientific academia, especially chemistry, physics, agronomy, etc. Who wrote most of the compositions for Elizabeth and me? It was you my beloved. And even though you knew we needed your thought process, you never were haughty, nasty or condescending to us.

These are the behaviors I will instill in my new workers. Their understanding of human nature and a world void of evilness and hatred can be realized if all people understand we need each other to grow, develop and fulfill the plans of humanity for all. Will all of my new workers be as academically savvy as you? Probably not, but they will have far better skills and trades than many of the inhabitant of this land.

On this land our schools will provide the best possible academic environment that anyone could imagine. Those who will benefit from higher academic education will be given those opportunities. Once achieved our workers will be given the freedom to mingle with other inhabitants of the land and saturated the environment with the good behavior that builds upon justice for all humanity.

Helga, intelligence is not unique to a specific ethnicity, but all ethnicities have innate abilities to be innovative, creative and progressive. They are barred from using these innate abilities by those who are prejudice against them because of their ethnicity.

The blending of ethnicities will break the theory that only specific ethnicities are entitled to the fat of the land and that diversity and indifference only weakens the foundation of the land.

Most negative behaviors are taught or they are learned behaviors from interacting with negative people. Remember our worker Jonathan who was one of the best furniture makers in the area. One of the plantation owners did not want him to build the furniture based upon his ethnicity. He chose someone different and then had to ask for Jonathan's assistance to correct all of the mistakes.

It is ironic, he wanted to pay Jonathan less than he had paid the other workers even though Jonathan had to remake many of the pieces.

Helga, my love, my blending research is for the good of the land. It really baffles me when those who are in charge do not understand that a divided land makes excellent prey for the enemy. The enemy can find plenty of loopholes and soft spots to penetrate and destroy due to those persons in power ignorance of wholeness and togetherness for all of mankind.

So, my beloved Helga, I hope you will understand and accept my thinking on the blending of ethnicity for the sake of bringing stability and wholeness to a land that is laced with evilness, deception, injustice, hatred, and unkindness to others. A bias idea based upon flawed documentation and ignorance citing that one is inferior and incapable of learning due to their ethnicity.

You have visited other countries with me and you have seen the progress of these countries in many areas of business and industrial ideals. Many of the inhabitants of those countries do not look like me, but have the same skills and abilities as me. Inclusiveness is a solid base for progression; exclusiveness is a sign of weakness.

Once you have read these documents, my beloved, we can talk about our decision. I do not want to upset you in any way for you are my rock and my support. You have helped me to become the outstanding person that I am. My achievements are saturated with your thoughts and your innovated ideas.

I love you and do not want to lose you. If it were not for the laws of the land, I would take you to be my beloved wife so that you could legally share my bed and my heart. Since it is illegal, you will always be the one who captured my heart for eternity.

Your Beloved Adolph

Jennifer carefully folded the document that she had just finished reading. How profound an explanation was this from Adolph Hamburg Jr.? I wish he was here today to see that nothing has changed and although there are many diverse ethnicities living on this land, the hearts of man had not changed one inch from the entitlement thinking during his lifetime. If it had, then you would not need civil rights attorneys like me to legally defend the injustices perpetrated others. You would not have people burning or destroying churches of other religions or ethnicities.

Adolph, you had a good theory, but believe me, it did not get into the crevices and cracks where needed. Evilness, unkindness, hatred, and injustice reared their ugly heads from the so-called established religions, to city government, to state government, to national government, and to the supreme courts.

In fact one supreme justice showed his prejudices by stating that one belonging to a specific ethnicity was inferior and should be only allowed to matriculate at HBCU's since they were unable to learn the progressive academia at the non-HBCU schools.

Jennifer shook her head, no Adolph we have not progressed. As she looked down at William's continued discussion of the historical lineage of his beloved wife, Katerina, she knew the pain he must have been experiencing attempting to write an account of his deceased wife's story.

She continued to read the contents of the package:

Even though Elizabeth returned to Hamburg with Adolph and Helga after their trip to Mississippi and Louisiana, her heart was more than heavy because Adolph did not ask for her hand in marriage nor did he suggest to her father he was romantically attracted to her.

Elizabeth's father was more excited and ecstatic with Adolph hybrid research. Adolph talked extensively about Elizabeth's work with the school on his plantation and her scientific skills and knowledge. He explained to Elizabeth's father how she was an asset to his research endeavors by helping him with his experiments, his produce business and her ability to discuss the results of his hybrid research with other farmers and scientists. Elizabeth's father, John Harvey DuPont could see the admiration Adolph held for Elizabeth and her scientific knowledge and skills, but he also saw the twinkle and the love in his eyes when he spoke about Helga and her assistance with the documenting of the scientific results. This was the same feelings he held deeply for Helga's mother. Mr. DuPont wished his daughter a safe trip back to Hamburg, for he was aware that due to her illness and physical condition, she would not be able to wed or produce an offspring for him; therefore he gave her his blessings. He knew she was happy teaching on the plantation and providing her assistance with the research. It was common knowledge that Elizabeth had learn to love the South Carolina area.

He could see that Helga loved her half sister and was providing her with the best of care and devotion. Mr. DuPont admired Adolph for not leading his daughter on romantically, but allowing her to use her scientific knowledge in his many business adventures.

Jennifer was so intrigued with the information in the package that she was not aware that Edwin was on the lanai and standing right behind her.

"You seem to be consumed by the contents of that brief. I am been standing here at least five minutes and you were unaware."

Jennifer place the bookmarker on the unfinished page, looked up at her husband. "This is one brief I would love to discuss with you, but I am trying to understand the reason for the brief and how it fits into my world as a civil rights attorney."

"Well I think you have done enough reading for today, my conference call went well, so let's grab us some lunch and do some tours before we get dress for our dinner engagement. This might be a good time for you to buy a dinner gown for our engagement tomorrow night."

With a twinkle in her eye, Jennifer asked, "Real lunch or real, real lunch?"

"I can settle for both, but are you up to the challenge?"

Jennifer winked. "Always with you."

As Edwin grabbed her arm, Jennifer reached down to pick up the package this is one brief she did not need Edwin to review at this time. Seductively the two of them walked into the dining area where the housekeep had completed the entrees for their late lunch.

She picked up one of the strawberries dipped it into the whipping cream and fed it to her husband. He did the same. With several helpings of strawberries and whipping cream, lunch was no longer a priority. Each longed for the other and they swiftly made haste to satisfy the desires that were building inside each of them.

When the housekeeper brought the salmon salads into the dining area she noticed the strawberries and the whipping cream had been removed from the table, she chuckled for she knew the salads would be eaten later. She also noticed the package that Mrs. Langley was reading had been left on the dining table. It was probably a case from her office; therefore she would secure it before it became misplaced. She picked up the package and placed it back on the table on the lanai. She would later place it in the Master Bedroom.

Jennifer had missed these intimate times with her husband where her mind could just wander to the places where only Edwin could take her. His hand explored the very depth of her soul as he gently kissed her lips, her neck, her breast, and the inside of her thighs. His hand sought her womanhood and she sighed loudly as his tongue and lips aroused the very marrow of her bones and soul. She gently pulled him down up on her, whispered in his ear, "Enter me now and take me to that special place where you and I can experience the essence of our love." As he entered her, their bodies moved rhythmically with the sounds of the ocean waves hitting the sand and the shore beneath their bedroom window. Their beautiful entangled bodies became one motion of love; each stroke built them up toward a climactic moment that was so pure and natural that both whispered, "I love you," in the same breath and at the same time.

As each laid there listening to the other's heart beat and feeling the warmth of love flowing from each other's body; both Jennifer and Edwin knew they had a strong love and bond that no circumstances or situations could alter.

Jennifer looked into her husband's eyes and wondered if he knew what she was reading, would the contents of the package impact a change in the tenor of their lovemaking as well as their family bond. She was not sure if she would ever reveal to him the contents of the package because she Never! Never! Wanted to lose him!

"Why are you looking at me with those beautiful green eyes? Did I not make your toes and finger curl?"

Jennifer laughed and covered her mouth. "My whole body, sir, was satisfied. I could not ask for anything better."

"I am glad, for a while there I was beginning to think I hadn't done my job." He winked kissed her forehead, but I can testify that you certainly did."

Jennifer's smile turned into a big grin. As she leaned on her elbows, she looked into her husband's eyes. "If you found out something about me that I had not share all of these twenty-nine years, would you still remain faithful to me?"

"Jen it depends on what it is, if it is something that would shatter the very foundations of the earth then I may have to think about it, but if it is something that deals with personality and behavior, we can always work through it."

"That is a good response, but what if it goes deeper and has something to do with my ancestral past?"

"We all have a little bit of past skeletons that we hope will stay buried in the closet forever. However, if it doesn't shatter the earth's foundation, then as two intelligent, loving people we should be able to work it out. Does this have anything to do with the brief you are reading?"

"No not really I was just thinking about another case of mine and how I should handle it."

"Jen, if the truth be told each of us hold back in reserve some behavior, personality or ancestral information. Many times this reserved information does not dictate the real you, but oftentimes only surface when it is a means to resolve some conflict or issue."

"You are absolutely correct. People use reserved information for all types of situations. Remember the one case where all the people in this one young lady's company had viewed her as one culture and had treated her thusly. However, when she was overlooked for a management position, she filed discrimination based on her ethnicity of being of Hispanic descent. Even though none of her employment application documents in the HR department supported her allegations, she had additional data to validate and prove her ancestral lineage. She won her case."

"I think we should get up and begin preparing ourselves for the dinner with Rosa and her sons. Did you find a dress for the dinner party at Mr. Kahuna's home on Thursday night? If not, we still have time for shopping."

"Edwin, you would be stunned by a strange item I found on the floor of the closet, while I was hanging up the dress I purchased on yesterday. I found Aunt Onnie's broach on the floor of the closet. Do you think Bria could have left it here on one of her visits? She is always borrowing something from me or Aunt Onnie."

Edwin looked away and smiled. "I am sure she probably left it here."

In his mind he was thinking this is one of the times you keep what you know in reserve. If you knew the truth about that broach, I am sure it would shatter the picture you've painted of your beloved Aunt.

"I could lay here forever in your arms, but you are right we need to get ourselves up and take a shower. Besides, we did not eat a proper lunch. We had the dessert before the entrée."

Jennifer pulled her husband out of the large king-size bed and they walked hand in hand into the Bathroom.

After eating their earlier prepared salmon salads, Edwin went out on the tennis courts to watch Rosa's two sons with their lessons and possibly talk the instructor into a match with him.

Jennifer retreated to her favorite spot, the lanai. She eyed her husband in his tennis outfit and a warm feeling ran through her entire body. At the age of fifty-five, soon-to-be fifty-six, her husband's body was as fit and trim when she first met him almost thirty-plus years ago. He loved to play golf, tennis and swim. His personal trainer often worked with him at least three days a week. She smiled. She had married such a wonderful, thoughtful, and logical man. She had liked his response today: "We all keep some areas of our behavior or personality in reserve and only allow them to surface when necessary." She had never thought about that aspect of people lives, but while reading this package, she was convenience that all people keep ideas, actions or events in reserve only to surface when it becomes necessary. She herself had a few aspects of her life she had kept hidden and as of today, she did not see any need to let them surface.

She looked on the table to retrieve the package and it was neither on the table or any of the chairs around the table. She became frantic and began to mentally retrace her steps of the morning and the afternoon. Then she remembered carrying the package with her to lunch. She quickly walked into the dining area, but the package was not in that room.

She walked into the kitchen; the housekeeper and the chef were discussing the evening meal.

"Has either of you seen a package of mine? I thought I had left it on the table on the lanai, but it's not there." Almost out of breath and in between breathing she said, "This is a very confidential and important package and I need to locate it immediately."

"Don't worry Mrs. Langley, you left it on the table in the dining room and I placed it on your reading table in the setting room of your bedroom. I can go and get it for you."

"Marie, please do and would you also bring me some of that delicious Chai tea you served with our late lunch."

She looked over at the chef. "Would you please change the evening dinner meat to a pork roast with red potatoes and some steamed vegetables? Thank you."

"Would you like soup or salad or both?"

"A mixed green salad with a Balsamic dressing would be wonderful."

"What would be your choice for dessert?"

"I think one of your delicious strawberry or blueberry cheesecake would be perfect."

Jennifer walked back out on the lanai just as Marie had placed the package and the tea on the table.

"Thank you and I will guard this package with my life"

Both she and Marie laughed.

As she picked up the package, she again wondered why William only wanted her to read the information and for her to make a decision about sharing it with the family. Did he think it would be too hard for Edwin to digest and then repeat the contents with his wife and children?

Out loud, she said to no one in particular, "My husband is strong, and I know he has dealt with situations more delicate, confidential, and exasperating than this information." She was thinking about the time he had to tell the several workers family members about the distraught fired factory worker that had killed their loved ones. The time he had to ponder over laying off hundreds of workers during the bad part of the recession. He was able to work it out that instead of laying them off, the union and the workers consented to work only three days a week. The tough one was when he had to fire his best quality control manager due to a sexually harassment allegations.

"Yes, I am more than sure he would have been able to discuss the content of this package with his family."

Jennifer was still puzzled why William Sr. chose her to reveal Edwin's true lineage. She knew that William was not shy of discussing issues of the day with any of his colleagues and top managers.

In fact one day he was really anger with his board of directors when they had a hard time approving someone he had recommended as the director of manufacturing for the millinery business. The young lady had worked in the fashion industry for years, had received several fashion awards, and helped coordinate the fashion weeks in New York and California. She was well recognized in the fashion industry area, but her walk, her talk and her ethnicity were not favorably accepted by many of the board members. This infuriated William and he used his ownership and executive privilege to select her.

She has been outstanding in this position and has increased productivity and sales for the millinery industry. In fact she was able to increase their export business and opened another manufacturing plant overseas.

THE ECEA PROJECT

J ennifer removed the book marker and her eyes fell on the last sentence she had read.

Jennifer, there is so much to this story that my dear Katerina revealed to me. I am attempting to give you a brief overview of the most essential parts. Due to the medication, I find myself struggling to remember some of the most intricate aspects of this unbelievable historical account. However, once I have slept and the medicine has decreased in my mind and my spirit, it appears that the dynamic facts of this historical story permeate my entire body. When this happens, the pen seems to flow over the paper with all of the intricate details.

Upon Adolph, Elizabeth and Helga's return back to the farm from their trip to Mississippi and Louisiana, Helga learned she was with child. There had been several miscarriages prior to this pregnancy and their two active and energetic sons were turning five and seven years old. In both she and Adolph's heart they felt that no more children would come from their union due to her several miscarriages. The mid-wife had assured her she would conceive again. Helga spoke to Adolph about her condition and he immediately moved her into his room in the column style antebellum house.

At first she resisted the idea, because she did not want to hurt her half sister Elizabeth's feelings. She was more than aware of Elizabeth's love for Adolph. Her second reason for being reluctant with his suggestion was the assistance Elizabeth would need for her daily activities. Although Adolph had his workers to build a very comfortable room on the lower left side of his big column home inclusive of all of the amenities needed for Elizabeth' conditions, Helga was still concerned.

Adolph allowed Helga to select one of the new workers to train as Elizabeth's assistant. She had selected a new worker by the name of

Thomasina Casell (soon-to-become Adkins) to provide the services for Elizabeth. Elizabeth was sad and resisted Thomasina's help initially. When her stubbornness brought on additional aches and pains she had no choice but to allow Thomasina to assist her. Even though Helga visited her daily and worked with her side by side in the research lab, Elizabeth became very distant with Helga and loathe being near her.

One day after several months of the new arrangements, Helga noticed that Elizabeth did not show up for their work in the school or the research lab. Helga inquired of the absence with Thomasina, who could not provide her an answer. When she entered Elizabeth's living space she knew why. Elizabeth was suffering from malnutrition and depression. She confided in Helga that she no longer wanted to survive and could not fathom Adolph not accepting her affection for him.

Although Helga tried to attend to her, it was futile and within six months she had died. The sudden death of Elizabeth had an effect on Helga's pregnancy and her baby girl was still born. She named this child Mary Elizabeth and buried her next to Elizabeth in the family plot.

Immediately follow the death of this child she became pregnant again. This child was an early deliverance coming in her eighth month. She and Adolph name this daughter Lillian Ann DuPont Hamburg.

Adolph now leaned heavily upon Helga for assistance with his work. She assisted him daily; therefore she had one of the female workers, Thomasina Casell Adkins, to provide assistance with the care of her newborn and her teenage sons. Since most of her days were filled with research and lab work, she trained two of the older schoolchildren to become teachers.

Adolph had also engaged the assistance of one of the medical doctors in the area to medically treat the workers on his farm. Dr. John Priestley Jr. a childhood friend of Adolph's had returned to Hamburg after medical school to continue in his father's practice.

Adolph showed him his research with the plants and animals and how he felt that his research could also transcends to the human race. He was determined that with continuous breeding of mixed cultures he would soon weaken the strength of the seed of the Nile as well as reduce the amount of melanin in all cultures. His was not attempting to create a new ethnicity, just one that would blend into the establishment to allow the humanitarian behaviors to become wide spread and to saturate many of the inhabitant's hearts. He called his research with the humans the ECEA project—education, culture, exposure, and adaptation.

Dr. Priestley was reluctant, but agreed to the delivery of the newborn babies of his other workers as well as those babies born to the members of the ECEA project. Dr. Priestly would record these births in the ledgers Adolph kept of his workers and the members of the ECEA project. Adolph's ledgers were the forerunner of the census report. Adolph's ledger information about the births was more detailed and extensive than the original census report.

Dr. Priestley was aware that Adolph ran his plantation much different from the other farmers in the area. His workers had better living quarters than most workers and were able to choose the type of skill or craft suitable to their knowledge and intellect. He allowed his workers to marry and live with their mates. All of his workers were provided some form of formal educations (the school provide studies equivalent to a ninth grade education) which he felt was necessary to run the business ventures of his plantation and to keep them from running away. Dr. Priestley was not quite sure if the main culture of the area were aware of Adolph's practices, since many of his workers did not wander off to other plantations and did not assimilate with other workers from different plantations.

Really it was no need since Adolph had provided all the necessities for his workers on his plantation. The town's people were only knowledgeable of Adolph's workers skill sets and their loyalty to Adolph. Many of his workers were contracted out to do work for other plantation owners or to train some of their workers; however, because of their loyalty to Adolph, none of his workers provide any insight into the operations of Adolph's business ventures.

Adolph and his family were some of the wealthiest plantation owners in the area, with a monopoly in the agriculture and export business. A number of the town's people were either employed in their tenant farming or sharecropping dynasty.

Adolph had overseers, but they were not of his culture or ethnicity and were not allowed to mete out any harsh punishment without consulting with him.

During the first year of Adolph's research with his workers, close to fifteen new babies were born. There were several sets of twins. Dr. Priestley and Adolph had worked out a special code to denote the ones where the seed of the Nile was waning. A successful mixed breed was based upon the following: hair texture and color, the color of the eyes (not dark brown), color of the cuticle around the fingers and toes (blended in with the skin tone) and the color of the ears (blended with the skin tones). At six months of age, Dr. Priestley would come back to check on the newborn. Those babies who met these criterions, Helga would neatly place in the ECEA ledger, the others in the workers ledger. The name of the child was provided by the parents. Once received, Helga would place the letters, A, R, or P next to the complete name of the newborn.

The codes used in the ledger were: A = accepted, the R = rejected and the P = possibilities. There were few Ps in the ECEA ledger, and as the birth increased, fewer Rs were recorded. Dr. Priestley always placed his initial beside each new entrance.

The surnames were also changed to accommodate the cultural rating. For instance, a newborn with the code A, the name was Adkins; Adkin was the surname for the ratings R or P. Other names found in the ledger were Haskins vs. Haskin, Hollins vs. Hollens, DuPont vs. DuPoint, Sharkey vs. Sharke, Ingram vs. Engram, Smith vs. Smyth or Smythe, Hartmann vs. Hartman, Petersen vs. Peterson, etc. I observed from reviewing the ledgers that the chosen surnames for the newborn follow a pattern of either affixing an s or interchanging a vowels with the same sound.

With his ECEA project, Adolph made sure that only those workers denoted as A's would become parents with other ECEA inhabitants. Workers not a part of the ECEA community, had the freedom to choose their mates and their choice of skills and trades. Most of the time a designated midwife with Dr. Priestley's approval would deliver the child while Helga or Elizabeth would record the births. If the delivery was complicated, Dr. Priestley was notified.

Dr. Priestly and Helga worked side by side delivering babies for a number of years. When Dr. Priestley's eye sight began to fail him, he suggested that Adolph secure a newly trained medical student from one of the Universities or engaged some of the new doctors in the area; however, Adolph refused and selected two of his category-A workers to attend medical school at several of the established medical schools. Helga continued to record the births in the ECEA ledger with the help of a trained midwife and the newly trained physicians.

Jennifer, I know this sounds unbelievable, but the original ledgers are in the safe hands of my attorney. If you would like to review ask him to deliver them to you. These are historical documents and you may think about loaning them to an African American museum once you have read the entire package. One day after reviewing the information, I wondered if the inhabitants of his project ever objective, but why should they? They had the best of both worlds and areas. He provided the same amenities for all of his workers, therefore none should complain.

Adolph's two sons by Helga were now teenagers, therefore he arranged for each of them to attend West Point, an army service academy founded in 1802 by George Washington and Thomas Jefferson. The school was located in the state of New York. His works on plant and animal hybrids were well-known throughout the country and at the finest of colleges and universities, so his requests for his sons were not denied.

Helga did not want her sons to leave, but knew she did not have the authority to hold them. She was even more disturbed when he advised his sons that once they finished the academy, he would give them a dowry and for them not to return to South Carolina, but assimilate with other cultures.

During the Civil War between the states, it was amazing how the little town of Hamburg was not greatly destroyed by the Union regiments. This was because of the river as well as the railway system that had been an asset to this city's economy. Therefore both the Union and the Confederates used these systems to their advantages. Adolph was able to continue with his research and his businesses by providing food substances and some clothing to the Union and Confederate regiments.

Although Adolph's research labs and communities were hidden far into the wooded portion of the town many miles from the established city, the high ranking officers of both armies would either stumble upon it or learn about it from others in their regiments. When this occurred Adolph would use his charm and his wits entertaining the high ranking officials from both of the armies at his home, thus keeping them from destroying what he had worked so hard to maintain.

Helga admitted to her great-granddaughter, Katerina, that some of the Union and Confederate soldiers intermingled with several of the women in the ECEA project as well as his other workers. Even with all of his money and resources he was unable to prevent this action.

Helga was fearful for her sons and wanted to know where each of them had settled. The oldest of them had stayed in the New York area and the youngest had gone to Texas. Each of them had married and had families of their own. In her heart she wanted to see her grandchildren and hold them, but she was aware of Adolph's instructions to both of his sons. During the time of the Civil War, there was no contact with her and Adolph from either son.

Katerina, had some information on her two great-uncles, but the private investigators could not find any traces of their offspring. One investigator thought he was on track, but then hit a block wall. Jennifer, I hope you will use the information in these documents to continue to look for Katerina's family so they may be introduced to their first cousin's offspring. Your office employees have the skills to locate lost or forgotten family members. Please assign this task to one of your employees.

To me, it is an eerie feeling when you know someone out there in this world is related to you and neither one of you has ever met. Please find them. This was not one of the main reasons for providing you with this information, but once I got more involved with writing the contents, I felt a personal need for my family to know all who contain the same DNA and genetic makeup. The world is so diverse and we cannot deny who we are and how we are an intricate part of contributing to this great nation.

LIFE AFTER THE ECEA PROJECT

The Civil War ended in 1865, thus freeing the workers. Adolph read them the Emancipation Proclamation written by the then president, Abraham Lincoln, and explained to each of them its meaning. Since all of his workers were literate to some degree, they understood the meaning of freedom, but did not feel they were ready to experience this freedom. The workers on the Adolph Hamburg farm were used to humane treatment; therefore they were not aware of what could or would exist outside of those walls.

Many of the ECEA workers and non-ECEA workers who had ventured outside of Hamburg to obtain additional training in higher education would come back and tell of the disparate treatment of those who showed evident of having the seed of the Nile. This frightened those who were not a part of the ECEA project. The non-ECEA workers had an extensive knowledge of how injustice looked and being free was not looking good to them.

Many of the workers on the Adolph Hamburg farm were equipped with skills and educational skills to venture into the free world. Adolph was a believer in higher education and had monetary provided assistance to the Quakers, progressive abolitionist and others who had established higher education schools for other ethnicities.

He and Helga did not show partiality to any of their workers who had the desire to go beyond the training provided on his farm. Those who felt they could survive in the free world without the help of Adolph and Helga did leave. Many of them stayed and continued to work for Adolph as hired workers in his many businesses.

A large majority of the cultural workers on Adolph brother's farm, Seifert Hamburg, wanted to taste freedom and left as soon as they learn of the emancipation. Although their father had been a very wealthy man with many acres of land and tenant farmers of other cultures, his brother Seifert was not fugal with preserving this wealth. Each of them had received a large dowry after their father's death, but Seifert and his family had spent most on lavish parties and travel.

Seifert and his family had used their wealth to give elaborate parties and travel out of the country. In addition, he and his wife had spent a large sum on the weddings for his three daughters. Seifert was not very good with running his business; therefore his wealth began to dissipate before the Civil War and after the Civil War. In fact he was just as broke as the tenant farmers on his land. Most of the workers left on his family farm were either too old or too young to provide the work he needed to rejuvenate his farm. The carpetbaggers and the high taxes had a very negative effect on Seifert maintain his family assets. Seifert's wife had died at least one year after the Civil War began and his health had begun to fail him. He was always jealous of his Brother Adolph's success and felt his father had catered to Adolph's every request.

Adolph loved his family, but his scientific work had kept him from interacting and visiting them on a continuous basis. Therefore when Seifert asked for assistance with money and a place to stay, Adolph felt guilty and let him move into the big house with he and Helga. Seifert was not nice to Helga; he treated her as though slavery was still in existence. Instead of complaining to Adolph, she assigned one of the physically fit male workers to assist him. Helga seldom visited his room but would often hear him grumbling to himself. She knew he had been a very weak and angry male figure and often used his deep male voice and his status to control his household and his workers. It was also known throughout the region that he was not kind to his workers and often punished them unmerciful. His current condition was the results of his treatment of others during his youthful and prosperous years.

During the time that Seifert moved into their home, Adolph's ECEA project had almost come to a standstill due to the Civil War and the Emancipation of Slavery. He and Helga was also getting up in age and no longer could stand the daily pace of keeping up with the results of their scientific studies.

Adolph felt he had achieved many of his goals for plants and animal hybrids. His work was known throughout the county and Europe. He had spoken about his hybrid research results in colleges throughout the South, the North, and the Midwest. The last entry in his ECEA project ledger showed that he had been successful in allowing several thousand of mixed ethnicities integrate the land without forethought or knowledge.

A number of the ECEA project offspring designates as (A's) had attended small colleges in the southern and eastern part of the country and some of the ones designated as P and R had attended colleges established for people of color as well as colleges for other ethnicities. These offspring had acquired degrees in medicine, other areas of science, education, engineering, nursing, architecture, etc. In fact one of the ECEA offspring had become a renowned architecture who helped develop the blueprints for the original White House buildings.

Jennifer, my attorney has a ledger that also contains information about the education and careers of several of the offspring of the ECEA project. After Katerina's death, I begin to review several of these documents. I could not believe the wealth of historical facts regarding the unspoken and undocumented activities of the inhabitants of this land.

In the documents are several letters from Adolph and Helga's two sons. Not only had they done well in their profession, but each had married and had several children. From reviewing the letters, their wives were not aware of their lineage.

Jennifer placed her bookmarker on the page and sighed. She had read some unbelievable information. She was wondering if anyone else in South Carolina knew about this research. How many people in South Carolina and other states were possible offspring of some of the inhabitants of this city?

From the contents, she was puzzled as to why no one in the area complained or was aware of the ECEA project. It was evident that he not only was well-known but had also acquired wealth from his work and the hybrid plants and animals he had created and produced.

Jennifer was aware that her grandmother had come from South Carolina, but from the city of Columbia. Was it is a possibility that her ancestors were a part of the ECEA project? She would make a note to ask her aunt Onnie, if her mother was born somewhere else and then moved to Columbia.

As she stood up she saw Edwin and Rosa's two sons leaving the tennis court. She knew that she had to get her countenance together since Edwin could sense her temperament and mood. This was some heavy and unsettling reading she had done today. She would have to put this on the back burner since she needed to be refresh and perky for the dinner party on Thursday at Mr. Kahuna's home.

Tonight they were having dinner with Rosa and her two sons. She wanted to discuss some of the contents with Rosa, but felt this might not be the right time or environment.

To cleanse her soul, thoughts, and mind of the information she had just ingested, Jennifer needed to feed her entire demeanor with thoughts of her beautiful family and friends. In fact she might call Nila about the atmosphere of the office and if she was till excited about the dinner date with her son Michael. She smiled to herself. Edwin had asked her to stay out of the matchmaking business; as a mother she still wanted the best for her children.

This package was stressing Jennifer so naturally she was really concern about her husband, Edwin's reaction to the content. How would Edwin react knowing that his chief of operations, Rosa and his landscape employee, Jacob was his aunt and first cousin?

Wow! This was too heavy for her to think about. How she wished that William Sr. had discussed this information prior to his demise. Just because her profession dealt with the civil rights of others, it did not mean she had the strength to open up the secrets and untold stories of the DeBeaux-Langley family.

Jennifer picked up her inspirational reading, something she had not done in a long time. She needed some words to sprinkle her thoughts with jovial, inspiring and heartfelt words. She felt the reading in this book would put her into another place and soothe her somnolent spirit.

The chef had fixed the entrée that Jennifer had suggested for the dinner meal. It appeared that all were enjoying the succulent taste of each morsel. Jennifer was having the time of her life listening to Rosa's sons discussed their tennis lesson and how one was better than the other. Each had played one set with Edwin and had won, but was beaten badly when they played Edwin and the tennis pro.

Rosa was smiling from ear to ear she was glad that her sons were enjoying their vacation. Neither was aware that they were close relatives of the Langley family. William Sr. had asked her and Jacob not to discuss until he had come up with a good way to apprise his immediate family.

Rosa knew well how to keep her conversations with William Sr. locked in her heart and mind; however, she was glad she and Jacob's families were able to enjoy some of the perks from William's knowledge of their relationship. William Sr. had wanted to tell the family before his demise, but Rosa knew he didn't because she had convinced him prior to his cancer treatment, that now was not the time since his family was dealing with his illness. She now wishes she had agreed with his timing.

She looked at her two sons engaged in a conversation with a person who was really their cousin. She now knew why her mother had been so evasive as well as so unclear when talking about her ancestors. William had shared some data, but it was still a little unclear to her about her complete heritage and lineage.

Jennifer tasted her Blueberry/Strawberry cheesecake (chef used both berries) and said, "The chef outdid himself on this cheesecake. I thought our chef back home made a scrumptious cheesecake, but this one is so light and fluffy."

"It sure is good, Mrs. Langley, I mean Jennifer. I need to ask him what his secret is so I can duplicate it at home. My sons have already eaten two pieces."

"Rosa, have you ever heard of the forgotten town of Hamburg, South Carolina? In this brief I am reading it mentions this town name."

"Yes, I have heard the name, but not sure if it was from some of my cleaning business clients or from my mother. Not really sure." She looked down at her cheesecake. "If I can remember anything related to this town, I will let you know."

"OK, you two, we are here on vacation, not to discuss work or anything related to it. Rosa I know you and the boys have other tours scheduled for tomorrow, so tonight I have planned for all of us to visit a botanical garden so the boys can learn about some of the beautiful floras that grow on the island."

"What time does the tour bus arrive, Edwin?"

"No tour bus, Mr. Kahuna's limo driver is taking us there. It is a private tour just for us and a few of his visiting managers. The driver should be here in about an hour. That will give us enough time to change into different attire for the evening."

"Sounds good to me, Rosa we will see you and the boys in about an hour. I hope you can remember who spoke to you about Hamburg. This information would surely help me."

Rosa and her sons headed for the cabana. In her heart she knew that Jennifer was fishing for some answers related to the package William Sr. had provided. How do you let your employer know that you are related to her husband? I am sure Jennifer has already figured out the relationship part.

William had confided in me that on her death bed, Katerina asked William to find some of her relatives and let them know about her and her family.

When discussion the information with Jacob and me, he revealed that he paid investigators and ancestry specialists to find us. Once he received the data, he used it to establish a business relationship with each of us. When he felt we were individuals who could be trusted with his secrets, he brought the two of us together with two of his trusted attorney to discuss the data from the investigators and the ancestry specialists.

As his attorneys began to read the information citing all of the different surnames related to our ancestors. I began to realize that my mother did not really have dementia, but was remembering the oral history of her youth. The door had just flung opened and the sound of the ancestors' voices came alive.

That was such a surreal and eerie feeling, knowing my employer was my oldest sister's husband. It was a much more eerie and surreal feeling when I met my youngest sister's son.

William's conversation with us provided evidence and documents on our relationship with his first wife, Katerina. Katerina was my mother's firstborn, the child she often spoke of that was taken from her. I wish my siblings and I could have met her before she died. The evidence and the documents proved that Katerina was the child my mother spoke about the wind taking away. I always thought she was dead, but she was physically taken away.

Yes, I had heard my mother speak of a Katerina DeBeaux, but I just felt it was someone she had known in her youth and I reminded her of this lady. Sometimes she would call me this name and then look away and begin to cry. I never will forget about three weeks prior to her death. I was helping the hospice nurse prepare her for bed. She looked at me with tears in her eyes and stated, "Katerina, you don't know how many nights I cried about you, blaming myself for allowing my grandmother to send you away. Yes, I was young and very much in love with your father, Raimond.

"My grandmother and her surrogate husband Adolph Hamburg would not consent for me to accompany Raimond to France. Instead they agreed with him that you should be raised by his sister Gabrielle. I cried day and night over this decision even ran away to Charleston to find you. I am glad you are with me today, because there has always been a hole in my heart and a longing to know who you had become. You are a perfect blend of your father and me, whom I still pine for after sixty years of separation.

"Katerina you are my firstborn, and I loathe how my grandmother stripped away from me the motherhood I never knew. I lived because I knew that one day you would return to me, erasing the guilt I've harbored all these years. Yes I did and still do feel you in my womb, holding you in my arms, kissing your beautiful eyes, and rubbing your little hands and toes."

Then she reached up kiss me all over my face and fell into a deep sleep or trance. For years I did not understand why she would continuously refer to me as Katerina and when I would ask, she would look into space and tell me the ancestors would soon come through the door and reveal to me the truth.

To no one in particular, Rose said, "It must be weighing heavy on Jennifer's heart how she is going to reveal to her family the real family lineage. I know for a fact in my culture, we are only aware of two to three generations past. For some odd reason we do not see the importance of knowing our genetic heritage. Oftentimes we have relied on oral history and most of it does not provide all the pieces to the puzzle.

Rosa watched as her sons entered the cabana to change their clothes for the botanical garden tour. A tear fell from both of her eyes and she wiped them with the back of hand. She felt the cool breeze flowing over her face; she was not sure if it was William Sr. or her mother. Looking up at the sky with tears engulfing her face she stated, "I am sure that both of you are aware that life is so funny, when you think you have figured it out, it throws you another curve and you have to start all over, reassembling the puzzle pieces.

"This is how I feel about my immediate family. There are other offspring out there in this big country who have no knowledge of our existence, my great-uncles and their families and my grandmother's maternal side."

Rosa looked up at the sky. "William, I hope you know what you are doing. This can of worms may be more than all of us can handle."

Rosa was glad to be going to the botanical gardens; this would take her mind off the contents in that package.

The ride through the floral gardens was very refreshing for Jennifer and it took her mind off the contents of the package. As she looked at the beautiful colors of the flowers as well as the different species occupying the same space, the same air, the same soil, the same water and most of the time the same botanist or horticulturalist hands, she thought why can't humans live harmoniously among each other. I wonder if Adolph plant research is among these beautiful florals.

The package had really stirred up the humanitarian side of Jennifer more than learning about the lineage of her husband's family. Her anger was usually minimum when reading many of her civil rights briefs, but those that demeaned and dehumanized people of another culture, she worked untiringly to ensure the mistreated culture received not only some compensation but also a ruling or decision that will help eliminate the repeated feelings of hopelessness, being unacceptable, and being treated inhumanely.

She looked around the members present in the botanical tour cart. They all were of different cultures, different economic status, various colors, similar or different interests, varied educational status and skills, but tonight each were enjoying the presence of the others, exchanging their fascinations with the various flowers in the gardens and even conversations on worldly events. Is this not the picture that one should focus on more than unkind words, evil expressions, and hateful actions?

Edwin looked at his wife. "You seem to be lost in a world of floral frenzy. They are quite beautiful, and even the fragrances seem to intoxicate you. I have never seen anything so beautiful except for you."

Rosa's sons looked at Edwin and begin to snicker at Edwin's remarks to his wife.

A big smile came over Edwin's face. "Boys, just live long enough, and I am sure the two of you will find that perfect girlfriend or wife that lights up your life with her beauty and her charm. You will continuous breathe her personal fragrance into your nostrils and carry the smell with you everywhere and like these flowers you will become intoxicated with her scent. Never just settle for beauty, but look for more behaviors and characteristics in a mate that you will love and admire until death separates the two of you."

Both of Rosa's sons smile turned into a serious look for they were both interested in girls and needed some male perspective on how to approach the situation. The oldest of them, Curtis spoke up. "Mr. Langley, I am interested in girls, but it's difficult to talk to my mother about these issues so I was wondering would you have time on our vacation or when we return home to provide some insight into dating and selecting the right mate. We do have an older brother, but he's not around for us to talk to and he is already married. I like a girl in my chemistry class, but I do need to ask you a few questions about how to approach her."

"Curtis, I will be more than happy to have that man to man discussion with you and George. I know the dating arena is much different from when I met my beloved Jennifer, but I know the principles and standards for finding the perfect mate still remain the same. Some times as men we are not observant to behaviors, we do not ask the right questions and society has us thinking that if we don't get intimate on the first or second date, there is something definite wrong with our manhood. I would love to speak to you and George, let's plan a tennis date and lunch at the club when we return to Charleston."

"Sounds good to me, Mr. Langley and thanks for agreeing to bring that male perspective into our lives. We do have a mentor at our church, but I think he is more interested in being close to Mom than mentoring us."

Curtis looked over at his mom and smiled. "You know I am telling the truth. When Mr. Morrison comes over he spends more quality time with you than with us. George and I laugh about it all the time. It's a good thing that you have also enrolled us in the male mentoring group sponsored by an African American fraternity group that has provided us with academic, humanitarian, and social perspectives on manhood."

"Mr. Langley, thank you very much for helping me out. The times, the environment and the legal and social injustices of this land toward males of our ethnicity make me aware that my sons need guidance from positive male roles and mentors. My oldest son did very well without one. However, I believe your father's influence helped him tremendously. I know my sons need a good male role model and I should have thought about you earlier, but did not want to impose upon my employer."

"Rosa, no problem, I had a role model and a father. Sometimes my father would be busy building up his business or going on business trips so his chauffeur and his wife would assist him with my summer activities. They had five children of their own, three sons and two daughters. When I returned home from boarding school, my days were filled with fun playing with his son and others in their neighborhood. It's amazing how well we all played together.

"In fact, Mr. Roberson's son Charles played tennis and golf with me at the country club. In fact his oldest son, Charles, was a much better golfer than me, and Dad got him a job as a caddy. He now owns several food franchises. His middle son, Warren, loved music and had formed a jazz combo. My father helped him get a number of gigs at the country and other places. He is now a well-known music composer and producer.

"His youngest son, James was more into the sciences and is now a practicing physician in New York. All five of his children were provided the opportunity to get an advance college degree. He did this on his salary as a chauffeur and his wife's salary as a caterer and seamstress.

"Yes, we can all learn from each other and believe me I gained a lot of knowledge from interacting with the friends and family of Mr. Roberson. It also gave me a different perspective on the cultural aspects of others. You can't believe all you hear and read you need to learn it firsthand, from the sources.

"My experience with the Roberson's family let me know that all people have the propensity and intellect to become success. All they need is the opportunity. All cultures of people are not looking for a handout. They, too, value their worth and their self-respect."

"OK, Edwin, the young men did not expect you to provide them an overview of your childhood or a lecture on love for one's neighbor. Don't alter the script on manhood—tips on dating and becoming a good and productive citizen."

"You are absolutely correct, Jennifer, I did interject too much, but I loved the times I spent with the Roberson family. I need to get in contact with them. It was good seeing some of his family at Bria's wedding."

"Edwin, I will have Rosa plan the outing for you and her sons when we get back to Charleston." Everyone continued to enjoy the botanical tour, except Jennifer, who was still tense regarding the contents of William's package. There were a string of questions she desperate needed answering.

She looked over at Rosa and could sense the tenseness in her body. Rosa had always been open and honest with her about Tessa and William Sr.'s relationship. I wonder if she will give me honest answers related to this package.

THE DINNER PARTY

Jennifer had rested most of the day before she and Edwin dressed for the dinner party at the Kahunas. She had tried to keep her wandering mind off the contents of the package. To diminish her uneasy soul and mind, Jennifer decided to take a walk along the beach and relax in the sauna. Even with all of these activities, she still felt a little tense as she begin dressing for the evening.

For some odd reason, the broach she had found earlier was pinned to the bolero of the evening dress. She was sure she had not done this and wondered how it got there. The last time she held this broach, she was placing it in her jewelry chest to return to her aunt Onnie. After breakfast she had asked Rosa to speak to Maria to ensure the dress did not need to be steam. She had not asked her to do any other task for her. It is strange how the broach got there. It does match the single strand diamond necklace and diamond stud earrings she had picked out for the evening. She had also decided to wear her hair up, a request from her husband Edwin.

She did not have time to puzzle her brains over the broach. It was there, so just wear it. Edwin would be out of the shower soon and wondering why she wasn't full dressed.

As Edwin walked out of the shower with a towel neatly draped around his waist showing his fifty plus year old sexy body, her blood rushed to her head and her private area became flushed. She had to talk to herself, not now, we cannot be late for the dinner party but at this moment all I want to do is wrap my legs around my handsome husband's body and love him senseless.

Jennifer picked up a magazine fanned herself and ran into the bathroom to cleanse herself of her want for her man.

By the time Edwin exited the walk-in closet, he was fully clothed in his black tuxedo. He was more than handsome and she knew what her ultimate goal would be after the dinner party. He walked over to Jennifer, placed the sweetest kiss on her cheek.

"You are so beautiful and you look amazing in that dress. I see you found a place for your auntie's broach. It looks good on the dress. I love the way you have put your hair up. I could forgo the dinner party and devour you."

"You still have a strong line, Mr. Langley and I am still falling for it, but we can't miss this dinner party. I thought the broach would add another dimension to this dress, that's why I chose to wear it."

She did not want him to know she did not place it on the bolero and wondered if he had since he brought attention to it. In her mind, Edwin usually doesn't assist her in her dress attire, so why would he on this night. She laughed inside, maybe I am reading too much into this and Marie thought it would look nice with the other jewelry I had picked out. If I have to say so, it does accentuate all of the other accessories that I am wearing.

"Jen, you seem to be staring in space, we don't want to be late for the dinner party. The limo from Mr. Kahuna is waiting outside."

As Edwin and Jennifer entered the Kahuna's home, several guests had already arrived. The home was fabulously decorated with the presence and accents of the Hawaiian culture. The aromas coming from the kitchen alerted Jennifer how hungry she was for her day had been spent dreaming and reflecting on the contents of the package.

Several of the female guests looked at her as though they knew her, but did not make any moves toward she and Edwin. Just when she was to talk to Edwin about her observation, Mr. and Mrs. Kahuna stepped forward and welcomed them to their home.

Mr. Kahuna introduced them to the guest in attendance and they all bowed with expressions of making their acquaintance. One older gentleman and his wife walked up to them and began a conversation about Edwin's father. He had met him on several occasions. He was once the head legal attorney for the Pineapple industry owned by the Langleys. The wife of the gentleman kept eying the broach on Jennifer's jacket. From her expressions, it appeared she had seen it before.

"Mrs. Langley, that is such a beautiful and unique broach that you have on. I am up in age, but it seems that I remember another lady at one of these dinner parties that may have worn one similar to yours. In fact she was a guest of the senior Mr. Langley and his friend Cromwell Pappas. You could be a younger version of this lady."

"Thank you for admiring my broach, but it belonged to my grandmother and I do believe my grandfather had Tiffany make it especially for her fortieth birthday. If there is another one, then the giver had two instead of one made."

"Dear, may I call you Jennifer? With these old eyes and attending so many of these dinner parties when Walter was the senior lawyer for the corporation, I could be mistaken."

"Of course, Mrs. Kaola, you may call me Jennifer and as you stated, our minds often play tricks with us as we age and try to remember past events. It was very nice meeting you and your husband, but it seems that Edwin needs my assistance to excuse him from the conversation with those guests. I do hope our paths meet again."

As Jennifer walked toward Edwin, she was puzzled; her aunt Onnie had never mentioned her attending a dinner party in Hawaii with William and Cromwell. This wasn't unusual, since Aunt Onnie was her own person and walked by her own internal music.

Jennifer grabbed Edwin's hand. "We need to mingle with the other guests prior to dinner being served. I see Robert and Marilyn Frank attempting to get out attention."

"Gentlemen, would you please excuse us?"

"You have such an elegant way of getting me out of situations. I love you for your charisma, thoughtfulness, and your way to not offend but to separate. That why I chose you to be my wife almost thirty years ago. Let's go and speak to the Frank's."

Hand in hand, they walked over to the Frank's and greeted them. They were about Edwin and Jennifer's age and had been to several Langley functions in Hawaii and on the main land. Both of them worked for the corporation in senior and executive management positions.

As Edwin reached over and shook Robert's hand, Jennifer hugged Marilyn and each provided a slight peck to the cheek.

"We are so glad to see the two of you. I was attempting to rid myself of the gentlemen standing by the bar, whose conversation was laced with politics, business, and religion and world affairs. Jennifer and I are here for a much needed vacation. Therefore I am trying to avoid those conversations and concentrate on enjoying Hawaii."

"How well we understand, Edwin, Marilyn and I was just laughing a moment ago how each of those gentlemen are still stuck in the past. It appears the nineteenth and twentieth centuries passed them by without them taking notice. They really need to come into the twenty-first century to see how all the landscapes, businesses, cultures and politics have evolved."

"It's like I say to Robert sometimes about the organizations I either belong to or volunteer for, we don't progress, because we are often stuck in what worked yesterday, when today is much different and the ideas and ideals of today's inhabitants are much different. When I suggest a course of action to take to alleviate the situation, the most common answer is, 'Oh, that won't work, we've tried it.'"

Jennifer smiled. "It's funny how the new presentation always come back to your suggestion, but the one who presents it put their personal twist on portions of it.

"Most of the time, I don't comment and let it slide, but on one issue which was my passion, I had to address the new proposal and even had done an overlay to show it was identical to mine with an additional paragraph. The room went totally silent."

Marilyn smirked. "Not only are they silent, but their facial expression shows contempt. I don't believe you embarrassed me in front of my friends and colleagues.' I just do my usual smile and continue with the agenda."

"Here we are, Marilyn, doing what we said we wouldn't, talking about societal, business, and political issues. I have had some restful days here doing nothing. After my daughter's wedding we both needed a break from the everyday grind of our professional world."

"I know, Jennifer. I was just admiring the beautiful broach on your jacket. It appears to be one of a kind, although in my mind I think I saw one like it on a guest, William Sr. brought to a function in New York prior to his illness. You know he always invited his best friend Cromwell Pappas. I think this lady was a good friend of his."

Edwin sort of looked away and waved at another couple that was talking to the Kahunas. His eyes and his expression did not reveal too much to Jennifer.

"This broach, belonged to my grandmother and according to my aunt Onnie, it was specially made for her by Tiffany's on her fortieth birthday."

"Well it certainly is elegant and beautiful. I hope you and I can have lunch before you depart the islands. It is always good to see you and

Edwin at these functions, since we are the most junior in our positions. We, too, need to mingle prior to dinner."

"Marilyn, I would love to have lunch with you, maybe at our home or a restaurant of your choosing. Give me a call tomorrow, and we can schedule the luncheon."

As Edwin and Jennifer walked around greeting other guests, her mind was on the discussions of the other two women regarding the broach. Why was she unaware of her aunt's invitations to a number of William's meeting in New York and Hawaii? If Edwin knew, why hadn't he discussed it with me? I know Cromwell often attended after his wife died and he did not take a companion with him. I hope I am nor reading too much into this. Cromwell is my aunt Onnie's half brother. Yes, it makes sense. He used his half sister to keep other women from approaching him.

Why am I concerned? All of them were seasoned people and they needed to have fun in the winter of their lives. Tessa missed out on a lot of opportunities because she could not accept her faults and her deceptions. William had tried to assure her that he held no malice in his heart, but would not forget how she had used him.

Jennifer's thoughts were interrupted with the announcement that dinner was being served. Each of the guests was directed toward a formal dinner room that seated at least thirty guests. The centerpieces were heavenly, as well as the table setting and the name plates. Each of us played musical chairs as the servers showed us our prospective seating.

I was grateful that the Kahuna's had sat us next to Robert and Marilyn Frank and another younger couple probable the age of my daughter Bria, James, and Marcella Woolfolk. They, too, seemed to be grateful that they were seated near us and not on the opposite side of the table.

As dinner was being served, the varied conversations began among the guests. I had tuned out the conversations and the noise and was thinking about the comments on the broach and how I favored an older guest of Cromwell Pappas. I felt Edwin's hand squeeze mine and I looked at him.

"You evidentially are in a world of your own. Mrs. Tinsley has complemented you several times on your broach."

"Please forgive me Mrs. Tinsley, yes I was thinking about a brief I have been studying for the past three day. Now I am back into the moment. Thank you for the compliment, it belonged to my grandmother."

Jennifer did not want to go into a long dissertation about the broach so made sure the comment was brief. However, she could see from Mrs. Tinsley's expression she wanted more.

As she lifted her fork to taste the roast pork, Hawaiian style, Mrs. Tinsley, blurted out, "It looks just like one I admired on a lady friend of William Sr. I think she lived in Santa Barbara, or maybe somewhere in the South like Texas or South Carolina. She was a special guest of one of William Sr. college friends. I think the man was her uncle or cousin. I can't remember. I admired it then and it is a perfect accessory for your dress."

Jennifer thanked her again and placed the forkful of delicious roast pork in her mouth.

Edwin changed the tenor of the conversation by commenting on the skills of the chef. Everyone else joined in by agreeing with his statement.

Jennifer was more than ready to get back into the limo and travel to their home. She had heard enough conversation about her broach and how she looked so much like one of William's friend's cousin or companion. She was a younger version of this lady.

As she laid her head on Edwin's shoulder she thought, I guess everyone does have a twin.

Edwin, too, was deep in thought. The dinner party had been great, but the conversation was one he could have done without. Why did he ask Maria to put the broach on Jennifer's jacket? Subconsciously did he want her to think about the comments and her aunt? His thoughts were how he had deceived his beautiful wife for years. He had known about his father's mistress since his sophomore year in college. He had never spoken to his father about it and had vowed never to reveal it to Jennifer.

"Yes, we wear the mask . . ." (Paul Lawrence Dunbar), and we keep guarded secrets. Most families have plenty of them stored in their memory bank and on their mental flash drive, but to keep peace and harmony in tack and confusion down, most families never insert the correct mental flash drive nor bring the information to the forefront of their brains.

I plan to go to my grave with this one, I never want this information to hurt or harm my wife or my children. How would Jen feel and react if she was aware that I kept this secret all of these years? Yes certain incidents are better off unspoken.

Jennifer had fallen asleep on Edwin's shoulder and he could hear her soft breathing as they turned into the gate of their Hawaiian estate. She looked so peaceful sleeping in his arms. This woman he has loved for more than twenty-nine years had been his stay and his strength. He could not let something like his father's extramarital affair drive a wedge through this relationship. He faulted his father and Aunt Onnie for not revealing their secret relationship to them. I know Jen knew he had a mistress. She was just not aware it was her aunt Onnie.

As he awakened his beautiful wife of more than twenty-nine years, he prayed that tonight's conversations from many of the guests would not arouse her curiosity and cause her to use her attorney and investigative skills to get to the root of the conversation.

Tonight he would hold her gently and peaceful in his arms and pray that they would leave this island without anyone else mentioning the broach or how she favors another woman that had been a guest of my dad.

Jennifer had awakened in the middle of the night because of a dream. She had seen her aunt Onnie in the arms of some man, but she was unable to make out his face. In the dream she could tell that her aunt was enamored with her male lover and he showed much love for her. As she wiped the sweat from her brow and felt the coldness in her hands, she thought about the Package and if something in it would help her to interpret this dream.

THE ECEA SAGA CONTINUES

As she turned over to look at the clock, it was 7:30 AM. She quietly got out of the bed and headed for the shower. She would be up and on the lanai before Edwin awoke. She was determined to read the remaining contents of the package so the final week of their vacation would not be so involved and stressful.

Jennifer had not touched the package in two days, so she knew she had to finish it before they returned home next week. A lot had happened this week and she had to brace herself to see if some other unexpected omens would show up.

Instead of a shower, Jennifer filled the Jacuzzi Tub and put in her favorite bath salts. Her body was tense, stiff, aching, and tired; therefore the jets would help relieve her of all of those symptoms. She smiled and stated to the wall, "I thought vacations were supposed to be stress-free."

The time has slipped away from her for when she opened her eyes it was 9:30 AM. She could not believe she had fallen asleep in the Jacuzzi. Edwin had Maria to prepare a light breakfast because the smell of the coffee has awakened her from this peaceful sleep. As she peeped out of the bathroom before entering her walk in closet, she observed that Maria had tastefully arranged the light breakfast on the balcony.

As she quickly dressed in one of Edwin's T-shirts, a pair of her jeans and a pair of Prada sandals, she felt the energy from the Jacuzzi relax her entire body. The smell and the breeze from the ocean penetrated her nasal passage, awakening all of her five senses, clearing her head of the dreadful dream, and bringing her back to a better place. The sounds of the ocean tide created a melody only she and the movement of her body could hear and feel. Jennifer knew this would be a better day for her.

She walked out on the balcony and kissed her wonderful husband. She wondered when did he come into the bathroom and take a shower for the smell of the mixture of his soap and his cologne continued to invigorate her spirit.

"Good morning to you Jen, I had Maria prepare us a light breakfast. I thought that we could take a long walk on the beach to clear both of our heads from the dinner party on last night. You may reprimand me when we get home, since this was a vacation for us to enjoy each other. Forgive me for accepting all of these invitations and arranging to have business meeting, but sometimes duty calls. Just like you are reviewing that briefing from my father, I had some business matters to resolve."

Edwin reached for her hand. "Today belongs to us exclusively and nothing will interfere."

Jennifer gave her husband another affectionate kiss and sat down to the light breakfast Maria had prepared.

"I don't know how I could have made it through the wedding without you at my side. In my prayers, tonight I am going to thank God for bringing you into my life. I love the way you pamper me. Don't worry about the other invitations and the meetings, I do understand. We have the early morning and the late night, enough time for us to explore what we've missed while rearing our children and taking care of our businesses. I love you, Mr. William Edwin Langley II, and this vacation to Hawaii has just melted away the everyday grind of life so each of us can touch the very essence of the other's soul, mind, and body."

Edwin placed a plate of food and a cup of coffee in front of the lady he knew could take him from zero to one hundred with just a smile.

"Eat up, lady, the beach awaits us."

The walk on the beach was what she needed. Not only did it dissipate her anxiousness, she was now ready to ingest and digest the remaining contents of the package from William Sr. As she walked on the lanai, she noted that Maria had placed on the table a pot of her favorite tea and some orange scones. Next to the refreshments was the package.

Edwin had gone into their bedroom to change into his golf attire for he had a tee time at 2:00 PM.

Jennifer poured herself a cup of tea, picked up the package, and focused at the place where she had placed the bookmark.

Jennifer, I am retrogressing a little for I remembered I left out some very valuable information regarding Katerina's mother.

Adolph and Helga were getting up in age and it appeared that their only offspring would consist of their two sons and their families. Even though neither of them had visited the farm since finishing West Point, Adolph and Helga had received several letters as well as pictures of their families. Their daughter Lillian Anne had left home to reside in New York. They had not heard from their daughter in almost two years.

Helga had miscarriage at least twice since her youngest daughter Lillian Anne's birth. Each had resided to the fact that another offspring was not possible so they would have to enjoy each other during the winter of their lives.

They had become content with this idea. It may have been 1912 or 1913, their daughter Lillian Anne returned to Hamburg advising them of her marriage and pregnancy. Her husband's name was Charles Henry Petersen and he was a known musician in the Harlem area of New York. Lillian Anne had returned home to give birth and to ask her parents to help with the early rearing of the child since both she and her husband were in the entertainment business.

During her eighth month of pregnancy, Lillian Anne had begun to spot, thus the physician had recommended continued bed rest. After several hours of intense labor pains, Lillian Anne gave birth to a beautiful baby girl whom she named Hettie Imelda Hamburg-Petersen.

As soon as Adolph and Helga saw the child their eyes met but no word were spoken, for the evidence showed that the Seed of the Nile was strong and ran deep within Lillian Anne's blood or her husband's.

This new baby girl could live in both cultures; she was not as fair as her uncles, her mother, her grandparents, or her deceased aunt, Elizabeth. Her skin tone had a slight tinge, her hair was more reddish-brown than blonde, and her eyes were a very light brown with a hint of green. She was beautifully adorned externally and did have some of the same facial features as her grandfather. Lillian Anne spoke very little of the child's father, neither did she know anything about the father's parents or ancestors. Adolph and Helga learned that the father had been raised in Massachusetts and moved to New York to pursue his musical career.

They named her Hettie Imelda DuPont Hamburg Petersen a combination of all of the cultural names and surnames of her ancestors. Within six months of the birth of this child, Lillian Anne had returned to New York.

In the beginning she communicated with her parents via mail, but eventually the letters stopped coming and no other words or communication was received from Lillian Anne. This beautiful child would eventually become the mother of Katerina Amelia Hamburg Petersen-DeBeaux.

Helga and Adolph adored their grandchild and provided her all the material things they could afford. Adolph often laughed about having to raise a child so beautiful in his old age. He and Helga knew that the spirit had provided them another chance to educate one of their offspring with knowledge of their different businesses in order to keep it flourishing long after their demise.

The child was kept occupied with studies and other cultural and social training and affairs that she very seldom asked about her mother and father. Helga and Adolph assured her that her parents loved her, but because of their profession, it would be difficult to provide her a proper upbringing.

Sometimes during the child's formative years Helga would hear her ask her sitter, "When will my parents return to get me?" Helga's heart would be heavy and her eyes teary knowing the child felt abandoned by her parents. She vowed that this child would grow up with more love and attention than any other child on their farm or within thirty miles of the farm.

The name Lillian Anne DuPont Hamburg-Petersen was never again spoken in their home.

Although the child was surrounded with much love from her grandparents, her sitter and others on the farm, the tears and the crying did not cease until she reached the age of thirteen. On this day, she announced to her grandparents that she knew and understood that her parents would never come after her and it did not matter, because no one could penetrate through the amount of love and affection she had for her grandparents.

Hettie had been well educated at the school her grandfather had on his property, but her grandparents' desire was for her to continue her formal training with a degree in one of the sciences. Helga had learned about a school that had opened up for children of color in the city of Atlanta, Georgia. At first Adolph was opposed to her attending this school. His sights were set on an all girls' school in the city of Charleston, thus allowing her to be closer to them. Since she would be his last known offspring, Adolph did not want her far from his sight.

Helga convinced Adolph that if she attended the school in Atlanta, she would become a multicultural citizen having exposure to both cultures.

The school in Atlanta was the Atlanta Baptist Female Seminary, found in 1881 by Sophia B. Packard. John D. Rockefeller and his wife, Laura Spelman had contributed monetarily to the purchase of the land to house the school. The school had been established to assist females of color to finish high school and subsequently complete a teaching certification. In the year 1924, the school's name was changed to Spelman College due to the antislavery activities of Laura Spelman Rockefeller and her parents.

The school that was established on Adolph's land for his many workers had provided Hettie with the best educational, musical and social training, but Helga wanted more for her granddaughter. She was a natural when learning about the plants and animals on her grandparents' farm, but her grandparents wanted her to secure higher training in the scientific field. Once he learned about the academic curriculum at the school, Adolph gave into Helga's wishes.

Although her grandfather was waning due to his age, visitors still came to the farm to learn more about his scientific methods. Whenever her grandfather was unable to articulate the process or provide insight on the process, Hettie who was always at his side would mercerize the visitors by providing the sought after answers.

At the age of fifteen, Hettie returned home from completing her high school classes at Atlanta Baptist Female Seminary. There were several of her grandfather's guests who were visiting from France. Although her grandfather was being pushed around by one of his hired workers, his mind was still sharp with the knowledge of his professional work. During this tour of her grandfather's grounds by the French visitors, one of her grandfather's workers who had matriculated at the University of Alabama and had received a bachelor of science and a master's in agriculture was completing the presentation. This young man was probably in his early twenties and stood as tall as the pine trees on her grandfather's property. Not only was he very handsome but quite knowledgeable about her grandfather's work.

Although Adolph has lived more than one hundred years of age, his legs and body were weak, but his mind was still sharp. He introduced the presenter as Jorge Michael McKinney. Hettie thought she knew most of the families working for her grandfather, but this young man was not very familiar to her.

She was fascinated with him and was fascinated with his statute and his knowledge of the hybrid research, there was one young Frenchman in the visitors group she could not keep her eyes from undressing him mentally and physical and it appeared his eyes were doing the same.

At dinner, she was seated next to the two of them: Jorge Michael McKinney and as she learned during dinner, the young Frenchman, Raimond Pierre DeBeaux. Raimond had read several of her grandfather's research manuscripts at the Sorbonne as well as at the University of New Orleans. He was intrigued with Adolph's results and wanted to meet him. While both men tried to keep Hettie's interest and attention, it was Raimond who obviously won time alone with her.

After dinner, she and Raimond walked through her grandfather's grounds and she pointed out some of the results of his research. She took him to the greenhouses and other important research sites on the farm for him to observe. On their way to the canning warehouse, Raimond held her hand and Hettie knew she was more than in love.

Hettie had spoken to her grandmother about Raimond's interest in the workers on the land. As much of the detail of the conversation that Katerina could remember between her mother Hettie and her great-grandmother Helga, is documented in this package.

Raimond had been very observant of his surrounds even the workers. From his matriculation at the University of New Orleans, he was very familiar with the terms Quadroons, Mulattos used for certain inhabitants of the different Parishes in Louisiana. He was inquisitive as to the origin and nationality of the workers.

Hettie's responses had some cynicism and sarcasm in them: "Why, they are human like you and me. I see no difference between your human makeup and theirs. They are good and loyal workers for my father. They have been vital entities of my grandfather's research and his business ventures. Many of their children have been academically trained and have become teachers, scientist and business men in other parts of the country."

Raimond asked, "Are they in anyway genetically attached to the Quadroons and Mulattos in the Louisiana Parishes?"

To his question she replied, "To my knowledge, no, many of their offspring were born on our land. After slavery, a large number of them migrated to others cities in South Carolina as well as other states."

Raimond had observed that much of the property was not productive and many of the homes had begun to deteriorate. "What will your grandfather do with his land and his research? I observe that he is doing very little with the hybrid project and have not produced any recent papers."

Hettie replied, "He has me to continue his legacy."

Raimond returned to New Orleans to complete his studies and Hettie returned to Atlanta Baptist Female Seminary to complete her studies in chemistry and math. They corresponded with each other via letters and often met secretly in New Orleans or Atlanta.

Upon her return to school for her second year, Hettie discovered she was pregnant. She immediately told Raimond and he assured her that he would take both she and his child back to France to live as a family. Hettie was only able to complete the first half of her studies and went home to deliver her child. Her grandfather was not doing well and at times did not recognize her. In fact he died before her child was born.

Helga did not want Hettie to have the stigma of trying to rear her child without the proper credentials; therefore after the birth of the child, Helga assumed the role of mother. Hettie was sent back to Atlanta to continue her studies at the Atlanta Baptist Female Seminary. Helga had envisioned her returning to the farm to teach the children and the workers.

Hettie wrote Raimond about the birth of the child and the name given to his child, Katerina Amelia DuPont Hamburg Petersen-DeBeaux. She provided a very clear and distinct description of the child and how her features were a blend of both of theirs. In her letters she pledged her deep love for him, promising him that no other would steal her heart for it was only for him. Hettie penned letters weekly including pictures of their love child. Even though she wrote weekly, she did not receive any correspondences from Raimond.

Raimond letters came to Hettie at least two years later to advise her he had returned to France after completing his degree in New Orleans and was now teaching agriculture at the Sorbonne. Her letters to him had been delayed in New Orleans and he had just received them.

In his letters he spoke of his marriage and his two sons, but assured her, upon his return to America he would come for her and his daughter. His letters still spoke of his love for her and for his daughter. His marriage had been an arranged one but his heart still belonged to her.

Helga was aware of these letters and vowed that Raimond would not take her granddaughter or her great-grandchild back to France. He was now a married man with a family of his own; this was not a life she desired for her granddaughter or her great-grandchild. She was aware of being in love with someone, but unable to have him completely. This was her life with Adolph. Yes, she knew he loved her, but her status as his mistress not his wife often made her feel unattached and dismantled. A feeling she did not wish upon her granddaughter or her great-grandchild.

Times were getting bad at the Hamburg farm; many of the workers were leaving for more advance work in the larger cities in the North, South, and Midwest. Helga was unable to find workers for the farm. Weeds had begun to outgrow the crops. Even the uptown and downtown areas of Hamburg began to become destitute due to the disastrous flood in the late 1920s. Many of the people left their farms and home to become a part of the industrial revolution and to build a better life in other cities in South Carolina. By the late 1930s, Hamburg was virtually unknown; however, since the Hamburg place was so far removed from the uptown and downtown, some of it still existed, especially the home house and a large garden several feet from the home.

The majority of the workers who were part of the ECEA project had left the farm and assimilated with other cultures and immigrants from other countries. Because of their training, skills and ability to articulate very well, each of them received good positions in the newly formed companies of the industrial revolution. Most cultures were unaware of the seed of the Nile running through their blood. It was unspoken and unrevealed by many of the members of the ECEA project.

Hettie wanted her grandmother and her daughter to move to Atlanta while she finished her last year of matriculation. Helga felt that was her home and she needed to carry on the work of her beloved Adolph. Hettie knew it was nothing to carry on since the only persons left on the land were her grandmother and several faithful workers. Helga was adamant that she and the few workers left would stay on the farm to keep the legacy alive.

Before Hettie had finished her last year of school, she received a letter from her grandmother telling her about Raimond's return to the states. The letter also revealed that Raimond had taken her daughter, Katerina to live with his sister Gabrielle who lived in Charleston. Katerina was nine when she was removed from her Hamburg home to live with her aunt in Charleston.

Hettie finished her training, but did not return to Hamburg, she became a teacher in the school system in August, Georgia. She wrote to her mother often, inquiring about the child Katerina and asking her to move to Augusta. She also learned that he had become not only a professor and lecturer in the agricultural school of the Sorbonne and the father of two sons but also part owner of a shipping business.

Helga was reluctant, but she allowed Raimond to take Katerina to his sister, Gabrielle Noelle DeBeaux home in Charleston, South Carolina. Her aunt immediately enrolled her into a girl's finishing school where she gained additional skills in education, ballet and piano training. She was also well trained in the French language and spoke it fluently.

At the age of fourteen, Katerina received a letter from one of her grand maman workers, telling her about her illness and near death situation. She begged her aunt to let her go for a visit. She was allowed to go with one of the workers of her aunt. During her week visit with her maman is when she was told the truth about her real mother and her ancestral lineage. Her grand Maman also provided her with documents regarding the Hybrid ECEA project that her grandfather had conducted. Katerina was to keep all this information a secret and never try to get in touch with her real mother or any of her other ancestors. She asked her not to come back for her funeral, for she was sure her mother would attend. No contact should ever be made between her and her mother.

A year later, her grand maman died. Katerina did attend the funeral, which was held in Augusta, Georgia. She sat in the back of mortuary where the service was held. One of her aunt's workers accompanied her to the funeral. Neither the face nor an image of her real mother was affixed in her mind or on her brain, but when she and the worker observed the lady on the front row whose face was a blueprint of hers, they both knew her identify. She instantly knew she was her mother. Katerina told me that "not only did she mirror the face of her Maman. Katerina could have been her twin. Her skin tone was a little darker than hers, but her eyes, nose, and mouth were the same. Now she knew why her father fell instantly in love with this lady."

According to Katerina she wanted to run up to her and kiss her face and her hands and just squeeze her, but she remembered the last words of her grand maman, never try to get in touch with your real mother.

Jennifer put the package on her lap. I can imagine how Katerina felt that day seeing her real mother's image for the first time. I do not know what I would do if I found out my mother and father were not my real parents. What a strong pill for a child of fifteen or seventeen to ingest and digest. I can also imagine how her real mother probably went through life wondering how it would feel to hold her child, kiss her child, and tell her child that she loved her.

Jennifer rubbed her chin and thought, I wonder did Hettie have internal hatred for her mother, since she kept her firstborn away from her. I believe modern-day psychologists would have a field day with this one.

The truth is at this moment, I cannot fathom how these two women went to their graves with such burdens and secrets; several cancerous secrets eating up their emotions and their sanity and changing their psychological state. Each had to live in different cultures because of the era and each could not reach out to the other because of cultural laws and practices.

It would be interesting if I could trace some of the ancestors of the ECEA project to let them know they are not who they believe they are. They have lived in a false culture for all of these centuries and never knew it. Would it be devastating for those offspring of the ECEA project who have been taught to despise and hate people of other cultures, to find out they, too, have the same DNA and genetic makeup of the culture they despise.

One of my worked told me about a daughter of a friend of hers who was of a mixed culture. The daughter hated the fact that she was of the mixed culture and after graduating from high school left her small town in Oklahoma, moved to Iowa and never contacted her family. It is believed that the daughter secured a new identity, to keep her parents from locating her. I can just feel the agony those parents are experiencing, knowing their own flesh and blood have denied not only herself but also her parents from having a loving relationship with her and possibly her children. Wow, the psychological and emotional baggage we hand to our children and we don't realize how it will affect them later on in life.

Jennifer picked the book back up looked at the sky and said, "William how could you have kept this information from your family? You are asking me to do something you did not do. This is a tall order and I am not sure how your son and your grandchildren are going to accept this information. Yes, the culture and ethnicity makeup of the land are changing daily and most of us have accepted this fact, but how do you go from believing you are one culture and find out in the prime of your life you are not. I pray that you had thought this out before you put pen to paper. However, this is still a heavy load for me to carry and an awesome task for me to carry out."

She began reading at the point where she had stopped.

Katerina explained to me that she did not begin reading the information and the documents until she was around the age of seventeen. From her trips to visit her father in France and living with her aunt, she knew about the DeBeaux ancestral lineage, but was she baffled when she begin reading about her mother's lineage. There are pictures of many of the ancestors on her mother's side of the family including pictures of Adolph's brother's family. My lawyer has secured them in a special place. Whatever is your decision about sharing this information with my family, there are additional documents and memorabilia with my attorney. There are some fascinating documents that will give you more insight into the ECEA project and the number of families that were a part of this project. There is also a separate ledger that recorded the name and possible ages and birthdays of his other workers.

During her illness, Katerina asked me to locate her mother. It was ironic that the year she asked me to complete this task, her mother was being honored by the school system for her contributions to the science and math disciplines. In fact several of her chemistry students who had won various prizes at the state's science fair were being honored with her. My corporation bought two tables for the affair and all except two tickets were given to several workers of the corporation. Although Katerina was not doing well, it seems that when she was made aware of the tickets, she gained strength and stamina from within.

I remember the occasion as though it happened yesterday on May 24, 1962, at the Marriott Hotel in downtown Charleston, I witness my wife's twin (her mother) accept accommodations and gifts not only for contributing to the science and math disciplines at her school but also for being a major contributor to the school system's science curriculum. From all of the presentations, I knew that Hettie Smyth had been a devoted and inspiring teacher, for many of her students had attested to that fact. My thought, her great-grandparents' and her mother's DNAs are where my wife got her business savvy, her tenacity, her determination, and her will to be successful in her millinery business.

Just seeing her mother accept those awards, put more light and twinkle in my wife's spirit. She began working part-time at her Millinery shops and she began having dinner with the family. I felt in my heart that maybe my prayers had been answered for her and my daughter. However, within six months of my wife's miraculous recovery, my daughter Olivia's illness took a turn for the worse.

Tears fell from Jennifer's eye and she wiped them away with her thumb. She was not aware that Maria was standing next to her with the phone.

"Mrs. Langley, there is a phone call from your son Michael. He says it is very important."

"Thank you Maria, I'll take it."

"Hi, Michael, is everything OK?"

"No, Mama Tessa had a major stroke, Dr. Epps, said she will need twenty-four-hour nursing care until she recuperates from the stroke. He has prescribed her some medication and has given directions to nurse Brown. Right now she is in the ICU unit and cannot be moved. He feels she needs to be in the hospital at this time so he can assess her recovery and her condition. I wanted you and Dad to know about her condition."

"Thanks Michael, your father is on the golf course and as soon as he returns, we will make a decision if we will leave for home tonight or tomorrow. I know that Rosa's sons will be disappointed, but they can stay or return another time. I'll call you back later on with our decision."

Jennifer laid the package on the table. She thought about her first meeting with Tessa. She had made other plans for Edwin regarding his choice of a girlfriend and wife. She was not unfriendly, but very reserved with her interaction and comments to me. I could feel the coldness and the disappointment when Edwin announced our engagement.

Tessa remained distant from Edwin and me for a long time. However, she showed much love for our children. In fact she and Michael have a very good relationship. He often defended her when she would not attend certain family gatherings. It's strange, even though I know he loved his grandfather William, it appeared he was more in tune to Tessa than his grandfather. Tessa and William Sr. often disagreed with her professional and outreach endeavors. However, Michael would often intercede on behalf of Tessa.

It was not until William Sr. began to make frequent business and social trips without her that Tessa began to soften up to me. I had become her listening and sounding board during those lonely and awkward moments.

"Lord, keep Tessa safe until we return home."

"Maria, I need you to locate Rosa and ask her to come see me on the lanai."

"Yes, I will Mrs. Langley."

Jennifer placed the bookmarker on the page where she stopped reading. Her mind was filled with questions about the package and with the worry of Tessa's condition. She was aware of the difficulties in the marriage between William and Tessa and she did not want her knowledge to cloud her decisions regarding Tessa.

She picked up her cell and phoned her son, Michael.

"Michael, would you please call Mr. Lambert, the family's Attorney and advise him of Tessa's condition. I know there were certain provisions in William's will that referenced the medical care of Tessa."

"I will mother, but I am aware that Tessa does not use Mr. Lambert as her Attorney. I think his name is Hamilton McGowan. I don't believe he is affiliated with the Lambert law firm. In fact three days ago she had requested his presence at the house."

"Thanks, Michael, forego speaking to Tessa's attorney, I will have Edwin speak to her about that on our return. Just call Mr. Lambert and advise him about our situation. Your father will provide the specifics when he returns."

Jennifer placed the bookmarker in the package. She could not believe that this was happening to her and her family. This was supposed to be an enjoyable time of rest and relaxation for her and Edwin.

She spoke out loudly, "Why are all of these situations crashing down on my family and me now? Jennifer began to inhale deeply the smell of the Pacific Ocean to invigorate my inner strength, but she looked out over the horizon and saw energy and her strength dip into the ocean."

Jennifer's weeping and sobbing was so loud that when Rosa and Maria entered the lanai, both took off running in her direction.

"Mrs. Langley may I fix you a fresh pot of tea? I still have several of your favorite scones in the kitchen. Would you like me to bring them out?"

Jennifer could not give Maria an audible answer she just nodded her head up and down.

Rosa was rubbing her back and provided her tissues to dry her tears and wipe her running nose.

"Jen, I mean Mrs. Langley (looking behind her to ensure Maria was not in close proximity), Ms. Tessa is going to be alright. She's had several ministrokes after her other major one, and she has always pulled through."

Still sobbing, "Rosa, I don't know about this one, she must have a premonition for Michael said she called her lawyer about two weeks ago."

"We all need to take precautions when these medical conditions occur, that's probably why she called him. Have you called Mr. Langley?"

"No, I have not, I will right now."

Jennifer picked up the cell phone and began dialing Edwin's number.

"We will probably cut our trip short and return home tomorrow."

"I do understand. I will tell the boys when I return to the cabana."

When Edwin answered the phone, all Jennifer said was, "Honey, I need you here right now. It is important." She disconnected the phone without another response.

The phone rang in the house, and Rosa answered it.

"Hi, Michael, I'll give the phone to your mom. She's on the lanai."

Rosa handed Jennifer the phone. "Mother, Tessa's nurse found her unresponsive this afternoon and the hospital has labeled her condition as very critical."

Tears began to flow heavily from Jennifer's eyes. "Michael, we will leave the island today as soon as your father gets back."

"Mrs. Langley, I can send the boys back with you and Mr. Langley and stay here with Maria to close up the house."

"Rosa, I cannot bear this alone. I will need your management and personal strength to get me through this. Maria can handle this, and I can get Mrs. Kahuna to provide additional assistance for Maria.

TRUTH TRUMPS CONFESSION

On the plane, Jennifer could not rest, although Mrs. Kahuna's personal physician had given her a sedative. Her mind vacillated between the Package and Tessa's condition. Her mind was not clear as to why Tessa needed her personal Attorney. From the Trust and the Will left by William Sr. all of Tessa's needs had been met. She was aware of personal properties left to her by her parents and other asset accounts, but Tessa had already advised her grandchildren of their inheritance.

Edwin squeezed his wife hand and kissed the salty tears running down her cheeks. He now had to be the strong one in the family. He knew that Tessa knew a lot about the Langley family and she was aware of his father's mistress. Edwin thought Tessa was a good woman to keep all of this dysfunction and uncharacteristic behavior away from the family. It always puzzled him why she did not divorce his father by honoring the contents of the prenuptial agreement and just move on with her life. Did she know something he was not privileged to? Or was my father holding an ace in his hand?

Edwin felt Jennifer's body tense as he pulled her closer to him.

Earlier Michael had texted the family to let them know that Tessa's condition was still considered as very critical. He looked at his cell phone and there were no new messages. He, too, began to feel a little worried.

The house felt surreal as they enter the foyer. The quietness of the large home brought chills to each of their bones. Edwin continued to hold on to a shivering and tense Jennifer, and Rosa stood next to the oil painting of William Sr. with her hands folded as though she was praying. Neither one spoke a word to the other. Rosa had asked the chauffer to take her two sons home. She was not sure how long Jennifer would need her support and strength.

It appeared that each of them had been standing the silent foyer for more than an hour. Soon the silence was broken as Michael shoes sounded against the wood floors in the foyer. He walked swiftly over to his mother and father and hugged them with so much intensity. He beckoned for Rosa to come and join the three of them.

"Mama Tessa's condition has not worsened. However, she is still medically classified as very critical and her vital signs are somewhat stable. I have kept the news media from putting it out on the airways. Our spokesperson asked them to wait until the head of the Langley family had returned home. Dad, I brought Regina with me so she can help you frame your statement and then she can summon the news media."

Regina Whitmark walked over to Edwin and extended her hand. "Mr. Langley, my prayers are with you and your family. As soon as you and your wife have settled in, we can begin the draft for the media."

Edwin's face turned from solemn to serious. "Son, I am very proud of you, as my eldest son you have taken charge of the situation. You have just demonstrated what I knew. You have great leadership skills and exceptional business savvy. Thanks so much for taking the helm in my absence."

"Dad, thanks for the vote of confidence, but cannot take full credit. I had help from Will, Regina, and Aunt Onnie. Each of them assisted me in getting the situation under control. I contacted Mr. Lambert the family Attorney he provided me some guidance. He will be here around three."

Edwin wore a big grin, he knew his son was doing a great job within their industrial and corporate chains, but now he was happy to see him step up to challenge family and personal situations.

Jennifer hugged her son again as she and Rosa ascended the stairs to her bedroom on the third floor. The household staff was busy unloading the limousine and carrying the contents to the appropriate rooms.

Edwin entered his father's library and sitting room where Michael and Will had assembled, Regina, the family spokesperson, and members of marketing and publicity departments. Each was in the stages of composing a statement for him to make regarding the condition of his stepmother. The chatter in the room helped awaken his spirit, mind, and disposition for he, too, had been in a state of disbelief, shock, and numbness from Maui to Charleston, South Carolina. He could feel his body showing signs of revival and rejuvenation.

As he began speaking to his marketing and publicity team, the phone rang. Simultaneously, Michael and Regina walked over to answer it.

"The Langley Residence, Michael speaking, may I help you. Hi Mr. Lambert, yes my mother and father have arrived home safely. Yes he is able to speak to you. I will get him to the phone."

Michael passed the phone to his father. He could not read the expressions on his father's face in relations to the conversation he and Mr. Lambert were having.

The silence in the large estate was beginning to wane for Rosa has reassumed her position as chief of the household and was providing directions to the staff. The chef was preparing refreshments for the marketing and publicity staff; Nurse Brown, Tessa's morning-shift nurse, was attending to Mrs. Langley. Rosa and the housekeep staff had begun preparing the sunroom for immediate friends, guests and the news media staff. She looked beyond the front gate entrance and noticed the lineup of personnel from the various TV stations and local newspapers.

Edwin turned around and each one in the room could see a change in his countenance. A smile could be seen on Edwin's face as he hung up the phone.

"Mr. Lambert said Tessa's condition is still very critical, but the doctors are hopeful. She opened her eyes about ten minutes ago, she is alerts and acknowledges one's presence with the moving of her eyes, but she is unable to speak or move any of her extremities."

"That's great news, Dad. I'll ask Rosa if Mom is stable so Will and I can give her the updated information."

"Please ask Nurse Brown before you speak to your mother."

"Regina, I think you and your staff should begin preparing my comments for the media. Let's get to work."

Onnie wanted to get to the hospital before any of the other family members. She had summoned Florence to get the driver to take her to the hospital to see Tessa. Florence did not ask any questions, just assisted her.

To Onnie the walk from the hospital elevator to Onnie's room felt very long. Her legs begin to grow unstable as though she could not make another step. She was not afraid of entering Tessa's room nor was she short on the words she had purpose in her heart to speak.

To no one in particular, she said, "Legs, this is not the time for you to go numb on me. I have something to do before the other members come to the hospital."

As she entered Tessa's room she noticed an unfamiliar personal nurse sitting next to Tessa.

"Good morning, I am Onnie Dusett, an acquaintance of Mrs. Langley. I wanted to visit Tessa before the rest of the family comes. Is she alert? Is she aware that someone is in the room? If so may I speak to her alone?"

"Good morning, Ms. Onnie, how are you. Ms. Tessa is aware of people's presence, but she is unable to speak. She often moves her eyes in the direction of the voice. I will be outside the door if you need me."

The nurse looked at Onnie strangely, for she had heard about the friction between Onnie and Tessa from her employer, Nurse Brown. She was guessing that Ms. Onnie wanted to amend things with Tessa before it was too late.

The nurse nodded her head to Onnie to show her approval and walked out of the room.

"Good morning, Tessa, this is Onnie. I thought I would come before the others to avoid a lot of commotion in your hospital room.

Onnie walked closer to Tessa's bed, she saw her eyes moved in her direction. They seemed to be sad one minute and angry the next.

Learning forward, Onnie carefully took Tessa's hand into hers.

She whispered into her ear, "Here we are alone together, two women who loved and adored the same man. We provided moments, hours and years that neither one of us could have done independent of the other. He was very special, loving, and kind. His tolerance of his situation was more than I could ever bear. My love for him would not succumb to the status of his marital situation. Since I was not young and foolish when I began the relationship, I weighed the pros and the cons, seeing more positive effects than negative ones.

For years I carried the secret of my love for him in my heart and my spirit. I can truly say he never made me feel unloved or not appreciated. In fact if I had all the times he confessed his love and devotion to me, I would own a small island in the Caribbean. William always made me feel special as though I was his light and his darkness. Even when we could not be together, his daily phone calls kept me in a place where I knew only he could fill. I understand now why I carried this secret for I never wanted any actions or decisions to hurt my precious William. I never intended for the relationship to adversely affect you, but longer the affair continued, the more I knew it did.

Sometimes I would look at him and see the strain and stress on his face. I knew it was the results of his double love life, especially since he did not bring disgrace to us nor hurt or harm either one of us. I had confessed to him on numerous times that I was very satisfied with my position in his life. If he had wanted something different for his life and I am sure he did, he could choose and it would not destroy my love for him. I know he was sincere when he often stated that he loved you for coming into his life during a difficult time, but he was in love with me and could bear to be apart from me. I know and I hope you understand, my William did what he had to do for his complicated life. He dealt with the hand that life, frustration and regrets had dealt him. Neither one of us wanted to free him so he had to endure the pain of his duel life.

He loved you for coming into his life when it was needed and he loved me for helping him to ease the pains and the hurt he was experiencing. I could feel his anguish, his uneasiness and I could see the strain of worry on his face whenever I was with him. My love for him grew strong and strong each time I held him or he held me. He would sometimes sit looking forlorn and distant and at those times, I often wondered why God had dealt him such a complicated life. All he longed for was to experience the love between a husband and a wife. Even though I was not legally his wife, I know I set the stage and the atmosphere for him to experience this joy. He always said he loved you and thanked you for coming into his life after the death of his first wife. However, his love for you had a different spin from the in love factor he had for me and Katerina. I had prayed that the two of you would work out your differences before his demise. Since this did not occur, I pray that the two of you will kindle that love connection again in heaven. I know you won't understand this and will never believe these words, but thanks for sharing him with me."

Tessa tried to free her hand but Onnie held it tightly.

"I know you will never forgive me for my role in this situation and I am not asking you to. I need your understanding that this was a symbiotic relationship where each of us benefited. I have never loved another man as I did William, and if you could express it, neither had you, but your pride, your image, and your status destroyed the love of a man who had dreams of having a wife who would be in love with him mind, body, and soul. He felt that your marriage was one of convenience.

"I hated you for years for not letting him go so he could be solely mine, but then I understood why you stayed. Although you would have acquired many material assets associated with your marriage to him, you understood the fact that the without sisters, loneliness and aloneness were bitches. How do I know? Because I had the same fear, when he expressed to me his quilt regarding our relationship and thought that maybe he would try to reconcile with you. For several months when we had no contact, all I could think about at night and see in my dreams were those two sisters: loneliness and aloneness.

"When the trial reconciliation did not yield success, upon his return to my arms and my bed, my love for him grew to a magnitude of overwhelming proportion. Even if he had stated I can only see you once per month, I would have been greatly satisfied. Whatever time I could spend with him would have eased my craving and longing for him.

"Yes, I had it bad and if I had to do it all over again, I would. William brought such joy and laughter to my life. So you see Tessa, both of us will have very fond memories of William Edwin Langley Sr. Just saying his name makes me miss him more and more. Do you know how it feels knowing that the man lying beside you has a wife? The man lying beside you must go back to his legal life. The man lying beside you continuously speaks of his love for you, but does nothing to make the love situation permanent."

It appeared that Tessa attempted to say something for Onnie saw her mouth moved, but no sound came forth. She squeeze Onnie's hand and Onnie saw a tear drop from her eye.

"Tessa, this conversation is more of a cleansing for me and an eradication of the burden I've carried for years. I know you were aware of our relationship, but I only learned several weeks ago that it was my great-nephew, Michael and not William who told you. William had wanted to, but I made him promise that he wouldn't. Now my mind is flooded with what if I had allowed him to tell you? Would he have left me for you or would I have been brave enough to let him take that step to divorce you? Let me assure you that I do not feel good about what I've done, but I don't hate the love and the sense of belonging that I gained from the relationship with William. May God have mercy on both of our souls for the emotional atmosphere we created."

Onnie attempted to release her hand from Tessa's but Tessa would not let go. As Onnie looked into Tessa's eyes and observed her body language, it seemed that Tessa was in agreement—my selfishness and hers had created the situation, and we both had to ask God for forgiveness and to forgive ourselves.

Tessa looked at Onnie and a big smile covered her face. It appeared that Tessa was having an out of the body experience. Onnie wondered where she had secured the thrust of energy.

She turned toward Onnie and with a very clear and concise voice spoke these words: "Yes, at first, I was very displeased with William's affair with you, but I channeled my anger into my charity work. There I found not only satisfaction in my work but also several suitors who gave me the satisfaction, the love, and the fun I was missing in my own marriage. Don't feel sorry for me, Ms. Onnie, because while you were in William's arms, I found solace in Charlie's arm. Yes, his secondary function was to assist me with the charities that I chaired, but his primary function was to alleviate the hurt and pain that you and William had caused me. In fact, I was not sure if the third miscarriage contained William or Charles' DNA. I found solace in knowing that even with William's adulteress affair with you, I was still respected as his wife and received all of the amenities of his wife. You on the other hand could only be viewed as his mistress or the other woman. If he truly loved you, he had the upper-hand. He could have easily divorce me without any complications. So you see Ms. Onnie, your conversation with me today, is just for you, because I made my peace with my husband's side piece long time ago."

Tessa turned her head to the wall and a big smirk filled the space where the smile once occupied.

Onnie was puzzled with this disposition of Tessa's, still holding her hand she could not understand the stance and position that Tessa had taken on this conversation. Was it really Tessa's audible voice or was Onnie hearing things? Still holding on to Tessa's hand, Onnie moved closer to the bed. She could see that Tessa looked as though she was in a deep sleep, with no expression on her face.

In her mind, Onnie asked, "Was that really the voice of Tessa or the voice of my conscience? It could not have been my conscience for I know for a fact that William and I thought that Charlie was not into women. Were we fooled? And yes, William did love me. I know for a fact that he did."

She squeezed Tessa's hand lean in closer to her ear to ask: "Was I really played all these years? I know William loved me and did not want to embarrass you with a divorce. Your words are a counterattack, but in my heart I know the real truth. I am not in denial, but my dear you are."

Again, Onnie experience the audible voice of Tessa.

"Believe whatever you want, but I know the truth. William played both of us, but I got the last laugh. Yes, he often visited my bedroom and most of the time it was not to talk."

Again she turned her face to the wall and assumed the same deep sleep position.

Onnie blinked her eyes twice for she was beginning to feel a little light headed. She was really confused: had she really been used by William. A tear began to fall from her eye. She had to discuss this situation with her brother Cromwell, William's best friend.

Edwin and Jennifer were taken aback when they walked into the hospital room and observed Onnie and Tessa not only looking at each other but also touching hands. They even saw Onnie take a tissue and wipe the tears from her eyes.

Walking over to her aunt Onnie, Jennifer placed a kiss on her cheek and bent down to kiss Tessa's cheek.

"Are you OK, Aunt Onnie?"

"Yes, I wanted to come see Tessa early before all of the other family arrived. Too many guests may tire her out. The driver is waiting for me. I will leave so you and Edwin may have some quality time with her. She doesn't speak, but her eyes follow your voice and your steps."

"Thanks, Aunt Onnie for coming to see Mama Tessa, I am sure your visit lifted her spirits, if I didn't know any better, I see a smile on her face. I hope the two of you have made peace."

"It was my pleasure, Edwin, some things you have to let go of and take actions that you know are morally and ethically correct. I'll check on her condition from you'll later on in the day."

As Edwin and Jennifer walked up to Tessa's bed both looked at each other without speaking a word but their expression noted – what just happen here between the two of them.

Tessa's countenance seemed much better than the condition the Doctor had described to them. Tears continued to flow from Tessa's face and it appeared that a bright light shone directly on it. As a big smile formed on her lips, the heart monitor stopped working as though Tessa had found her peace.

Edwin ran to the nurse's station and explained about the monitor. They heard code Blue being announced throughout the hospital and several hospital workers made their way to Tessa's room.

After several minutes, the Physician came out. His eyes told them what they had feared. Tessa had taken her final breath.

Tessa came from a very small family, and the only relatives Edwin and Jennifer knew of was a first cousin, Darla Suzanne Manfred, on her father's side. Tessa's lawyer was immediately contacted to see if there were other relatives of Tessa. He was only aware of her cousin Darla Suzanne Adkins Manfred.

"To my knowledge, Jennifer she has only one first cousin on her father's side, Darla Suzanne Manfred who lives in Columbia, South Carolina. I can contact her or you may have Rosa contact her."

"Thanks for the information, Hamilton—Mr. McGowan, but either Edwin or I will contact her. Please e-mail or text any phone number or address you may have on Mrs. Manfred."

"Hamilton is acceptable for you to call me, Jennifer. I will have my administrative assistance send that over immediately via e-mail. I also need to talk to the family about Tessa's will and the new additions she signed off on about a week ago. I will have my assistant set up a time for the reading of the will to the family."

"Thanks again, Hamilton for the information. As soon as you send over the information, I will contact her cousin. Once we receive it, Edwin can complete the news release apprising the community of her passing. During her better days she was quite a fund-raiser for the causes of children's diseases and several other philanthropic interests."

Darla Suzanne Manfred acknowledged that she was Tessa's first cousin, but it had been some time since they had spoken. Tessa often sent her Christmas cards and occasionally, thinking of you cards, but they rarely visited or spoke on the phone.

In fact while speaking to Jennifer, Darla was very opened and candid about her family.

"My father, Keith Lawrence Adkins and Tessa's father, Joseph Phillip Adkins were brothers. When we were younger, our families would visit each other, but something happened when I was about fourteen and our family visits became less and less. Tessa and I were the only great-grandchildren of Thomasina Adkins and her only son our grandfather, Joseph Lawrence Adkins. I would ask my mother about the reason for us not seeing much of my cousin Tessa, but she would not discuss it. I think I am about two or three years younger than Tessa."

"Sometimes, Darla, it is best when there are misunderstandings in the family that—those misunderstands are best resolved by the affected parties."

"You are quite right about that, because I think Uncle Joseph and my father reconciled, because he and Aunt Cora attended my father and my mother's funerals. Tessa did not come, but sent flowers, several gifts and arranged for the catered repast."

"Would any of your other family members be attending Tessa's funeral?"

"Yes, my daughter Marilyn, and her three children, Joseph, James and Nila."

"Please extend an invitation to your daughter and her children that I would like them to remain after the funeral for a family dinner."

"I will Jennifer and I will see you next Tuesday."

The name Thomasina Adkins sounded familiar to Jennifer, but was not sure if it had something to do with one of the cases she was working on. She could not dwell on this name she had to assist Edwin with the funeral arrangements for Tessa.

The lawyer for Tessa had sent over the obituary and the funeral program for Tessa. Tessa had submitted all this information to Mr. Hamilton a week after she and Edwin left for Hawaii. It seemed strange to Jennifer, but again these were Tessa's wishes and neither she nor any member of her family had the rights to change them. In fact, Mr. Hamilton had politely and legally addressed that issue.

Again Jennifer honed in on the name Thomasina Adkins, for it did sound so familiar. Could it have been a name included in the package from William or was it one of the new cases Nila had spoken to her about while she was vacationing in Hawaii?

Whatever, this was not the time to dwell on this name. Edwin and the children would need her to help coordinate Tessa's funeral; therefore she needed to stay focused and remain strong.

Rosa entered the library where Jennifer had been using the phone. She could still see worry in her face and was sure that Jennifer needed a massage to relax her.

"Rosa, have you ever hear of a person named Thomasina Adkins?"

"No I have not Jennifer and if it has something to do with the package from William, you need to clear your thoughts and concentrate on the farewell celebration for Tessa."

"You are absolutely correct. I am going to see if William needs me to assist him with any of the arrangements. I saw the attire you had chosen for her and we will carry it to the mortuary this afternoon."

"That was one of her favorite dress ensembles and that was the reason for my choosing it. Before you go to the mortuary, I have engaged the services of your massage therapist. He is in the exercise room waiting for you. Upon your return, I will have the chef prepare you and Edwin a light lunch."

"Rosa you are so thoughtful, I do not know what I would do without arranging service and events I need to stay stable."

Rosa hoped that her arrangements with the massage therapist would bring calm to Jennifer's Soul. Rosa picked up the phone in the library and called the exercise room.

"Hi Claude, Jennifer is on her way down for her massage. She needs it badly. Thanks for coming over in an expedient manner."

No problem Rosa, I am ready and hope my magical fingers will do the trick on Mrs. Langley's stressful spots."

TESSA'S FAREWELL

As Jennifer and the family, gathered in the foyer and the library of their home prior to going to the First Presbyterian Church in downtown Charleston, she glanced as Rosa opened the front door and to her surprise walked in her new legal assistant Nila and it must have been some of her family members.

Jennifer thought it was very nice of her to come to Tessa's funeral, she must have promised Michael she would come. I must go over and greet her. She looked around for Michael, but he must have been in the Library with his father.

"Nila, thank you so much for coming. I really appreciate it."

"You are welcome, Mrs. Langley. Let me introduce you to my family, my grandmother Darla Manfred, my mother Marilyn Johnston, and my two brothers Joseph and James Johnston. Mrs. Jennifer Langley, Tessa's daughter-in-law."

Jennifer extended her hand to Darla. "Nice meeting each of you. We are not quite ready to proceed to the church, but I would like for each of you to meet my husband. Excuse me as I get him."

Walking toward the Library, Jennifer was all confused. This could not be possible. Only in make believe or fantasy worlds could this happen in one family. Why had I not noticed some resemblance of Nila to Tessa? I need to talk to Michael. Did he ever take Nila upstairs to meet Tessa? Did he ever mention her name to Tessa? I can't think about all of this now. Tessa and William, the two of you have created a big puzzle for this family to resolve.

"Excuse me Edwin, Will and Michael, Tessa's cousin and her family has arrived, I would like you to come and meet them. Has anyone received a call from Marcus and Bria? I hope they didn't miss their plane."

As each of them entered the foyer, Michael's expression changed when he noticed Nila; as their eyes met with expressions of wow, the foyer seemed to have gotten brighter!

"Mrs. Manfred, Darla, I would like you to meet my husband Edwin Langley, my two sons Michael and Will, and my daughter and her husband, who just arrived—Bria and Michael. This is Tessa's cousin and her family, Darla Manfred, her daughter Marilyn Johnston, her two sons Joseph and James, and her daughter Nila."

Warm welcomes were extended by each of the family members.

Michael eased Nila toward an empty space in the foyer.

"Why didn't you tell me you knew my grandmother? I had to find out on this solemn occasion that you are related."

"I was not aware either, Michael, my grandmother seldom talked about her cousin. There was no relationship with them. Besides, during the short time of our relationship you never introduced me to your grandmother Tessa."

"Let's talk about this after the funeral. Tessa was not my blood grandmother. She was my grandfather's second wife."

As the funeral director began placing the family members in the limousines, the atmosphere took on a sorrowful nature for this was a funeral of a person who was not easy to love or communicate with. What a sad commentary for this was a person who had lots of talents she could have shared with her family and others.

Jennifer looked around the room for she felt the same cold breeze flowing over her face, the day of Bria's wedding. As she entered the limousine, she whispered, "Now you can mend the pieces of the heart that was broken all these year. Asking for forgiveness isn't easy, but you can do it."

In her mind she thought, just knowing a little about Tessa's formative years is helping me to understand her behavior toward her marriage, having children and the acceptance of her by others. She wanted to feel physical love, but since she had never experienced it with her parents she was unable to give or receive it. What a psychological trip we as parents or care givers put on those we profess to love and cherish. I wonder if any one understands how we as parents, shape the lives of our future generations with the drama, lies and deceptions we burden them with each day.

Edwin looked at her strange. "Why are you asking God for forgiveness? Is there something about you and Tessa's relationship I do not know about?

"No, the forgiveness I whispered was for William Sr. they will be together again and he can mend the brokenness and hurt she experienced on earth."

"Let's all get through this funeral and then you and I can discuss this thought."

"It's not just a thought, Edwin. We both knew the bond between them dissipated long before we married. I never knew the reason, but I am sure both of them took it to their graves."

"You are correct, but we need to concentrate on making sure this funeral is conducted appropriately. The way Tessa would have wanted it."

Edwin kissed her on her forehead and held her hand through the processional and the funeral program.

Tessa had written her own Obituary, her eulogy and has design her Farewell program. It was a surreal program with only organ music of her choosing and the silent reading of her obituary. The only persons who spoke were the CEO of the Memorial Hospital and the Pastor who read her hand written eulogy. The eulogy was based on the following Bible verses found in Matthew 6:14, Ephesians 4:31–32, and Colossians 3:13. Her subject was: Forgiving yourself and others.

Many who attended the services listened very attentively to the contents of this message, but very few were aware of the turmoil and strife that existed in the Langleys' household between William Sr. and Tessa.

From the content of the eulogy, not only had she made her peace with the Lord, but she encouraged others to make sure that any anger, malice, or envy harboring in their heart against others, to make it right before they depart their earthly home. Kindness and compassion should penetrate our entire being so our words, our actions, and our deeds can build up and not destroy others.

It was evident to Jennifer that the contents of the eulogy were saying to the family, that she had finally found peace within her soul. Jennifer was not aware that she had been silently weeping, for in her heart and mind she knew firsthand of the conflicts between William and Tessa as well as from the package how it revealed some of the ways Tessa and William Sr. had hurt each other. Her silent tears were not consciously brought forth until Edwin used his handkerchief to wipe the teardrops from her face.

There was much solemn and quietness as each of the family members ate their delicious meals. Mr. McGowan, Tessa's Attorney, broke the silence with his announcement.

"I would like to let each of you know that the reading of Tessa's will and last Testament will be held at my office on next Wednesday at 5:00 PM. I will send out a reminder to all who are recipients and those who have been mentioned in the will."

"Thank you, Hamilton, I am sure all that are affected will be there next Wednesday."

"You are welcome Edwin, and I am going to depart so the family may have some quality time with each other. See each of you next Wednesday."

As the family exited the dining area into the Sun room or the great room, Michael guided Nila quietly to the foyer of the home.

"How are we going to play this out? Is there anyone in your family that knows we have been dating? This is going to be a bit awkward don't you think?"

"Nila looked at him with a weary smile. Is this your way of releasing me easy? I do not believe that my kinship to Tessa would in any way affect our relationship. As you stated, she was not your blood relative."

"I like what we have currently, but how do you think the others will feel?"

"It's not about them it is about us and where we see this relationship going."

"I would like to keep seeing you, but I do think that we should allow your family to know about us."

"Let's make the grand entrance and tell everyone, especially my family about our relationship."

Most of the family had moved into the sun room carrying on individual conversations. Michael and Nila walked into the room and it appears that there was instant silence.

Holding her hand in his, Michael looked around for courage as he focused in on his father's face. He had so wanted to be more like his father, who was not overbearing, but knew how to use his charm, wit, charisma, intellect and knowledge to persuade the business corporate board to accept many of his changes and new ideas. Today he was trying to get his head around how his father would handle this serious situation.

Michael cleared his throat but continued to hold on to Nila's hand.

"To the Johnston's family, although we are here for one occasion, I have some other information to discuss with you. My mother introduced me to Nila about three or four weeks ago. I am not sure if you'll are aware that she works in my mother's law firm: Dusett and Langley Civil Rights Law Firm. Dusett is my mother's maiden name and she often uses it when she is defending her clients in court. Since our introduction, Nila and I have begun dating and we enjoy each other's company. Upon our initial meeting neither one of us was aware of her relationship to Mama Tessa or do we feel that-that affiliation should hinder our relationship. We have decided to continue seeing each other."

Michael looked over at his father and he had a very broad grin. He idolized his father and wanted his father to acknowledge the maturity he was showing in his professional and personal lives. Michael leaned over and kissed Nila softly on her cheek; the room begun to fill with laughter, chatter, and congratulations.

Edwin and Jennifer walked over to their eldest son and hugged him. Jennifer planted a kiss on both he and Nila's cheeks. She placed her arm into Nila's and walker over to Nila's family.

"Son, I admire you for what you just did. It is showing me that you are maturing on all levels. However, there are some items we need to discuss before this relationship become serious."

Michael watched as his mother walked arm in arm with Nila over to her family.

"Dad, what items are you talking about?"

"Don't play me Michael, although, I have not confronted you before, but it took all I could along with Tessa to keep your mischievous activities out of the news. Yes, Tessa confided in me some time ago about her paying off your gambling debts and some of your suits by your mistresses."

"Dad, please don't tell mother and I do not want Nila to find out. I know I have been playing the rich bad boy games with my frat brothers and my buddies from graduate school and some of the activities I took too far, but I assure you I have gotten that syndrome out of my system and ready to settle down with a special friend, companion and lover."

"I can see the maturity, but I always tried to tell you that there are consequences you have to endure when you are involved in unsavory activities. Tessa and I did the best we could, but when you go public with these activities, your past is sure to surface. How do you think Nila and her family and even your mother would react if they found out about your wild side?"

"Dad, I know I owe you and mama Tessa a lot, but I like Nila and do not want her or mother to gain knowledge of these actions. I need your help and your influence to help me make them go away."

"We'll talk later, but I can't guarantee I can make all of them go away. I think you need to go over to the Johnston family, you know your mom. She likes Nila and may be talking marriage prematurely."

Michael walked over to Nila, placed her hand in his and began a conversation with her family. Jennifer excused herself and made her way over to Edwin.

"Is Michael OK? The two of you seemed to be in a deep and emotional conversation. In fact I see the worry on both of your faces."

Edwin gave his wife a big grin. "Just men talk, you know his first serious relationship. He needed to know how I felt about his announcement. We need to not make decisions for him but provide support when needed. It's Déjà vu for me."

"How is that?"

"The same situation happened to me. I was so pleased when Dad acknowledged you as my soul mate and supported me in my relationship with you. This is something that we as men do. Girls want their mother's approval and support. Guys also seek their dads."

"Well, what was the outcome?"

"Look over there, he's all smiles."

The room was full of laughter and joy as each began saying their good-byes. Michael and Nila walked her family to their cars and then returned to the Sun room. Edwin and Jennifer departed for their bedroom.

This was a day filled with surprises from the funeral services of Tessa to the announcement from Michael. What other secrets in this family could be hidden in the many rooms and closets of this estate. She dare not ask. As Jennifer began to disrobe herself, the presence of William Sr. in the form of a cool breeze enveloped her body and her soul. She knew this was not the end of the secrets; there were more secrets and evidence lurking in the rooms on the third floor of this mansion.

Jennifer sat on her king-size bed and removed her garter and stockings. Her mind began to wander back to the package she had received from William Sr. The crux of the family secrets had been revealed, but there were several more pages in the document that she had not read.

She looked at the silhouette of her wonderful and handsome husband in his walk-in closet. Can his broad shoulders, sharp mind and calm disposition remain intact once she reveals to him the secrets of the Langley family? Knowing her husband and the relationship he had with William Sr. the package may have been more for her and not Edwin.

William Sr. had stated the writing of the package had been a way of cleansing his soul and his conscience. A way of asking for forgiveness before he departed this earth and a way of righting the wrong he had done in this life.

Jennifer walked over to her dressing table to remove her makeup. Her mind was so full of the package information and her attempts to interpret William's reason for writing it, that she was not aware that her conscious thoughts had become audible.

"I wonder if William ever made amends with Tessa before he passed from this life to the next. If he did I wonder how she reacted. William, William, why are you still filling this atmosphere with questions and complications? Death should silence these complications, but with you and Tessa, the silence had become more audible than before. Did you ask Tessa for forgiveness for the years you neglected her with your mistress? Did Tessa ask you for forgiveness for her deceitful acts and her hidden secrets? Will your package bring resolve to the secrets of the Langley family?"

"Jen, who are you talking to?

"No one just thinking out loud about William Sr. and Tessa."

"Thinking and wondering about their life style is not going to change it. We need to make sure that the chain of deception, lies, mistrust, adultery and secrets are broken by discussing the facts and consequences with our children. This is something I have thought about from the day I discovered my father had a mistress, but who was I to challenge my father?"

"You knew about your father mistress?"

"Yes, since my sophomore year in college. I wanted to confront him, but it might have complicated other things that were going on in my life."

"Did you ever meet her?"

"At the time, being ignorant of the situation was better for me than being knowledgeable of the situation."

"Change never comes if one doesn't address the injustice."

"OK, Ms. Civil Rights Attorney, you are absolutely correct, but when the injustice involves your father it becomes too difficult to address. I tried once when he was ill and was in a very loquacious mood talking about his father and his mother, but I held my thoughts."

Edwin walked over to Jennifer and placed his hands on her shoulder, and then he kissed the top of her head.

"Today has been long and challenging. Let's leave this conversation for another day. I suggest we go to bed hold each other sweetly and sexy and let nature handle our emotions and our desires."

Jen turned around to face her husband and saw the wanting in his eyes the same feeling that was welling up in her. As she slowly arose from her chair, Edwin pulled her close to his naked body and planted kisses in places she knew existed, but didn't know a kiss could make them feel that way.

As each of them touch, held, kissed and caressed, the desire to make passionate love was more apparent in their touches than to talk about issues and concerns.

As her husband entered her in a loving and seductive manner, she released the burdens of the months, weeks and days as her body responded to the rhythmic pattern of his. Life's issues seemed like a faraway place as she responded to the fulfillment of her husband's loving making ability. He was sending her to a height she had not soared before and she emphatically loved it. As each of their bodies began to experience the joy and ecstasy of their lovemaking, their orgasms lit the candles of the here and now. As they both held each other tightly, she knew no matter what information she had gleaned from the pack, or the surprise from the reading of Tessa's will, she will always love this man and would never, never release him due to past or present situations and circumstances.

Jenifer kissed her husband on the forehead as she listen to him softly snore. This was her lifeline and she vowed to never let anything cut her off from this supply. Whatever Tessa may reveal in her will or any other writings, she could and would accept it and live with it. Edwin had always been her source of light and energy and she was his. They had worked together to keep this energy flowing and no matter what, the light of love for Edwin would never dim or flicker.

She moved in closer to her husband, whispered, "Good night, my love," and fell asleep in the arms of the one who mattered most.

Morning came too soon; however, Jennifer had given notice to her office that she would work from home for the next week. She had two good legal assistances consisting of Nila and John. Each was very capable of completing research for the cases scheduled for court. Nila had provided her with the legal references for the case pertaining to the land suit and was working on the case related to race and ethnicity.

She woke up smiling, and Edwin mistook her smile for his sexual ability last night.

"Was I really that good, that you awoke with such a broad grin and smile? Then I may need to stay with my fair maiden today to let her know that fifty-six is only a number and the twenty-sixes have nothing on me. Especially when you have a sexy and fine wife like I do."

"I must admit, I was wowed last night by your skills and yes, the grin is for you and because of you."

"I could call in and move the meeting to a later time."

"Your board members are waiting for you and several have flown in to attend this meeting. I would suggest that you attend your meeting and return home to a surprise."

Edwin, smiled patted her naked butt and entered the bathroom. She put on her robe and sat down on the side of the bed.

Her thoughts wandered to the package. She wanted to finish the contents so she could move on with her professional and personal endeavors. The real reason was she did not want her mind to be cluttered with the information from the package and what may be in store for the family during the reading of Tessa's will.

She smiled again; although Tessa did not like her initially and did not want Edwin to marry her, she had become Tessa's pillow of comfort. Whenever Tessa had an altercation with William Sr., Tessa would come to her for a listening ear and for consolation. She never took sides, but used her legal skills to diffuse the fire that was raging inside Tessa.

One time Tessa had confronted Jennifer about William's mistress. Tessa thought she was hiding the fact that she was aware of William's mistress and would often asked questions to see if Jennifer would reveal her identity. One day Tessa began her tirade about William's mistress and stated how the family thought she was oblivious to William's infidelity. She looked at Jennifer with malice in her eyes and stated, "You know who she is and probably help them to arrange their meeting places."

How well I remembered that day. I was taken aback at her accusatory tone and began to stare her down. Finally I said to her, "Tessa if I were aware of his mistress, I would not conspire with him to arrange meeting places for them. In fact if he would ever confide in me about her, I would express my disgust with his infidelity and his disrespect for you."

Tessa looked at me strangely, but I could see from her expressions that she knew I was being truthful. In fact she said to me, "You really don't know his mistress, do you." Again I answered her, "No, and do not wish to know her. If the situation arises, I would immediately express my distain for both of their actions."

I remember looking at Tessa and saying emphatically to her, "I do not know the circumstances of you and William's in house separation, but if I ever learn that Edwin has disrespected me with a mistress or has been unfaithful to me in any manner, I know I would not be around for any reasons. It is not worth me staying for show or status. I can make my own way, having a man does not define me, or make me better.

Edwin and I need and depend on each other for personal, family, religious and sometime business decisions. We made a decision early in our marriage to never go to bed angry with each other. We openly communicate our needs and concerns to each other and we discussed the way we need to rear or discipline our children. It was never a one sided discussion.

I grew up watching my aunt Onnie being her own person and taking change of her life, her financial and business endeavors. I would often pray that God would send her a special person in her life. I know she had several male acquaintances/ friends but marriage was never a part of the equation. She never allowed their friendship to overshadow who she was nor did it keep her from being a strong and determined woman. You see I had a wonderful role model to teach me how to be tender yet strong, that's why I feel Edwin and I have had more than twenty years of a good, solid, and loving marriage."

I personally saw the stress and the strain in Tess's face as she tried to hold back the tears. One of the lessons, I did learn from her was when she reached out and touched my face and said, "Never say never, for you cannot see nor determine your future reaction until it happens in your life. I never imagined my marriage to man whom I admired, adored and love would end up being such as fiasco. I played a part also, but the communication piece is where I fell short, thus giving him the opportunity to walk through the door of infidelity."

It appears after that conversation, Tessa never brought up the subject and I remained her sounding board when she was disgruntled or disgusted. In fact she confided in me that she had a slight bout of depression after her three miscarriages.

Her thoughts went directly to the package. I wondered was it depression or guilt, especially since I have read William's account of the miscarriages. I don't believe William in his condition would write an untruth about those situations. In fact he stated this writing was helping him to cleanse his soul. Would he lie even in his state?

Jennifer pushed herself up from the bed still with a fog of wonderment. Wondering about the two documents, the package and Tessa's will, would they coincide, or would they bring another element of surprise or perspective to the table? The prospect of her having to handle another lineage crisis for this family was more than she could bear.

Walking in the bathroom, all she wanted to do was sit in her Jacuzzi, and let the jets pulsate on her weary muscles. She was in a fog and did not notice her naked husband standing there with a smile on his face.

She walked directly to the Jacuzzi tub and began to prepare it for her sore and aching muscles.

Edwin watched his wife rub her forehead and press against her temples. He felt earlier during their lovemaking that she was a little tense but now he noticed her mental state, being unaware of her surroundings. It was as though she was in a faraway zone, hearing voices or seeing the departed. He placed his hands on her shoulders.

"Are you OK? Do I need to stay with you today?"

"No, I am OK, just wondering what is in Tessa's Will and why all of a certain she decided to change it. I'll be fine. Remember I am working from home this week so I can catch up on the research that my staff completed for the two cases. The court dates have been set for next month and I need to be ready."

"You will be fine. In most of your cases you are often overprepared. That is why you have such winning statistics." Edwin kissed her on her forehead and retreated to his walk in closet.

He stood there for a moment. He was concerned about his wife for he had never seen her in such disarray. She was always the calm one in the family, the one able to bring balance and stability to situations. From observing her today, she is the one who needed a shoulder to lean on. He made a mental note to send her flowers and to come home early from the office. He loved Jennifer and did not want any of the current situations to affect her mentally or physically. In fact he looked around and thought how could I survive without my Jen?

His mind wandered to his father and his grandfather, both had not been good role models when it came to loving and respecting their wife or their significant other. His grandfather had dated many women after the death of his grandmother and his aunt Olivia, but never thought about marrying any of them. Although he had kept the secret of the identity of his father's mistress, he never wanted to be that dishonest and bold in his marriage. Jennifer was the best thing that had happened to him and he would never do anything to destroy the relationship and the love and respect he had for her. No his father or grandfather were not role models, so he learn to be a good father and husband form observing others that he admired.

Edwin finished tying his Windsor knot on his favorite tie. It was a tie that Michael had given him one Father's Day. He believes Michael was about sixteen or seventeen years old. In fact, Michael was really proud of the tie, shirt and socks, since he had earned the money by working at one of the Millenary shops. Edwin looked at himself in the long mirror and saw a younger Michael. He would have to plan some time to talk to Michael about his past rendezvous, if he was going to continue to date Nila and be true to this relationship. His past behavior must end immediately. Edwin wondered could this infidelity and womanizing behavior be inherited or was it learned behavior? He hoped not and he would make sure that his son eliminates if from his inner being. It was important that both of his sons, Michael and Will become stellar men of the business and community worlds.

As he walked out of his closet, he thought, I need to have my secretary plan a weekend trip with both of my sons to go deep sea fishing and scuba diving at our estate in Miami. While Will is outdoing his thing, this will give me time to talk to Michael.

The day had come for the reading of Tessa's Will. Jennifer had wanted the surroundings to be more familiar and cozier, therefore she asked Mr. McGowan to conduct the business at the estate. She had Rosa and her culinary staff to prepare a wonderful light Brunch consisting mostly of different types of salads, breads, individual fruit tartlets and flavored teas.

It was a beautiful September day; therefore Edwin had instructed Rosa and the staff to serve the Brunch in the Sunroom. The staff had arranged the Sunroom into a mini dining area with each table's centerpiece decorated with fresh autumn floras. The waitstaff was ready for the Langleys' guests.

Jennifer looked around the Sunroom and smiled, she must thank Rosa for all the hard work she does to ensure all of her gatherings have an ambience of love, elegance and excellence.

Hamilton McGowan, Tessa's Attorney, was the first to arrive. He was casually dressed in a light brown cardigan sweater, a beige shirt, brown trousers and light brown loafers. Jennifer had not notice before, but Hamilton was a handsome man with a buff body. He looked as though he may have been in his early or middle thirties. She had to blink for a moment for Edwin was the only man she had ogled like this and the only body she loved to explores. She looked in the directions of the sunroom and used her hand to gesture that the brunch would be served in this room. When she followed his gait into the room, she noticed he had "swagger" when he walked. As she led him to the beautifully adorned tables she followed his strong masculine hands as he placed his attaché case and a wooden box on the floor next to his seat. Jennifer greeted him and asked, "Would you like some ice tea before the others arrived?"

"Yes, I would, it will calm the dryness in my mouth."

Jennifer motioned to the waitstaff. "Mr. McGowan and I would like a glass of tea."

Jennifer needed the tea, not for the dryness in her mouth for the fire she was feeling in her inner being. This had never happened before and she was silently praying this feeling would go away. She had only known one man and wanted it to stay that way.

She looked at his buff body again over the top of the glass as she gulped down at least a fourth of the tea. She hoped he had not notice her emotional state. If he did she could state it was her anticipation of the reading of the will. She needed Edwin to arrive shortly or she may say something to him that later she might regret.

"Jen, the room is simply breathtaking, for my next dinner party I may have to borrow Rosa to plan and decorate for my wife and me when we decide to give another soiree. Rosa and Jacob could go into business together with all the skills and experiences, I have observed of their handiwork over the years."

"Thank you, Hamilton. The operative word is 'borrow' since Rosa and Jacob have been here so long, they are part of the family. I would be so lost without their assistance.

Within minutes the Sun room was filled with the persons that were summoned for the reading of Tessa's Will. All of Edwin and Jennifer's children were present, Tessa's cousin, Darla, Rosa, Jacob and the CEO from the children wing of the Memorial Hospital.

Jennifer walked over to her husband and put her arm into his. She leaned over and kissed him on his cheeks. He returned the kiss, but she never let go of his arm.

He whispered into her ear, "Are you OK, your pulse is beating fast?"

"Yes, I am OK just anticipating the reading of Tessa's Will and wondering why my aunt Onnie just walked in."

To her surprise, in walked her aunt Onnie. As always, stately dressed and looking much younger than her age. Florence was walking beside her and the two were engaged in a funny conversation.

From the corner of her eye, she could see Hamilton watching her aunt as Florence guided her to her seat. She gestured a hello wave to all in attendance, except Hamilton. She threw him a sexy smile.

"Nice to see you again, Hamilton and you look stunning in your attire. I know you must work out at the gym daily for it shows."

"Thanks, Ms. Dusett, for the compliment, but you also look stunning. I am sure your personal trainer marvels at the work he has done with keeping your body in physical shape."

She moved her name plate from her original table and placed it next to Hamilton.

She looked at her niece and batted her eyes. "Jen, I hope you don't mind."

Jennifer hurried over to the table and greeted her aunt with a kiss and so did Edwin and the others. To settle the inquisitive looks and the heat in the sun room Jen calmed it by introducing her aunt to Tessa's cousin, Darla. A look of surprise was on the waitstaff's faces, wondering why she was attending the reading of Tessa's will; however, Rose and Florence were laughing inside and out.

Leave it to Aunt Onnie, she knew how to work a room and turn boring to lively. That was exactly what she was doing while the waitstaff served and the others in attendance gazed upon her.

"My dear Jennifer, don't you think a brunch goes better with soft music? Ask Rose to put on some smooth jazz while we eat and chat."

Rose immediately left the room, to adjust her composure. Instead of asking the staff, she turned on the Sirius Smooth Jazz Station because she needed to vacate the room to calm her fast beating heart. She adjusted the volume to ensure it did not overshadow the conversations at the table.

Jennifer kept a watchful eye on Aunt Onnie for she was animated in her conversation with Hamilton. In fact, most of the time Onnie's hand was touched Hamilton's hand during their animated conversation.

Everyone was in a jovial mood as they brunched on the various salads, breads and teas. Jennifer heart felt like it was going to beat out of her chest. Not because of the reading of the will, but her initial reaction to Hamilton and now her aunt's flirtatious behavior with him. It appears that Hamilton and her aunt had crossed paths before. After today, she was going to confront her aunt about her behavior with Hamilton.

In fact, she was wondering why was her aunt present at this reading and what could Tessa have left her? As she looked around the room she noticed only one person with a worried look, her son Michael.

"Does he know something that I don't?"

Edwin leaned over to her and said, "You are doing it again, talking out loud to yourself. You need to eat something for I am sure you were nervous about the brunch menu and skipped breakfast to work with the staff. Eat please."

"Do you know why my aunt Onnie is here?"

"No and I am sure you have no reason to be concern. Tessa may have wanted her to hear what she is leaving our children or she may have a special piece of jewelry she wants to give Aunt Onnie. Stop worrying and eat. Everything is going to be fine."

Edwin tried to control his concerns, he was aware that Tessa knew of his father's affair with Onnie. Prior to his father's death and before her death, the two of them had discussed the matter. Tessa had assured him that she would carry the information to her grave. She also confided in him that two of the miscarriages were induced, but the third one wasn't. She had really wanted to mend her and my father's marriage by giving him another heir. Edwin was not aware, until she told him, that she had carried the third child for six months before she miscarriage. It was another son and God had punished her for the miscarriage of the first two.

After the brunch, all of the individuals headed for the Large Library where William Sr. spent a great deal of his time. Aunt Onnie took a seat next to Bria and her husband. She still had that beautiful smile on her face and did not look uncomfortable.

As Hamilton began to read the beginning of the will, Jennifer and Rosa looked at each other. Each was experiencing the cool breeze they felt on Bria's wedding day. They were sure William Sr. was letting them know it's OK.

Jennifer and Rosa let out a big sigh of relief as they realize the will was a mere declaration of how she wanted her assets to be distributed.

Most of her shares in the various companies were split among the grandchildren, Rosa and Jacob. Special pieces of jewelry were divided among Jennifer, Bria and Darla, Tessa's cousin. Her land holdings were given to Michael and Will but a special piece of property in the Augusta, Georgia area that was once owned by her grandparents, but had been bought by her father and mother was given to Darla. The special directions stated that this was heir property and could not be sold to anyone outside the Adkins family.

There was timber on this land that had been sold and all the proceeds had been placed in an endowment for Darla's oldest granddaughter, Nila. Who could not receive it until she had been married for five years; otherwise it would transfer back to the Langleys' holdings. The separate bank accounts and investment accounts were divided equally among Edwin, Jennifer and the grandchildren. She had also established a small investment account for Rosa and Jacob.

Hamilton was concluding the reading of the will, when he placed his hands on the midsize wooden chest that he had brought into the room. He opened the chest and took out a large white envelope that was address to Onnie Dusett. Hamilton handed the envelope to Onnie and stated, "The information contained in this package is for you only and should never be seen or shared with the rest of the family. The only person who is aware of the contents is my professional secretary. I was not made aware of the contents.

Onnie smiled and took the package from Hamilton. Whatever was in the package she still had some unfinished business with her great-nephew, Michael.

"Ms. Dusett, there is also a special broach that Tessa wanted you to have. It is a replica of the one you lost on your many trips outside of the mainland. She knew it would not have the same sentimental value as the original one since it belonged to your mother, but it might ease some of the pain over your loss."

As Hamilton passed the black velvet box to Onnie, her smile did not waver, but she discreetly opened the box to see if Tessa's jewelry piece had capture the beauty and essence of her mother's broach. She knew in her soul that Michael had discovered the piece in Maui and had apprised Tessa of his find. Why didn't he just give it back to me? I wonder if he still has the broach. I will have a long and stern talk with Mr. Michael.

Jennifer let out a loud sigh as she looked at the broach; it was identical to the one she had found in the estate at Maui. Something was not right about this. How did Tessa know Aunt Onnie had lost the broach? The only person that knew about her find was Edwin and Tessa was in a coma when they had arrived state side. She looked over at her aunt who did not have a worried look on her face, but a broader smile. She then reached over and patted her niece's hand.

She looked at Edwin, who only shrugged his shoulders.

In her mind, Jennifer thought, *Now how am I going to approach the subject of the broach that I found in the estate in Maui? Maybe I should talk to Bria first before I speak to Aunt Onnie.*

Hamilton then walked over to Michael with the wooden chest. "Michael, per Mrs. Langley's request the contents of this chest have been destroyed, you are no longer indebted to her but to yourself. She wanted me to express her thanks to you for always being there when she needed a listening ear. She will never forget the many hours the two of you spent together."

In her mind Onnie thought, I bet the original broach is in that chest. I will have to find a way to get that chest to retrieve my mother's original broach. This was a gift given to her by my biological father, Mr. Cromwell Pappas.

Michael took the chest from Hamilton's hand. He looked around at his family who all had a puzzled look on their face.

"OK, I know all of you are wondering about the contents of the chest. Well, you see, during my earlier years in undergraduate and graduate school, I was obsessed with betting on the college football and basketball teams which resulted in me owing large sums to a number of bookies. Mama Tessa helped me pay them back and I was paying her the money she had loaned me. I have matured and don't have that urge anymore."

He looked over at Nila's grandmother. "Mrs. Manfred, would you please not tell Nila? This is something I will discuss with her. Thank you."

Edwin looked at his son. "Michael, I do hope it was an obsession back then, for your mother and I will not put up with such habits and if I had known that was why you were so close to Tessa, I would have put a stop to it. Son, this is the last I want to hear about you and your betting obsession."

"I promise you, Dad, it is over. I want you and Mom to respect me as a prominent and successful business man and, someday, a good and loving husband and dad."

Then he looked at his father and smiled. "I also need to be a good influence on my baby brother Will"

Everyone in the room laughed.

Hamilton concluded his reading of the will by acknowledging that all stock certificates, land deeds, etc., were in his possession and each person must come and obtain them from him. Each will also be required to sign for said documents and to record them with the state of South Carolina. He would also be available or someone in his office to assist them with the process.

Before he left the estate, Onnie walked up to him and whispered into his ear. The two of them laughed loudly.

"Florence and I will be by your office on Monday of next week. I would prefer to speak to you and not one of your associates."

"Just call my secretary and make the appointment. I will forewarn her of your call. Have a good afternoon each of you."

Something was not sitting right with this scene that just played in front of her and Jennifer knew she had to review the script and discuss it with her aunt. No one else in the room seemed to be bothered by her aunt's behavior. Do they know something she didn't?

Rosa walked over to her, placing her hand on Jennifer's shoulder. "Your aunt has all of her faculties. Dementia is a convenience when she wants it to be. In one of her loquacious moods, she may or may not let you in on her secret."

"How do you know this Rosa?"

"Someday, I will share with you my many conversations with Florence about your aunt's ability to remember and articulate at her convenience. Yes aging causes you to forget sometimes, but that is the only thing that is affecting your aunt's ability to remember. It just like the rest of us we sometimes forget, but if we think about it, it often comes back to our memory. When she is in one of her Onnie moods, Florence had confided in me that she tells her, 'I was an opera singer who often played a variety of parts. I can become whomever I want to.' I know you love her, but don't be alarmed by that last stage performance."

Jennifer was even more bewildered, had she become so ingrained with her work that she had missed some signs within her own family. She had to be more observant. She thought she was in tune to her family, something she prided herself on. Had she really been oblivious to her aunt's acting ability, or did she just love and adore her so much she was blind to it?

Jennifer moved her head from side to side and thought. *There is too much going on in this head of mine right now. I have to finish up with William Sr.'s package, my two court cases, and discuss my son's gambling behavior before I try to tackle my aunt Onnie's behavior.*

She was aware that Rosa was still standing near her. "Rosa, do you know why she prefers Hamilton as her lawyer instead of the family lawyer, Mr. Lambert?"

"No, I do not, but think about it, Mr. Lambert has been with the family for years, Hamilton is younger and doesn't know much about the Langleys' or the Dusetts' holdings except for the legal work he has done for Tessa. Your aunt, I am sure has her reasons and she is quite the charmer when it comes to protecting herself and her family. Mr. Lambert might not be as loyal to her since he has for many years been the Langleys' main attorney. I've also notice that Hamilton is a great listener, something that is not in Mr. Lambert's nature. You know your aunt wants all the attention when she is speaking." They both laughed.

"To change the subject, I still have not completed the package from William Sr., but there are some grey areas I need to discuss with you in private. I am also having a problem deciding if I should share the contents with my family."

"Jennifer, I will attempt to help you with some of the grey areas, but I am not sure William gave me all the facts. I am really not the one to discuss family heritage, for I have never provided my boys with the names of their fathers nor have I talked extensively about their grandmother's ancestors. I have no idea of what happened to my sister Helen, Jacob's mother or my father after my mother left Augusta, Georgia. I know the name on the birth certificate, but have never seen him in person nor have I tried to locate him. I am sure I can find out something about him on ancestory.com, but I have no desire. Therefore you are asking the wrong person about disclosing or discussing one's lineage. You may need to discuss this with your friend Myrtle Goodsome, the renowned psychologist. She would have the best directions and guidance for that question."

"Rosa, I come to you because you are so practical in your thinking and in the advice you give to others."

Rosa shook her head, Jennifer is a dynamic civil rights attorney, but she has no clue about the realities of life. I think her aunt shielded her on purpose. I would not say she is naïve, but her thinking of the world and human nature sometimes lacks the critical thinking piece she needs to read people. She shows her innocence within the real world, but not in the legal world. I guess we all have a little bit of naivety in us.

Jennifer woke up refreshed after a good night sleep ready to tackle the briefs for her two court cases and the additional research information Nila and her assistance had provided. Edwin had already gone to work and the house was very quiet since Michael and Will had also departed for their prospective jobs. No nurses or additional staff was stirring; therefore she had a quiet house to concentrate on her work.

As she began to walk toward the bathroom, she heard a light knock on her door.

"Yes"

"Good morning, Jennifer, it's Rosa. I've brought you some tea and breads for your morning walk-up."

"Thank you, Rosa, please come in. Place them in the sitting area. I was just about to begin my morning stretches and then take me a hot bath."

Rosa entered the room and saw that the daze that was once in Jennifer's eyes was gone and there was a glow all over her countenance. She had to discuss with her about the clearing out of Tessa's room, but today did not look like the right time.

"Jennifer, I'll just leave these items in the sitting area. If you need something else let me know. Oh, the nurse is in Tessa's room removing most of the medical equipment. When she has finished I will let you know."

Rosa look to the ceiling for this was a slip she did not want to happen. She hoped this slip would not put a damper on Jennifer's day.

"Just let me know when she has finished. Rosa, I may need your assistance later, but right now I must concentrate on the briefs for my new court cases."

As Rosa closed the door, she was glad that her slip of the tongue did not disturb Jennifer. She had been worried about her and her quiet demeanor all week-end; this was not like Jennifer.

Rosa knew that Jennifer's personal trainer had suggested a masseuse since her muscles were so tight. A day of rest and relaxation was also recommended even by her personal physician. On Saturday she and Edwin had spent most of the day having massages, sitting in the steam room and relaxing in the Jacuzzi. Even her color has come back to her face, for she was so flush after Tessa's funeral.

Rosa paused in the hallway next to Tessa's bedroom suite. She looked in and realized there was finality in this room. No more nurses around the clock, no more bells ringing from Tessa and no more attitude and tantrums when she did not have her way.

Rosa had her three sons who were constantly around her, but she thought about the lonely life Tessa lived. It was really of her own choosing, because she had a first cousin and her family. There might have been others, but she was too stubborn to reach out to them. From my experiences, I do not want to live a life of aloneness and loneliness in my old age. Therefore I have to begin getting my family to reach out to their relatives before I close my eyes. It is going to be a shock to my sons when they realize that Jacob and I are related. He is my nephew and their first cousin.

As she moved closer into Tessa's room, William's spirit appeared as the cool breeze she had felt on Bria's wedding day and the day of Tessa's funeral. "What are you telling me William? Is it time for the family to really know their lineage and to come face-to-face with their ancestors. I have to get myself ready for this before I can spring it upon my children and Jacob's children. Why didn't you do all of this before you died? This is too hard for me and I can see it its wearing Jennifer down. You should have thought about it before you wrote that damn package."

Rosa looked around to see if the nurse and her helpers had heard any of her conversation with the deceased, William Sr. They were so engrossed with dismantling the equipment and packing other medical supplied, they really did not know she was in the suite.

Rosa walked down into the small lounge area of the suite, it was bare of pictures, there was not one of Tessa's parents, herself or of William Sr. I agree with Jennifer, loneliness and being alone is a bitch. All it does is help you to conger up grieve and mischief for yourself and others. I now know that Tessa's outward hatred was her acting out of the inward hatred she had for herself. This is the reason I need to let my sons know about their heritage and especially their fathers. Before I can help someone else, I need help. I will discuss with Jacob our need to make an appointment with Myrtle Goodsome, the friend of Jennifer who is a psychologist. She can help us walk through this process.

There are a lot of Mom's documents in the attic that I have never gone through or read. I know many of them may hold the key to who we are and how did we get here. I know I cannot go through them alone. I am going to need the strength and the support from Jacob.

Rose sat down on the leather chaise with her hands under her chin. I must make it a point to do the following things this week: talk to Jacob about my decision, make an appointment with Myrtle Goodsome, retrieve the documents from the attic, discuss family with my children and grandchildren, contact the fathers of my sons and start my own healing process by visiting my mother, brother and sister's graves. It's never too late. I need to break the trend and the pattern of my mother. This is going to be a difficult task, but I must start the process soon . . . I cannot keep putting it off.

It's really funny before I can start to break the cycle begun by my great-grandmother, my grandmother and my mother I may need to get some counseling for myself. I wonder if it is too late. We as humans know the best path to take but often put it off until a crisis arises. It has been years since I've really thought about my family, but my conversation with Jennifer at Tessa's funeral opened up a can of worms even for me.

Tears flowed down Rosa's face as she began to think about her family. The nurse walked over to her and handed her a tissue.

"I know she was a handful, but on certain days, I could feel her reaching out to me to express her appreciation. Sometime she would ask me to give her those photos she had hidden in the chest in front of her bed and she would shed many tears. You may want to give them to the family and they can distribute them to some of her immediate family. Tessa was such a beautiful young lady growing up. She looked more like her father than her mother. There was another young lady in the picture, but she would always say, it was a neighbor. Now I know it was her cousin Darla. I wonder why she could not audibly speak about her cousin."

Rosa wiped her tears and blew her nose. She hugged the nurse for almost five minutes.

"Sunday, I will have a family dinner, something the Smyth's has not done in several years. I will hug all of my children and my grandchildren. I will advise them that life is too short and we need to do better with family gatherings. Oftentimes we get too caught up in our careers and our social outreaches and spend less time with those we need to. In the long run, nothing matters more than family. I know Mrs. Tessa understood this, but she had spent too many years not expressing what she felt to her husband or her family."

"I bet some of the things you have seen and possibly heard could be an eye opener to this family. On her good days, she would say little things about her mother and father. One such discussion that sticks in my mind is when she revealed that her personality mirrored her father's."

"Yes, there are things I observed and heard in this house. Many I will keep safely in my heart and mind. Behind these walls was so much hurt, heartaches, bitterness, mistrust and buckets of tears. The ones who could erase these memories from the walls of this estate are no longer here.

"Look at the pictures of this little girl. Observing her big smile and the twinkle in her eyes, would never suggest the demeanor or the behavior of the grown up child, Tessa."

"As a nurse, Ms. Brown, you understand that most times, people formative environment and atmosphere set the stage for their adult lifestyles. That's why this Sunday dinner for my family is so vital. My two youngest sons are not very close to my oldest son and his family. Therefore as the mother I must find ways to relink the family chain. Sunday's dinner is my way to start the mending and bonding process for my family. Thanks for the tissues, the conversation and these pictures.

"I will give the pictures to Ms. Jennifer so she may share them with Tessa's cousin and her grandchildren. I need to go check on Ms. Jennifer. When you finish in Tessa's or Mrs. Langley room let me know."

Rosa knew she did not have to see Jennifer, but her conversation with the nurse was making her feel guiltier. She was already feeling that way; therefore she did not need anyone to put more salt on her wound.

Rosa ascended the steps of the sitting room into Tessa's bedroom suite. She walked over to the chest in front of Tessa's bed and pulled out several drawers. She was surprised and amazed at what she saw. Tessa had a chest full of pictures of her family and many pictures when she and William Sr. were experiencing happier times. She decided to take one of the photo albums and several loose pictures sitting on top of the various albums. One loose picture was of an older person, probably in the early 1900s. Turning the picture over, she saw the name: Grandmother Thomasina Adkins. Jennifer had asked her some days ago if she was familiar with that name. I wonder where Jennifer learned about Thomasina Adkins.

As she was leaving the room, Michael came in. He had a strange look on his face.

"Hi Rosa, I know you will have the staff clean up this room, but there are some documents in mama Tessa' safe that I need to retrieve."

"I don't have the combination to Ms. Tessa's safe we may need to ask Mr. McGowan if she provided him with it."

"There is no need to call Mr. McGowan, mama Tessa gave it to me, because I often opened it up for her when she needed things."

"Well go ahead and get the documents you need. I was just getting some of her personal items and pictures. Your mother or father will advise me on the storing and distribution process. Rosa held up one of the loose pictures. See this picture, it's Ms. Tessa with her cousin, Darla. This was taken about forty or forty-five years ago. Did Tessa ever talk to you about her cousin and her family?"

"No, she did not. I never knew she had any family no more than her mother and father. I am not trying to avoid your questions, but I must get those documents and leave, because I have a conference callback at the office at 2:00 PM."

"Go ahead, Michael. I need to check on the culinary staff to discuss lunch and dinner."

Rosa was on her way down the steps when she heard Michael calling her name.

"Rosa, Rosa, wait a moment!"

"Yes, Michael is something wrong?"

"Are you aware of someone taking additional documents out of Mama Tessa's safe? It is completely empty and it was opened."

"I can't imagine anyone who would be interested in taking some documents out of Ms. Tessa's safe. She distributed her jewelry pieces per the reading of the will, so maybe she also gave those documents to Mr. McGowan."

"No, he doesn't have them. I have already inquired and he advised me that all she gave him for me were the documents showing she had paid off my betting debts. Do you think Mr. McGowan gave them to my father?"

"Michael, I believe you need to ask your father. What type of documents are you looking for? I may locate them while I am clearing out Tessa's personal items. Would she have another place she housed important papers?"

"I will ask my father, but after the nurse leaves would you secure this room until I can come and look for those documents. I need them to resolve some overdo personal actions."

"Yes, Michael, I can do that for you."

Michael walked down the hall with a dejected look on his face. He wondered what mama Tessa had done with those documents. He prayed that his father did not get them. His father knew about his gambling debts, but he was not aware of the two women who were blackmailing him and especially the one who claimed he was the father of her daughter, but would not let the child take a DNA test. He knew he had to resolve this matter, since he was now involved in a monogamy relationship and he really like the way the relationship was flourishing with Nila. If fact even though they had not been dating for a long time, he was thinking possible marriage. She was a wholesome and pure girl the example of one his parents especially his mother would want him to date and to marry. Right now he had to resolve all of his issues from his previous riotous life and activities. He prayed that his father did not have those files.

Then his mind wandered to his aunt Onnie.

"She is vindictive and if she knows that I revealed her identity to mama Tessa, she probably knows about some of my other activities. I have a streak of her in my DNA, so I need to get on her good side. I know she will know how to resolve this issue. Put on your thinking cap Michael. You need your aunt Onnie's shrewdness."

Michael had spoken this out loud, he turned around but the hallway was clear. He was glad for he did not want anyone else in the family to know about this dark side of his life.

MICHAEL'S INDEBTEDNESS

It felt like the business conference call was dragging on and on. Michael was glad he was able to sit in his office and listen, because his mind had drifted back to the documents. He was glad he had told his administrative assistant to take notes during this call, so if there were any action items he would be able to respond. His mind drifted again, how I could have let myself get into this situation, I don't know.

I remember how both my mom and my dad looked disgusted and upset with me, a look I shall never forget, when I wrecked my new car. The plain truth and even though I attempted to lie was because I was trying to show off for the fellows and had drank too many beers. The punishment was not as severe as the look. Although my parent could afford to buy me another car, it became my responsibility to work to pay for the car and the insurance on the new one. To please my parents and to stay in their graces was my desire, but it appeared that I was always the one who placed my parental guidance and directions on the back burner and did my own thing.

I was sneaky with my bad habits and only showed the side I knew would be favorable to my parents. Finishing college and grad schools at the top of my class, being a model employee and a successful manager of my department. I wanted them to have bragging rights about me so I played the part of "good boy during the day and bad boy at night." Michael felt the heat rush over his body, this was not a scene of his life that he ever wanted revealed to his parents. He had to find those files and find them soon.

Michael was deep into thought but something told him to look up. His administrative assistant was trying to get my attention. It seems that a person on the conference call was asking him a question about the division of the company under his management.

"Melvin, let me research the information and I will get back to you. If we are both OK with the projections, then we can send a final draft to all the principle players."

"Michael, that sounds good to me."

"Then I will contact you no later than 9:00 EST tomorrow to discuss the data and the final draft."

Michael gestured to his assistant to get the files and bring them to him for his review. The conference call was almost over and he was glad. His day was not going good. If anyone in the family finds those documents it would put him in deeper trouble with his family, especially his mother and father. They had not been strict parents, but there were certain behaviors they did not tolerate.

He sat back in his chair as he listened to all the others say, "Good-bye," "Good conference call," etc. He could not wait to hang up the phone and call Hamilton McGowan to quiz him about the missing documents; however, he knew not to bring suspicion to his probing and to not disclose the contents of the files.

His assistant walked into his office. Not only did she have the files, she had the research and the specs he needed to answer Melvin's questions.

"Thanks Becky, I am glad I hired you for this job. See I told you working on that MBA would pay off and I see a raise and a promotion in your future. You just keep me looking good. Once I read all of the supporting documents, we can draft a response to Melvin. Do me a favor would you get Hamilton McGowan on the phone for me."

Becky returned to her desk with a glowing smile. Not only did she like Michael as her manager, but her body and her mind visualized how she would soon have an intimate encounter with his masculine and muscular body. In less than a minute, she had Hamilton on the phone for Michael.

"Good afternoon Hamilton, thanks for taking my call. I was wondering if there were some additional documents that mama Tessa had left for me. It appears they were not inside the chest that you gave me."

"No Michael, no additional documents were given to me by Mrs. Langley specifically for you. I do have an extra file she wanted me to give to your father privately. Therefore I have arranged for that meeting."

Sweat poured down Michael's brow and his heart began to beat rapidly. "Hamilton, if you would just look through the files for Mama Tessa, to see if it is there, I would really appreciate it. Sometimes our assistants misplace items or put them in the wrong folders."

You know it is ironic you are asking about another file because on the day that I went to see her, it appears she was looking for another set of files. She had the nurse look in several locations, but to no avail. I will have my secretary to look back through the files I have on Mrs. Langley to see if we overlooked a file addressed to you. If I locate it, I will send it over to your officer by a courier."

"Thanks Hamilton, I hope to hear from you soon."

Now Michael was really getting worried, could mama Tessa have misplaced these files or provided them to my dad before the reading of the will. I hope neither Rosa nor the nurse found them and gave them to my dad. Could this be the reason Dad is planning a trip with Will and me to Miami? I need to think of some reason to get out of this trip until after I find those documents.

Michael was in a fog until he heard his assistant buzz him.

"Mr. Langley you have a call on line three from your aunt Onnie."

"Thanks Becky, after this call, hold all of my others, I need to work on these projections and perspectives for Melvin."

"Yes, I will."

Before answering the phone, Michael tried to put a little joy in his voice. "Hi, Aunt Onnie, are you fixing a dinner for Nila and me tonight? Is this the reason for your call?"

"Hi Michael, not this night but maybe some other night. I do need to see you to discuss some personal matters. I hope you are not busy tonight, if so then maybe tomorrow night."

"I had planned on taking Nila out to dinner tonight but if it is urgent, then I can cancel and reschedule."

"No that want be necessary, just make sure you come visit me before my dementia get out of hand and I begin discussing this personal matter with your parents."

"Aunt Onnie, you do sound a little serious. Yes I can come over tomorrow at dinner time. Have Florence ask the chef to cook that meatloaf that I like with all of the trimmings."

"Would you like a bottle of wine also? You may need it."

"Just a glass would be fine. Can you give me a hint regarding this personal matter, Aunt Onnie?"

"No, for right now, I'll just let you think about it. See you tomorrow Michael."

Onnie looked at the documents that Tessa had put in the box that held the replica of her broach. She wondered why she had given it to her or was it a mistake. Then she saw the additional note written by Tessa: "It's now your time to keep him clean."

Tessa knew about these items way before she had her stroke. Why didn't she handle these through to resolution? Michael was her favorite grandson ... But he has a lot of me running through his blood. Could this be her reasoning?

Onnie looked at herself in the mirror, she still looked good for her age, but her body was getting tired of manipulating people, situations and circumstances. Yes she knew how to make this go away as with other cancers she had eradicated for her and her family. However, these two were tall orders.

Then she smiled and looked at herself in the mirror, she was still a stately women.

She spoke into the mirror stating: "But not too tall an order for me and my brother Cromwell to resolve. We may be aging, but shrewdness and eradication of problems are our specialties. I can hear Cromwell now: 'Onnie, my sister, just a piece of cake and a matter of time we won't hear any more about these situations.'"

Cromwell and Onnie's father had been one of the leading persons in the organized crime activity on the Chattahoochee River during the '30s, '40s, and '50s. Cromwell had learned a lot from our father. However, Dad made sure that his son's profile was not tainted. Thus, Cromwell II had become mayor, governor, and now a long-term U.S. senator from Alabama. If anyone knew how to fix these situations he and his associates did. Although the times and the methods had changed regarding the resolution of specific situations but the terminators still had ways to perfect the disappearing act.

Tessa was just too soft and did not know how to play the game. If I had dealt with these situations, neither one of these ladies would have seen a dime of the Langleys' money. If I have my way this time, they may have to clean out their bank accounts.

Onnie walked out of her library with a smirk and smile on her face. Yes she would toy with Mr. Michael first, but she loved her nephew and none of these situations would taint his reputation. After she get her restitution for him ratting her out to Tessa, then she would tell him how they will restore his dignity.

She sat down at her desk to retrieve her brother's private number. Her mind was working overtime. She had met the young lady Nila only twice, but she liked her spunk and her aspiration. She works for Jennifer, and not only does she have confidence in her professional ability, but Jennifer has shown she would love to have her as a daughter-in-law. Well, all she need is a clue from Jennifer and she would intervene and make it happen. Right now she had to eradicate the unsavory mess her nephew had gotten himself into. She hope it doesn't take long, because she was getting old and wanted to attend another wedding before her time expired.

She put her hand on Crowell's number and a broad smile crossed her face. During one of her many conversations with Crowell she remembers him stating, "As cunning, shrewd, and manipulative as you are, you will live forever. In fact, I think God is afraid that if he brings you to heaven, you would be plotting to take his seat at the right hand of the father." Maybe he is right I may live to see Michael and William get married.

Onnie leaned back in her chair as she listened to the ringing of Crowell's phone. This one call is vital to the continuation of the Langley family's clean global image, integrity, and morality. She left an urgent message on Cromwell's phone to return her call.

"Florence, we are going to have a guest for dinner tomorrow night, my nephew Michael. Let the chef know he wants his famous meatloaf with all the trimmings."

Florence looked at her a little puzzled, she knew that Michael was Tessa's favorite, so Ms. Dusett must have something up her sleeve. "Is someone else attending besides Mr. Michael?"

With attitude in her voice, "No, Florence, just Michael. We will be dining together. You can have the evening off tomorrow, because I need to talk to my nephew in private."

Florence's entire disposition changed. She knew Ms. Onnie had a mission to accomplish and did not want any witnesses to her little rendezvous with her great-nephew.

Onnie observed the smirk on Florence's face as well as her body language. "You don't have to worry. It's just an innocent dinner. I may be next in line to leave this family. Therefore I need to discuss some personal items with the eldest male of my immediate family. William hasn't matured enough to handle the family business and Bria is now married, so the one left is Michael."

Florence left the room smiling. In her mind she thought, Ms. Onnie must think I am very dumb, Michael is the one who has almost tainted the Langley name. Ms. Tessa kept his deplorable actions from going public. Ms. Tessa's nurse often spoke to me about his sordid behavior and how Ms. Tessa was using her money to pay off gambling debts and even some woman who claimed she had a son for him.

She looked around and spoke out loudly, "Nothing was sacred or a secret in the Langley household. Whoever overheard or harbored the secret often told it to a trusted worker."

Michael could not concentrate on the file in front of him. Although his administrative assistance had done an excellent job of putting the package together with graphs and pie charts, comparisons and future projections, he just could not keep his mind on the contents. He laid the package down and closed his eyes. He couldn't mess up on explaining the projections to his colleagues since he had already expressed his ideas via the conference call. Melvin was one of those guys who was aggressive and probably wanted his position or one like his. It would never happen as long as he was the son of the owner, but he had to show his father he was responsible and had the acumen to perform in that position.

He opened his eyes and looked out the window. He could see the Charleston Harbor and on a clear day the Atlantic Ocean from his office window. He often watched the swelling tides when he needed something to take his mind off his troubles. However, today, the waters in the harbor and the ocean were still and were doing nothing for his disposition and his stress. A thought passed through his mind, Becky had been an asset to him by doing most of his research and explaining the pros and cons of this project. Why don't I let her present it and I can fill in when there is a need? This would also give me leverage when I go to the board to suggest a promotion for her in my department

Why was he so nervous about having dinner with his aunt Onnie? He was aware of many of her personal secrets. So they were even. He just did not know how to play his cards as well as she. His aunt Onnie had been at the game a long time and what a pro she was. Instead of showing fear, I need to turn the table around and let her know I need her to help me resolve some mistakes I have made in my life. If I start the conversation, this may trip her up and she'll forget the real reason for our dinner party.

He looked around his office with a smiled and loudly said, "Yes, that is what I will do. Now let me prepare myself for my conference call with Melvin."

He punched in the intercom button for Becky. "Becky, would you come into the office so we can begin preparing the briefing for tomorrow's conference call with Melvin. In fact, I was thinking that maybe you should take the lead on this one. It will help me convince the board of the new position I would like to create in the department and the selection of you to fill that position."

"I will be right in, Mr. Langley." Becky had more than the promotion in mind. She liked him very much and was looking for a way to have him pay more of a personal attention to her than a professional one. Her last friend had told her she had skills in the bedroom. If she could only use those skills to win Michael over, her plan to become Mrs. Michel Langley would work. He never brought his personal life into the office; therefore she was not sure if he was seriously dating.

Becky picked up her package, yes she knew she was very proficient in her work and had helped cover many of his oversights on reports and briefs. He owed her and she wanted her just reward; therefore she had to work this presentation to her advantage.

As Becky sat close to Michael going over the contents of the briefing, he was half listening and halfway plotting his plan for his aunt Onnie. He was brought back to reality when he felt Becky hands massage his shoulders. At first it felt good because he was tense due to his upcoming dinner engagement with his aunt Onnie, but he did not want to give Becky the wrong impression. He was not in any way interested in her romantically, only professionally.

He reached up and removed both of her hands from his shoulder.

"This is not the time or the place for this action. This is a professional meeting and I intend for it to stay that way. If I need a massage, my father has a personal one that comes to our home. Now let's get back to the presentation."

Becky batted her eyes and looked at him with a puzzled look. "I can see how tense you have been since the conference call this morning and the phone call from your aunt Onnie. I just thought a quick massage would ease some of the stress. Nothing else was intended."

"Now that we have that cleared up, let's continue with the briefing. I will be able to follow along better if you would pull it up on the projector.

I was thinking more of a video conference with Melvin as well as inviting two other project managers to be on the call. So why don't we start from the beginning."

"Sounds like a great idea, therefore, Melvin would not be able to over simplify the contents of the project nor change or alter some of the guidelines, timelines and the projections."

As Becky began displaying the briefing on the projector, she thought, he sidestepped this forward approach, but there will be other times when we are outside of the professional setting and I can spin my web again. After the presentation, I will suggest that we go out for a celebration. I will be ready for you then Mr. Michael.

Michael was restless tossing and turning in his bed. He finally decided he would not get any sleep and opened up the briefing for tomorrow's video conference. As he began reading the documents, his mind began to work overtime. On the margin of each page, he responded to what if questions that one of the attendees may ask. He was really surprised how sharp his mind was even though he had not gotten any sleep. In a way he was glad he couldn't sleep since he had sent an invitation to his father to attend the presentation. He looked over at the clock next to his bed; it was 3:00 AM, and he would have to be at the office no later than 9:00 AM.

What could he do to relax himself? He did not want to think about his dinner with his aunt Onnie and he felt he had a handle on the presentation. He walked into his bathroom and began filling his Jacuzzi Tub. Sitting in this tub with the jets pulsating over his body should relax him and allow him to look rested for his meeting.

As he lowered himself into the tub, his mind wandered to Nila. He was glad his mom had introduced him to her. She would be the calmness to help him focus and relax. He loved everything about her. She had a light and airy spirit, she enjoyed her work, had a passion for helping others, and she looked at situations in a practical manner, finding positive results instead of always focusing on the negative. Yes, she would make a wonderful wife and mother. That's the way he had to make his past disappear so his future could be filled with Ms. Nila Patrice Johnston. As he began to fantasize on how his life would be having Nila as his partner, companion, lover, wife, and mother, his body began to relax. He awoke to someone knocking at his door. It was his brother William asking to borrow one of his jackets. He did not realize it was now 6:45 AM and he needed to get dressed for work.

"Just a minute, William, let me get out of the tub and you can come in and get that jacket."

William walked into Michael's room. "While you are drying off, I can have on the jacket and out of here. You must have overslept, brother, or is there someone in the room with you?"

"Just get the jacket and leave me alone. You wear it more than I do, so just keep it in your room."

"It's a good thing I needed this jacket, because you would be late for work. Oh by the way Dad asked me to be on the video conference today. He thinks I can learn something from my big brother. See you later on at the office."

Michael walked into his bedroom with the large bathe towel wrapped around him just as his brother was leaving out of his room. Why would his dad ask William to sit in on the conference? It was not like he wasn't ready for the presentation, but now he would have to alter the plans instead of Becky being the lead; he would have to take the helm. He dressed quickly for work for his first task of the day was to advise Becky of the changes.

He had to be diplomatic in his delivery for he did not need any woman drama this morning. His countenance would have to ready for the stage scene this afternoon with his aunt Onnie.

As he entered his office, Becky and the specialist from IT was already there getting the video equipment set up for the conference call.

"Good morning, Becky and Timothy. Thanks for getting the equipment set up for my presentation. Becky when you and Timothy finish, I would like to speak to you."

"We are finished. Thanks Timothy, I'll send an e-mail to your manager thanking him for allowing you to help me."

"Becky, I will take the lead on presenting the project today. Additional key project managers and specialist have been invites, so since it is coming from my department, I need to be the key presenter. There are some parts I will defer to you so let me show you where I penciled in your name."

"Why the sudden change, Michael? Are you upset with me because of yesterday? I was just trying to relieve you of your stress."

"Becky this had nothing to do with yesterday. If you want to be promoted into a project manager's position, your thinking should be more business minded and less feeling minded."

"I thought when I left here on yesterday, everything was OK."

"And it is, sometimes we have to change the presentation as well as the presenter when the audience changes. Do not take this personal, take it as a learning experience. As a project manager, you will need to look at revisions and changes from the planning stage to the critical implementation steps and to the finish products. Sometimes you also have to change personnel depending on skills and knowledge needed during a strategic part of the development. Again take this as a learning experience and not as a way to deflate you. Let's look at my notes so we can prepare ourselves for this video conference."

In her mind, Becky knew Michael was correct; however, she still would try the after work drink to toast their success. She was more interested in getting him to notice her personally and not professionally. She was very skilled in her job and always did an exceptional job on completing his project packages and any research needed. She had to find a way for him to notice her personally.

The meeting had gone very well. Each person in attendance was excited about the new project and knew it would help increase production in the textile industry and would give them a global visibility by partnering with several Asian countries. Michael's father had called him after the meeting to congratulate him on such an excellent presentation. Even Melvin had sent him a congratulations e-mail. He was all smiles.

"Becky, thank you for all of your assistance, the presentation was a success and we should begin the new project procedures the first of the year. I will check with HR to see when I can announce the two quality control positions, the two engineering positions and the two chemist positions. I know you recorded the two revisions suggested on the time line and the need to get the IT department involved in the process."

"Michael, it was a good video conference and we should go out after work to celebrate our success."

"Becky, why don't you work on setting up a celebration luncheon on Friday for the department? This is a better way to express our gratitude to the whole department instead of the two of us going out. Remember, it took all the workers in this department to analyze the data and submit suggestion on ways to improve products and production in our division."

"I know we reviewed their submitted reports and held meetings with key people, but the two of us basically put the proposal together."

"Becky I thought you were ready for promotion into a management position, but I see now you may need to take a few management classes.

A department or a division does not function on I, but on we. It is the input of all the employees in the department to ensure a quality, efficient and effective product or service. Check with HR and let me know when the next management training classes will begin and I will ensure you are enrolled."

With attitude in her voice and disposition, Becky looked at Michael and stated, "I know it takes the total input of the department to ensure the department is functioning efficiently, but my suggestion was to celebrate the success of our presentation. However, we can do it your way. What catering company would you like for me to contact for Friday's celebration?"

Michael ignored the attitude in her voice and her body language. He had to laugh internally. He could not believe Becky was upset that he is refusing her suggestion. He had never, never shown her he was personally interested in her, the three years she had been his administrative assistance. If he did submit a promotional request to HR for her it would be out of his department. He did not need any other drama in his life to mess up his chance with Nila.

"Becky, maybe you and John and I can have a long lunch together tomorrow, but I have another engagement tonight. You and John can go without me. We need to get this video equipment back to IT, please call John to come and get it. Again, I thank you for all of the time you have put into the preparation of the package and assisting me with the presentation."

"With additional attitude in her voice, she stated, "I'll get right on those tasks, Mr. Langley. If you have any additional follow up actions on the presentations, I'll be at my desk."

"Before you start on the tasks, I detect a little disappointment because I am unable to celebrate our success tonight. Yes, we work well together and we have done well on this project. However, we need to keep our working relationship on a professional basis. As I discussed with you earlier, your contributions made on this project were exceptional and I would be looking into a possible promotion for you. Don't take my professional assessment of your work as something different. Thank you for this morning and if I need assistance with other matters, I will let you know."

Becky walked out of Michael not very happy. She still had time to work on getting him interested in her. However, she did not want to do anything rash to make him change his mind regarding her promotion. She needed the raise since she had just purchased a BMW similar to the one he was driving. In fact she was going to show it to him tonight and suggest that she would drive them to the restaurant.

As he got out of his chair, he heard a knock on his door. John from IT opened the door and entered.

"Mr. Langley, this is one of my colleagues, Sylvia, she is here to help me pack up the video conferencing equipment."

Michael extended his hand. "Nice meeting you, Sylvia. John is one of my best IT specialists, so learn all you can from him. I have to go to HR to check on some paperwork. I should be back in about thirty minutes. If you need any assistance, my administrative assistant Becky will be able to provide it."

Thank you, Mr. Langley, but it shouldn't take us more than fifteen minutes to complete this task.

Michael exited his office, he looked over at Becky's desk and she was not there. He wondered where she could have gone. Usually she advised him when she was leaving her desk.

Today was not the day he needed drama with Becky. He had to keep his mind fresh for his dinner date with his aunt Onnie. He could not imagine why she wanted to see him alone. After he leaves HR, he was going to have a quiet lunch at his favorite Deli. This may be a good time to ask Nila to meet him there. I need a conversation with her to distract me from my woes. Nila was growing on him, even at work and at home his thoughts were on her. Maybe I'll have lunch somewhere else, since the deli is so close to the office. I do not want to run into any of my workers, especially Becky. I still cannot get over her attitude. I'll ask Nila to select a restaurant closer to her office.

Michel sat in his car outside of the Italian Restaurant that Nila had suggested. When he saw her car pulled into the parking lot his heart began to beat faster. He did not realize how he was growing fond of this lady. And a lady she was. He was opening her car door before she could put her car in park. As she exited the car he lightly kissed her on her cheek.

"I'm glad you could meet me for lunch. This morning I completed a successful new project presentation and it went over very well. I needed someone to celebrate with and my first choice was you."

"Thank you for including me in your celebration. The food here is wonderful, but I would like to hear all about this successful presentation."

He placed her hand in his and they walked hand in hand into the restaurant. The waitress showed them to a secluded table in the bar area.

"I come here a lot for lunch and they know I like seclusion. I usually eat and review my briefs and don't like to be disturbed."

"This is perfect, because I need to run something pass you regarding my administrative assistant. Her behavior was a little strange today, when I did not accept her invitation to go out after work to celebrate the success of our presentation. I have never gone to any happy hours or made any gestures to her that I had a personal interest in her. She does very good work and I often compliment her on it and have provided her several accommodations, but always in a professional manner. I do not discuss my personal business at work. What do you think?"

The waitress walked up to the table and each of them ordered the lunch lasagna and a glass of tea.

"I do not know the young lady, but oftentimes, female workers sometimes take their bosses' compliments to another level. Even though you have kept your relationship on a professional level, she is reading more into your compliments. This lady could have a mad crush on you because you are a good looking man and she likes what she sees."

Nila smiled. "Are you sure you have not winked at her or given her a sexy smile?"

"I promise you nothing like that has happened. In fact I was stunned a little when she displayed that attitude. It was a first for her or maybe I just have not noticed it. She is a good worker. She has caught a number of errors in some of my production compilations and she has made corrections on some of my written documents. She has very good research and analysis skills. She had been an asset to my department and I have often voiced this."

"You don't see it do you? She figured her detail work has made you look good and you should be more than grateful for her having your back. Whether you have openly made any intimate gestures toward her, in her mind not only do you like her work, but you like her romantically. She just has to use her feminist accents and behavior to show you."

The waitress brought their lunch orders to the table and looked at Michael as though she knew him. She kept looking at him.

"I don't think we ordered anything else. Is there something you need?"

"No, you remind me of someone, but I don't think you are that person. Sorry for staring."

"It's OK"

"OK, Michael you can now confess up, do you know the waitress?"

"No I do not, but she is the least of my worries, I need to know how to keep Becky happy until I can get her a promotion into another division or with one of the other managers in my division."

"Just do not buy into her advances, keep all of your responses and directions to her on a professional basis. If it is necessary to work with her on another project get two other persons from the department to assist her. This way you can avoid not only her advances but also her wolf cry of sexual harassment. She'll soon get the message."

"What if she refuses the promotion to another department?"

"Use your management jargon to convince her and to assure her that this promotion is best for her to move up the corporate ladder." Nila put her fork into a piece of lasagna and brought it close to her mouth. She looked at him with a smirk. "If all this doesn't work then call me over. I'll use my legal mind to show her the light." Then she slowly and sexy put the fork of lasagna into her mouth.

Michael was sexually aroused with that gesture, but he knew he had to take this relationship slowly until his past activities were no longer an issue.

Walking out to their cars, Michael felt a lot less tense. He was falling for this lady and he did not need any of his past activities to affect their relationship. Yes, he had done some things he was not proud of, but he was young and foolish and had not weighed the consequences of his actions. He did not want to lose Nila, so his dinner with Aunt Onnie this evening would be the key to making sure his past never, never upstage his relationship with Nila.

He opened the door of Nila's car. Before he helped her into the car, he leaned down and kissed her lips with such deep passion. She accepted it and opened her mouth to receive the sweetness of his tongue. Her body warmed up to his kiss, but she also needed to take this slow. This was her boss's son, and she did not was to jeopardize her professional career over sexual passion and feelings.

They agreed to dinner and a concert on Friday night.

Michael watched her as she drove away. Yes, this was going to be his wife, and he had to set the stage for this to become a reality tonight with Aunt Onnie.

Onnie took the scarf and broach out of the box and placed them on the coffee table in her great room. These two items had revealed her secret not only to her nephew but also to her lover's wife. It may have been the best thing that could have happened. These two items will now obtain her eldest nephew loyalty to her. Yes she is going to make his past go away, but it is going to cost him dearly. I think I will just toy with him for a while before I assure him that his past is just that his past and it's gone. I have already contacted the right people and within weeks, his worst nightmares will become a thing of the past.

Onnie picked up the two documents that Tessa had placed in the box that contained the scarf. No Tessa was never as clever, crafty or as shrewd as she. William's comments were "How could one with so much book sense have little common sense."

Once she had learned of Michael's situation she should have spoken to her husband to help her implement an ingenious plan that would have cleaned his slate. Instead, she kept paying off his debts to the bookies and the two women. This was not going to happen under her watch. This was her blood, her immediate family and since they had survived the Dusett's skeletons in the closets all these years, nothing on her watch would ever be revealed. If it killed her, she would make sure Michael's past goes away and those Dusett's skeletons stayed in the closet. On this very day, she declared that neither skeletons nor past actions would stain or destroy any of the members of her immediate family.

A smile formed on her lips, I was not just an opera singer, but I have impeccable acting skills that could charm the spots off any leopard. Tonight will be my night to accept my Oscar for a best dramatic female part.

"Florence, thanks for not taking the evening off. I know I had promised, but you can have tomorrow off. I am on my way to get dress for dinner with my nephew. When he comes, direct him to the great room. You may offer him a glass of wine or a glass of cognac. I think he likes both of them."

"Yes, Ms. Dusett, I will."

Florence walked into the great room; she saw the scarf, the broach, and two pieces of documents neatly placed in the center of the coffee table. *I wonder what she is up to. Why would she have those items on the table for him to look at before she makes her grand entry?*

Florence looked around to ensure that Ms. Dusett was not standing in the doorway. As soon as she picked up the two pieces of documents, she heard Ms. Dusett's voice.

"Florence, give those to me, they are not for you or Michael to read. I left them there by mistake."

Florence handed the two documents to Ms. Dusett.

"I was going to bring them to you. I knew you had left them there by mistake."

"I am sure you would have after you had read the contents. Florence you and I are too much alike, that's why we can tolerate each other. I hear the door bell, let my nephew in. Don't forget to sit him in the great room and offer him a glass of wine or cognac. He's going to need one of them."

Michel was directed into his aunt's great room and as soon as he sat down on the soft leather coach, he noticed the scarf and the broach in the center of the coffee table. His heart began to beat fast in his chest and it appeared that no air was getting into his lungs.

"Michael, would you like a glass of wine or a glass of cognac before dinner?"

"Florence, I believe a glass of cognac is what I need right now."

As Florence gave him the glass of cognac, she saw the flush look on his face and how tense he had become. *There was something about those two items on the coffee table and I aim to find out about them. Ms. Onnie isn't the only one that knows how to snoop and pry. She is just more polish with her nosey approach.*

"Michael, is everything alright? You seem a little startled about something. Your aunt should be down shortly. Can I get you another cognac?"

"I am fine Florence, had a very intense day at work, but my presentation went over fine. I just need to exhale. Yes another glass of cognac would be great."

Florence refilled the brandy sniffer and handed it to Michael.

"I'm going to check with the chef to see about the meal for you and Ms. Dusett's."

Michael was alone with his thoughts. *How could Aunt Onnie have these two items?*

William spotted them in the bedroom suite at the estate in Maui. This was the week William and I had taken Granddaddy to the island prior to his death. He wanted us to go with him, sort of a final visit with his grandsons. Instead of him sleeping in the large bedroom suite, he allowed one of us to use it. William chose to sleep there because of the large bay window and the beautiful scene of the ocean and the beach. While putting away his clothes he came across the scarf and the broach. I should have known better, but I advised William that it was probably Mama Tessa's and we should take them to her when we leave. In fact I suggested that I would give them to her since I had more of a relationship with her than William.

Yes, I should have known who it belong to, simply because of the fragrance of the perfume on the scarf. Again, young and foolish, thinking this would add another feather in my cap with Mama Tessa if I got into trouble again.

He was wondering what was taking his aunt so long to come down, but he wanted to touch the two items to ensure they were the same ones he brought back from Maui. He looked around at the entrance of the room, and Aunt Onnie was not there. He exited the sofa and picked up the scarf and then the broach. On the broach was the word replica. Wondering again why would Mama Tessa give them to her? Why didn't she just give them back to him? He thought he heard footsteps so he immediately put the items back onto the coffee table.

Onnie was standing outside the great room watching all of Michael's moves and expressions. She loved her nephew because he was of her lineage. She did not like to see him squirm, but today she would teach him about loyalty to his immediate DNA donor. She watched him as he looked at the broach with the word, replica. He kept looking back to ensure she was not walking in the room.

As always, Onnie made a grand entrance to every function she attended. Intentionally she was always late so others could admire not only her attire but also her flawless seventy-plus-year-old beauty. This was not plastic surgery, but genes that produced cells that did not age quickly.

Onnie walked effortless into the room with a beautiful St. John's pant ensemble. She walked over to her nephew and placed a warm kiss on his cheek. She had the two documents in her and he noticed them as she bent over to kiss him. Taking a seat across from him on the other chair, Michael noticed a cunning smile on her face.

She had recently sprayed her favorite perfume on her; therefore Michael knew immediately the scarf was hers.

"Good evening my handsome nephew. I hope you had a wonderful day."

With softness and love in her voice, "I did. Please pour me a glass of whatever you are drinking? I am sure we both may need it after our little chat."

"Good Evening, Aunt Onnie, don't you look stunning in that sky blue pant ensemble. You should be on the cover of *Vogue* magazine."

He stood up and placed a warm kiss on her cheek.

"I am drinking cognac. Would you also like a glass?"

"That would be perfect because wine may not be the right choice for our conversation tonight."

As Michael began to pour the cognac in the brandy sniffer, he could not believe his hands were shaking. Aunt Onnie was not a person you wanted on your bad side and he had known this. Why didn't he just return the items to her, but still inform mama Tessa so he would stay in her good graces?

"Here you are my beautiful Aunt."

"Aunt Onnie, if I had known those items were yours, I never would have given them to mama Tessa. William and I found them in the bedroom suite at the Maui estate. Really the only reason I brought them back is because I knew mama Tessa did not want to or had not traveled in years to the island or any other place in her condition."

"Michael, I should warn you not to dig yourself into a hole that you cannot get out of. You were aware that the two items on that table did not belong to Tessa, even the smell of the perfume on the scarf was not Tessa's. You did it to stay in safe graces with her and I can understand your reasoning. But don't you know we are blood relatives and I would have helped you out of any situation. Tessa did not have the connections that I have. Therefore your worries would never disappear with her attempting to handle them."

"I was afraid that if I came to you for assistance, you would probably tell my parents."

"Michael you are a grown man, I would have counseled you about your escapades, but unless it would have tainted the Langley or Dusett's names, your parents would have never known. You didn't know until after the reading of the will that Tessa had told your father about your gambling debts. Your grandfather also knew. In fact, he helped pay off several of your bookies. Although your grandparents did not sleep in the same room and had a dysfunctional relationship, they often talked about the cancerous issues that ruined their marriage and how they could keep the plagues from harming the next generation."

"Aunt Onnie, I am not judging you or your lifestyle. I knew what I was doing was against the principles and teaching of my parents, but for some reason, I could not shake the behavior from my system. Mama Tessa was a fall back, because I knew she would welcome my attention since she felt isolated from the core of the family. Was I smart enough to know this move was wrong? Yes, but to me it was my only option. And once I saw how receptive she was to my attention and to my needs, I kept exhibiting the same crazy behavior. She was aware each time I messed up, but I was sure she would never reveal my riotous lifestyle to the family. She was an enabler to my behavior."

"No matter how smart and intelligent we are Michael, we never want to appear as the bad guy to our family. Have you been looking for these two files? I believed you called Tessa's lawyer inquiring about them. But before we discuss these files, why is the broach a replica and what happened to the original one?"

"Mama Tessa called me into her room about a month after I gave her the items. She asked me not to tell anyone about them and on my next trip to Maul to take the broach and put it back in the large suite of the estate. I was a little taken aback, but I did as he ordered."

Onnie laid the documents on the table next to the scarf and the broach. "I also know about the issues you are facing with these two young ladies. Tessa included the information in the box that contained the scarf and broach. She was frantic because her methods to make them disappear were not working. The more money she gave the more money they wanted. I've known about these situations for some time, but only after the reading of the will did I have possession of the two documents. You do know I have contacts and means of making life threatening issues disappear."

Onnie got up from her chair, walked over to her great-nephew and put her hands on his shoulder. She could feel the tenseness in his body.

"I will not go into any details, for I do not want you aware of my contacts, but rest assured that they have already begun working on these two issues. Just to calm your nerves, we received the DNA sample from your suppose son and he is not your child. There are no remaining pictures of you and your friends having fun and will never ever make the tabloids, all known ones have disappeared. If there are any other women involved in your early years of fun, I will need the names to ensure the Enquirer or any of those other papers will ever air your dirty laundry."

"I don't know of any others. They were the only two who made noise in the last three years."

Michael turned around and looked at his aunt; tears were streaming down his face. At that moment all he could do was reach up and hug his aunt. No spoken words would be adequate for the burden she had just lifted from his soul and his mind. In fact he felt like he had lost the weights that had been dragging him down for the last three years.

The only others words, that came out were: "I love you, Aunt Onnie, and I would never forget your involvement of making me whole again."

Onnie hugged him back.

"This is our secret and it is my intention to take all this to the grave with me. I know you are the one who used your knowledge of your grandfather's relationship with me to your advantage. This was your ticket to getting Tessa to help you with your issues. I expect you to carefully erase this knowledge from your memory bank. Your mother or father should never be privileged to this information."

Onnie did not give him an opportunity to respond. She placed her arm in his. "Now let's go eat your favorite meal. Go wash your face so we can enjoy what the chef has prepared."

As Michael and Onnie were enjoying their meal, Florence walked into the dining room to see if they were ready for dessert and coffee. She noticed that they were happily engaged in a conversation and neither had finished their entrees. She slipped quietly out of the dining room. She saw the two documents lying on the coffee table. She quietly opened each document and scanned the contents. She could not believe what she had read. From where Onnie was seated in the dining room, she observed Florence holding the documents.

In her mind Florence knew something real and wonderful had transpired between aunt and nephew and she now knew it had something to do with the items on the coffee table. She would have to keep her eyes and ears open, because she would soon learn the significant and the real story behind those three items.

"Aunt Onnie, now that we have cleared the air between us, there is another personal issue I would like to broach with you soon. I know you will have the voice of reasoning, expertise and wisdom to share with me. Tonight has been a good night for me and I can now relax knowing you have my good interest at heart. Forgive me for not coming to you earlier. I now know that was a mistake."

He leaned over and kissed her gently on the cheek.

"Good night and I will call you soon."

Florence walked into the great room. The atmosphere was much different from when the night started. Onnie was sitting in her favorite chair still sipping on her coffee.

"Come in Florence and have some coffee and a cherry tartlet with me. I just had a very refreshing discussing with my nephew and that in itself is a reason to celebrate. Why don't you take the day off tomorrow and the next day since you stayed over tonight. I have some business I need to attend to and the driver can take me to the places I need to go. Do not tell my niece that you are those two days. Don't answer your cell if she calls. I left an envelope in the foyer for you. Go have a massage and a facial."

"Wow, what happened in this room Ms. Dusett? I have never seen you in such a good mood. No I'll take that back. I have notice you when you returned from trips and vacations, how different you responded to me and the other staff."

"Florence be careful, you are walking on a thin line between professional and personal. I have good eyesight and saw you holding those documents."

"I only picked them up, Ms. Dusett. I did not see the contents."

"Florence we are too much alike, but I know your lips are sealed tightly about my nephew's visit. Yes, tonight has been phenomenal and I plan to continue to mentor my nephew on life's challenges and the consequences one must bear when he or she exercises too much inappropriate freedom."

"Thanks, I think I will have that cup of coffee and one of the tartlets and then I will head for home. The staff has cleaned up the kitchen and has left for the night."

"Now that you are comfortable with your cup of coffee, if you ever mentioned what you read on those two documents, you will have me to really deal with."

Florence opened her mouth to speak, but Onnie put up her hand.

"Don't try to deny it. I saw you. I love my family and I will do everything to protect them from any scandals. I have assisted you with your son's incident at the University of Alabama, but if you breathe the contents of those documents to Rosa, I can reverse my assistance for your son with a single phone call."

Florence looked at Onnie with a bewildered expression. "The contents of those files will remain in my heart and my head. I will not reveal it to anyone. You have been good to me and my family and I shall always respect you for it."

"Yes, I have been more than good to you and your family. I've arranged for you and your husband to be present at all of the games, you have access to one of my relatives' summer cottage when you are in Tuscaloosa and even a car. Yes, I have been more than your employer and don't you ever forget that."

"Ms. Dusett, I have no intentions of violating the trust you have in me. I have heard and seen a lot since becoming your personal assistant (LPN), but I would not in any shape or form divulge information that I have seen or heard."

"Florence you were so interested in knowing what was contained on those two documents, have you and your husband taken the time to review the success of your son academically? It would be disastrous if your son uses up his eligibility at U of A not drafted into the pros and still don't have saleable skills to be productive in the workforce."

"We have talked about it, but per my son, his coach does not want him to declare a major since it may take away from his practice time. You know he is one of the most talked about running backs in the NCAA league. They are even talking about a possible Heisman Trophy winner for the 2016 season."

"Florence you need to get your head out of the sand. Your son needs to declare a major and begin taking classes toward that major. What is he classified as today? A sophomore? He has wasted two years of his academic year by taking worthless classes."

"Ms. Dusett, even if he doesn't get a degree, we are sure he will be drafted into the pros."

"How many other boys have this dream and it's shattered by an injury during their college years or even when they make it to the pros. Your son needs an education to fall back on. These Big ten schools do not care about your son or anyone else's son. It's more about using the skills and talents of these young men to place more money in the school's coffers. Do you and your husband realize that the athletic department bottom line is about keeping the alumnus happy so they can contribute more to the school?"

"I really had not looked at it that way. I was happy that he received an athletic scholarship toward his tuition. We had saved some, but not enough and when the U of A recruited him as one of their running backs, we were more than happy."

"Florence I am not going to have this conversation with you again, but upon your next visit to Tuscaloosa, I want you and your husband to meet with his coach, academic counselor and one of my friends who teaches there to ensure your son will graduate in a good field. Did you not tell me he made good grades in high school?"

"Yes, he did and he was on the debate team and members of other social and academic clubs. You are always helping me out, Ms. Onnie. I really appreciate it and tonight's conversation about those two documents will never cross my lips again."

I know it will not because you owe me too much and will never be able to repay me. You are forever in my debt. I think it's time for me to turn in. Have a good and restful time on your days off."

On his drive home, Michael's mind drifted toward Nila. Lately he has been unable to get her out of his mind or his system. The kiss at lunch had his manly hormones in an uproar. However, he knew he had to walk the line of cautious on this relationship. He did not want anything to affect it.

Yes, he would have to talk to Aunt Onnie about his feelings and his desires for this lady. He knew she would have some great wisdom to impart to him. He was not unaware that she had a big part in the courtship of his parents. He smiled. I know she can do the same for Nila and me. But he had to deal with Becky and her advancements. He was glad he had broached the subject to Nila. He could see in her eyes that she had gained respect for him on certain subject matters.

Even when discussing his relationship with his aunt Onnie, he would have to use caution, since she is now aware of how close his relationship was to mama Tessa. She may be baiting him for other information and he vowed to mama Tessa he would never reveal her secrets.

I wonder if anyone in the family knows about mama Tessa's secrets or am I the only one she had enough confidence in to tell. She took them to her grave. I know I will have to do the same. Although Mr. Charles is still living, I doubt if he would confess to anyone about mama Tessa's and his real relationship. Wow, I never realized how many skeletons are really in the Langley/Adkins/Dusett's closets.

As he drove into the grounds of the Langley estate he began to whistle a tune by Taylor Swift, something about Forever and Always. He looked up and saw that the lights were still on in his parent's bedroom suite. It was after twelve midnight they were usually asleep at this hour. I hope they are OK.

He smiled, speaking to no one in particular, "I am too old for them to wait up for me."

A LESSON ON MANHOOD

Jennifer and Edwin had just returned from a dinner party held at the home of one of his senior executives in the Textile Division. Jennifer was so exhausted she could hardly remove her evening wear. As she began removing her garments, she thought about the long day she had on her return to the office. It appeared that she was getting more and more civil rights cases. Nila had brought her three new cases to review. Nila was a welcome addition to her firm; she had already done some minimum research on the cases and had highlighted some significant points in the body of the case file.

Her mind wandered to her son Michael. Why was he having dinner with Aunt Onnie tonight? I now understand why he was so close to Tessa, but Aunt Onnie is too shrewd and knowledgeable for him to attempt to sugarcoat her. I bet she sweetly put him in his place. He will have no other recourse but come to his father and me.

Her eyes wandered over to her handsome and muscular husband of twenty-six-plus years. Although he had aged, he was still the perfect gentleman and prince charming she fell in love with more than thirty years ago. How she wished that her son Michael would see the example they had set in their marriage and follow suit. I must discuss this with Edwin and we need to have a long talk with our son Michael.

She walked over to him and pointed toward the back zipper of her dress.

"Edwin, the dinner party at the Katrons was just wonderful. I know he has just been promoted as the president of manufacturing in the textile international market, but has he been with this division long or is he newly hired into that position? He and his wife look fairly young."

"The dinner party was nice and this was Warren's way of getting to know the other managers and executives in his department. I believe he has been with the company at least seven or eight years. When Joseph Leeward decided to retire last year, he was the one that recommended Warren Katron to the board as the next president of this market."

"Why did he have it on a Monday night instead of later in the week or the weekend?"

"He's flying out tomorrow to China, Japan and other countries to discuss our reorganization plans for the textile international market. I suggested to him to have it on Monday since he will be gone for the next two weeks."

In her mind she really wasn't interested in Mr. Katron. She wanted to know where her husband's thoughts were on their son, Michael.

"Did you see Michael at work today?"

"Yes, he had a video conference discussing some of the production changes he will begin implementing the beginning of the year. He did a phenomenal job, and all in attendance were pleased with not only his presentation but also his choices for project managers for each phase of the project. I am really proud of him. He is doing a good job of learning the business."

"Did you discuss with him the dinner date with Aunt Onnie?"

"No, why should I? Maybe Michael and Aunt Onnie had some professional business to discuss. You know she still has all of her land holdings in Alabama and some of her other investments. There is a need for her to decide if she will keep them or begin to sell off her land holdings and her investments. This may be something she will let Michael handle."

"I don't know if her conversation with him tonight was about land holdings. It appears during the reading of Tessa's will, almost everyone in the room knew of Michael's gambling addiction, but me."

"Jennifer you do not need to worry about his addiction. Father and I have handled it, and Michael has assured me that his sessions with the psychologist have helped channel his interest in another direction."

"Edwin, I guess this will be the first time in more than twenty-six years of marriage that we have not discussed a matter together and come up with a solution. Why? Did you and your father think I would be unable to handle it? Michael is my son also."

"Too many opinions about his situation could have caused him to become more adamant about continuing down the wrong path. Our last conversation with Michael was to tell him that no one else in the family would get him out of another situation with his bookies. He needed to grow up and face his own demons. I also advised him that it might jeopardize his position with the company. It was Dad that suggested the psychologist."

"I am glad you and your father had the conversation, but I still don't understand why the information was kept from me."

"I know what I am about to say will not satisfy your curiosity, but some situations with young adult men should be discussed with and resolved by older men. Michael would have respectively listened to you, but not necessarily adhered to your guidance and directions. Why, because he sees himself as a man and not as mother's little boy. Look at his pattern with Tessa. I am sure she counseled him about his addiction with gambling and probably told him that she would not provide another dime for his addiction. However, he knew that if he fell back into temptation, Tessa would bail him out over and over again. Remember the Oedipus complex? You may be tough in the court room and with many of your employees, but when it comes to your son and his happiness, you would forego your ultimatum to him with another last chance"

"You think I am that weak, Edwin?"

"No baby, it is not weakness, but a mother's love for her son. What has your psychology friend always told you? Most women cannot raise a man. At a certain age, the mother needs to turn the reins over to the father or to a father figure."

"I can see the look on your face, the one you always gave me when you were upset with me. Like the time I agreed with your aunt on not wanting to move into the estate but having a place of her own. I don't believe she would have been comfortable living under the same roof with Tessa. Now don't you agree?

"Yes, but it seems that the relationship got better as they got older."

"I think the best way to put it is they began to tolerate each other."

Edwin pulled her close to him. "You remember we made an agreement when we got married that we would never go to bed angry or without a comfortable resolution. Therefore if you need to keep talking it out, we can."

"No, I know certain conversations are best resolved when the father or the male figure discusses it. I am just hurt that he did not have enough faith in me to talk to me about his situations, but chose Tessa, William and you."

"Jennifer, again, it is not that he did not have faith in you. He did not want to disappoint you or shatter your ideals of who he had become. A male child, no matter how old he is still wants to please his mother and never wants to lose that mother's love and bond connection. Think about it, even the worst of mothers, their sons still want their affection, attention and their love. They often seek them out to find that connection and that bond."

She hugged her husband and placed a seductive kiss on his cheek.

"Now I know why I love you and need you in my life, you continue to surprise me with the way you handle difficulties in our lives. I also am stunned how your gentleness and wisdom keep me from exercising the female tantrum position. I love you William Edwin Langley Jr. Let's get some sleep."

Although Jennifer's body had retired for the night her mind was working overtime. She looked over at her husband who not only was snoring but was also in a deep sleep. Is there something she is missing with Michael having dinner with Aunt Onnie? Edwin did not seem to think it was all that serious. Can I be that unobservant of situations that are happening right here in my home or am I too involved with my civil rights cases that I have blocked the everyday events of my family out of my world. When was the last time I talked to Edwin about nis job and his work? I go to visit Aunt Onnie, but I am preoccupied with ensuring that her staff is taking care of all of her needs. We never have an aunt-to-niece conversation.

Jennifer turned over in the bed hoping she would not disturb Edwin's sleep. Then she smiled to herself, he doesn't even know I am next to him. He must have had a long day.

As she tossed and turned most of the night her mind wandered back to the package. She had to finish that document. There could be some clues to the reason way Michael is behaving as he is and other clues about the secrets of the Langley family. I know we tried not to spoil our children materially, just because we had money. I thought we had done a good job of preparing them for the real world. Bria seems as though she has taken our foundations and our blessings and had begun to carve out her niche with her new husband.

She doesn't know when she drifted off to sleep, but Edwin's movement in the bed awaken her.

Yes, she had to finish that package; there might be some reasons in the document why Edwin had kept certain family issues from her. She felt he was just like her aunt Onnie. Both of them wanted to shield her from the perils of life. They had taken her bumps and falls for too long. It was time that she understood what it really feels like to be in some of the conditions and situations of her clients. Yes, she does an excellent job of defending her clients and helping them to realize their civil right as a citizen of these United States, but she doesn't fully understand how certain people's heart could be so filled with hatred and evilness for another human being. Her victories were won through passion for the ones who had been dealt an uneven and unjust hand in life, not from experience or understanding.

As she rolled over to exit the warmth of her husband's body he pulled her back over to plant a sweet kiss on her forehead.

He smiled. "I would kiss you on the lips, but I know sleep dwells."

She lovingly patted him on his cheek.

"I can remember in law school when morning breath was not an issue."

"Shhh, don't say that too loudly. Remember we were the model couple!" He looked at her and winked.

"Yes, if only we could turn back the hands of time, a lot of things we felt were not issues should have been priorities for our life. Good thing God was watching over us. Are you playing hooky from work today? I know you have two very important cases on the docket for next month that you and Nila have worked very hard on."

"No, Nila and I have a 1:00 PM conference today. I am going to use the morning to review some of my notes to discuss with her and John. Before I go into the office, I am going to stop and have lunch with Aunt Onnie."

"Stay out of it, Jennifer, if Aunt Onnie does not broach the subject, don't ask about it. The less you know about their conversation the better it is for you."

"What are you, Michael, and Aunt Onnie trying to keep away from me?"

"You already know about his gambling debts and how they were resolved. The details don't matter as long as we can keep him away from his old bookies. I know he is ashamed of his past actions, but being focused on a good relationship with Nila had begun to peel away the core of his past sins."

"So you just want me to take this as a fix and not hear the details."

"Isn't that the modem operand of every good defense lawyer? To give you only the facts with fewer details to create a reasonable doubt mind-set for the twelve people sitting as the jury."

As Jennifer exited the bed, she looked Edwin in his eyes. "As the defense attorney, details make the difference in winning my case. I may not ask directly, but I intend to find out what was behind his meeting with Aunt Onnie."

"As my attorney, there are certain details you may not want to know, because it may hinder or taint your defense for me. Just go and have a good lunch with your aunt. Aunt Onnie is too shrewd for you to get her to reveal her reasons for having dinner with Michael. She had been in this game much longer than you. Therefore she is an old pro at only giving you the need to know information."

"OK, if you say so, but I may not be finished with you regarding this conversation. I don't want my loving husband to be late."

As they said their parting good-byes, Jennifer thought, *I hope he doesn't think this is the end of this conversation.*

After finishing her bath, she heard a knock on the bedroom door.

"Yes, come in."

"Good morning, Jennifer, Edwin thought you may want a light breakfast in the sitting area this morning. So I had the chef prepare something light for you."

"Thank you, Rose."

"If you need anything else, just let me know."

"Rose, were you aware of Michael's gambling problem? If so why did you and the rest of my family keep it from me?"

"Jennifer, um, Mrs. Langley, the first I heard of this issue was at the reading of Mrs. Langley's will. Why do you think anyone in your family would discuss that with me?"

"I know Tessa would not have, because she felt you were loyal to me and Edwin, but what about things discussed with Aunt Onnie?"

"Florence does lend a listening ear to your aunt, but I think this issue was a surprise to your aunt. Didn't you see the look of shame when Michael expressed his regrets and sorrowfulness to each of us in attendance?"

"Mrs. Langley"

Jennifer put up her hand. "Just call me Jennifer."

"Jennifer, sometimes just knowing issues have been resolved is better than knowing the sordid details. If you attempt to dig for the details, they might not be pretty. Mrs. Langley and Edwin have resolved the issue. Let well enough alone."

"It hurts Rosa that I was kept out of the loop."

"And it's OK. Think about your work for human and civil right. What if this had gotten into the news? If you keep pushing it, it just might land there. There are a lot of people who once had a gambling problem. He isn't the first nor will he be the last. At least he is getting help for his addiction. My advice is to stay out of it."

"I feel my right as a mother has been violated. I am furious with Edwin for keeping this from me."

"Do you really think your grown children share everything with you? If you do, you are living in a very false world. They did not share things when they became an adolescent and they really don't share as a young adult. It is only revealed when there is an issue. A lot of times we stumble upon them or we hear bits and pieces at the dinner table."

"I know Bria and William confided in me when they needed a mother's opinion or a solution to their issues. Why is Michael so different? It hurts he did not come to me."

"Jennifer, think about your life. Are there things you kept from your aunt Onnie when you were in boarding school, undergraduate school and law school? Are you really sure that Bria and William have told you everything about their lives?"

"Yes, there were things but nothing like a gambling debt."

"Whatever they were, you kept them away from her. Have Bria and William confided in you and asked you not to tell William?"

Yes, but . . .

"Then you violated his right as a father. Those are his children also. You just admitted you did not want to violate your children's confidence by speaking to their father. This is the same thing Edwin did. He kept his knowledge of Michael's gambling issue confidential."

With attitude in her voice Jennifer looked at Rosa. "I need to get dressed, because I have a luncheon date with Aunt Onnie."

"Try and keep the conversation light, you know your aunt Onnie."

"Rosa, I still have not finished William's package, but when I do, I may need your take on how to broach the subject with my family. This can become a really big issue personally and professionally."

"Most people would love to know about their rich heritage. You might be over thinking this because of the persons involved. Think of this as one of your human and civil rights cases. How would you explain the contents of your research to the family involved? The same tactics you use with your clients, use with your family only on a more loving and personal level. Family members may get angry for a little while and soon forget and begin the caring and loving piece again after the anger dissipates."

With less inflection and anger in her voice, Jennifer stated, "I am glad you came in to bring me my breakfast. I feel ready to meet Aunt Onnie and the world."

"Have a good day and I will see you at dinner. Do you really have much more to read in William's package?"

"No I have just a few more pages. With my two heavy cases for next month, I have not found the time to read them. I hope I can get through them before the holidays set in, if not, I will have to wait until next year to discuss the contents with my family."

If it is only a few pages, I am sure you will be able to get through them before the holiday. You know it's always a little busy and hectic around here during those times. You need to block off two days in November and December to take your aunt shopping. She will really be disappointed if you forget. In fact I will discuss your calendar with your administrative assistant at work to coordinate those four days around your work calendar. Have a wonderful lunch with your aunt and give her my regards."

"OK, let me go I did not realize the time had flown by this quickly. Thanks Rosa for always helping me to calm down before visiting my aunt. I feel I can now handle whatever Aunt Onnie hits me with today."

As Jennifer began to input the code to Aunt Onnie's electronic surveillance gate, her cell phone began to ring. It was Nila calling from the office.

"Hi, Nila, I will be at the office right after lunch. Is there a crisis that I need to address right now?"

"Good Afternoon, Mrs. Langley, no there isn't. Your secretary just received a message from Judge Bush, she had granted a continuation to the opposing party on the Land ownership case. She has scheduled it for the first of next year. I think the opposing team really sees the light and cannot find a way to win this case. The main members of the opposing team are vacationing out of the country and will not return until the end of December."

"Wonderful news, Nila, therefore, the only case on the docket for November is the race/ethnicity identification case filed by the ten-year-old young man. You have assembled some very detail data and specific court cases pertaining to this case. I am sure with the information and evidence we have assembled we will only be in court one day for the Judge to provide his opinion."

"We did get another case in today regarding discrimination in the housing market, but I have not read the contents of the brief yet. Have a good lunch with your aunt, and I will see you tomorrow. There is no need for you to come in today. The office is quiet and John and I are working on the three new cases you received last month. If anything comes up that need your attention, I will call."

"Nila, thank you very much. I will see you tomorrow."

A cloud of calmness swept over her entire body. She felt like she could take on not only Aunt Onnie but also any injustices that crossed her path on this day. She would have a nice and fruitful luncheon with her aunt, return to her home and finish the rest of the package from William Sr. This was going to be a good day for her.

Jennifer walked into her aunt's home; whatever the chef had prepared for lunch had filled the house with a sweet aroma. This aroma also told Jennifer just how hungry she was. As soon as her aunt walked up to kiss and greet her, her stomach began to rumble and growl.

As Onnie placed a kiss on Jennifer's face, she smiled and said, "My goodness child when was the last time they fed you? I am glad the chef made us a good meal for lunch. We have grill chicken with a Mango sauce, smashed red potatoes, sauté mixed vegetables, spinach/raspberry/strawberry salad, rolls, white chocolate cheesecake, and spice tea. Doesn't that sound good?"

"Oh yes it does. I have had so much on my mind lately since Tessa's death that some night I have either forgotten to eat or did not feel like eating a full meal."

"What could be pressing you down to keep you from putting nourishments in your body? Remember you are in the prime of your life, probably going through menopause. You need to keep your mind and your body physically fit."

"You are right. Between the office and some personal things, like finding out my son Michael had or has a gambling problem and wondering is there something else he and his father had not divulged, which has caused me to stress out."

"You can control your stress. For one thing, you really don't have to be in that office on a daily basis. I know it's your passion, but you can find someone to be the first chair lawyer and you can always sit second chair. Only on specific cases do you need to be first chair. You have made a reputation for yourself handling human and civil rights cases that I am sure, reducing your number of days at the office will not decrease your caseload."

As she and her aunt walked arm in arm into the dining room, she smiled; once again her aunt had done it. She easily slipped another subject into the conversation to avoid the real subject matter, my son Michael. At her age she is still sharp and knows how to control people and conversations.

"Aunt Onnie, I heard you had dinner with my son Michael. Did you and he discuss anything exciting?"

"Michael is such a charming young man. He just wanted to ensure as the eldest great-nephew in the family that all of my needs were being met. In fact I am going to invite him and that young lady—what is her name?"

"Nila"

"Yes! Nila! Such a beautiful young lady, beautiful smile, much charisma and a wonderful personality. I want to know more about her." She winked at me. "That why I am preparing a dinner for the three of us so I can find out more about her. Let's eat before the food gets cold. Florence, would you please serve us out salad?"

How does she do it? I thought she had dementia, but like Rosa said to me, it is convenient to claim when she doesn't want to adhere to our suggestions for her life. Well I am a product of her teachings and environment and I will get the response I came here for.

"Aunt Onnie, you know I need to get to the crux of the matter."

"Listen to my niece, the lawyer, the crux of what matter, dear?"

"You are quite aware of my question. The disastrous situation that is about to ruin my son, Michael's personal life."

"Jennifer, I know you are concerned, but this matter needs to be resolved by your husband. Sometimes too much of a female's influence does not support the masculine maturity a young or mature male child needs to become a functional man in society. Yes, you endured the pain to bring him into this world, but you are female and he is male. You cannot teach him to be a man."

She looked at Jennifer and slowly sipped some of her ice tea.

"I am glad that you were of the same gender as me, because I know that a male child under my care would not have been fit to be let out into society. You know my friend Freda? Her husband Carl had little input in the rearing of her son. Carl Jr., who is your age, has never secured tenure on a job and now he and his girlfriend are living off his father and mother's retirement funds. She complains to me, and you know me, I don't do a lot of listening. I tell her the reason for this debacle."

Onnie picked up her napkin and placed it in her lap. "Listen to your wise old aunt. Let Edwin handle it and when it is resolved he will give you the need to know information. Now let's eat child."

Jennifer sat there with her mouth wide open. Her aunt in her most sophisticated way had told her to leave this situation alone and let her husband take care of it. Am I hearing this correctly? My aunt is suggesting that my input would adversely affect my son's masculinity. Let me exhale before I address this.

"I resent the fact that you think my input on my son's situation could hinder the resolution. I know that a young male needs a male figure but as his mother, I do have the right to address this. Edwin said that to me just the other night. I guess you and he had been discussing my involvement."

"Watch the way you address me dear, I am still your aunt and being disrespectful is one of my pet peeves."

"Sorry Aunt Onnie, I am not being disrespectful, but I am hurt that you think only Edwin should address this situation."

"You are a brilliant lawyer who has won a large number of meaningful cases, so I know you are intelligent enough to understand my stance on this matter. Would you allow Edwin to take care of a female concern for Bria? I think not! Let's not belabor this and be petty about this situation. Michael needs a male prospective and he does not need an emotional premenopause lady attempting to give him solutions."

Jennifer removed the napkin from her lap and began to wipe the tears that were flowing down her face. Her aunt had never talked to her in this manner. "Rosa often suggests that I was shielded from the real world by my aunt. If this is the real world, I don't want any more of its experiences."

Onnie raised her hand. "Before you speak again, I took all of the bumps and bruises for you during your formative years. It was my mistake to not allow you to fall and learn to cope with your own bruises and bumps. I was overprotective since both of your parents died when you were young. I was overprotective because of my own rearing. I was overprotective because I did not want you to experience life as I had. Yes I was your enabler, protecting you from real pitfalls, inhumanitarian actions, schemes and injustices of the real world. When you suggested to me that you had a desire to be a civil rights attorney, I was a little concerned. There would be no way you could look at circumstances of the underdog and figure out ways to get them the most out of this unjust and cruel world. I am proud of you, because you have an innate ability to discern the uncanny lies from the truth."

"I have learned so much from you. I love you more than you realize for all you have taught me. I guess today, it appears that you are turning against me instead of agreeing with me on this matter."

"Baby, your aunt would never, never turn against you. I am trying to show you that in order for your son to be whole as a man, it is best that the resolution comes from his father. He has already wasted too many years allowing a woman, Tessa to resolve his gambling issue. She should have sent him to his father or his grandfather. Do you understand what that action does to a growing male child? He feels he can always go to some woman to get himself out of a situation instead of personally solving it."

"I hear what you are saying, but it doesn't feel good right now."

"No, it doesn't, but you have to accept it as it is and move on. Our entrée is going to get cold, let's eat and talk."

"Are you saying that I should push back and let Edwin control this issue? I'm not there yet. I still feel that I am intelligent, knowledgeable, and mature enough to help out."

"Yes, you are all those things, but you are missing the most important piece. You are a woman trying to address a problem of your grown male son. Too much female estrogen would add on to the amount that Tessa has already sprinkled on him. Only Edwin can provide him the cure for the too much estrogen he has already inhaled."

"I see I can't win with you on this subject. I will stay out of it. But I need to understand, do I not question Edwin about the progress?"

"Jennifer, no, absolutely not! Did you just tell me that next week Edwin and his sons were going to Miami for a father-and-sons bonding?"

"Yes."

"Then let them bond and I assure you your wonderful husband will discuss the results. If you nag him, he will never discuss the resolution with you. You've always let him be the head of the home. Don't try to pull that plug on this issue nor strip him of position. I assure you he will talk to you after he has had a discussion with his son. Remember it is OK if he doesn't do it right away or in the presence of his son."

"I was thinking about going with them so I could at least provide some support for my husband"

"Your husband doesn't need your support on this he needs your trust. By staying home and allowing him to resolve this issue and any other issue shows him that you have trust and confidence in him to handle the situation appropriately."

Jennifer again dabbed away the tears that were flowing down her face. She felt helpless. As a woman would she be a hindrance to the appropriate resolution?

"Let me ask you something Jennifer? When you are preparing for specific cases do you have to drill your clients to have them provide you with the truth and accurate facts of the case?"

"Yes at times it becomes difficult, like they do not want past or hidden family secrets to surface. Sometimes it is information they have not shared with the immediately family, afraid that if the family knew it will sever or tarnish their relationships or their good name and reputation."

"Then you know that all families including Edwin and mine have skeletons in our closets that we have not talked about for years. Most of us only give the good information and superficially give part of the bad. You knew my real father, right? Did you know he was a part of the crime scene on the Chattahoochee River? He was one of the main players for the gambling and racketeering on the river front. He kept it away from his family by being a legal business owner and medical doctor. He never allowed the consequences of his illegal actions to taint his legal family and his mistress's family. How do you think Cromwell moved up the political ranks in Alabama? The skeletons in Daddy's closet helped move him in that direction. There were a lot of influential families that owed him a favor and those favors were repaid through his son's political career."

"Did you know all of this growing up as a child?"

"Bits and pieces, but no details. It was kept far, far away from his two families. Neither Cromwell's mother nor my mother ever gave us any clues about his outside business activities. Even when the FBI and others investigated the criminal activities on the Chattahoochee River, his name never surfaced. To this day, I believed that one of his buddies took the blame so he and his family could be spared. Cromwell and I knew something was not right, but we only became aware of the real deal when we became young adults.

By this time, our father was old, but could still pull stings for his family and others. He was never convicted, because he ran a profitable business that kept a lot of people in the community with jobs and he was one of the best doctors in Barbour County. Who was going to bite the hand that fed them? Remember, my father was instrumental in building the first small hospital in the area that accepted all ethnicity, the poor, the rich the good and the bad.

"How do you feel about it now that you know the illegal situations your father was involved in?"

"Since it did not really impact me socially, personally or professionally as I matured, I can't say I really dwelt on it. My bad taste came with selecting a good male friend because I did not exclusively have my father on a daily basis and I was more than aware of his relationship with my mother and his wife. When I became an adult, I often wondered why my mother accepted this life. There were times I wanted to ask her, but kept silent. You don't know how it felt as a young child to not have your father exclusively on holidays, or to stay with us more than overnight or a couple of hours. No we did not want for material things, but those minutes and hours spent with my father did not fill the longing in my heart for a full-time daddy."

"How did my father cope with the situation?"

"My brother never let it show on his face, but inside I knew he was hurting. He and father never saw eye to eye and mother would always have to come between them. My brother released his anger through sports and academics. He was an excellent tennis player—probably could have gone pro—and he excelled in science and math. He never allowed his father to hug or touch him. Daddy only attended his graduation from medical school, since Dad had also finished the University of Alabama Medical School."

"You are such a beautiful and classy woman. Is that the reason you never married?"

"No, I had suitors, and one even asked me to marry him, but it appeared that I catered to men like my father."

"Your father when he became a young adult would sometimes bring up the subject about Dad with our mother. Her sweet answer in a nutshell was basically, 'It is none of your concern.' Your dad, like I said, never really fostered a relationship with our father. He became a doctor at the insistence of both Mom and Dad. Plus my dad had big-time connections with the right people at the University of Alabama Medical School.

"Listen, we have totally gotten off the subject. This is not about me but about you allowing your husband to help Michael with his male issues."

"I know, but I always wanted to understand how you could accept your father as part-time."

"It's what you do and what you come to accept. If you want to break the mold then you find another road for your life. I created that road for you so you would not exist under the shadow of your grandmother and grandfather's past mistakes. Somewhere in the Bible it talks about the sins of the father are visited upon the son. I believe that some of the skeletons in our family closets often leave the closet and take up residence in one or more of the ancestors. No matter how hard we work to provide the future generations with a stellar environment, the bad characteristics or behavior often manifest itself in one or more of the offspring. My dad was a gambler. His spirit of gambling had shown up in Michael. When we know of these behaviors, it is our responsibility to create an environment to combat the skeletons from escaping from the closet. It is up to the family to provide the therapy or the counseling needed to stop that behavior from surfacing in the next generation."

"Like being a female abuser, the son often observes his father's behavior toward his mother or other women in his life. His mother or the other woman often accepts the fact that her husband or significant other loves her even though he is an abuser. Her reason for accepting this behavior she observed from an abused mother, grandmother or aunt."

Onnie looked down at her napkin, picked it up and wiped her mouth. "There are in my opinion, two types of skeletons, one that needs to be revealed since its spirit may dwell in one of the future generation and one that needs to stay in the closet since it may cause instability and hatred within the family structure."

"Aunt Onnie, I don't really think I understand the second one."

"Jennifer, there may be one in the family that is looked upon as almost perfect. However, there may be situations in that person's life that reveals the human side of them. Instead of tarnishing the person's reputation, upstaging the near-perfect persona, and maybe hurting others in the family, it is best these skeletons stay buried in the closet or the backyard."

Onnie was sure that Jennifer did not understand her reasoning for expressing the second one. After her conversation with Tessa before her demise, she has felt guilty about her affair with Tessa's husband. This is one secret that she hopes stays buried in the backyard. She must remember to have Hamilton draw up a legal document assuring that Michael would never tell his father, mother or sibling about this secret. In fact once Jennifer leaves, I will call Hamilton to set up the appointment.

Jennifer walked over to her aunt and hugged her. "Thank you for this conversation. I came here expecting you to tell me why you had lunch with Michael, but you opened my eyes to another dimension of the situation. I won't say I feel good about the directions to allow Edwin to totally resolve Michael's issue, but I am going to be mature about it."

Onnie reached up and hugged her favorite niece back. She was glad she had this conversation; however, nothing hits her blindsided. When Jennifer called to have lunch with her on today, she knew Jennifer had an ulterior motive. Inside she laughed; Jennifer would never be able to get her to reveal her reasons for meeting with Michael. Now her next move is to ensure that Ms. Florence does not discuss the dinner with Rosa.

THE ACCIDENT

As Jennifer got into her Bentley, she looked at her face in the rearview mirror. Her eyes were red and puffy, tearstains had dried on her face, and her makeup was half gone. She looked a mess. It was a good thing that she did not have to go into her office, because after today's lunch, she would be unable to concentrate on any of her docketed cases. She tossed her purse on the passenger's seat after she retrieved her compact. At least she could try and remove some of the tearstains from her face. At all cost she would avoid Rosa until she had the opportunity to revive herself from the deep conversation she had with Aunt Onnie. She put the car in gear, but her mind was distracted with today's conversation. She heard the horns from the oncoming cars, as they swerved to avoid an accident. What she did not realized it was her car. She focused noticing her car had landed halfway in the construction site on the other side of the road. She felt something wet moving down her face, and when she touched it, it appeared to be blood. Her next remembrance was awakening in the hospital bed surrounded by her husband, her sons, and Aunt Onnie.

"How do you feel Jen? The doctor says you are lucky, only a few minor bumps and bruises, the cut on your forehead, a small fracture in your left wrist, and two cracked ribs. They want to keep you here for a couple of days to observe you and to ensure there are no other internal damages from the accident."

"My head is really throbbing badly. What happened? I remember moving out of the way of the oncoming car, but nothing else. Why am I here? Did I total the car?"

"Jen, your head hurts from the cut and the bump on the forehead. It occurred when you lost control of the car and landed in the ditch on the other side of the road. Jen, cars can be fixed or a new one bought. I am glad you are OK."

Michael walked over to the bed and kissed his mother on her cheek. "You may be working too hard on those court cases. Nila tells me that sometimes you miss lunch to complete additional research or a conference with potential clients. Mom we have enough money for you to work part-time and start taking care of you. I can always go back and get my law degree and run the office for you. If you are concerned about me and my past situations, I am now working on it with my psychologist."

"She held out her hand and pulled him closer to her. You are always my main concern since you are my son, but I am not sure your situation was the only thought running through my head at the moment. Nila is very capable of running the office in my absence and I trust her to do the right thing."

William (aka Will) who had a close bond with his mother's boy, could not contain his weeping. He walked over to his mother and just fell in to her chest.

Jennifer let out a weak yell.

"I am sorry mother, I am so distraught about your accident, I forgot about your two crack ribs."

Jennifer smiled as she looked at her youngest son, her baby boy. The image of his dad—he looked more like Edwin than Michael.

Through tears and sniffing, William declared, "I prayed the whole time I was driving over here that you would be OK. I talked out loudly stating that I would be lost if I did not have both of my parents to talk to about my life situations. I am thankful you are alive. I promise you, Mom, I will do better by completing college. I'll finish my degree by next year and start working on an advance degree. I know that I have procrastinated by not taking a full load and then dropping certain classes. I knew there would always be a place for me in the various businesses owned by the family. However, this accident has caused me to reflect upon my immature behavior and actions. I love you mother and please mend so you can come home soon."

His love and his guilt were intertwined in his speech of compassion.

"I love you also Will and I am going to get well. My aunt Onnie once told me a long time ago that God has to bring suffering into our lives so he can strengthen us to deal with the bumps and bruises along life's journey. Being rich does not keep us from the pitfalls that life often throws in our pathway. We must be equipped to handle it so we can move on to accomplish our dreams and visions. Today's accident was a test of our faith, our insecurities, our boastfulness, our haughtiness and our attitudes of – it will never happen to me or anyone in my family. Riches do not entirely shield you from failures and long, unending falls."

"You are right mother and that is how I viewed life. Yes, based on my inheritance, my mind-set was I had the capital to keep me from failing and falling. Even if I never finished college, my trust fund from my grandfather was enough to keep me happy for years to come. That was the Wrong Attitude!"

"Life has a way of painting a picture to show us that none of us rich, poor, educated or uneducated can escape the imperfect seasons of life."

Aunt Onnie, who was sitting in the chair next to her bed, never took her eyes off her niece. Two hours ago she was having lunch and a very candid conversation with her and now she was looking at her niece lying in a hospital bed. Her face was swollen, eyes red and puffy, bandage on her forehead, a cast on her left wrist and bandages around her ribcage. Her heart was heavy for she knew her discussion with her niece had clouded her thoughts, thus the cause of the accident. Why didn't she just give Jennifer the answers she was seeking about Michael instead of being her true self by skirting around the issue?

She leaned over and began to wipe the tears from Jennifer's face. She whispered softly into Jennifer's ear.

"I am sorry, it is entirely my fault. I should never have filled your mind with the past skeletons of my family. We should have had a lunch filled with fun and laughter and this would have never happened."

Jennifer put her right hand on top of her aunt's left hand.

"Shhh . . . it's time that the truth comes out. We all live in a false and evil world, hard to discern truth from lies, and when this world falls down on us, we are unable to handle it due to misconceptions of our past heritage and past experiences—the skeletons we kept hidden in the closets. Thank you for sharing, for this will help me decide about another pressing matter. In my heart I want it to stay in the closet but in my legal mind, it needs to be shared. None of us no matter how intelligent and rich we are cannot fathom how our past actions and reactions to life's pathways and journeys can adversely affect the next generation. I love you for sharing with me today and I hope soon you will continue with the sharing."

Onnie looked at her niece with a weird look. She knew in her heart there was a secret that she would take to her grave. She also knew she needed to do a little blackmailing of her own with her nephew Michael. She never ever wanted her niece to find out about her relationship with William Sr. It would truly affect the way she felt about her, tarnish her belief in her and see her as a clone of her father. There were two other persons she had to make sure they kept her little secret, Florence and Rosa.

Edwin walked over to his wife and kissed her on her lips.

"You need to get some rest. I am going to take Aunt Onnie back home and will return in about two hours. We don't want to tire you out."

"I can take a nap, but I don't want you to leave yet. Michael or William, will one of you drive Aunt Onnie home?"

Aunt Onnie looked around the private room with attitude in her voice and control on her face. "I am not leaving. I can go to the waiting area or sleep in this room. If I need to go home, I can call my driver. In fact, I can ask for another bed if needed. I am not going anywhere."

While all of them were around Jennifer's bed, her private physician, Dr. Stephen McCastler, and his intern, Dr. Krystal Hervey, entered the room.

"Hi, everyone, my patient may need some rest, but I need to examine her right now. Meet the new physician to my practice, Dr. Krystal Hervey, she is a graduate of NYU medical school and is beginning her residency here at Memorial with me."

Together each of them said hello to Dr. Hervey. Especially William, he was unable to keep his eyes off her. In fact his entire inside warmed as he glanced upon her beautiful face and shapely body.

Edwin shook Dr. McCastler's hand and offered a welcome and words of congratulations to Dr. Hervey. "We will go to the waiting area until you finish, Dr. McCastler."

Edwin noticed his two sons move over into the corner of the waiting area. He had noticed Will's reaction to Dr. Hervey and he was sure that was going to be the crux of their conversation. She was a beautiful young lady, but was he ready for another in-law outside of his ethnicity? As he shook his head back and forth he thought, my father brought me up to respect all people and he would be ashamed of me for such thoughts. He was thinking not only about his feelings but also about his associates and colleagues. How would they view the Langley family?

Multiethnic and multicultural! This should not really matter since there was a growing population of multiethnic and multicultural people not only in the United States but all over the world. These types of thoughts had never come into his mind when hiring the best possible employees for his companies. Why now?

In fact, Colby Jerome Miller had been his best friend through prep school, college and law school. They met at the prestigious male boarding school in Mass. Instantly they became friends since each loved jazz (old and contemporary), were on the golf and tennis teams in high school and college and each had a desire to one day become a lawyer or a business leader. In college, Colby majored in biochemical engineering due to his family owning a chemical company in Massachusetts. Colby was more than an average student in math and science. Therefore he tutored me in my calculus classes. After undergraduate, Colby completed a degree in law from the University of South Carolina to equip him with the science and legal background to be a part of the family business.

Colby's family owned a medium size Chemical business and supplied specific chemicals to several fertilizer corporations, paint corporations and a small pharmaceutical corporation. His formative experiences mirrored those of Edwin. In fact, Edwin's father and Colby's father had become not only friends but also associates in each other's business venues.

Edwin stood there for a moment and a frown formed on his face. Did we become friends because of the capital that he and his family had, his ability to help me with my math classes, or did I like him because of his personality and his character?

Colby was and still is practical about personal and professional decisions. In fact in high school and in college, he kept me grounded and kept me from sowing my seeds in the wrong orchard. No, I gravitated to him for his down to earth nature and our ability to click on all levels. His family and mine have practically been inseparable. We have even been on vacations together. His children and mine are good friends. Why are these thoughts haunting my mind now?

I am not sure that my son William is even interested in Dr. Hervey. He currently has been taking his best friend's sister on dates. I may be getting worked up over nothing . . . But do I need to check my thoughts and my motives?

He walked toward the waiting room and observed his sons again in conversation. His first notion was to go and listen to their conversation. Then it hit him! Let me wait and see the action William takes. We have accepted Marcus into our family I am sure we can weather the storm to welcome Dr. Hervey into our lives if it comes to that.

Colby would not believe I am having this conversation with myself. We have been friends for over thirty years and our difference in ethnicity has never been an issue. I may need to discuss these thought with Jennifer when she gets well. I don't need to add any other burdens to her condition at this time.

He followed the others into the waiting room to give Dr. McCastler the privacy he needed to examine Jennifer.

"Jennifer, I need to talk to you about a lump I detected on your right breast when you were brought into the hospital. I reviewed your last Mammography film and the radiologist did not see any malfunctions. However, when we did the full-body scan after your accident we detected the lump. I will need to do a biopsy on the lump to determine if it is malignant or benign."

"Was another mammogram done after I was brought into the hospital?"

"Yes, to make sure the X-ray had picked up what Dr. Hervey and I observed. The film, this time picked up the same abnormality shown on the MRI. Dr. Hervey, the radiologist and I conferred and felt we needed to complete a biopsy on the abnormality we saw on both films."

"Have you spoken to Edwin?"

"No, I needed to discuss it with you first and then bring Edwin in to discuss the procedures."

Jennifer turned her face toward the window as a tear rolled down her face. What was happening to her and her family? This was too much for her to comprehend and handle. Michael's gambling situation and now, the lump on her breast. Why was her family being attacked?

"Dr. McCastler, I would like all of my family to be present when you discuss the lump in my breast. My daughter is a medical research physician in Maryland. I will have Edwin put her on the cell phone or the room phone to listen."

Dr. McCastler entered the waiting room to summon the Langley and Dusett families into Jennifer's room. Each of them arose once he appeared.

"I need each of you to return to Jennifer's room, there is something I need to discuss with her family."

The quietness from Jennifer's family as they followed the doctor into her room caused the hospital walls to close in on each of them, as the medicinal smell of the hospital burned through the tears that were forming at the base of each of their eyes. It felt as though God has sent his angels to synchronize the beat of their hearts and the expansion of their chests.

To Edwin, even though the room was only a short distance from the waiting room, it took forever for them to walk down the hospital halls to Jennifer's room. Each of them stopped short of Jennifer's bed and looked from Dr. McCastler to Jennifer to Dr. Hervey to Jennifer. There was no way to read what was on either of their minds from their facial expressions.

Dr. McCastler looked over at Aunt Onnie. "Ms. Dusett, take a seat in the chair next to the Jennifer's bed." The others followed suit and place themselves around Jennifer's bed.

"Edwin, Jennifer would like for you to call Bria so she may be included in this conversation."

Edwin's hand began to shake as he reached into his coat pocket and retrieved his cell phone. As he dialed Bria's number he could see the worry on his family's face. He knew he had to be the strongest whatever news the doctor was about to provide to them.

"Hi, Bria, this is Dad, we are all in your mother's room after the accident. She has several broken ribs, a cut on her forehead and a fractured bone in her wrist. She is doing well and I don't think you should come just yet. Dr. McCastler has summoned us into the room to discuss another medical condition. Your mother wanted you on the phone to listen to the report."

Dr. McCastler looked around the room and noticed the same worried faces that Edwin had observed earlier. He needed to enlighten them of their mother's condition, but did not want to increase their fear.

"During the body scan MRI following your mother's accident we observed a lump in her right breast. We followed up with an X-ray and the radiologist again confirmed there was a small lump in the breast. We need to do a biopsy to determine if the lump is benign or malignant. We plan on completing the biopsy tomorrow. Keep in mind that we have been very successful in the diagnosis and the treating of breast cancer, so we are hopeful that if it is malignant, that we can treat it very effectively."

Silence filled the room and all you could hear was the noise from the machine monitoring her vital signs. Even though the temperature has been in the upper seventies, a cool breeze was felt by all in the room. In fact Aunt Onnie folded her hand around her body to help block out the coolness.

Bria broke the silence: "Dr. McCastler is correct about the treatment for breast cancer. However, this has not been confirmed so let's be hopeful that the biopsy will show that the lump is benign. Let's keep our faith that God knows what is best and he will see all of us through this situation. Dr. McCastler, my father will give you my cell and work number, please keep me informed."

"I will Bria and thanks for assuring your family that with the new treatment we have thousands of breast cancer survivors. Some of them have been survivors for more than twenty years."

Edwin held his hand out and each of his sons fell into his chest and then walked over to Aunt Onnie to embrace her. She rose from her seat and each of them walked closer to the side of Jennifer's bed. As she placed her hand over the cast on Jennifer's left hand, each one in the room bowed their head as she said a short prayer over her niece.

She again placed a kiss upon her niece's forehead. "I know that this too shall pass. You will come out of this victoriously."

"I know I will and whatever is the diagnosis, I have the most loving family in the world that will stand by my side through it all. Now I want each of you to go home get some rest and I will see you tomorrow. Michael or William, would you please drive Aunt Onnie home."

"I am not going home. I will stay here with you."

"I insist that you go home and get some rest. Edwin will stay until visiting hours are over and I will be sending him home. I feel OK and knowing each day I will get stronger, but I will need the strength of my family for right now and if they are tired, we all will need a hospital bed. Go home."

Reluctantly, Aunt Onnie picked up her purse and walked toward the door.

"Dr. McCastler, what time are you completing the biopsy?"

Before he could answer, she continued, "Whatever time it is, I will be back here at 8:00 A.M. Michael or William, which one of you will drive me home? Good-bye, Bria, and I will call you later on tonight."

Will stared intensely at his mother with a face laced with affection and love. "Good evening to each of you, Mother, you know I love you and will talk to you tomorrow. Please get some rest. Dad, do not let her get tired. Make sure she gets some rest. I am sure the pain medication will take effect soon."

As Edwin said thank you to both of the doctors, he made a point to look closely at Dr. Hervey. He was somewhat perplexed and upset with himself for his earlier thoughts. He noticed that she was of a mixed ethnicity. He was wondering, what was the ethnicity of her parents. Whatever it was, she had a beautiful disposition and a very warm smile.

She slowly turned and looked at Jennifer and Edwin. "I know everything is going to be fine. My mother is a breast cancer survivor and I believe it has been more than twenty years since her diagnosis and treatment. She is very active in many academic and social organizations and she is having fun spoiling her grandchildren. Dr. McCastler and his staff will do everything to make Mrs. Langley comfortable and to keep the family informed about her condition. Prayer is always a good conduit. See each of you tomorrow."

Dr. McCastler shook Edwin's hand. "I will call you tomorrow regarding the time of the biopsy. Dr. Hervey is going to be a welcome addition to my practice. She has a certain aura that seems to help the patience combat their fears of the diagnosis and the prognosis. I am grateful she chose to work in my practice. See you tomorrow."

Edwin felt ashamed of his earlier thoughts about Dr. Hervey. He had condemned her based on ethnicity and he did not know the young lady. It appears that he was going to see a lot of her since Dr. McCastler had already voiced his approval of her talents and skills. When did this nonacceptance of others begin to surface in his spirit or was it always there and he kept it in abeyance because of his father's acceptance of others, his wife's chosen work profession and his best friend Colby?

I don't think I am nonaccepting of others, it is more of I want my family to have the best. What is the best according to my limited knowledge of others? Has negative comments and actions of others penetrated my psyche and now I am re-thinking my beliefs about certain inhabitants of this world? I hope not!

There are good, bad and evil in all ethnicities, not one ethnic has a monopoly on these personal behaviors and characteristic. He looked around the corridors while walking toward the nurses' station to the elevator. His mind wandered back to Dr. Hervey. I wonder if she is the first generation of her family to finish college. And why would that matter? Colby was not the first generation in his family. In fact, his great-grandfather was a product of Hampton University, Howard and Harvard. He was president of one of the HBCU colleges. His grandmother was a dentist. Why am I tripping over this? Has society and social media changed my way of seeing others? Most of these comments are just that and many have no validity or proof to support it, but because of our gullibility and eagerness to harbor hate we grab hold to anything. I do not want to become a grabber of idiotic thoughts.

As he walked down the corridor toward the elevators, he shook his head in disbelief. Why all of a sudden this matter is consuming his entire being. Once Jen gets well, I will need to discuss my thoughts with her. I have to and I must, because I do not want it to consume me as a person. As he entered the elevator, he felt a cool breeze sweep across his face. It was as though someone was trying to get his attention. His thoughts crowded his head, his soul, his spirit and his heart. Even though he was in the elevator alone, it felt like all the air was being sucked out and the space in the elevator was closing in on him. He heard himself let out a large gasp of air. He could not wait until the elevation stopped in the parking area. In fact his forehead was wet as well as his underarms as he exited the elevation. Why?

Edwin opened the door of his Mercedes, climbed into the driver's seat, closed the door and place his head on the steering wheel and began to weep openly. This had not happened to him in a long time since the death of his mother and his father. But why was he weeping so openly now? He had been reassured about his wife's condition; he was concerned, but why the tears?

He needed someone to talk to and he thought about his best friend Colby. Would he really be the best person to talk to? He did not believe he harbored any prejudices against other ethnicities, but today's thought to his son's reaction to Dr. Hervey has caused him to have doubt. Maybe I am not ready to have my nest empty. I want to hold on to my children forever. A little known fact is I accepted Bria's marriage, but I was not ready for her to get married. This may be the cause of my today's anxiety. I am concerned not only about the health of my wife but also knowing it is time for all of my children to begin living their own lives.

I am still concerned about my thoughts about the ethnicity of Dr. Hervey. Why don't I harbor the same thoughts about Nila? Maybe because I feel comfortable knowing her family lineage. This thought has never surfaced in my mind before. In fact, I always believed that I was more than liberal when it came to the civil rights of others. Edwin blinked twice for he was aware that tears were freely flowing down his face.

As he walked into the foyer of his home, Edwin's feet took him toward his father's library and study. There over the fireplace in this room were two oil paintings one of his father and the other of his mother. He looked at his father's picture first and then at his mother's. He stared for a long time at this portrait. There was something he was seeing in his mother's eyes that he had not seen before. She was looking at him with much distained. She had often talked to him about not judging people based upon other's opinion, but to look for the good in all. She often encouraged me to play with or interact with some of the workers children, because we can learn from all people. I wonder what her eyes are saying to me tonight. It appeared that her stare was penetrated his heart. He had an urge and a need to touch her picture and ask for forgiveness. When he reached up to touch her picture, a cool breeze passed over his face and the hardness and hurt that surrounded his heart began to dissipate.

Edwin was sitting in the leather wing back chair in his father's library when his two sons walked into the house. Both walked over to him and put their arms around him.

The eldest, Michael, looked up at the oil paintings of his grandparents.

"Daddy, everything with mother's medical condition is going to be OK. I remember when Granddaddy used to ask me to bring him into his library during the latter stages of his cancer. He said that it was always some spirit in this room that calmed him and assured him that life for his family would be great and he should not worry about them. Then he would look at grandmother's portrait and say, 'I wish your grandchildren could have known you for you were some special lady.' Then a single tear would drop from his eye while he said, 'I loved you more than I could ever express.'"

"I guess that was the reason, I came into this room. It was not my intention, but my body automatically came into the library. My father would bring me here and sit me in this wing back chair when we would have serious discussions about life and his desire for my future. The day that my mother died, before I could go to her room to have our daily talks, he brought me into this room to tell me about her death. So much has gone on in this room. I used to watch my mother and father dance, laugh, kiss, and show love and affection in this room. It is ironic, but he informed me about his marriage to Tessa in this room, and I confessed to him about my love for your mother and my desire to marry her in this room. If the walls could talk, they would probably have enough words to fill a short novel."

William place his hand on his father's back and began to massage it. His father exhaled the air that had inflated his lungs and kept him from breathing.

"Daddy, I also know that mother is going to be OK. She is in the hands of two capable doctors and don't forget your oldest daughter and her husband have medical degrees. Our concern should be how we are going to keep mother from going back to work full-time once she comes home. The three of us need to be on the same page and yes Aunt Onnie should be included, because we all know mother does not want to ruffles Aunt Onnie's feathers."

All three of them let out a loud laughter, and together they all said, "No one wants to ruffle her feathers."

"OK, sons, we all need to get some sleep so we can be at the hospital by 8:00 AM. I have already called my administrative assistant to let her know about my not coming into the office. I also informed her that my reason for not coming to the office is not public knowledge for right now. Maybe the two of you should also call your office. By the way, Michael, I have spoken to Nila and she will begin rescheduling any docketed cases and take the lead on all old and new cases in your mother's office. She is something else. You may need to call her tomorrow while we are at the hospital."

"Good night, Dad, thanks for taking care of all us. I will call Nila tomorrow. I know William is going to be there bright and early so he can drool over Dr. Hervey. Did you see him give her the make-believe full-body scan while we were in Mother's room. She is hot!"

"Good night, Dad, and do not listen to your son Michael. He is always reading more into a look and an action than he should. See you in the morning. I know you will inform Rosa when she arrives in the morning."

"I've already called her and she is going to meet us at the hospital. Good night Michael and William. Remember to send up a prayer for your mother."

When Edwin awoke the next morning, he felt like he had been fighting in his sleep. His whole body was not relaxed, but tense and tight. He needed to shake off the tiredness, because he needed a double dose of strength for his two sons, Jen, and Aunt Onnie. As he walked into the bathroom, he inhaled Jen's aromatic body wash and bath salts. Oh how he loved that women. No other women could measure up to the love he had for his wife. He looked up at the sun roof over the Jacuzzi tub and whispered, "Lord you know she is my strength, the air I breathe and the sun that warms my heart. Keep her safe for my family and me. I pray for the healing of my beautiful wife Jennifer."

He stepped into the shower to let the heat from the water soothe the tense and tight spots on his body. The steam opened up his bronchial tubes so he could inhale and exhale better. In his heart he knew that God had heard his prayer and his Jen would be OK.

When he arrived at the hospital, Aunt Onnie, William and Michael were there in the waiting room. His son William handed him a cup of Starbuck's coffee and an Orange Scone.

"Thanks son, how did you know I needed this?"

"We all left home around the same time so I knew all of us would need some Starbuck's to awaken us. Aunt Onnie had her morning coffee per Florence, because she did not sleep at all last night."

Edwin walked over and put his arms around Aunt Onnie. "Good morning, Aunt Onnie, once we hear from the doctor about the biopsy, I am taking you home so you can get some rest."

"Rest is not what I need at this moment. What I need is to know my little girl is going to be fine and free of cancer. I was up all night praying and asking for healing for my little girl. Rest will come as soon as I hear from the Doctor. Are you OK, Edwin?"

"Didn't sleep a wink last night, but once I walked into this hospital, it appeared that a load was lifted from me. In my inner soul, I feel that everything is going to be OK. In fact while I was showering this morning, a rainbow appeared through the dome over the Jacuzzi tub and there was not a rain drop in sight. To me that was an omen that all is well with my family."

"It sounds like an omen to me. Let's all sit together and enjoy our Starbuck's coffee."

Onnie pointed toward a couch and several chairs in the corner away from the others in the waiting room. As she walked toward the area, the others followed her.

No word had been spoken between the four of them since they sat down. Michael looked up and saw Nila walking through the door. His pulse speeded up so rapidly that he felt as though all the blood had rushed to his head. In fact he was very lightheaded. Did this woman really make him feel this way? Was it love or lust? When he was around her he was such a different person. Sometimes he didn't know himself. In his inner spirit as he arose to meet Nila, he kept saying calm down, calm down, calm down. It is too early to show your hand.

Michael walked over to Nila and placed a sweet kiss upon her cheek. She immediately took his arm and they walked over to the others.

"Good morning, all. I could not concentrate on work so I decided to come and sit with Mrs. Langley family. I hope you will not mind. The office is in good hands with John and if he runs into any obstacles, he was informed to call me immediately."

Onnie did not speak immediately, but patted a spot next to her on the couch.

"We welcome you here. The more strength and love vibes we have in one space is truly a good sign. Come and sit beside me. There is a Starbuck vendor in the hall, I am sure Michael will go and get you your favorite kind."

"Thank you, Ms. Dusett, I don't drink coffee, but a cup of chai tea (Oprah's blend) would be wonderful. Thanks, Michael."

As Edwin began to walk toward Nila, he saw Dr. Hervey approaching them. In his mind he wondered why her and not Dr. McCastler. He knew why because he was doing the surgery to remove the lump from Jennifer's breast. Again he had to channel his thoughts away from the ethnicity of this lady and more toward her ability as a doctor.

"Good morning, Dr. Hervey, I believe you are acquainted with everyone except Nila Johnston. She is one of the employees at my wife's law firm. Nila Johnston, Krystal Hervey. She is one of the residents with Dr. McCastler."

"It is nice meeting you, Nila. Please refer to me as Krystal. Dr. McCastler is still in surgery. I did not want the family to assume the worst because it is more than the normal one-hour procedure. There are no complications, but the surgeon found a second lump that was not detected by the X-Ray lodging behind the one detected. Once they have been sent to the lab for a diagnostic evaluation, Dr. McCastler and I will speak to you."

As she turned to exit, she saw Michael and William returning with fresh cups of coffee. Immediately a smile graced William's face.

"Good morning Dr. Hervey did Michael and I miss the report on our mother?"

"No, I was just updating your father, your aunt, and Nila on the timeframe for the surgery and to inform them that a second lump was detected. However, there is no concern for alarm at this time."

"Thank you so much for coming in to give us an update, we really appreciate the information. I do have an extra cup of chai tea. Would you like it?"

"Thanks, I can only stay for a while. I have to complete Dr. McCastler's rounds while he is in surgery."

As Michael and William passed out the coffee and tea, Krystal sat in the chair next to Edwin. She noticed that Edwin's right cheek was moving rapidly, but thought it was due to the stress created by his wife's condition. She reached over and touched his hand, and Edwin not only froze but also politely removed her hand from his.

"Mr. Langley, I see that you are stressed and I know this is an ordeal for each of you. Your right cheek is moving rapidly, I was just attempting to feel you pulse."

"I am sorry Dr. Hervey, I mean Krystal, my reaction was not normal. I am just concerned about my wife. If I don't calm down shortly then I will allow you to take my pulse."

As she stood to leave the waiting room she looked directly at Edwin then focused on William.

"If any of you need my professional assistance, you may ask someone at the nurse's station to page me. William thanks for the tea and I hope to return with Dr. McCastler after he has completed the surgery. Your mother is going to be in recovery for at least two hours before any of you can visit."

William stood up and walked over to Dr. Hervey and said something softly to her. She smiled and nodded her head.

Edwin felt a knot in his stomach and heaviness in his chest. Had he lost his clear thinking? He did not hear the remark to Krystal. Perhaps his son was thanking her personally for providing us with the update. I have to shake this feeling and these thoughts from my inner soul. Jennifer would be so upset with me. There is absolutely nothing wrong with Dr. Hervey except she is of mixed heritage. Are we all mixed with other ethnicities? Look at me French, European and German. These are the ones I know for sure. I could be mixed with something else.

"William, my son what was that soft spoken word about to Dr. Hervey?"

"Nothing really, Dad just asked her if she would be interested in having lunch with Michael, Nila, and me sometimes or maybe later on today. She said sure, but would let me know about her schedule."

"What about Robert's sister? I thought you were in a relationship with her."

"No, Dad, she is a good friend of mine, but no love interest. In fact she has been dating a guy in one of her college classes. I think his name is Charles. But can we talk about this later. It's only a friendly lunch outing. Nothing more!"

"OK, son, just saw how your whole persona lit up when you returned from Starbucks and saw Dr. Hervey."

Everyone in their corner laughed.

Later in the afternoon, Dr. McCastler entered the waiting room and asked the family to follow him to Jennifer's room. As the family stood up and begin following Dr. McCastler. Nila remain seated. Michael walked over to her reached out his hand and she took it. A smile graced the face of Aunt Onnie and Edwin. Both welcomed the change and the new Michael Langley.

Jennifer was still a little incoherent, but she knew her family was entering and her smile brighten up the whole room. Each of them walked over and placed a loving kiss on her forehead. As each one was smiling and being thankful for Jennifer's recovery, in walked Dr. Hervey with the patient's chart for Dr. McCastler.

All eyes were upon this stunning young lady and one in particular could not keep his focus or his eyes off the stunning and beautiful Dr. Hervey.

As she approached Dr. McCastler, her eyes first made contact with Edwin and then with William.

"Dr. McCastler here is the patient's file and the report from the lab. All of the lab reports are not ready, but they have assured me I may pick them up in about an hour. It is good seeing each of you again."

As she turned to leave the room, Dr. McCastler placed his hands on her arm. "Don't leave this is going to be one of your special patients and I need you to be aware of all of the directions I am giving the patient as well as her family."

Dr. Hervey nodded her head in agreement with Dr. McCastler and took her place beside him. She could feel the warmth of William's eyes upon her and the tenseness of his father's aura near her. Was she missing something about Mr. Langley or was he just nervous about his wife's health? Does he feel she is not seasoned enough to be assigned his wife's case? She hoped the latter was the reason for his tightness and his tenseness around him. She thought I will address this with him later to help ease his worries.

Edwin dialed Bria cell phone to ensure she would be among them to hear the news about his wife and her mother. As soon as Bria answered, Edwin nodded his head for the doctor to begin his prognosis.

Dr. McCastler walked over to Jennifer's bedside and focused in on the worried faces of her family.

"Jennifer's conditions from the car accident are healing very well. Her vital signs are in normal range and there is no internal bleeding or a concussion from the bump on the head. While completing the surgery to remove the lump from her breast, we discovered another one right behind it that had been detected by the MRI or the Mammogram X-ray. All of the lab work from the biopsy has not been finalized, but the preliminary work shows that what we removed is benign. As soon as the additional results are in, I will notify the family through Edwin. Right now I want my patient to get some rest because she has been through a great ordeal. I would suggest that each of you go home get some rest and come back in about three hours. Jennifer will be in very capable hands between Dr. Hervey and me."

The silence in the room had almost caved in on each of them but as soon as they heard the report from Dr. McCastler, it appears that the air began to fill the room and the walls began to recede. You could almost hear the magic of the happy breaths as each person inhaled and exhaled. The dimness no longer lingered over each of their heads and it felt as though God had just released the warmth and the light from the sun into Jennifer's room.

Together each of the family members walked over to Jennifer's bed and began to kiss and hug her. The tears flowing from each of their eyes was enough to fill a pint size jar and then some. You could hear Bria over the cell phone laughing and crying.

Nila and Krystal stood together as they watched a family filled with love and emotions. Without a word spoken, Nila walked forward and stood beside Michael. Krystal stood quietly in the same spot until she felt the warmth of eyes upon her and a hand on her shoulder. He softly spoke these words, "Thank you!"

She smiled and softly spoke, "You are welcome." The two of them walked together toward Jennifer's bed.

It appeared that everyone else in the room was not conscious of what had transpired between William and Krystal, no one but Edwin. Again he tried to shake his thoughts and feelings, but it was getting very difficult. He had to do something about this, but he did not want to upset his family or his friend Colby. Why was William's attraction to this young lady affecting him in this manner? He needed to know more about her before he began prejudging her, her foundation and her family.

Edwin walked over to Dr. McCastler. "Do you have any time this afternoon that I may speak to you in private? I am concerned about Jennifer and would like to discuss her medical condition with you."

"Yes, of course. I will be finished with my rounds and my appointments at five thirty today. Six would be a great time for you to meet at my office."

"Thank you Dr. McCastler, I will be there."

Michael and William looked at their father and together asked, "Do you need us to attend with you?"

"No, I want to discuss this matter alone with Dr. McCastler. Take your aunt Onnie home to get some rest and then have her driver bring her back to the hospital around 6:00 PM. We can all have dinner together after we visit your mother. I am going to the office and then meet Dr. McCastler at 6:00 PM. William, would you make a reservation at our favorite steak and lobster restaurant for 7:00 today? Don't worry about me. I am fine and grateful for the news from Dr. McCastler."

Edwin flipped through the papers on his desk, but his mind was not on business this day. How could he possibly broach the subject of his assistant Dr. Hervey to Dr. McCastler? He has known the doctor for some time and he would not select an assistant not up to his medical standards. In his mind he kept going back and forth on the ways to discuss his concerns with Dr. McCastler. In his heart he knew it had nothing to do with her medical skills, but this was the only logical way to really get to the information he wanted to know about her.

Edwin looked at the clock it was only 4:00 PM, he had at least an hour before he returned to the hospital. In fact he should leave now and visit Jennifer before his meeting with Dr. McCastler. He was not getting anything done at the office, so it was useless to continue to shuffle the papers on his desk.

As he arrived in Jennifer's room he noted that she was sound asleep. Instead of awakening her, he sat by her bedside and watched her as she slept. This was the woman he loved and adored. If she knew of the thoughts in his head about Krystal, she would be so disappointed. He was sure he could resolve this and shake these thoughts from his whole being before Jennifer returned home. That is why his conversation with Dr. McCastler today was so essential.

Jennifer stirred in her sleep. Even in the hospital, he thought she was the most beautiful and sexy woman with or without added adornment. If she even had a premonition of his thoughts at this moment, she would look at him with an expression of "I don't believe you." He reached over to touch her but stopped in midair. If he awakens her now, he would have to explain his meeting with Dr. McCastler. He did not want to make up something that was not true. His meeting with the doctor should not last very long, so he will stop back in Jennifer's room before he goes to dinner. He softly kissed her forehead and started down the hallway to Dr. McCastler's office.

As he approached Dr. McCastler's office, he noticed Dr. Hervey leaving. He slowed down his gait to ensure he did not have to stop and speak to her. Again he was appalled at his attitude. Why does he feel so uncomfortable around this lady? Was he having anxiety attaches, because his daughter Bria had announced that she was six weeks pregnant, and he was concerned with the grandchildren and his/her perceived ethnicity? Why should he care? He loves his daughter and he respected his new son-in-law so why are these thoughts clouding his judgment.

He had to discuss it with someone because his grandchildren will be of mixed ethnicity and he only wanted to show real and true love to them, because part of their genetic makeup came from him. He remember watching holly wood movies related to slavery showing how the mixed breed children were dismissed by their father, sold off or either abused by the owners' wives. He did not want to relive the past with his grandchildren. But it was just something about Krystal's presence and statute that made the marrow in his bone turn icy. He wondered if his talk with Stephen would help shake this feeling.

As he entered Dr. McCastler's office, he observed Dr. Hervey looking back but not showing any type of emotions. In fact she didn't even wave to him. Could she have the same feelings toward him? He could not read her and he thought he was so good at reading people's character, but this one had him baffled. It almost appeared that she instantly put up a red flag and barrier when she met him. I couldn't have been that transparent. I think my entire disposition is because of Jennifer's accident, the lumps in her breast and my anxiety of becoming a grandfather. His feet felt like lead as he shuffled them toward the empty seat in Stephen's office.

"Hi Edwin, come in and have a seat. Dr. Hervey and I just looked in on Jennifer and she is doing well. She will be able to go home in about three days. I would suggest that you have a part time medical person to come in at least twice a week to keep her from getting too involved with her work. She needs plenty of rest to heal. The lab work came back and the tests were benign, but we will still have to watch her closely. I intend to discuss it with her tomorrow around 10:00 AM. I would like you to be present and the other members of your family if you feel it is necessary."

"Whatever directions you ask me to follow I will see that it is done to your specification. I definitely will let my family know the good needs and yes we all will be here tomorrow morning. However, my reason for visiting with you today was to discuss Dr. Hervey as the physician assigned to Jennifer. I know you feel that she is an asset to your practice, but does she really have the experiences and skills to deal with Jennifer's condition."

"Edwin, I knew by your expression that you were concerned about Dr. Hervey being assigned to Jennifer but I have confidence in Krystal. She finished first in her undergraduate class with a degree in microbiology, she was also first in her medical class. Dr. Hervey comes from a long line of medical professions. Her maternal grandfather was a physician, her maternal great-aunt was a dentist, her father is a physician, owns one of the largest medical lab corporations and is one of the salaried physicians on the New York Giants staff. Her mother is a pediatrician and an instructor at NYU medical school. Both the mother and father finished the University of Pennsylvania Medical School. I believe her two older sisters are in the medical field and her oldest brother runs the medical labs.

Although she doesn't discuss her paternal grandparents, her grandfather was a top executive in the Oil industry and her grandmother owned a top modeling agency and a well-known clothing line. She has been exposed and has worked in the medical field since the age of sixteen. She is very capable and very knowledgeable. I am sure her life experiences mirror that of your family."

"Stephen, I know you have confidence in your new intern, but I would feel at ease with a more experienced physician."

"Edwin, are you really concern with her medical experience or your son William's interest in Dr. Hervey. Yes, I have noticed how William has paid much attention to Krystal and that he has asked her to have lunch or dinner with Michael and his friend. You may be worried about nothing. In this twenty-first century, the young adults love attention span is very short. This young lady is very level headed and her first love is medicine. She will not let anything block her success in this area. I know she has gone out on several dates with a person that attended medical school with her. He is a pediatrician in the children's ward. However, I don't believe it is serious."

Edwin sort of moved nervously in his seat. Were his thoughts and concerns that obvious? He wondered if his behavior and concern had been noticed by his family.

Before he could respond to Dr. McCastler's question. Dr. McCastler put his hand up.

"I don't really want you to respond to me. It was more of a rhetorical question to let you think about your concerns. I believe the youth and young adults of today don't really buy into the past thinking of their ancestors when it comes to dating someone of another ethnicity. Did you have the same thoughts with Bria's choice or knowing her father was a well-known orthopedic surgeon made a difference? If it makes any difference, Krystal's father is of European descent and her mother is a mixture of African American, American Indian and French."

"Stephen does my concern show that much? I am only concerned about my grandchildren. You know Bria is now six weeks pregnant. I don't want my grandchildren to be labeled or to be hated by others.

"Edwin, with all of the money you have, I am sure you can shield them from any form of mistreatment. The fabric of the world is changing and in the next century we probably won't be able to describe people with the terms of race and ethnicity we current use. In fact we should be in the process of coining different ones for the twenty-first-century population.

Don't worry about Jennifer she is in very capable hands. If you show signs of not wanting William to date Krystal, you will just push them closer together. Edwin, let nature take its course."

"Thanks for talking to me I know I may have to discuss this with Jennifer. However, I'll have to wait until she is completely well."

"Give Jennifer time to heal from her accident and from the news of her biopsy. I don't want her stressed over anything. The visiting nurse will make sure her vital signs are within the level for her age and weight. Do not allow her to work on any cases while she is recuperating. I know there is someone in the office that can take care of her cases. She does not need the stress."

"Rest assured, Stephen, between her aunt Onnie, her children, and me, she will be so pampered that she may never want to go back to her office. There is a young lady she has been training the past year, and she is very capable of running her office. In fact one of the cases that concerned Jennifer, her assistant, Nila, was able to get a settlement without going to court. We will do everything to keep her mind off the office."

"Nila, is she the young lady that was with Michael?"

"Yes, and we just found out that she is Tessa's great-niece."

"Do you have a problem with her ethnicity?"

"No, I just told you she is Tessa's great-niece. She really isn't a blood relative, so I have no problem with Michael dating her. In fact since she has come into his life he has changed some of his errant behaviors."

Dr. McCastler looked at Edwin. Here this man is almost sixty years old, and he has not noticed the change in the fabric of America and other countries. I almost spilled the beans about Tessa. I guess his father never told him. I hope he opens his eyes soon.

Dr. McCastler walked over to Edwin, placed his hand on his shoulder and looked straight into his greenish gray eyes.

"You are aware I have been the family's physician for more than thirty years. In fact we may be the same age, or I may be a couple years older. However, when I started here as a resident, your father embraced me completely. He had been a faithful patient of Dr. Beauchamp. However, once I set up my practice at the end of my residency, he began seeing me for medical advice.

"One day he confided in me that he liked my bedside manners and my honesty. In fact over the years and through his days of cancer, he began to confide in me more and more. I think if your father were still alive, he would not be pleased with the way your heart and mind are carrying you in a direction opposite of his teachings and his actions. Look at how he helped Rosa and Jacob with their small businesses.

"Look at the diversity of his workforce, inclusive of management and executive managers. He chose competent employees based on their ability to carry out the task of the position and not on who they were. It was not about nepotism, but about your ability, experience, skills, and your forward thinking. You need to reflect upon how your father ran his business and his personal life."

"Stephen, you are absolutely correct, and I know Father would have sat me down in his leather wing chair in his study and do what Rosa always said when he discussed his disapproval of something with her—a come-to-Jesus meeting."

They both laughed, but Stephen still could see the worry on Edwin's face.

"Have you ever thought that sometimes when situations like this arise in our spirit, that there is a deeper reason for it? Keep living and I am sure the real reason will be revealed."

"You are aware that my best friend through boarding school, college and law school, was of another ethnicity and I never questioned his loyalty or our love and bond for each other. That's the same attitude I have with Rosa and Jacob. In fact Rosa is more like a relative or a long-lost cousin that I have accepted. In fact I know she and my father were very close."

Stephen smile again and took his hand from Edwin's shoulder. He walked over to the window overlooking the Charleston Harbor. The place he went so many times after his discussion with the Sr. Langley. His mind was racing at this point.

Why didn't William Sr. tell his son about his lineage and his bloodline? It was not his place to open the Pandora's box on the Langley family lineage. In fact this was a chapter that should never be opened by him—doctor and patient confidentiality. The sun was going down on the Harbor and it always helped him inhale and exhale the worries of the day. At this moment he had inhale, but the exhale would not come. He wanted so much to put Edwin at ease with his concern about Krystal, but it was not his place.

"I hope our discussion today will help you to work on your concerns about Krystal. She is a wonderful lady and she may have some insight into your feelings. Bring yourself to just talk to her on a casual basis. Nothing too heavy! She is a very personable and bright young lady. Give her a chance. By the way, how is Bria doing with her pregnancy?"

"Thanks for the talk, Stephen, there is a lot of self-talk I will need to complete to be open with this relationship. You are right about my father. He would not be pleased with my concerns at this moment. In fact I can hear him in my mind telling me this is not the way I was reared. I must gravitate more toward understanding others and their plight and not letting society's hatred of other ethnicities penetrate my soul by depositing their concepts of hatred, evilness, and mistrust in the fibers of my body. His treatment of others should be a model for me and my family, no matter what is exhibited in this country and in this world. This is where my mind should be at this moment. Believe me, I will take your advice and talk to Krystal."

It appeared that Edwin's body had aged about ten years, for he was slow to get up out of the chair. He knew he had to shake this feeling and concentrate more on Jennifer getting well and running the corporations his father has left under his watchful eye.

He walked over to Stephen and extended his hand.

"Thank you for a listening ear. I will take in consideration your advice to me. I know it is not going to change my feelings overnight, but I have to start somewhere."

As he walked back into Jennifer's room. Krystal was there discussing her progress. Edwin stopped for a moment to get a second wind. He closed his eyes and visualized his father's face. He knew his whole attitude and demeanor would cause his father much disgust. "All humans have a right to be treated with respect. Each of us has the right to be given a fair playing field. It is up to each individual to take advantage of this field to soar to the heights of their visions and their dreams. Those of us who have been successful in our flight should always reach down and pull another individual up. The more we reach down the wider the playing field becomes."

Yes, I could have played this tune on my saxophone, for it was like a broken record that my father played over and over again. This rhythmic prose was not only quoted but also acted out on the Langleys' theatric stage daily.

When the shaking in the arm ceased, Edwin walked over to Krystal, extended his arm.

"Thank you for taking very good care of my Jen. She is my whole life and I need her around a bit longer to keep me straight. If I have seemed aloof lately, it is because I have had so much on my mind. Please forgive me for being distant."

"You are welcome, Mr. Langley, for I love what I do. My purpose in life is to heal those who may be experiencing some medical condition."

"Would you mind having lunch one day so I can formally ask you to forgive my attitude? I am sure you are aware that I asked Stephen to assign another physician from his staff to my wife's case."

"Mr. Langley, that won't be necessary. In my profession, patients are encouraged to get a second opinion or be assigned to another doctor in the office. I have to be professional and mature enough to accept that fact."

"Krystal it is more for me than for you. I am ashamed of my attitude not only for medical reason but also for a personal reason."

"I would love to have lunch with you under one condition, that the participants would include your wife. We will have to wait until Mrs. Langley is dismissed from the hospital."

Before Edwin could respond, Jennifer looked at Edwin and then at Krystal.

"It may be sometime before I am ready to frequent a restaurant. The discussion should be between you and Edwin. When and if it is necessary then I can join you."

"But, Mrs. Langley, I would feel . . ." Jennifer cut her off in the middle of her sentence.

"Edwin and I have had more than twenty-six years of love and affection. I know him and he's trying to free some built up thoughts and discernments that have been learned more than taught. He needs to work through this with you. Enjoy your lunch with Edwin."

"Mrs. Langley, you are healing and progressing quite well. All signs show that you may be out sooner than you think. I will have lunch with Mr. Langley under one condition. After our luncheon, the two of you will dine with me. I know that William has asked me to have lunch with Michael, Nila and he. If there is a friendship growing then I would love to cook one of my Krystal Hervey's special cuisines."

"Yes, if the situation does arise we would greatly accept your invitation. I know you have other patients so I will see you tomorrow."

Krystal placed Jennifer's medical chart back on her bed and typed some information into her portable tablet.

As she exited Jennifer's hospital room, she looked at Edwin and smiled.

"Call me when you are ready to have lunch."

No words were exchange between Edwin and Jennifer. In fact, Edwin walked over to her bedside and pulled her close to his body. The warmth and the fresh smell of his wife helped him be at ease. She was so special and could always calm his distraught with a smile, a wink of an eye or a sight rub of her finger across his lips. He loved this woman, more than words could express. If something had happened to his Jennifer, he would be unable to breathe.

He could not remember how long he held Jennifer, but when he looked he saw a sleeping beauty in his arms. Her soft snoring penetrated his ears and her warm breathing brought some solace to his weary soul. Was he really so uneasy about William and Krystal's pending friendship? Has the world really taught him to look at other ethnicities different even though he had been taught to give all a fair chance?

He doesn't think he had been faking his devotion and affection for his friend, Colby Jerome Miller. Each of them made sure they spoke at least once per week catching up on happenings in both families. In fact Colby and his wife expressed concern over Jennifer's condition and will visit as soon as Jennifer is released from the hospital. His wife Danielle, asked me not to alert Jennifer about the visit because she may get too excited.

Edwin pulled Jen closer to him so that he could hear and feel her heartbeat. She has been the only one who could read his thoughts and give him options about some of his business decisions. His mind wandered to the time he was trying to make a decision about the next VP of quality in one of his companies. I was having a difficult time deciding between two members of my management team that had been with the company for ten years or more. I knew the accomplishments of the best qualified candidate, but some of my top executive managers were whispering things in my ear regarding my candidate of choice. My choice was a hard worker who had been able to increase productivity in two departments, improved customer service statistics, partner with highly effective companies, and rearranged his staffing to pair high achievers with potential high achievers. This manager had a quiet nature, not much on social gatherings and spoke very little about her family. Her focus was on her position and her contribution to the company. During conference calls and management meetings she was not intimidated; she often provided pros and cons regarding a new idea or thought.

One day, Jen saw the wrinkles on my forehead and asked was there an issue at work that was keeping me so preoccupied. I explained my dilemma. I had observed the profession acumen of both candidates and each projected the insight of being able to carry out the duties of the new position. There were only three of us on the executive team who felt that Vanessa was the better candidate. In my mind I visualized the executive team and there was very little diversity, gender and ethnicity. I felt this would be a welcome change and balance. Instead of making a quick decision, Jen suggested that I give both candidates a project to work on related to the new position. They could choose their own staff to work with them and must have a thorough proposal to present to the executive team within six weeks. The components should have been tested, outcomes of the test should prove that the new process/procedure was ready to implement.

There was no question after the presentation that Vanessa's proposal was more superior and her complied raw data showed the outcome of the tested model would yield a tremendous increase in quality and service. My executive board had no alternative, but to accept my decision.

Now I know why my love for this woman grows stronger and stronger each day. She is not only my soul mate but also my helpmate and a keep-me-grounded-mate.

Jennifer stirred in Edwin's arms. "You are still here? I'll be fine, go home and get some rest. I'll see you in the morning." She slightly pushed Edwin toward the edge of the bed.

"You have a luncheon date to arrange with a special person, to help you overcome your fears of losing another one of your children to marriage. I don't think you want an empty nest."

There she did it again. She put another thought in my head—an empty nest or ethnicity. What is the real reason for my uneasiness?

He leaned over and kissed his beloved Jennifer with much passion. "Your clear focus and level head is why I will never ever stop loving you and believing in you."

As he walked out into the fresh air of Charleston, South Carolina, his body was no longer tense, his head was not aching, and his heart had a more normal beat. His obsession with Krystal Hervey had placed undue burdens on him. He had several corporations to keep stable and productive. That was where he should refocus his energy and his thoughts. After the luncheon with Krystal, I am determined to let life have its perfect will.

Jennifer turned over in bed and reach into the drawer of the stand next to her hospital bed. She retrieved the package from the drawer and began to look at it. No one in her family knew she had asked Rosa to bring this package to her. It was her desire to complete the final pages before she was discharged from the hospital. If Edwin only knew the contents of this package would he still have these haunting thoughts about Krystal?

Yes I do need to complete this package so I can be equipped with facts and thoughts to help Edwin move on to a better and more productive place. In a few months he is going to be the grandfather of a child with several ethnicities. I do not want his inhibitions to cloud his role as the greatest grandfather on this earth.

Yes, let me finish this great piece of personal work so I may be the catalyst to ensure my immediate family and my future families are happy and secure in who they are and what they can achieve.

Jennifer looked up toward the ceiling of her hospital room. As her eyes focused on an area that seemed like a reflection of William Sr., her breathing became louder and faster. Her heart monitor went off, and several nurses rushed into her room.

As the nurse checked the monitor, which was now stable, she asked Jennifer, "Are you OK, Mrs. Langley? Did you know why the monitor went off?"

"Yes, I am fine, I was thinking about my accident and the stress could have caused the monitor to react. Thanks for coming in to check on me."

PAST REVEALS THE FUTURE

In removing the book mark from the package, two pictures fell in her lap. She did not remember those pictures being a part of the package. Where did they come from and how did they get there. Then she remembered, Rosa brought her the book and possibly placed the pictures for her to see other members of Edwin's mother lineage. As she looked at the first two pictures she saw so much of Edwin and Bria in the face of the girl and the stately looking lady. On the back of one picture, Rosa had written, a younger Katerina, my mother's oldest child. On the back of the other picture was written, my mother at the age of twenty-two. Tears rolled down Jennifer's face.

Yes, Edwin, you need to become acquainted with who you really are and the strengths you acquired from such a strong and brazen family. Our children have been given the nutrients from the best of soils. Therefore I will never despair over who they will become, for their future has already been outline in the DNA helix of their ancestors. Failure is not an option for them, because each of their lineages has succeeded in spite of the obstacles and the odds.

The third picture was of a younger German male holding the hand of a stately young lady. It was a black and white old photo so I could not see hair color, eye color or skin texture and color. I could see features of both people in Rosa, Jacob, Edwin and my own children. The picture it appeared was taken in front of a school building. On the back was written, my great-great-grandparents in front of the school on their property. It was a little unnerving seeing the past and knowing my children and husband were unaware of their ancestral lineage. It was uncanny that the woman in that picture looked so much like my daughter Bria. They could have been twins.

Jennifer turned to the page of the package to begin reading the final pages. She looked at the handwriting of William Sr. She imagine it probably was difficult for him to remember all of the information his beloved Katerina had shared. She imagined how his mind wandered to remember and how the tears flowed once he remembered.

During their quiet discussions, William often spoke of his love for Katerina and how there has never been another to fill the void of her leaving him. His mistress had come very close to it. In fact he had stated to me that her personality and witty character almost mirrored that of Katerina. Katerina was soft spoken, but very strong in her opinions. His mistress was also strong willed about specific topics. Both were very successful in their business ventures. That is what drew him to his mistress. Whenever he would bring up his mistress, I would sit quietly, but almost never responded in a negative way.

One day, during his fatal illness, William confided in me that he had tried to fill Katerina's void with his relationship with Tessa, but her secrets kept her from giving her entire mind, body, and soul to him.

Tears would fill his eyes when he spoke fondly of his precious Katerina. He felt she was such a free spirit. She loved people and found ways to interact with the many people she employed and those she came into contact at her business. Her millinery clientele loved her and would often recommend additional clients to her. William felt she was not only a good business person but also an excellent people person. Her communication and business skills, something she learned from her aunt, helped grow her business beyond their wildest imagination. They never dreamed that this business would become an international staple.

She looked at the final words on the printed pages, she could feel from the slanting and the shape of the letters that his age and his illness had affected his ability to write more legible. Affectionately she ran her fingers across each of the letters hoping she could feel his presence and his warmth. The cool breeze she felt on the day of Bria's wedding entered the room and slowly drifted across her face. "William I know you are here with me for your presence I feel daily. You were our stabilizer and now you have passed the baton to me. I will try to walk in your shoes. However, it is going to be difficult. Some of my family members have that same stubborn shield that you possessed when you did not want to concede."

She looked up at the ceiling of her room and noticed the bright shadow. Yes, his presence was even in her hospital room.

In her mind she pondered, *Why had William kept this information to himself all of these years, and why did he feel it was necessary to share the day of Bria's wedding?* William had met Marcus months before his death, and his eyes and smile expressed to Bria that she definitely had picked someone he liked. Two days before his death, he reconfirmed to her his approval of her marrying Marcus with his hands and his eyes. In fact he placed both of their hands in his and nodded his head.

She laid her head back on the pillow. This is going to be the longest twenty pages she had every read. It is the ending of a past generation and the beginning of a new one. Can they measure up to the accomplishments of the past generation, will they walk in the humanitarian pathway trodden by their ancestors, will they become inventors, discover cures for several diseases, add to the global markets of their corporations and teach their children that the same hard work and determination exhibited by their forefathers is the same behavior that will keep the Langley family going for generations to generations.

A tear fell from her eyes and she looked around, speaking to no one in particular but the spirit and the warmth in the room. "I am glad I married into this family."

She continued with her reading of the package.

I hope you can read the remaining pages of this package. My strength is getting weaker and sometimes the pen slips out of my hand. I really wanted to finish the contents of this document so my offspring and the next generations will know their family history and be proud of who they are and embrace the blood and DNA running through their veins.

My father did not speak much of his grandparents, but I knew each were of Irish descent. His mother was not married, but was the mother to three other children, Jonathan, Jason and Mildred. Her name was Elizabeth Anne Langley. When I was born, because I favored my grandfather, she gave me his name, William Edwin Langley. She would often say you look so much like him and your personality is so my father. Thus his name has been passed along the Langley generations—me and my son Edwin and your son Will.

My grandmother, Margaret Elizabeth, died shortly after her daughter (my mother) gave birth to her oldest son, Jonathan. My grandfather, who owned a mercantile/bakery business, after the death of his wife, my grandmother, began spending a large portion of the profit on other women and whiskey. Thus my mother Elizabeth Anne took over the daily operations.

There was a secret that my Uncle Jonathan would hint about how his grandfather became the owner of that bakery. My grandfather's family rented the top portion of the bakery from the owner. Most of the family members worked in the bakery for the owner. Something happened with the original owner and the owner's wife. I never knew the real story but it had something to do with the operation of the bakery. The original owner's wife later moved into the bakery apartment with my grandfather's family after the death of my grandmother. When the original owner died, the shop was taken over by my grandfather and his widow.

According to my father, his mother, Elizabeth Anne, learned to feed the family on very little to save money to buy a three bedroom home in the neighborhood and to increase the size of the bakery. She possessed an internal passion and drive for business ownership. Prior to her purchasing the home, the five of them (including the original owner's widow) lived over the mercantile/bakery shop, this often included one of more of the grandparents' siblings.

The mercantile/bakery became a staple in the neighborhood thus providing a number of jobs to the neighborhood residents. According to my uncle, grandfather capitalized on the growing business and began joining business organizations in the area to learn about other business ventures. His ability to interact with those in the business area, paved way for his daughter to build upon their business holdings.

During his turbulent childhood, my father would often hear my grandfather and his mistress arguing. He remembers his grandfather would leave the house and not return for two or three days. His mother and his grandfather's mistress would have to tend to his businesses which now included a mercantile shop, a bakery and a neighborhood grocery store.

On one of his missing in action stints, he was not around when my father's oldest brother Jonathan, arm was caught in one of the bakery machines. Since he was unable to get medical help immediately, his arm was amputated. He was never the same and died when I was about sixteen years old.

I think my grandfather was sorrowful about the loss of his grandson, because he would often bring up the situation with his mistress accusing her of not overseeing the workers in the bakery, after the incident, my grandfather stayed home more but his consumption of alcohol increased.

When my father was attending college, his grandfather died. Several years later, his mistress left and my grandmother never heard from her, thus gaining total control of the businesses. Without any formal education my grandmother used her wit, business and survival sense to keep the business afloat. This was unheard of in the early 1900s.

My grandmother worked hard to keep the grocery, mercantile and bakery businesses successful and growing. She also encouraged each of her children to further their education. As you know, Dad's youngest brother, Uncle Jason, became an engineer and his sister, Aunt Mildred, was a schoolteacher. Uncle Jonathan wanted no part of higher education and continued to oversee the bakery until his death. Only Aunt Mildred had two children, my cousins Jeremiah and Evelyn.

My dad continued in the footsteps of his mother and grandfather in the business world. None of his siblings were interested in the business, so after the death of his mom, he bought them out. Once he saw how profitable the grocery store and the mercantile/bakery were, he began opening other types of businesses, thus our variety of business ventures.

I am sure there is more to the story about how my great-grandfather gained control of the businesses, but I must enlighten you about my mother Angela Olivia Corbett Langley and my little sister Olivia Elizabeth Langley.

As the story goes, my father met my mother at a summer outing at one of his college friend's home. She was the cousin of his friend visiting from Buford, South Carolina. She, too, was a college student studying to become an elementary school teacher. From some of the pictures my father had retained, my mother was a small boned tall brunette with a very sensuous smile. My father often told me she was a chain smoker and showed signs of nervousness when meeting new people.

The two of them exchanged letters and my father often drove to Buford to see her. They wedded the year after each had finished their degrees. My father began to oversee the businesses since his mother was getting up in age. My mother wanted to teach school, but my father felt she should stay at home and have babies. The first four years, no children had arrived due to several miscarriages. My father was distraught over not having a male heir to inherit the business; thus he began to have extramarital affairs.

Because the businesses begin to grow and his name was well-known in the business world, he and my mother would often attend business trips in New York, Atlanta, Los Angeles, etc. Shortly after one of these trips, I was conceived and my father was ecstatic. Even though he now had a male heir, he continued with his extramarital affairs.

Jennifer eyes were getting tired, but she wanted to finish the last ten pages of the package. Again she wondered why had she been the chosen one to learn about William Sr.'s family history. Yes he had given his family a brief history of the family, but not as detailed as the package. She thought about the size of her bedroom suite, which was on the third floor of the estate—how far the Langley family had come. In fact, in retrospect, William Sr. married up since Katerina was born into a more affluent family. She knew she had been truly blessed, but she was concerned about the strange thoughts and attitudes her husband was challenged with due to Will's interest in Dr. Krystal Hervey.

Her eyelids were getting heavy, but she wanted to finish prior to Edwin having lunch with Dr. Hervey. The contents of this package would allow him to reflect on his attitude and to see that many of us in these United State are mixed with different ethnicities and a plethora of experiences and backgrounds. It was puzzling her why Edwin, all of a sudden was so concern with this subject. It had not disturbed him when Bria brought Marcus home. Or had it and he just didn't voice his opinion because Marcus's grandparents and parents had acquired wealth and was able to pass an inheritance on to all of the offspring. Each of them had been very successful in their professional endeavors and their business investments.

His best friend now and in college, Colby was of the same ethnicity. Had he thought about talking to his friend about his reluctant acceptance of Krystal Hervey, or will tomorrow's luncheon bring to light his unjust feelings and thoughts about her?

Jennifer laid the book across her chest and began to drift into a twilight sleep. Her mind focused on her aunt Onnie and how she had been so in tuned to all the people who rented from her and farmed her land. Jennifer had never heard her say a cross word about any of the tenant farmers or other people who lived in the surrounding areas. Even when they were unable to pay off their debts either at the independent grocery she ran or for the renting of the farm, she had the same demeanor when dealing with those issues.

The way she dealt with each individual was based on merit not on ethnicity. Jennifer sat straight up in the bed. A look of wonder engulfed her face. Has Aunt Onnie told me all of the finite details of my heritage? Are there some missing pieces or excluded information regarding the Dusett family? I must make a point to discuss this with Aunt Onnie.

Jennifer tried hard to keep her eyes open so she could continue to read, but due to her pain medication and the tiredness of her body, sleep won out.

The ride home from the hospital to her home went smoothly. Her family made sure that her bedroom suite was prepared for her arrival. Edwin had engaged the services of Nurse Brown, the same nurse who had been Tessa's medical provider.

Rosa was in the bedroom suite adjusting the room to accommodate some medical equipment, Dr. Hervey had ordered. She wanted to ensure that Jennifer would heal well.

After being settled in the room, the nurse advised each member that Jennifer needed her rest; therefore the sons and the father returned to their offices.

Jennifer had tried to continue to read the ending of the package, but each time she opened it, it appeared that sleep won out. The package was sleeping beside her when Edwin returned home from the office.

Edwin walked into their bedroom. He marveled at the natural beauty of his wife even when she was ill and sleeping. Yes, he had a jewel sleeping in the bed with him and he did not want to lose her. She had sensed his confusion over accepting Will's pending friendship with Dr. Hervey. Was he concerned about a statement he had overheard from one of the lawyers in his corporation whom he had considered a good acquaintance? He was not sure but it sure did cause him some concern. He knew that Colby, his good friend from undergraduate and graduate school would never do anything to undermine him. However, such a statement was made in a conversation he was having with one of the attorney's in his corporation. All people regardless of their ethnicity have ulterior motives to sabotage their way into an established business and attempt to take over or destroy if they think the timing is right.

Again, he only caught a little of the conversation the labor attorney was having with an employee who had been counseled several times about using language and descriptions in opposition to the standards of the company. This employee had been suspended for several weeks, but given another chance because of this lawyer's conversation with his manager regarding the skill level and experience of the employee. Edwin thought I need to have my administrative assistant look into this employee's HR records and his performance on the job.

He walked over to the bed and saw the brief that his wife had been reading prior to falling to sleep. Again, the writing looked almost like his father's penmanship, but why would a brief from my father end up in her civil rights law firm? A lot of puzzling things had begun to happen to him; therefore he needed to talk candidly to his friend Colby about his thoughts and concerns. He enclosed the book marker on the opened page and laid the brief on Jennifer's nightstand. She stirred in her sleep and rolled over to see her husband glaring down at her with the sexiest smile she had ever seen.

"How was your day?"

"It was good and eventful. I had a number of conference calls and had to meet with my lawyers and financial staff regarding our last-quarter profits."

"I hope the corporations are doing well"—she winked at him—"since I won't be able to consume my job at the firm for some time."

Edwin laughed out loudly. "No worries, sweetheart, we are not at that point, and I hope we never get there."

"Just checking, because sometimes you men can be so secretive about business matters around your wives, thinking we do not have the same business acumen you do!"

"Please leave me out of that configuration, for I know there are females who can handle more pressure than a lot of the men I've encountered. You, my love, happen to be one of them."

He bent over and kissed her with much affection. As he began to retreat, Jennifer pulled him closer into her and began to explore his mouth and his tongue with such passion that his whole body came alive.

"Whoa, sweetheart, we must take it easy. You are not completely well."

"Edwin, I am recuperating from an accident and the removal of a benign growth, I am not dead."

"I think a little affection from my husband will be a good prescription from the doctor."

"Are you sure?"

"Let's test the waters."

Holding Jennifer in his arms after making passionate love to her had ease his conscience regarding his dilemma. He still was not sure how he was going to approach his luncheon conversation with Krystal. It wasn't that he did not like her, but the overheard conversation from one of the lawyers on his staff had caused him to worry.

"Something is taking your attention from me and whatever it is, I command it to disappear. Tonight is my night to cuddle and snuggle with my wonderful mate."

"Sorry, my mind did wander for a minute. I was thinking about the approach I should use tomorrow when having lunch with Krystal, I mean Dr. Hervey."

"Edwin, this should not be an issue. First of all why would you need an approach, she is only trying to clear the air with you being reluctant with her dating your son and secondly do not insult the young lady by addressing her as Dr. Hervey, she has asked several time that you call her Krystal."

"Do you ever think sometimes you have the right attitude and compassion for a particular situation and you hear a discussion and think maybe your thought and ideals are not normal?"

"Most of the time, you need to consider the source of the comments. Many people give personal comments without considering the facts of the situation. When I am surrounded by a diverse group, I often open up my mental filters. You know the conversation is going to be filled with opinions and few facts and experiences. Those that have merit you file in the 'think about it' section of your mind, and those with no merit you allow the filters to take and dump in the 'I cannot and will not use' container."

"I know, but these off the wall comments, sometimes come from people whose earlier opinion and suggestions have been on point."

"That is true, but sometimes our assimilation and association with others teach us that many of us play the role of Dr. Jekyll and Mr. Hyde. I once read a poem by an African American writer, Paul Lawrence Dunbar entitled, "We Wear the Mask." In your spare time, read this poem, it is true to life for all of us. We change like a chameleon depending upon our intended audience."

"I am aware of everything you are saying that I need to be less closed-minded and hear what she has to say."

"Edwin darling, do not overwork or overthink this. I do not believe that Krystal is losing any sleep over your luncheon date." However, as she leaned toward her husband, she continued, "I do feel that your thoughts of her are taking priority over our quality time together. Bring your sexy and handsome self over here, and let's see if we can replay the last scene."

Edwin awoke with a renewed spirit. He was not going to allow some misplaced remarks cloud his thought pattern and his ability to listen objectively to Krystal's conversation with him.

He had already informed his administrative assistant he would be out of the office all day. She had all of his numbers if he was needed; however, her directions were to either called Michael or William to put out any business mishaps.

Today, he was going to have a leisurely breakfast with his beloved, Jennifer, then call his friend Colby to invite him and his wife down for the weekend. He had not played golf with him for some time and it would do Jennifer some good to interact with his wife Danielle.

Colby was an early riser like him. He usually spent at least one to two hours with his personal trainer before going into the office.

"Good morning Colby, how is your workout going?"

"Good morning, Edwin, I was just trying to catch my breath. My trainer really overworked me this morning. I must let him know that I am not as young as I used to be. I may have to cut this down to less than two hours. OK, Ed, why the call this early in the morning? I hope Jennifer has not had a setback."

"No, but I am calling to see if you and Danielle can come down for the weekend. Jennifer would love to spend some time with her and we can play maybe two rounds of golf."

"Sounds good to me, I will talk to Danielle and get back to you today. I know you are probably rusty with your game so I will try not to beat you so badly."

"You know I always let you win."

"Yes, that what you tell Jennifer, but we know better. How are your children doing?"

"They are all doing well and busy with their lives. In fact Bria is expecting, can you believe twins?"

"Well, being a grandparent is the best thing that can happen in your life. I love mine with all of my heart and feel sad when I have to take them home to their parents. You know we now have four. My oldest son has two sons and my youngest daughter has a son and daughter. My older daughter has had some complications, but we are praying that her last procedure will help her to conceive. We have been discussing adoption with her and her husband."

"I hope you and Danielle will be able to come down for the weekend. There is so much we need to catch up on, especially with our growing families. Take care and hope to see you and Danielle this weekend."

A sense of relief was experience in Edwin's spirit for he knew he could discuss almost anything with Colby without offending him or being offended. As he tied the Windsor knot in his favorite tie, he began reflecting on him and Colby's friendship, a true friendship that extended over thirty-some years. It was a true friendship for they never agreed on everything, but they never let their disagreement hinder their friendship. He wondered what single aspect of their life had kept them true friends for this long.

Some of their upbringing did mirror each other's, and both of their fathers were successful businessmen and entrepreneurs. Edwin and Colby had attended a private all male preparatory school in Massachusetts as well as undergraduate and graduate schools. Each had been expected to become the Chairman of the board for their father's corporations. Was this the reason they were close or did it go deeper than just having status and money.

As he began putting on his suit coat, he thought, it did not. When he met Colby, his thinking was like the rest of the privileged students, Colby and the two other minority students were there on a minority scholarship. Colby would often ask pointed questions in his philosophy, history and humanities classes. His direct questioning on specific aspects was not in a negative way but it made the professors more aware of Colby's analytical and critical thinking abilities. Colby was also an excellent student in math and would most of the time excel in all of his mathematic classes. My main reason for befriending him was to get some help with my math. However, the connection turned into a friendship of a lifetime. Yes, we talked about everything from girls, to social issues, to injustice and hatred, to politics. I remember that Colby was always careful in the way he expressed his thoughts or in the way he responded to my questions.

During our years at the preparatory school in Massachusetts, I visited Colby's home on many occasions, but did not have the courage to invite him to mine. I was not sure how my father would accept Colby as my friend, although he was more than nice to Rosa and Jacob. In fact he had literally helped Rosa and Jacob to improve their own businesses as well as secured some prominent clients for each of them.

Colby had convinced me to attend Brown University for my undergraduate degree. It was not until after our freshman year at Brown that our families met. On this day, I became aware of Colby's environment and all of the same privileges I had experienced, so had Colby. The difference Colby was reared by his biological mother and father. I on the other hand had been basically reared by my father and a nanny until I was twelve, no input from my stepmother Tessa. On this day my father and Colby's father became friends and business associates, investing in each other's corporation. Although Tessa was cordial to Colby's mother, she did not try to form a friendship and Colby's mother did not force one.

After Colby and I finished our undergraduate at Brown, I convinced him to obtain a law degree at the University of South Carolina. Since he was going to acquire the CEO position of his father's company, he needed his chemical engineering degree as well as his law degree.

As Edwin walked out his closet into the bedroom suite, with his mind on his friendship with Colby, a thought came to him: *Wow, I bet Colby's mother knew about Dad and Onnie.*

A shocked look engulfed his face for he had never openly admitted he knew about their relationship, and he hoped that Jennifer was not close enough to hear it.

Yes, he had discussed it with his best friend Colby, and again, he had given him solid advice. It is not your concern and your business, I know it hurts to know about your father's affair and with your wife's aunt, but think how your questioning his behavior may affect not one family, but two. Is it wrong, of course it is! Think about the repercussions that my follow once you broach that subject. You may not know all of the reasons he chose this behavior, but I am sure you know many. Your presence in that environment and household has provided you with enough evidence to see why he chose this path. No it is not the right one, but he has to pay for it.

On one occasion when I was discussing the matter with my friend, Colby asked me this question that penetrated my soul, "How much do you love your wife and family? I'll just let you ponder that while I continue to beat you in this game of golf."

My friend Colby, I do value his foresight, his wisdom, and his candid answers.

Edwin entered the breakfast area and looked directly into the eyes of his beautiful wife, Jennifer. Now he knew why he had kept his knowledge of his father's affair to himself. Last night was magical and even though I know she problem felt pain during our lovemaking, she endured the pain to satisfy her soul mate, me! That is another reason I have kept this knowledge away from her. I do not want to lose her.

Edwin walked over to Jennifer plated a long and intimate kiss on her, their tongues met and taste each other's sweetness, at that very moment he knew the secret would travel with him to his grave. "Did you rest well last night, Jen?"

"Let's just say last night was my therapy for getting well so I can indulge more and longer."

"I can't wait for your full recover, because I have gigantic plans for the two of us."

"How do you feel about your meeting with Krystal?"

"Wonderful, I know I can handle whatever thoughts and ideas she may broach at the luncheon. I decided to go with an open mind, be more attentive to her conversation, listen fully and clarify when necessary."

Jenifer laughed out loud. "Now I know why you received an A+ in Dr. Graham's communication class. Your statement just proved it to me. You just cited the components of a good communicator. Go to the head of your class."

"I did sound like I was reciting a page out of Dr. Graham's textbook. I loved that man's class for it was more than regurgitation, but a demonstration of how those components would work in the real business and professional world. Colby and Danielle were great team mates."

"Speaking of Colby, Danielle called this morning while you were in the shower, they will be here to visit us this weekend. Thanks for inviting them. I needed this, some time to spend with my college friend Danielle. We are going to have a good time catching up while you and Colby decide who beats whom on the golf course."

"You are welcome. Their presence here will help us to concentrate on having fun."

A LESSON IN HUMILITY

As they both sat in silence eating their breakfast, Edwin's mind was still on his luncheon date with Krystal. Should he follow the brilliant steps that Danielle and Jennifer prepared their presentations for each communication project? No he did not need them. He was now the president and owner of the Langleys' conglomerations, why would a meeting with a resident at the hospital have his nerves on edge? I think it has more to do with me allowing the world to have me second-guessing my treatment of others. This hurdle I will conquer even if I have to use some of the components of a good communicator.

"Jen, continue to get some rest, I am going into my home office and make some calls prior to me leaving for my luncheon appointment with Krystal. I'll let you know when I am leaving."

He walked over to Jennifer and placed a kiss on her cheeks and neck before proceeding to his office on the second floor of the southeast corner of the estate.

"Have a good lunch and remember to use your impeccable communication and listening skills."

I could have chosen any restaurant downtown Charleston to dine with Krystal, but I chose the Magnolias on Bay Street for its ambience, its view of the harbor and its cuisine. I loved its freshly made bread loaf, the Tomato Bisque, the shrimp and grits, the pear salad, the fried green tomatoes, the buttermilk fried chicken and its delicious pecan pie. Yes they did have a vegetable plate for those who were watching their intake of calories and of course all types of sea food cuisines. This was the perfect place to take your clients, your wife, a friend or a new acquaintance. I am sure Krystal would love this place.

As I entered the foyer of the restaurant, I looked around to see if Krystal had arrived. I did not see her. The maître d' addressed me by name: "Mr. Langley, good afternoon, may I show you to your table, the one with the perfect view of the harbor. I believe your luncheon guest has already arrived."

Walking toward the table that had been reserved for me I looked at Krystal dressed in a beautiful multicolored dress. She was such a stunning and attractive young lady. Her beautiful coiffured light auburn hair was following down her back. Why was I so afraid of my son building a relationship with this beautiful and stunning lady?

As she saw me approaching the table she emitted a smile that almost had me tripping over my feet and the maître d'. Krystal extended her hand, I took it and did something I had not planned to do, I planted a kiss on and it and said, "Thanks for accepting my invitation."

"You are welcome, Mr. Langley and how did you know this was one of my favorite restaurants? Had you discussed my food choices with William?"

"I am glad this is one of your favorites and it is also one of my favorites. I enjoy the ambience and the food choices here. And don't tell anyone, but I personally know the manager. If this is one of your favorites then I know you are more than familiar with all of the wonderful entrees on the menu."

Krystal smiled as the waitress placed the napkins in both of their laps and refilled her water glass. She watched Mr. Langley as he ordered a bottle of white wine. The waitress departed leaving them in silence for a few moments.

"Mr. Langley, I can understand your concern with me as a recent medical graduate being in charge of your wife's medical care, but I assure you that my focus is always on the best for my patients."

"Krystal, I was concerned about your inexperience. However, Stephen assured me that you would do an excellent job."

"I have this internal feeling that it is more to our luncheon engagement than your apprehension of my medical skills. Does it also have to do with William's attraction to me?"

"Will is my youngest sibling and I am a little more protective of him. I know that Bria and Michael can handle many of life's situations, but, William has been sheltered by his mother and me."

"Mr. Langley, I know he has been sheltered, but I know he is able to handle the perils of life. He has told me about his selfish ways of not finishing school because of his family's ability to maintain him financially.

He has been working hard to complete his BS by this fall and start on his MBA in the fall."

"Yes, that was one of my concerns. I do feel his degrees are necessary to continue in any of the management or executive positions in our companies."

"What is your other concern? His friendship with me may blossom into more than friendship?"

Edwin sort of shifted in his chair, for he did not expect this young lady to get straight to the crux of the reason for their lunch date. He was glad the waitress came with the bottle of wine he had ordered. This would give him time to reflect on his next statement.

There was dead silence at the table as he tasted the wine and provided the approval to the waitress.

"Krystal, I am concerned about Will, because he has never been in a serious relationship and it has taken him sometime to mature into the adult status professionally and personally."

"Mr. Langley, I hope I do not offend you with my response, but Will and I are just getting to know each other and being friends is one item on the agenda. Currently we are enjoying each other's company. Although I like his friendship and enjoy spending time with him, my main focus is on trying to cultivate my chosen profession. My friendship with your son will not affect my desired professional calling of becoming the best oncologist I can be. I have known from my early childhood that I wanted to become an oncologist, working with cancer patients. You see I come from a long line of medical doctors on both sides of my family."

Krystal paused and took a sip from her wineglass. She hoped this would give her the courage to continue with her thought.

"I know you can look at me and tell that I am a mixture of several ethnicities. This may be a reason for your reluctance when it comes to your son's interest in me. I can assure you that once you hear about my childhood experiences, you will understand why you do not have to worry about my motives for forming a friendship with your son."

Edwin needed a sip of his wine before he continued the conversation. He could see that Dr. Hervey also had taken a class in communication. Jen was right remembering the components of a good communicator are very essential for this conversation.

As he carefully placed the wineglass on the table, he noticed the waitress approaching the table to take their order.

"Mr. Langley, are you ready to place your orders."

He looked over at Krystal.

"Mr. Langley, I think we have similar taste, why don't you order for the two of us."

As I watched Mr. Langley give our orders to the waitress, I saw more and more of William in him. In fact, his son William had more of his disposition than Michael. I did not know Bria, but from William's description she was a good combination of his mother and father. From our many conversations, I know that I am about three months older that William, but even if I were younger, he would be my choice of a soul mate. He was kind, compassionate, a good listener, a gentleman, a good conversationalist, witty, and caring. Yes, his father is showing some of those same characteristics.

As the waitress departed, Krystal picked up my wineglass and looked at Mr. Langley.

"Mr. Langley, there is no need for you to be concerned with William's status of maturity. It appears that he has grown up tremendously in the past months and you did not realize it. William and yes he wants to be called William instead of the nickname Will. He feels growing up he was always in the shadow of his two oldest siblings. Therefore he remained in the background knowing the last child usually gets the royal treatment. How do I know? We have discussed his position in the family and how he views himself."

"Wow, I did not see that coming. It appears that the two of you have been having some challenging conversations. Will, I mean William has always been the quiet one and the less out going, so my wife and I never pushed him until lately regarding his academic endeavors, his career and his social life."

"You may be surprised that he and Michael are very close and they do share things with each other. He often allowed Bria and Michael to orally contribute to the conversation pieces for the Langley family after their private discussions. William is his own person and yes we have discussed his professional and personal goals. He admires you, his mother and his late grandfather. He does not want to disappoint you and Mrs. Langley."

"I would say that you and Will have had some heavy discussions. I knew you and he had been on several dates, but he seems to have formed a relationship with you that I would not have guess."

"Yes, we have discussed a plethora of personal and professional items, some I will share and others were for my ears only. Today's lunch engagement is about openness and honesty. Those things I can provide during our conversation."

Krystal took a sip of wine to give her the added courage she needed to continue the conversation, Mr. Langley followed my lead.

"Mr. Langley, I know you are concerned with my ethnicity and your son's attraction to me. I assure you I know what strength, humility and endurance fells like just being a member of the Hervey family. I have had to endure looks, stares and remarks since I was a child. In fact my immediate family has weathered the storm of inappropriate remarks, gestures and stares, not just from strangers, but from other family members."

The waitress approached with our bread and our pear salads.

"It would take me all day and part of tomorrow to relay my story, but I will be as brief as possible. My father's background is a long line of ancestors from Ireland. My mother's lineage is a little more expansive, consisting of African, English, Indian, and somewhere a little Asian. My parents met in school at the University of Pennsylvania, both majored in premed with a concentration in microbiology and chemistry. Each had noticed the other in their various classes but never connected until they were place on a science project together during their junior year. Both of my parents are very successful doctors."

Krystal paused and took a bite of her Pear Salad. She could see Edwin looking at her intently. Inside she was smiling for she knew he was not ready for a history lesson on her family.

"My father's father was the COO of one of the major Oil companies and openly declared himself as a staunch conservative Republican. His wife started out as a professor, teaching Inorganic and organic chemistry. Later on she opened a boutique and began designing her own clothing line. He had wanted her to give up her career, but she was a strong willed person and did not give into to his intimidation."

"So are your grandparents on your father side still living?"

"My grandmother is, but my grandfather died two years ago. He had pancreatic cancer."

"Were you close to your paternal grandparents?"

"I was close to my grandmother, but not my grandfather. He refused to accept my sisters and my brothers in any manner. Our cousins on my father's side often went on vacation with the grandparents and spent more time with them at the summer home in Florida than my family. We had quality time with the grandmother, but the grandfather never paid too much attention to us. Our father had told us it would be hard to crack the exterior and interior structure and attitude of his father, so do not attempt."

"How did it make you and your other siblings feel?"

"During our younger years, it did not seem to affect either of us since we often interacted with our cousins, but as we became old enough to observe the difference, then we began asking questions. In fact, the Hervey family inclusive of my paternal grandmother had quarterly gatherings with my father siblings and their children to ensure there were a connection and a bond. My father's middle sister was a psychologist/psychiatrist who often facilitated the discussions and the interactive role play."

"Do you think those discussion and fellowship with your family helped you to become a whole person and not be antagonist to your grandfather?"

"For me, it helped me to understand my environment and the social barometer I would encounter, but I still felt the void in my life of the love of my grandfather. Not only did he ostracize us, but often he was aloof with his son."

"How do you mean?"

As Krystal took a spoonful of her Grits and shrimps, she looked direct at Edwin.

"I think I was about eleven or twelve years old when I overheard this conversation. The younger offspring were playing on the lawn of my paternal grandparent's home in Virginia Beach. We were playing tag or something like tag. One of my twin cousins Robert fell and broke his front tooth. My mother asked me to find my father and let him know that he and Aunt Kaitlin were on their way to the hospital emergency room.

Walking into the large house, I heard voices coming from the Library. The door was ajar so I slipped in quietly. My father and his father were in a heated conversation. I only heard parts of it, but it has stayed with me to this day."

"What exactly did you hear or thought you heard from the two of them?"

"My father was talking and he said something like, from the day I brought Marcella here as my intended wife you have been so negative to her and to our children. I cannot believe how you treat them in comparison to your other grandchildren. I know it haunts you nightly that your ingrained thought of her and our children have been a false misconception of your upbringing, your environment and your friends whose flaming breath is consumed with prejudice and hatred for those who do not look like them. You would never admit it and I would not want you to pretend to have changed when your heart is still so wicked. You are growing old and one of my children may be the one that you may have to call for assistance."

"You married her out of hatred for me, because you knew I did not want any foreign blood in my lineage. As my eldest son I could not believe that you would be the one to taint my bloodline."

"No, Dad, I married Marcella because I love her and I love everything she represents. Contrary to you, I treat her as an equal, not as someone I could control. As I matured, I often wondered why Mom accepted you telling her what to do instead of discussing the situations and coming to a mutual agreement."

"Is that what she has reduced you do, not being the man of your household?"

"No father, I am the man of my household but it is not a dictatorship, it is mutually working together to ensure we have created a healthy environment for our children. It is far better than the one I grew up in. In fact Marcella and her family has taught me more about a wholesome family than you ever did."

"So you are saying I did not present myself as a loving father?"

"Presents and expensive gifts are not acts of love, just like you do not touch or hug or kiss my children, you never did it to your own. You may have told Mom how much you love her, but never in front of us. Most of the time, we only witness you and Mom in heated arguments."

"Son, why are we having this conversation now and on this day? Look outside at least I let them come over to my home and play with their cousins. I don't need to interact with them. They know I am their grandfather."

"Dad, do you hear yourself, calling your offspring them? Sometimes I wonder if you would have accepted my children if I had married someone from another ethnicity? I doubt it, since you have so much ingrained hatred and misconception, societal poisoning, and media biases regarding people who do not look like us."

"It is not right for you to marry outside of your bloodline. I am disappointed with my eldest son choice of a wife and tainting my blood with another."

My daddy tuned to leave and saw me standing there but managed to say to his father with a shocked look on his face, "I hope before you die that you never find out that your genetic makeup is not as pure as you think it is." He walked toward me and hugged me tightly.

"How long have you been standing there?"

I lied and said, "Just a few minutes. Mom and Aunt Kaitlin took Robert to the hospital. He fell and broke his front tooth."

Krystal picked up her wineglass drank a sip placed it back down. She took the napkin and wiped the tear from her eye.

"My grandfather never acknowledged that I was present, in fact he walked by me and summoned Aunt Kaitlin's husband."

"Before your grandfather's demise, did you ever discuss your feelings with him?"

"No, because I did not feel it would have made a difference. He did make an attempt to see us about six months before his demise. By the time my family and I had arrived he was in a comatose stage not aware of his surrounds. He left all of his grandchildren stock in the oil company and other types of mutual funds. In my card and my other siblings' cards he wrote, 'Love may be demonstrated in a plethora of ways. This is one way.' I still have the card and often look at it to help me understand why my grandfather never attempted to show me and my siblings love."

Edwin retrieved his napkin to wipe his mouth. At this time so much was running through his mind. I knew my grandfather and I had a good relationship him. I cannot fathom how Krystal felt knowing her grandfather's dislike for her was based on her genetic makeup. How can you abuse your own?

I pray this never happens with my grandchildren from Bria and Marcus. You never know what others have experienced and had to endure during their formative years. We only look at surface to form an opinion and a dislike for others. Is this what I am doing to a young lady who has endured a lot from her paternal side of the family?

Krystal notice that Edwin's facial expression had changed and he seemed a little flushed. She was not trying to make him feel guilty just wanted to acquaint him with her environment and atmosphere when it came to her mixed ethnicity.

"Mr. Langley, I know I have provided you a brief description of my growing up in a family where one member's bias, prejudice and racism could have had a negative effect on me. However, I downloaded those negative behaviors on my memory chip as a learning experience to never treat another human the way I was treated and to realize no amount of injustice will hamper my will to achieve success. Not all of my mother's side of the family treated us favorably, but my maternal grandparents filled the voids that I missed with my paternal grandfather."

"I appreciate your candor with me and you have opened some pores that maybe I kept closed for specific reasons. Look at the time, it is almost three, and I am sure you may have another engagement. I really enjoyed our time together. Let me walk you out while the waitress completes our luncheon transaction."

"Thank you for a listening ear, oftentimes one's memory chip needs to be cleared of clutter pasted on it from yesterday's trials, injustices, evil acts, etc. You have provided the forum and the atmosphere to allow me to do just that. Please tell Mrs. Langley that I asked about her and praying for a speedy recovery."

Edwin made his way back to the table just as the waitress brought him the completed transaction. He looked up at the waitress; this was the first time he noticed her the whole evening. She, too, was of a mixed ethnicity and had such a sweet disposition and a lovely smile. Had he been living in a vacuum for the past ten years? The world has change around me and I did not notice. It was Bria's marriage that brought it to my eyes.

He smiled and signed his name on the transaction and ordered a Hennessey with a wet back. It had been a long time since he had this type of drink. Wow, had he been living in darkness all of these years? He did not like the word liberal, he preferred a person who loved and respected all people. He looked at character, behavior, experiences and drives to make quality decision when hiring qualified employees to his many corporations. Had he begun to overlook these amenities and now looking at others bases upon the bias, prejudice and racism that is silently spoken, yet often acted out during important meetings and discussions?

Turning the glass of libation around in the palm of his hand, his mind wandered to advertisements that paint an unreal picture of the fabric of America. He thought, even the media controlled by staunch conservatives paint such a dismal picture of those ethnicities that do not mirror them. The daily news regarding people of other ethnicities portrays only the negative aspects, never presenting a balanced picture.

Those who watched it can only glean from this limited information negative thoughts. Is this the reason I am having this internal conflict? I am putting more credence on social media information than the truth. Sometimes when watching the national news, in my mind I think, *Is this the news or the comedy hour.*

Edwin picked up his drink and gulped it down quickly. He could use another one to clear his head. He motioned for the waitress to bring him another one. This was unusual for him. He can't remember the last time he had Hennessey.

The whiskey sort of masked the guilt he was feeling at this moment. Had he forgotten his father's teachings by surrounded himself with more negative thoughts than positive ones? His father had often counseled him to build his coalition with diversity and not with tunnel vision and thinking. He needed to evaluate his board and assess where he had gone wrong. In fact he had sort of allowed his executive managers to do more of the hiring. It was another reality that his father had counseled him on; it was time for him to put the reins back in his control. Now might be the opportune time to elevate both of his sons to a more prominent status in the company. He also needed to have the same talk with them that his father had with him.

In fact his emphasis will be strictly on hiring practices and diversity. He may need to assess the hiring practice of the top management in the HR department to ensure hiring has been above par. In fact this may be a good position for William to take over and reorganized. The Affirmative Action stance that once helped people of other ethnicity to obtain stellar positions has been eradicated by impractical and unfair governmental conservative laws. Yes, once I review and analyze the makeup of my employees in several of my industries, I will share with my management team on how we can bring parity to certain areas.

He picked up his Hennessey, took a sip and smiled. I will have to be more observant when I make this announcement to see how many of my present top executives' entire persona will change. I am glad I had this luncheon engagement with Dr. Hervey.

Edward motion to his waitress to bring him his check for the two drinks. He wondered if she was working her way through college. If so he could arrange for her to receive an anonymous scholarship. He was an acquaintance of the owner of the chain and had a very good rapport with the manager. All he needed was to get her name.

"Thank you for your excellent service today. And whom do I thank for this service?"

"You are welcome, Mr. Langley, I was told by my manager, Mr. Langford that I should be on my best behavior as your waitress." She extended her hand toward Edwin. My name is Lori Watson and I have been working for this establishment for the past six months."

"Nice meeting you Ms. Watson and I will let your manager know about your excellent service. Are you attending any of the colleges around here?"

"Not yet, but I plan to in the fall. I just completed my application for Clemson and hope to be accepted in the engineering program. I finished high school last year but did not have the finances to enroll immediately. Thank you so much for the Tip it will definitely go toward my college finances."

Edwin left the restaurant feeling as though a load had been lifted off his chest. He was not out of the woods, but at least it was a start toward reassessing his thoughts and actions. This weekend with his buddy Colby and the hitting of the little white ball should begin to help him break through and find the old Edwin. He made a mental note to talk to his community outreach chairperson to discuss setting up a scholarship fund for Lori Watson.

Jennifer was sitting in the Sun Room hoping that Edwin's lunch with Krystal was going well. This attitude of his was haunting her like a room full of bats. If William Sr. had talked to him about his mother and her lineage would Edwin be fighting these demons?

She looked at the package that was lying on the table in front of her. The contents would open up a foreign world to him compounded with his thoughts toward Krystal. I hope he will be open minded and accept these facts or will we as a family have to attend counseling sessions to help us accept the facts of our heritage. I can accept it and I am sure the children will, but how will Edwin react, especially since he is having difficulty digesting Will and Krystal's friendship.

Jennifer picked up the package, she only had a few pages to go and she wanted to finish so she could decide how she would introduce it to Edwin first and then her children.

WILLIAM SR.'S FINAL CLEANSING

As she viewed the last few pages, she noticed that the penmanship of William Sr. was getting less and less legible. He must have written these last few pages days before his comatose period.

He began by stating, Jennifer my arms are getting weak and my mind is beginning to fight forgetfulness. If I repeat anything I have already told you, it's due to the medication and my condition. I know I should have been the one to tell William about his heritage, but each time I attempted, something always got in the way. I tried to live an example of who I was and how I viewed humanity. My actions with Rosa and Jacob and the diversity of my workforce should have sent a clear message to everyone that I believed in treating all people fairly and equitable. In my opinion this was a clear picture.

I know I had other short comings, but when it came to justice for all I tried to portray a very clear and loud voice. I know this is a heavy task for you to perform, but I would not have asked if I did not believe you were the perfect one to handle it. Sometimes I lie awake in my bed and openly talk to a spiritual being higher than me. I have asked for forgiveness of my personal sins and ask that my sins will not be immediately visited upon my offspring. I cannot redo the past, but I can ask for forgiveness and hope my seed will not be tarnished by my pass misgivings.

The story related to my family about the death of my mother and sister Olivia was not the entire story. Yes she did jump out of the third floor of the hotel room due to a fire and yes she had my three year old sister in her arms, but here is the total truth.

My mother was not just a chain smoker. She was also an acute alcoholic and an abuser of prescribed medication. These behaviors came as a result of my father's many affairs with other women and only showcasing my mother around his associates and colleagues during the appropriate times.

While attending a business meeting in Chicago, my father had not informed his mistress that my mother would be attending. Thus an altercation occurred. My mother attended all of the affairs with my father and appeared as the model wife to all. Many of my father constituents knew about my mother's addictions. In fact a number of them had wives whose behavior mirrored those of my mother.

The next day after the confusion with my dad's mistress, Mom drank and smoked a little too much. She had sent Olivia's nanny to purchase her more cigarettes and more whiskey. While the nanny was out, she had fallen asleep, and the burning cigarettes caused a fire on the bedspread and the clothes on the bed. When she awoke and saw the fire, she must have become disoriented. Instead of using the door to escape the room, she thought she could save herself and the baby by jumping out of the fourth floor window. My sister Olivia, named after my grandmother, died instantly. My mother survived three or four days.

It is odd how we deal with tragedy. My father never smoked or consumed any form of alcohol after that incident. That was a small price to pay since his actions caused the entire tragedy. Since I was only twelve at the time and in boarding school, the reality of what really happened did not permeate my brains until I was in business school working on my MBA. I overheard the conversation my father was having with his lawyer about my never finding out the truth about my mother and sister's death. From that day forward, I vowed that I would not follow in my father's footsteps and parade mistresses over my wife. I failed gravely in that area, not with my beloved Katerina, but with Tessa.

Today, as I write the final words to this package, I am aware that my behavior was just like my grandfather and father's. I do not want the rest of the men in the Langley family to follow suit. I was not a good role model for them, so I pray that they observe the love and devotion you and Edwin have for each other and pattern their lives after the two of you.

I know these are my last days and I have purged as much as I can from years of carry a heavy heart. Whatever you do, make sure that my son and my grandchildren and my great-grandchildren do not repeat my pass sins. Teach them to uphold themselves to a higher standard.

My spirit and my love will always be among you and in the walls of this house—no, home!

I know if my beloved Katerina had lived the walls would be dripping of love and unity.

I must digress again for this is where my thoughts and brain are taking me. I don't think I ever revealed the debilitating illness that took my precious Katerina and my beautiful daughter Olivia.

Katherine not only had the gene but had also transmitted the genes for a rare hemophilia disorder unique to French descendants and related to factor X antigens and other scientific terms I could not remember or pronounce. It caused severe bleeding in Katerina and Olivia's body. It appeared that it did not manifest itself in Katerina's body until after the birth of our daughter. She also had a trace of something called Beta Thalassemia, but not sure if it contributed to her illness. This factor can also be traced back to French descendants

Along with the rare hemophilia gene, Olivia was also diagnosed with an acute case of Sickle Cell disease which is common in those who may have African descendants. Olivia's young body was not able to fight off both of these illnesses.

I never fully discussed it with Edwin just told him that his mother and sister died of an acute blood disorder.

Jennifer, you and Edwin will always be my connection from the past, to the present and to the future. I have, through these documents, started the new chain of life to be intertwined with truth, love, forgiveness, honesty, morality, justice, humanity and a belief in self and fellow man.

Yes, I attended church most Sundays with my family. However, I do not think I got it right in this area. Maybe my offspring will do a better job with their relationship to the spiritual one.

I love you and my family. His signature—William Edwin Langley Sr.—was so illegible that Jennifer stared at it for about twenty seconds.

As she closed the book and placed it back on the table she heard Edwin's footsteps coming toward the sunroom. She silently prayed that his lunch with Krystal had been good. If not the finishing of this document had undergird her with the strength the two of them would need to get over this life's hurdle and the next one.

Several months had passed since Edwin's lunch date with Krystal and his rejuvenating weekend with Colby and Danielle. Jennifer's health was improving daily and she had resigned to working three days of the week. Edwin and Jennifer could not be any happier, their daughter Bria and son-in-law Marcus had two beautiful twin daughters. It appeared Edwin and Jennifer was in Columbia, Maryland more than Charleston, South Carolina. Tessa's room had been turned into a nursery for the children and Jacob had rearranged the garden so a Doll house could be built on the estate. This would be a special place for Mimi and her granddaughters to bond.

Michael and Nila was more of an everyday item. Michael was being groomed to acquire his father's position at the corporation. Nila was basically running the civil rights law office and had hired at least two new lawyers to help with the caseload.

How proud Edwin was of William. He had assumed the executive manager's position of the Human Resource Department and had uncovered several unethical and illegal practices that had been enacted in that department. In fact the former executive manager had confessed about these practices and had indicated several executives on Edwin's board of operations. She even had kept the e-mails and the voicemails that helped solidify her confessions.

Edwin smile as he read the briefs from the former executive manager of Human Resources, he wondered why people thought they could get away with illegal practices forever. It is funny that you need to be more cautious and not allow your surroundings to become saturated with people who are not in tune to your actions and ways of respecting others. His father had often told him that diversity keeps you on your toes but make sure you have staff and employees who understand your professional and personal philosophy when dealing with business and people.

He pulled Jennifer closer to him as he and she were snuggled up on the chaise lounge chair in the sunroom. It was specially made for them so both would be able to recline together. He was listening to the soft snoring of his beloved Jennifer. How could he have ever functioned effectively without her in his life? She was nothing like her aunt Onnie. However, Aunt Onnie was needed to keep us all in a thinking mode and not a relaxed mode. It appeared that her onset of dementia had dissipated and her thought process was as sharp as ever. As Jennifer stirred a little his mind reflected upon the weekend with his friend Colby.

"Friend, you have been real quiet. Are you afraid I am going to beat you as I always do? You seem to be in a place where I cannot find an entry point into your thoughts. This has never happen to us. Would you like to talk about it?"

"You could always read my moods. Yes, there is a matter I need to discuss with you. I need more of a sounding board, a listening ear and a realistic response. But I don't need to tell you that. Even in your soft spoken ways, your words are so powerful, even the strongest bow bends to acknowledge your wisdom."

"Why don't we finish this hole, go get some lunch and return to complete our game?"

"After then I will be more refreshed, since I have not been able to concentrate on this game. That is the only reason you are five strokes ahead of me."

"Yes, Edwin, put it on concentration and not the real reason you have become rusty."

I remember walking to the clubhouse, my feet felt like rubber and my heart was racing. I did not want my best friend of over thirty years to think I had become one of those rightwing liberals, thinking that only people like me mattered and the hell with everyone else. It appeared that like Jennifer said, for years I had been walking around with my head in the sand thinking that everyone's views mirrored mine. In fact her question was "Why do you think I opened a civil rights law office?" Then she looked at me and shook her head.

As we got closer to the clubhouse, it seemed like my stride had gotten shorter or the path to the dining room has become longer.

I was still in a fog of disbelief when Colby stated, "Are you going to follow the waitress and me or continue to think how you can improve your game this afternoon?"

"No, my mind was on Jennifer and Danielle. I know they have planned a formal dinner for us this afternoon with the rest of the family. I hope Jennifer does not tire herself out. She is such a perfectionist."

"Don't you worry, Danielle will keep her grounded. I believe your household operations chief, Rosa has everything under control."

I can remember as though it was today, as we both sat down and ordered our meal, I looked at Colby and said, "I just need to confront this head on and I need you to be more open as you listen."

"Confront what, Edwin?"

"My negative thoughts about William's involvement with Jennifer's oncologist, not because she is Jennifer's doctor but because of her mixed heritage. For some odd reason, I accepted Marcus, but I have a huge challenge accepting Krystal."

"Is your challenge regarding your offspring or what others may think? I am sure your colleagues and others have been having these thoughts about you for years, that you have overexposed your family to various ethnicities and your best friend for more than thirty years is of a different ethnicity."

"I believe it is a combination of both. I mean, I am going to love my grandchildren regardless of their mixed ethnicity, but will it affect my interaction with others in the business world?"

"Listen to you, I own a business and yes, it may block a deal you may have wanted to perfect. However, there is always ways to circumvent negative business behaviors and find another interested partner who may bring more to the table then the one you wanted the most.

Think about when you wanted to go global with your textile industry. There were several small textile companies that helped you to get the market moving in that direction in contrast with the larger ones you thought you needed to get you started in the global or international market. Yes they had the contact, but you had the business savvy and the conglomeration of small businesses that had implemented some new research and development practices to improve the durability and the feel of the new synthetic silk and cotton blends.

One of the companies even had a person that was a powerful negotiator, another one skilled in preparing reorganization proposals for international market and another one did an outstanding presentation to the investors on how the integration of these two markets would satisfy the supply and demand for these blends. The merging of those three small companies and placing them under your corporation were a great business decision for you and the small business owners."

"Colby, that's why we have been friends for so long. You always cut through the darkness and bring in the light. I have been in a dark place over my feelings and inhibitions regarding Dr. Hervey, but you placed my thoughts on another spectrum when you brought to my remembrance the skilled integration of the small textile businesses with mine. Those small companies were owned by men of various ethnicities who had done well, but my proposal to them not only helped increase their sizes but also gave them the opportunities to become visible in the global market."

"Edwin, oftentimes we allow the new technology of social media and the convoluted news articles from the various news media penetrate our psyche and we subconsciously buy into the negative because that is all we hear day in and day out. Don't let these false and unscrupulous articles and comments inhibit or ruin a now solid and beautiful relationship with your son. Are you second-guessing what you were taught by your father? The more you show openly your concern due to Krystal's mixed heritage, then the more Will is going to become more involved with the young lady."

"It was an eye opening for me when she related the behavior of her late grandfather's estranged behavior toward her and her siblings. He never told either of them that he loved them and never embraced any of them. He died before he could express such an endearing term as 'I love you' to his grandchildren. I do not want to be in any way like him."

"Then don't mirror his attitude. Do you want William to have a healthy relationship with his family and his possibly intended girlfriend? Then learn to accept the differences and move on. The young lady is secure in who she is, she loves her profession and her wisdom, knowledge, and understanding of others is reflected in her conversation and her actions.

"Face it, Ed, the only negative so far in your eyes is her mixed heritage. None of us are pure. You may be surprised that you are not totally made up of French and Irish blood. Believe me we would not be having this conversation if Krystal with all of her credentials and other amenities looked like Jennifer."

"Wow, are you aware of your DNA makeup?"

"No, and I don't care, I choose my friends and acquaintances not based on heritage, but other human qualities that we all have in common. If that had been the case I would have never befriended you, because you were leaning toward the geek side until you hooked up with me." Colby laughed and then stated, "Eat your food so we can finish our game. We are going to let nature take its course with Will and Krystal's friendship."

I knew Colby would view my reaction as something lite and the behavior could be fixed by me not allowing other's people's definition of a perfect world mess with my psyche. As Colby said to me, "Look at the current fabric and makeup of the people of the world. No one is pure. Each of us has a mixed heritage. Some of us do not want to accept our mixed heritage, nor do we want to grasp the concept that the world's population is changing. Ethnicity is no longer a single factor but a mixture of several ethnicities. Look around you, my friend, those who resemble you, the population base is shrinking and it is a frightening reality for many."

Jennifer opened her eyes and looked at me.

"Have you been watching me the whole time I have been sleeping?"

"Yes, I have and also remembering my conversation with Colby regarding Krystal."

"You really need to bring closure to that matter because Krystal is going to be a permanent fixture in this family. Do you remember the brief or package that I had been reading for some time?"

"Yes, and you would always put it aside when I entered the room. Have you received a ruling on the case?"

"No, not yet, but once you have read it, then we can discuss what are our options regarding the ruling."

"Honey I think your pills are having you talk a little crazy. When have I ever read one of your briefs and helped you out with a case. I know very little about civil law."

"You can definitely help me with this one. You see the brief was actually prepared by your father. His directions were for me to read it first and make a legal decision on how to enlighten the other family members."

"Why can't you just give me an overview?"

"For you to get a clearer picture, you will need to read the entire package."

Jennifer picked up the package off the table. Here, once you have completed the package, then we can discuss the contents. It may help you with the feelings and issues you may be experiencing at this time."

Edwin picked up the package and opened up the first page. He knew it was something strange about the package since it was handwritten and the writing mirrored his father's penmanship. He was not ready for some heavy reading; he just wanted to cuddle up with his wife.

"Jen, I will have to put this on my to-do list. Right now I just want to spend some time with my beautiful wife before the others arrive for dinner. I must have a clear mind especially with your aunt Onnie coming and it will be her first time with the twins."

"Rest assured, I will keep reminding you about the package. The contents will be a powerful eye opener for you and the rest of the family."

"If this package is where my father is cleaning his conscience and his soul about his extramarital affairs, then it can wait, because I know all about his mistress and their extravagant trips. You should have been the first one who read the contents, and I don't understand why you are not angry over the contents."

"For you, Mr. Know It All, it has nothing to do with his mistress, and if you were aware of her identity, why haven't you discussed it with me?"

"I did not say I knew her identity. I said I knew about the extramarital affair for years."

Edwin paused without making another statement; he did not want to reveal the truth about this matter.

"Why should I be upset about his mistress? If your father had wanted me to know about this mystery women he would have told me about her during our late night talks. What are you holding back from me? Do you have knowledge of the mysterious one?"

"Jen, don't make this bigger than what it is. What I should have said is we all knew he has a mistress. Who she is, is probably still a mystery to all of us. At this point it would not matter, because I am sure she is either dead or too old to remember."

"Again, my sweet and wonderful husband, the package on the table has some very important information and its contents may be the pill the doctor ordered for you to help you with your Krystal syndrome."

"Now you are being funny. Yes, you have jokes. Don't worry you have piqued my interest therefore, I shall carved out some time next week to start reading this package. At this moment, I just want to hold the most adorable women in my life, the only woman in my life and the beautiful mother of my wonderful children."

Edwin pulled Jennifer close to him and began to passionately kiss her. He hoped his comments had not caused Jennifer to mistrust him about his knowledge of his dad's mistress. No, he never wanted to open that can of worms, because he would never be able to exist without Jennifer in his life and if he became truthful on this matter, he was sure it would put a strain on their marriage. He pulled her even close and whispered something in her ear. Hand in hand and with a smile on their lips, they ascended the steps to their bedroom suite.

DIVERSITY AT THE DINNER TABLE

Edwin felt like he was in a twilight, but he saw the cloud and he heard the voice. He looked over to see if Jennifer was aware, but all he heard was her light snore. He sat straight up in bed as the cloud and the voice came near.

"I am the seed of the Nile. I have bred new and distinct cultures all over the world. Humans have tried desperately to break my power, but that ability was only given to the one who is greater than you and I.

Yes, I have been bred many times over and each time my characteristics, my personality, my strength and my determination still hold dominance to the hybrids of this world.

The seed of the Nile is so very strong that it will never, never dissipate for I will surface in the next generations to come. I am powerful, I am unbroken, I will not be forgotten. I am the seed of the Nile. My cells will always be ingrained in all people."

It disappeared as quickly as it had appeared.

The sweat was pouring off Edwin's brow. What had just happened here? He looked at the clock it was a little after 5:00 PM and the dinner guest would be arriving soon. Jennifer must be already up and dressing for he did not see her in the room. Had she attempted to awake him from the dream or the nightmare? He was not sure which one it was.

Whatever happened, I will keep it in my heart and mind. It may be an omen that I need to read that package from my father.

Edwin wiped the sweat from his brow, refocused his eyes and started to the bathroom to begin preparation for the dinner party. He felt that the hot steaming water from the shower would clear his thoughts to make him more alert for the conversations around the dinner table.

Immediately he looked back at the package sitting on his nightstand. There was something spooky about the cover so he could not imagine what the contents contained. What did his father need to reveal to him about the family and the business? I hope it a cleansing of his soul related to his treatment of Tessa and his extramarital affair. Even if it were, what was so puzzling is why he had chosen Jennifer to read the contents before him.

As he walked toward the bathroom, he tried to focus himself, but the book seemed to be pulling him toward it. Again he felt the wind on his face a voice sounding like his father's. "It can wait until tomorrow for what you are about to read you need to have a clear head and an opened mind."

Edwin turned toward the voice and he could see a silhouette of his father leaving the room. He knew he would have to take a couple of days off work to see just what information his father had transcribed in the package.

To no one in particular, Edwin said, "I need to clear my spirit, my thoughts, my facial expressions and my ideology regarding Krystal. I do not want my internal feelings and my thoughts to put a damper on this dinner party. I have to remain focused because Aunt Onnie is coming and even though she's nearing eighty, she is still sharp and alert."

Jennifer walked into the room looking more beautiful and stunning the day he met her. He often wondered how he had captured such a charming and intelligent young lady. Even though he felt he was handsome and smart, there were others on campus that had eyes for Jennifer, she often expressed the others were friends but there was a different bond she felt for him.

"My don't you look lovely, I may not let you out of this room for this dinner party."

"Stop joking around, and why is it that you are not dressed? Some of our guests have already arrived."

"Sorry, I got involved thinking about a proposal for one of the businesses and time just slipped away."

"Was it really a proposal or the contents of the package? Whatever, you need to hurry up. I left Aunt Onnie with the guests and you know how she talks. She can amuse them for hours or she can put them to sleep. I will lay out your clothes, now hurry and take your shower. Oh, William brought Dr. Hervey as his guest."

"You think you know me well. It was the proposal and not the package. Whatever my father wrote will get my undivided attention after the dinner party. I do not want anything to interfere with this night. I will be on my best behavior even with Dr. Hervey."

"Then to whom were you speaking when I entered the bedroom? Was there a breeze that crossed your face and a voice that sounded like William? I bet you even saw his silhouette leaving the room once he ceased speaking to you."

"Jennifer you sound so spooky about this package. Why don't you go rescue our dinner guest from the jaws of Aunt Onnie and I will be down in less than twenty minutes. Have Colby to prepare drinks for the guests."

Edwin leaned over kissed Jennifer on her cheek.

"Just because we've been together thirty years or more, you still cannot read my thoughts or my actions. Now Mrs. Langley, go entertain our guest."

Edwin walked into the shower with a surprised look on his face. How did she know about the cool breeze and the voice? Did Dad come to her while she was reading the package?

He felt that this reading may be more complicated or hard to ingest and swallow than he could imagine.

He turned the shower on adjusted the jet sprays to pulsate heavily on his aching muscles. Yes this is what he needed to clear his head and have a mind free of the contents of that package.

As he descended the stairs he could hear the chatter of the guests in his father's study. He wondered why they had congregated there instead of the sun room.

Immediately his eyes focused in on Krystal who looked radiantly in her pale blue cocktail dress. Will's arm was resting on her bare right shoulder and both seem to be enjoying the other company.

Colby walked toward his friend and handed him a dry martini.

"Look like you could use this before you meet your dinner guests. Sip it slowly as you mix and mingle with each of them and I am sure it will calm you down. I made it just like you like it."

"Thanks Colby. I am familiar with all of the other people here, but who is the gentleman talking to Aunt Onnie?"

"Oh, I forgot to tell you, I was bringing a friend of mine. That is Jonathan Wesley, one of our retired corporate lawyers. He and his now deceased wife moved here from Massachusetts almost five years ago. He has been widowed almost two years. His wife died from stomach cancer.

I thought he would be good company for Aunt Onnie and my thought was correct."

"We don't need any match making from you Colby."

Edwin walked farther into the room. Clearing his throat, he said, "Good evening, all, welcome to my home and please forgive me for being late to my own dinner party. I know each must be hungry, but let us lift our glasses and toast to friends and family and long-lasting relationships."

As the guest followed him into the dining room, he thought Colby has always been there to rescue me. His dry martini has calmed my nerves and will help me be myself tonight.

The dinner party went off without any slip ups by him. He was attentive to all who was in attendance. He looked around the dinner table to take in the atmosphere of the guests: Bria and Marcus were beaming with joy about their twin girls; Michael and Nila were looking forward to their wedding in the next year; Colby and Danielle were ecstatic that their youngest son Andre had announced his engagement to a wonderful investment banker; William and Krystal looked as though their relationship was blossoming; Aunt Onnie had been especially quiet for she was enamored with Jonathan's charm, wit, and his undivided attention to her and Jennifer; and I were just delighted to be among family and friends.

As the guests begin to leave, I asked Aunt Onnie, would she like for my driver to take her home or was she staying over tonight?"

She looked at me with a smirk and a smile. "Thank you, Edwin, but Jonathan has offered to see me home." She winked and stated, "You may be seeing him again at the family gatherings."

Marcus and Bria left ascending the stairs to the third floor guest room, Michael and Nila said their goodnight as well as William and Krystal.

As Danielle and Jennifer walked toward the Sun room, Colby caught his friend's arm.

"You were not your usual self tonight a little more reserved than I have seen you. Is there something bothering you besides the relationship of Will and Krystal?"

"There is, but this is not the right moment to discuss it with you. There was a package my father left for Jennifer and me to read. Jennifer has already read it and has given me a deadline to finish it. I am unsure of the contents, but I feel uneasy about what I may discover about some dark Langley secrets and my father's unfaithfulness to his second wife."

"In that case, I think you need to isolate yourself from familiar surroundings and read the package. It may also give you some insight on why he allowed Jennifer to read it first."

"The reason I was late to dinner, I thought I heard my father's voice as well as his silhouette in my bedroom. It was an eerie feeling because I also experience a gust of cool wind flowing over my face."

"It may be true that our deceased loved ones come back to help us when we are burdened with making personal or business decisions. On many occasions when I have had a dilemma on making a business decision, Dad either comes to me in a dream or I audibly hear his voice telling me what decision I should embrace."

"I have heard from others that the dead are aware of the living and comes to assist when there is a crisis in their life. This is not a crisis, but I do need some clarification and some questions to be answered regarding this package and why now."

"Well Edwin, whatever is in that package, I am sure your father's elucidation will make it clear. He was not one to beat around the bush. He was always a straight arrow man. Let's go join the ladies and when you need to talk again, there is text, Twitter, Skype, or the phone"

"Colby you always reminded me of my father's personality, he was short on words, but their meaning lingered in your head forever. You get right to the point to avoid inferences or unneeded clarification."

"OK, you two what type of travel plans have you made for us. Danielle and I think we may want to explore the Greek Islands again. What about a Mediterranean Cruise? We can spend one week on the Santorini islands and several days on the Mykonos and Symi islands before returning home. We had such a peaceful and beautiful time the last time we visited there."

"We were not really planning a trip. However, Jen, why don't you and Danielle make the travel arrangements, and Colby and I will follow your plans?"

"Since each of us have almost handed the baton over to our offspring, I know Edwin and I can spend at least two weeks in the Greek Islands."

"Sounds wonderful to me, I have been working part-time since my accident and diagnosis and I know Danielle must have a lot of vacation time at the hospital. We will make it happen."

Colby placed his arm securely around his wife's waist and they ascended the stairs to the east wing guest room.

Jennifer brushed her lips over Edwin's and winked.

"A week or two in Greek should be an ideal place for you to read your father's writing and understand his reasons for writing such a document."

Edwin smiled but he silently felt that he was set up by Jennifer. The vacation was a way to get him away from his familiar terrain so nothing would interfere with him reading the package.

He kissed her very affectionate and guided her gently to their bedroom suit on the west wing's third floor. He knew he should have drunk another one of Colby's dry martinis because it was going to be a long restless night.

As soon as he entered the suite, he felt the cool breeze flow over his face and it appeared that someone's spirit has entered the room with him and Jennifer. He froze in his track and surveyed the room with his eyes. There was no one there but him and Jennifer.

Jennifer saw the bewildered look on his face and smiled. She knew that William Sr. presence had startled Edwin. Just as she began to enter her closet to change for the night, she knew William's spirit was there for she also experienced the cool breeze flowing over her face.

Softly she said, "It is arranged, he will read the package and learn more about his heritage and why his recent thoughts should no longer haunt him. In our world today, few people can claim complete purity. We are all mixed with several ethnicities. As the poem goes all of us have some of the Nile ingrained within our DNA. I hope that my husband can accept these facts and move on with his life. I will be here to support him until he becomes comfortable with knowing who he is chemically . . . a very potent bloodline."

THE GREEK ISLAND VACATION

The vacation to the Greek Islands could not come fast enough for Edwin. He had done nothing productive at work for the past three weeks. In fact he had done more soul searching than working. He had delegated a number of issues to his sons and to his department heads. Even though he had reviewed them, he was not going to sign off on them until he had completed a thorough and detail review.

Edwin prided himself in being a detailed, organized manager, but for some reason these past three weeks he was unable to concentrate. He looked at his father picture that hung over the beautiful leather wingback chair in his office. This man had taught him all he needed to know about being savvy and wise in the business arena; however, he had disclosed some of the skeletons in the Langleys' closet.

He picked up the phone to call Jennifer's best friend who was a psychologist. He felt he needed to speak to someone after he finished reading his father's confession of his sins. He placed the phone down; no, he would rather speak about this situation to someone who was not a friend of the family. He needed an unbiased and frank opinion. Maybe he should just wait until after he had read the entire package before contacting a psychologist. In fact he would not tell anyone including Colby that he plans on seeing a psychologist after he finishes the package. His inability to handle the contents of the package would never be revealed to his family or his friends.

Edwin decided that he would find a secluded place on the Ship while it was sailing to the first island Mykonos to begin the reading of the package. He had already informed his wife and friends that he wanted to take in the sites of the coast of Greece before they docked at the first port or island. Each had been OK with his schedule for the day. They would all have breakfast, lunch, and dinner and maybe after dinner visit the lounges or the casinos.

On the plane to Athens, Edwin began to read the beginning of the package, he chuckled and laughed out loud as his father explained to Jennifer why she was chosen and how the penning of this information had helped him release some of the sins and anger he had been harboring all of these years.

He looked over at Jennifer who was sleeping soundly in the first class window seat. To no one in particular, Edwin stated, "I know you did this to clear your conscience, but did you remember to ask God for forgiveness for all of your years of infidelity and adultery? Knowing you, you put it more in the form of a business decision than a humble request."

Jennifer stirred in her seat but did not awake. At that point, the cool breeze that he had felt in his bedroom suite at home now flowed gently over his face and he was sure someone was standing behind him with their hand on his right shoulder. When he turned around to see if Colby was standing next to him there was no one there. In fact Colby was still in his seat, very involved in the reading of a historical novel, *The Warmth of Other Suns*, by Isabel Wilkerson.

He turned his attention to the window of the plane and inhaled as he looked at the beautiful ocean and beaches and they began to descend into the Athens airport.

"Dad I know your spirit is here with me on this plane as I read your account of cleansing your soul, but give me time to get to the crux of the content and then you can visit me. I do not need any distractions while I am reading this package."

It appeared that as soon as he made that statement, he felt the breeze dissipate and the heavy hand was lifted from his shoulder.

Edwin continued to read the package as the plane continued to descend. It was amazing how his father could see all of the reasons why his relationship with Tessa went sour and how he did or did not feel any remorse with his infidelity and his mystery lady.

He kept mentioning it was a way to cleanse his soul. Then he changed directions by stating that this document was more about my mother Katerina and her heritage. He had provided some information to his immediate family, but not the most intricate details.

His writing explained a little bit about the paternal bloodline of the Langley family. Then he change gears and started cleansing his soul again.

He spouted on about his relationship with Tessa and how it was not his intent to hurt her. He did not love her like his dearly beloved Katerina, but felt she would be a good mother to me, his son, since Tessa was so good with the babies and small tots in the children's wing of the hospital.

The interesting part was an account of how my father met my mother and her aunt. I never met my great-aunt but was aware that she reared my mother from age ten to age twenty-one when she met my father.

I could infer from the writing that my father was not in the best of health for he often started a piece on my mother and then switched to either Tessa or his family.

I was aware of this part that my mother's father was from France and he met the granddaughter of a renowned hybrid scientist while he was visiting his farm and laboratory in Hamburg, South Carolina. The city, Hamburg, no longer exists. I think it was dissolved in the late 1930s.

What was interesting was how my father's memory went from him meeting his beloved Katerina and her aunt to an account of a rare blood disease that took the life of both my mother and my sister Olivia. I knew my mother and sister were ill, but I was not aware of the medical reason for their demise. Maybe he wanted his family to know about this disease and we should all be checked since it may be an inherited illness.

But now the document was taking a new twist for he had begun to tell the story of my mother's great-grandfather and his obsession with creating hybrids for animals and plants. My great-great grandfather's obsession with this technique had made his father, my great-great-great grandfather a rich inhabitant of Hamburg, South Carolina.

Edwin sat straight up in his seat on the airplane. The plan had just landed and was taxing to the gate. He wanted so much to continue with his reading but he knew he had to put a mark in the document so he could deplane and get to the hotel in Athens.

As the first class passengers begin to deplane he secured his computer case and slipped the package into the side pocket. He extended his hand to Jennifer to help her out of her seat. He had already retrieved their two small carryon bags.

Once inside the airport, they noticed the limo driver holding up the Langley and Miller's name. Edwin thought Jennifer and Danielle did an excellent job of planning this trip. They included minute details that Colby and I would have overlooked. It was a joy to see the limousine driver holding up a sign with the names: Langley and Miller. This minuscule detail will ensure we get to the right place and rest before we begin our tours in the city of Athens.

While the limousine was traveling toward the hotel in Athens, each of them pointed out the beautiful sites of the inland of Athens as well as the coastlines. Their hotel was built on the coastline of the Mediterranean Sea and their suites overlooked the adjoining seas with a view of the many beautiful building.

Entering into the Hotel suite, Jennifer observed the beautiful welcome package on the large king-size bed, the beautiful floral arrangements and the small table adorned with snacks and a chilled bottle of wine.

At the moment all she wanted to do was take a hot shower and rest before they prepare for their lunch and the first set of tours to points of interest in Athens. They would be in Athens for two days before boarding the ship to several islands along the coast of the Mediterranean Sea.

The couple enjoyed the two days stay in Athens. During those two days they had visited the following Greek historical sites: the Parthenon, the Temple of Poseidon, the National Archeologist Museum, the Temple of Olympian Zeus, as well as several Greek restaurants and wine tasting at Ancient Corinth and the Papagiannakos Winery.

Edwin was excited about boarding the ship the day after their tour of the Acropolis Museum. He had fought off the urge to miss some of the tours so he could get back to reading the package. However, this one day at sea until they get to the Mykonos Islands will give him the opportunity to learn more about the Hamburg and DuPont families. Although it was only a five hour trip from Athens to the island of Mykonos, the ship would stop at several smaller islands before continuing on to the island of Mykonos. He was still a little confused as to how these families were the bloodline of his mother Katerina.

After breakfast, the others begin scattering to find some activity or adventure to explore on the ship or they could tour the small island where the shipped had docked. Edwin had announced that he was going to find a chair on the deck and inhale the sea air and visually take in the beauty of the coastline on the way to Mykonos.

Jennifer smiled and kissed him passionately on his lips. She knew he was anxious to get back to reading the package.

As he settled himself on the deck next to the area where people were swimming or sun bathing, Edwin opened the package to the place where he had placed his book marker.

At this spot is where when he began reading about how his great-grandfather (at this point did not realize the connection) met his great-grandmother. Adolph Hamburg matriculated at the University of Georgia School of Agriculture and Environmental Science to learn all he could about Horticulture and Animal life. While there he met a young lady by the name of Mary Elizabeth DuPont and her attendant Helga DuPont a Creole/mulatto from Biloxi, Mississippi. It appeared that Adolph was interested in the young lady, Elizabeth who was confined to a wheelchair since the age of five. After becoming acquainted with the two young ladies he discovered that Elizabeth's father was a large contributor to the school and had gotten permission for Elizabeth to attend the school even though women could not officially enroll in the school. The attendant was Elizabeth's half sister and was four years older than she.

The story continued to unfold to reveal that Adolph was really enamored with Helga and not with Elizabeth. Although he spent time with both women, his full attention was on Helga. During Adolph's interaction with the women, he learned that Helga was a much better student than Elizabeth and wrote most of Helga's compositions. Once Adolph and Elizabeth had completed their four years at the University of Georgia, Elizabeth asked Adolph to request to her father to allow her and Helga to visit his farm in South Carolina to learn more about his hybrid experiments. Elizabeth's father agreed and all three of them traveled to Hamburg, South Carolina.

Edwin smiled as he read this account for he was so sure that Mary Elizabeth DuPont and Adolph Hamburg were his great-grandparents. However, the story took a sudden turn and Edwin was surprised to see that upon their arrival to the plantation, Helga discovered that she was pregnant.

Edwin had to reread this section more than once for it was not clearly registering in his head that his great-grandmother was a product of a mulatto slave and the Plantation owner. He thought that maybe Helga had gotten pregnant by another male slave attendant assisting his owner or the owner's son.

He wanted to continue to read to discover if his interpretation was valid, but his eyes were not only tired but also burning from the continuous reading of the document.

Edwin looked out into the beautiful blue sky with very little cloud covering. The blue in the sky match the perfect blue of the water and the sunshine revealed how crisp and clear the Aegean and the Mediterranean seas were. He looked at his watch to see if it was nearing lunch time. He really was not hungry and he wanted to learn more about the DuPont Hamburg DeBeaux family. It was eleven forty-five by his watch and they were to meet in the VIP dining room for twelve thirty. He thought that's good I still have at least another thirty minutes before I need to leave and find the dining room.

As he opened the package up to the point where he has cease reading, he heard his name.

"Edwin, it's close to the time for us to meet the ladies for lunch. Are you enjoying the contents of the package? I just know you did not bring work with you on this trip."

"Hi Colby, this has nothing to do with work. It is a document my father left for me to read prior to his demise and I have been procrastinated long enough on reading the contents. I thought the air and the sea breeze would open up my head and I would be able to soar through this document with the greatest of ease. I must say there are some very interesting and intriguing points in this document."

"Well put a marker in the point where you left off, we can go by your cabin and leave it there before we attempt to find the VIP dining room. You have a smirk and a smile on your face was your father attempting to confess his sinful ways to you?"

"I guess while he was bedridden with cancer his mind must have thought about his behavior over the past thirty –five years and he wrote this document per his words as a way to cleanse his soul."

"Have you gotten to the part where he reveals his mystery lady? Did he paint you a clear picture as to why he felt it was necessary to have her all of these years? However, there is one thing I often wondered. With all the money your father had, why didn't he just divorce Tessa, give her a settlement, and go on with his life?"

"I have not gotten to that point, but it seems that it was a bit more complicated than just a divorce and a settlement. There was a prenuptial agreement, but remember Tessa had her own dowry and really did not need a lot of Dad's money."

"Hey here are our suites. I am going in to take a quick shower since I have been to the gym, the sauna and the swimming pool. Let's meet here in the next twenty-five minutes."

"Sounds like a plan to me. See you in twenty-five minutes, Colby."

"As Edwin entered the room, he thought, I should be a little more selective in revealing to Colby what is in this document. If there are incidents and information I do not want anyone to know, I have to be cautious with my comments."

Edwin took a quick shower and put on a fresh short set. He was feeling a bit sentimental after looking at his father's handwriting and reading part of the document.

As he stepped outside of his suite, he glanced up and saw Colby exiting his and Danielle's suite. He had to chuckle. Not only was his friend handsome as the women during their college days had often said, but at fifty-seven years old, he had not aged and his body was buff and tight. He smiled, I must find me some me time so I can stay as fit as my friend. No one would believe that Colby is fifty-seven years old, has a full head of hair and very few gray strands. I will be turning fifty-seven soon. However, Colby is about five months older than me, my hair is thinning, and the gray has practically taken over.

As we began walking toward the elevators to go down to the dining room, two younger ladies passed us smiled and continued to look back at us. Colby and I did a fist bump and together said, "I guess we still have that sex appeal."

"You are just a little more buff than me, but yes we are still turning the ladies heads. Remember when we had our choice of dates on Brown campus, but you only had eyes for Danielle."

"Really you cannot talk, once you were introduced to Jennifer, you did not look at another woman on campus. Your nose was more than wide opened."

Colby lightly touched Edwin on his shoulder. "Do you remember the young lady, Brenda Ward in our communication class? She tried everything in her power to capture your attention. She even volunteered to be your partner for the special communications project."

"Yes, I knew she was hurt when I told Dr. Graham that I had already started my project with another student in the class. In fact after class she walked up to me and asked me why I didn't want her as a partner. I just told her I chose my partner the week he provided us the syllabus. She was never the same after I rejected her advances."

"Look, there are our beautiful better halves over by the dining room door. Why are they holding up their arms and pointing at their watches?"

"I would say because it is one instead of twelve thirty. Let's pretend we thought they said one."

Together each walked up to their wife, planted a kiss on the cheek, and stated, "We made it on time. We are starving, so let's go and dine."

Both ladies just shook their heads and walked arm in arm with their husbands.

Out of the corner of their eyes Edwin and Colby saw the two ladies that had passed them in the hallway. In fact their table assignment was directly across from theirs. They tried to make eye contact but both Edwin and Colby remained focused on their prospective wives.

During the serving of the dessert, one of them became brave and walked over to our table.-

"Good afternoon, my name is Helena Goodman and extended her hand toward Danielle. I saw the two of you playing bridge today and it appears that you are furious partners. My friend Susan Webb and I would like to challenge the two of you to a bridge game. I hope that is OK with the two of you."

Danielle was amused but with a straight face she stated, "It is very nice meeting you Ms. or Mrs. Goodman, but we have a number of activities planned with our husbands and if we find some free time, I will contact you."

"Thank you Mrs., I did not get your name."

"I know because I did not provide it. If my friend and I decide to play bridge with you we will contact you. Especially since your assigned dining room table is across from us."

Everyone at the table smiled after Ms. Goodman face dropped and she returned to her table as a rebel who had lost her cause.

Jennifer looked at Edwin and Colby.

"What was that all about? I do not remember the two of them in the room playing bridge. We won a lot of games and rotated to several tables. If they had been there playing, I would have noticed them."

"Jennifer you should not filter too much into this. I believe the lady was trying to show her hand. When Colby and I were on our way to meet the two of you, they passed by us in the hallway. They looked and smile but did not speak."

"She had a lot of nerve coming over to our table. With Danielle's response, I bet she will not try that again."

Danielle bumped fist with Jennifer and then looked at Colby and at Edwin.

"You know that the two of you are handsome and she was really letting the two of you know she was available."

Colby looked at his wife and with a broad grin he stated, "Do you really think we are interested, we have the best looking women on the ship."

"Let's take a stroll around the deck of the ship for in a few hours the ship will dock at the island of Mykonos."

During their walk each began to point out possible events and activities of interest on the ship. All of a sudden, Jennifer began to laugh uncontrollable. Everyone looked at her. She pointed toward an area near the third deck pool. It was the same two ladies whom they had encountered in the dining room. They had changed into some very skimpy swim suits and had cornered two older gentlemen in a very seductive manner. At that point all of them began to laugh. It was obvious that the two of them came on this cruise to catch men of prominence.

Danielle looked at her husband. "I wish I was evil. I would have a little fun with them. Jen, do you remember the girl Brenda, who had eyes for Edwin? She loathed you, and you were not even moved by her haughty and inhumane actions toward you."

"Ms. Danielle, you can talk! What about Regina Patton, who told you how she was going to take Colby from you?"

"Look at us now. We are still with our first love. If you don't play the game with the black widow spider, you'll never get caught in her web."

Edwin was enjoying the small talk as well as the reminiscing of things that happened during their time together at Brown, but his mind kept gravitating to the document. His interest in the contents of the package was really piqued.

The four of them entered the casino of the ship. Edwin was not really interested in gambling, but he needed to play along with them until he could disappear and start back reading the document.

Jen and Colby headed for the Black Jack table and Danielle and Edwin decided they would only play a short time at the slots. They were to meet back in one hour at the cocktail lounge across from the casino. As Danielle sat down, a young woman approached her.

"Good afternoon Dr. Miller, my name is Shannon McCullers. I have read so much about your work regarding the premature babies you have saved at Hampton Medical Center in Massachusetts. In fact I am reading your latest book and if you don't mind, I would love for you to autograph it for me. I have a number of mothers I see professionally due to the death of their child, or children born with specific medical condition or defects. Your books have helped me tremendously in my work. I am a clinical psychologist from Sumter, South Carolina, not far from Columbia."

"Dr. McCullers, it is a pleasure meeting you. I would love to autograph your book."

"Please call me Shannon and here is my card. On the back I will give you my personal cell phone number so we can meet either at the next port or on ship so I can get your autograph."

"Oh, thank you and please forgive me. This is a very dear friend of the family, Mr. Edwin Langley. Mr. Langley, this is Dr. Shannon McCullers."

Edwin extended his hand to Dr. McCullers.

"Nice meeting you, Dr. McCullers. I would love to have one of your cards. This may become handy for some of the workers at my factory who often need counseling related to family, work, and medical situations."

"Certainly, Mr. Langley, even though my practice is in Sumter, I do have small satellite offices in Charleston, Summerville, Kingstree, and Hollywood. It's ironic because I do work with a number of HR personnel with referrals from their companies. I would love to get some referrals from one of your conglomeration of businesses."

"Shannon reached into her purse and handed Edwin several of her business cards. If your HR staff needs additional information from me, please have them to call me."

As she turned to leave she looked over her shoulder.

"Hope you will have better luck on the machines than I did."

Together they both said thanks.

"She seemed like a nice young lady with a real cause, I will alert my staff about her and probably work up some type of agreement to use her exclusively for our company."

"You can do that Edwin, but remember you live in South Carolina and no matter how good you are in your job, some of your workers may not want to discuss their personal situations with a person of another ethnicity."

"Danielle, I have been friends of you and Colby so long, that thought did not enter my mind. I still will discuss her with my staff and see how we can incorporate her into our employees counseling packages."

"Sounds good, now let's win some money on these slot machines."

Edwin played a little at the machine, but he was more elated as to how fate had just played into his hand with the Dr. Shannon McCullers. He did not need to look for a clinical psychologist one had just walked into his life. He knew just from reading portions of his father's document he may need the help of a clinical psychologist to help him understand the whys, the hows, and the what-ifs. It still puzzled him as to how he did not have a problem accepting Shannon as a possible counselor for his workers, but he could not cope with William and Krystal's involvement. He would hold on to her cards for a little while before he distributes them to his HR staff.

Edwin placed another five dollar bet into the machine and several bells and whistles begin to go off. He was not conscious it was his machine, for his mind was still on his father's document and Dr. McCullers.

Danielle walked over to him and put her hand on his shoulder.

"For one who did not like the casino, you just won the jackpot. I cannot believe it you hit the jackpot my friend."

Edwin looked at the machine with much amazement and it finally clicked in, he had won the jackpot on the five dollar slot machine.

"I bet Jen and Colby have not done this well playing poker. Let's go and show them."

"We can't until the attendant cash you out and then we can show them your winnings. I am sure Jen will use it to buy some souvenirs when we dock at Mykonos."

Playing the slot machine had kept his mind free of the document, but he would have to find some time tonight to sneak away to read more of its content. Maybe if he pretended to be falling asleep in the jazz concert tonight, Jen will take him back to the suite early. He smiled to himself as he neared the cash out window. That sounded like a good plan to him.

In fact, Jen and Colby may be tired since they had ventured off the ship after his win in the casino. In fact, the ship had docked at two smaller islands before the final dock at the island of Mykonos.

Edwin ate very little of his food and kept his contribution to the conversation to a minimum. His mind and thoughts were filled with the contents of the package. The other two couples that had been assigned to their table were from Scotland and Australia. The couple from Scotland was on the cruise celebrating their fiftieth wedding anniversary. Their children and grandchildren felt they needed the time away from his

business. He owned a company that made parts for washing machines
and dryers. The Australian couple taught classes at the university. He
was an engineering professor, and she was a business professor. They
needed a break from work and decided to take the Mediterranean cruise.
It was a good thing that each of them was so engrossed with the others
experiences on the cruise and their love for their occupation that no
one noticed that he was a nonparticipating entity. Every once in a while
Edwin would either laugh with the others or offer a nod of the head, but
a contributor he was not.

As dinner was coming to a close, Jennifer invited the couples to come
to the jazz concert with them. The Australian couple declined for they
were going to a poetry reading session/open mike night. The Scottish
couple accepted the invitation.

When Edwin heard this, he was wondering if his plan would work,
for he did not have a plan B.

Neither plan A or B was a factor, because Edwin was totally involved
in the jazz concert. Jennifer had introduced him to jazz while they were
dating at Brown and he fell in love with the rhythmic movement of this
form of music. In fact he had begun buying up all of the old school jazz
artist as well as the now contemporary and smooth jazz sounds. His
favorite jazz instruments were all varieties of the saxophone, the acoustic
guitar and the piano. Some of his favorite jazz artists are Dave Koz, Rick
Braun, Mindi Abair, Kirk Whalum, Dave Brubeck, Dave Sanborn, Wes
Montgomery, Gerald Albright, Candy Dulfer, Spyro Gyra, Joe Sample,
and many others. In fact the family theater in their home houses more
variety of jazz music inclusive of the old 45s, albums, 8-tracks, cassettes,
and CDs. The room also included signed autographs of the jazz musicians
he had met throughout the years. He was proud of his collection and
showed it off when the opportunity arose. Their love for jazz can now be
seen in their children's love for a variety of music. Michael is more into
the smooth jazz sound, William loves smooth jazz and contemporary jazz,
and Bria goes from classics, R & B, to smooth jazz.

Not once did Edwin feel or try to fake tiredness for he was so into the
concert that he was not ready for it to be over. He was so wired that he
knew he did not need a plan to stay up and read some more of his father's
soul cleansing document. He could not wait to pick up the package.

As the Langleys said good night to the Millers, Edwin's mind was on
the document he had placed on the nightstand.

Once he entered the suite he immediately undressed and put on the bottoms to his pajamas. He picked up the document and made his way to the Chaise in the sitting room of the suite.

He saw Jennifer coming out of the bathroom wearing a very beautiful and sexy white gown.

"Are you coming to bed or have you decided to sleep on the chaise?"

"Yes, I'll be there in a minute but I have such a high from the jazz concert and I wanted to read a little more of my father's soul stirring confession."

"Don't stay up too late for we dock at the Mykonos islands shortly and the tours start at 10:00 AM. You need to be refreshed and ready to do some sightseeing. Remember we stay on the Mykonos islands for two or three days."

"I'll be fine Jen, I just want to finish reading about Elizabeth, Helga and Adolph, It seems like it is a very weird or interesting relationship." When I get to a place I can stop, then I will come and snuggle up with you."

Jen smile for she knew just where he was and if she knew her husband this was not going to be a good stopping place for him.

Edwin open up the document, he was curious as to who was the father of Helga's baby. He knew Adolph was more than infatuated with her, but marrying Elizabeth would be the smart thing since she had money and was interested in his scientific experiments.

Edwin looked at the clock. It was close to 3:00 AM, and he had learn more than he wanted to about the Hamburg family. It seemed that all of Adolph's offspring came from the union between him and Helga. Although they were never married he and Helga lived as husband and wife. They were very nice to Elizabeth. However, she knew Adolph would never marry her; thus she became weak and sick from a broken heart. She was very much in love with Adolph but realized after his third child with Helga that his heart belonged only to her.

Up to this point he still had not made a connection between the Hamburg family and his mother Katerina. His eyes were tired and he needed to get some sleep because tomorrow would be a day filled with touring the Mykonos Islands. In fact since they were going to be there two or three days, the four of them had booked a reservation at one of the five star hotels so they could also tour the island on their own.

He crawled into bed beside his lovely wife; she stirred for a moment, moved closer to him, and continued with her sleep. At this point he knew he had been the luckiest man in the world by marrying Jennifer Dusett, now Langley. Even in her sleep at fifty-five years old, she was still the prettiest and sexiest woman alive.

While reading a magazine on the flight over to Greece, he came across a picture of Jane Fonda who was in her seventies. The article noted how young and beautiful she looked. From the photo it showed how she had maintained not only her weight but also her ageless smile. This is how he pictured his beloved Jennifer. As he drifted off to sleep, he dreamed that the same article would be written about his lovely wife, Jennifer, the famous civil rights attorney.

On day one of the tour, the couples explored some of the rustic towns observing different styles of wind mills and whitewashed housed. In each of the towns visited they did some shopping for their children, grandchild or grandchildren. Several packages were purchased for Aunt Onnie. Each of them had fun tasting the special cuisines prepared by the Greek chefs. At the end of the tour, the couples decided to eat at their hotel and visit some of the nightspots the hotel concierge had suggested.

At the nightspots, Edwin had not thought about the package until he saw a young man who could have been his half brother. The young man if he had been a young lady has some similar facial features of his mother. He closed his eyes and visualized the face of his mother as he remembered from his childhood. When she was ill, he would often say in his mind, why God would give such a beautiful woman such a deadly and dreadful disease. He had taken away his sister, wasn't that enough? Why would he bring so much grief to the Langley family? As he turned to take another look at the young man he standing very close to their table. His could make out some of the French words spoken by the young man and his friends and he heard his name Jacques DeBeaux. He wanted to speak to the young man, but did not want to make a scene. He hoped that he would become visible again before they decide to leave.

As the couple began to leave the one nightspot and venture to another one, he saw the young man to the left of him with several friends. It seemed eerie that all of them communicated in the French language. Something funny must had been relayed to the group for when the young man smiled, he reminded him of his mother's. He began to wonder if this was a relative of his living in France that his father would make known in the document or maybe he was reading more into the facial features of the young man. Maybe he was so involved with the document that his mind was playing tricks on him.

His mother has often spoken of the children by her father and his wife. In fact he and his family had visited his family in France prior to his mother's demise. However, he and his father lost contact shortly after his mother's death. Could this young man be a distant relative on his mother's daddy's side of the family or just a mirage?

Colby pulled him out of his thought zone.

"You know you have no sense of directions. The way to the next nightspot is in front of us and our hotel is behind us. Just one more stop and then back to the hotel for some much needed sleep. We have a long day tomorrow."

"I was just waiting for you to take the lead my man."

After leaving the second nightspot, Edwin and Jennifer prepared for bed; however, the face of the young man Edwin had seen at the nightspot began to haunt him. Even though he thought that he had fallen into a deep sleep after his passionate lovemaking with his wife, out of nowhere he sat straight up in the bed as he saw his mother's face and the face of the young man pass before him. He knew it was a nightmare or a dream but wondered if it had any connection to his father's famous package.

In about two hours this would all be in the past for they were beginning to dock on the Mykonos Islands, part of the Cyclades between the Aegean and the Mediterranean seas. There were several tour attractions that he was beaming to enjoy, thus taking his mind off the package and the young man at the nightspot.

Jennifer turned over and smiled.

"Is it time for us to explore the beautiful terrain and tourist spots of the Mykonos Islands?"

"Yes, it is. I know this island was named for the grandson of Apollo and has some wonderful sites on it and the other small island that make up the Cyclades Islands."

"Well, let's get up. We do not want to be late, or Colby and Danielle will have a few choice words."

The tour on the Mykonos islands and the surrounding small islands was very exciting. The couple explored the beautiful mansions with various colorful balconies and stylish windows in Little Venus, took a short boat over to the island of Delos to see the birthplace of Apollo and

Artemis, relaxing on the beautiful beaches and enjoying the open terrain of the island of Mykonos.

Even though Edwin enjoyed the tours of some of the historical churches, observed the birthplaces of several Greek gods, Edwin's mind began to drift back to the package. He closed his eyes and laid his head on Jennifer's shoulder. There on the beach with the sound of the waves, the song of the birds and the chatter of the people he drifted away into a semiconscious sleep that revealed to him a connection between the young man at the night club and his mother. In fact there they stood before him, Katerina holding her father's hand and the young man sitting at his feet. Right before his mother Katerina was about to speak, he felt someone softly shaking him.

"I guess the breeze from the sea put you into a restful and peaceful sleep. It is time that we leave for the hotel and get ready for dinner and a night out at the Greek theater."

"Do you know what play we are seeing tonight?"

"Yes, the story of a Greek goddess named Clytemnestra or Clytaemnestra, legendary wife of Agamemnon, a Greek warrior. Different stories or voices have been written about this goddess who was the sister of Helen of Troy as well as Castor and Pollux. While her husband was away at war, she began a love affair with another and upon his return she and her lover plotted to kill him."

"This should be an interesting play."

"For what Danielle and I could gather from reading the brief details of the play, it is much more descriptive than her subdued role in Homer's Odyssey."

"I am glad I took my nap earlier so I can be fully awake to enjoy the plot of this play."

Edwin pulled his wife up from the sandy beach, kissed her slight on her lips and they began walking toward their hotel room.

On his way to the room he ran the words "subdued role" over and over in his head. Had his father imagined this reputable heritage due to his disgrace of his marriage vows to Tessa? If he made it up, then why wait until after his death to spring on his offspring.

As he opened the hotel suite and entered after his wife, he was hoping that this play would alter his angry thoughts about his father's lack of diplomacy regarding his extramarital affair and his heritage. The package has aroused some angry feelings he has suppressed for too long.

Edwin awoke so refreshed. He had thoroughly enjoyed the Greek festival and the Play, Clytemnestra. His eyes were not strained from attempting to stay awake for he had been so intrigued with the story line of the play. He could not imagine someone being as evil as the main character Clytemnestra who had plotted with another to kill her husband upon his return from war. He could not imagine living in a world of mistrust and hate that was so vividly displayed in the play.

He smiled, as he walked past the package on his way to the bathroom before meeting the gang for breakfast. He could not wait to bid the others good-bye as they toured other parts of the city. This would give him a free day to indulge in more details of the euphonious package of his father. Maybe my father's intention was to glean a little sanity for himself—not plotting to kill but to make sport of his behavior and to reveal to us how sorrowful he was of his errant ways.

Today was the day that the others would roam the city of Mykonos and buy an assortment of souvenirs for their family and friends. He had expressed to Jennifer that he would stay in the hotel and read some more of the package. He also wanted to check on a merger that his sons were coordinating while he was away. Not that he did not trust their judgment, but wanted to make sure this was an appropriate and solid business move for the company.

While the women exited the hotel for souvenir shopping, Colby had set up a tee off time for him and some of the men he had met aboard the ship. Edwin made his way to the hotel reading lounge that overlooked the seas and provided a breathtaking portrait of the Mykonos islands, its captivating shoreline, ornate and colorful houses built on the cliff, the sapphire water, the white sand on the beaches and the nearby beauty of the other islands that made up the Cyclades Islands. This breathtaking scene would help him concentrate on the contents.

Edwin settled in a chair whereby he could scope all of this beauty with an easy movement of the head. His real reason for choosing this location was to obtain beauty and privacy during the merger meeting and an atmosphere that would keep him engaged with the reading of the package.

As he listened in on the merger meeting adding his approval or asking pointed questions for clarification, his cheeks seemed to puff up quite a bit for he was proud of the research work his sons had completed to sell the merger to the board. Although it was a small manufacturing company, their products and business structure would easily acquiesce into theirs and with increased production the product would be a hot item for the millennial generation. He had to chuckle, his sons had been listening to him and learning from him. At this point he was a proud daddy. The board had decided to read the proposal and arrange for a meeting the next two weeks to give their decision. He would be back in Charleston at that time and would be able to discuss the proposal with each individual board member. This way he would be able to sway those who might not be feeling the merger.

The contents took him to a place where he did not want to go or did not believe. He was aware of the female daughter of Helga and Adolphus but like the rest of their children had been told not to return to the farm but assimilate into the world of the majority.

Lillian had gone to New York to work as an actress; there she had married someone by the name of Petersen. Petersen probably did not know her heritage therefore, she returned to Hamburg to have the child. A baby girl name Hettie Petersen. Lillian left the nine month old child with her aged parents and assured them she would return for her soon.

Edwin sat straight up, he could hear his mother telling him, "Your grandmother's name is Hettie Peterson, your great-grandmother is Lillian Peterson, and your great-great-grandmother is Helga Malveaux-DuPont." He had heard this all of his life, but this is the first time the ethnicity of his bloodline was revealed to him.

He had to reread this for he missed something in the translation or the content. Each time he read it and it had to have been five or six times, he came to the same conclusion. He was not the pure Irish, French, and German descendant he had so often spoke of to his children and other who knew him. There was another lineage he was just made aware of: the seed of the Nile.

Edwin now was baffled, why is his father speaking to him about his heritage from the grave? Was he trying to shield me from the evil tongues of American or was it to save face with his business world colleagues?

Out loud to no one in particular, Edwin stated, "My lineage is not what I had envisioned. Although the land is a blend of many, many ethnicities, I see myself as an imposter, not telling my wife, my friends or my colleagues what blood truly runs in my family."

A tear begin to run down Edwin's face, he wiped it with the back of his hand. All of a sudden it hit him; Jennifer read it first. What does she think of me now and our marriage? Will she apply for a divorce once we return to the states?

Again, not speaking to anyone in particular, "She deals with this daily. Maybe I am just overreacting. I am angry with my father, if he knew this almost forty years ago, why is he now revealing it to me? Does he expect me to be the bearer of this news?"

He looked at the package; he was almost three quarters finished with the contents. He wondered what else would be in the last quarter pages to upset him. He felt like throwing the package in the water for it to never surface again. What harm would that do? Then he, too, could conceal all evilness and hatred from his family once they become aware of their true lineage.

In his mind he knew he could not destroy the contents of this package for it held the hidden secrets and origin of his strength, power, endurance, stamina and bloodline.

He picked up the package and slammed it loudly against the table in front of him. The impact was so great that it caused the lunch dishes to fall off the table onto the floor of the hotel.

This information would haunt him forever, and trying to speak to Jen about it or discussing it with his family would not be easy. Yes, not only had he seen success on both sides of the family, but would this revealing document shake the foundation and the confidence that had made this family connection and business solid and successful. Could this information become an adverse factor against the stability of this family?

In spite of the number of colleagues he and his father had assisted, people may use this information to plant obstacles, traps and other circumstances to upstage their business standing in the global market.

Another tear fell from his eye, was he made of the same stamina as his father, his grandfather and his great-grandmother? Could he endure any adversity that may arise in his business and personal world? Yes, he could and the knowledge of his bloodline will not affect these standings. As we look at the global market, there are many ethnicities who have honed out them a very productive portion of the global market. Diversity is very prevalent in the global market.

Again, he picked up the package and looked at the beautiful white sand on the beaches below. "Why, Dad, are you putting such a heavy burden on me. I am not sure if I will be able to fully grasp what is happening to me."

I must finish this before I get back to the states. We have a couple of days here before we sale back to Athens and board the plane for South Carolina. South Carolina, the state where the Confederate flag still flies on the capitol grounds, the state that still believes in white supremacy, the state that has passed laws to keep other ethnicities from experiencing justice and equality, and the state that has embraced my forefathers and their businesses! How will they treat me now? Will they continue to support my cause and my businesses? My family has built a large conglomerate of businesses will they try to dismantle them and destroy us?

"Dad, what have you done to me? Why is it important during the twenty-first century for me to know my true heritage? Will this knowledge be effective in attempts to reinstate equality and justice to all mankind? I need some answers."

The courtship between his grandmother and the French gentleman was quite a story. Although he imagine that his grandfather, the French gentleman love his grandmother, it was during a time that she could only be his mistress and not his wife. His best recourse to ensuring his daughter, my mother Katerina would be provided the appropriate, skills and etiquette to blend into the land of America was to allow his sister to rear her. My great-grandmother was reluctant, but agreed to the arrangement.

My anger grew more and more as I learned about other factors surrounding my mother, my grandmother, and my other relatives: two aunts and an uncle. As I closed my eyes and visualize Rosa, she and my mother had so much in common. She looked like my mother, she had mannerisms like my mother and now I realized why my father and I would always bounce ideas off Rosa to ascertain her train of thought. It was as though my mother was speaking to me through Rosa. I wonder now if that was the same way my father felt?

Edwin then turned his attention to his first cousin, Jacob. He had the same business drive as his mother, he was able to take the simplest of ideas about landscaping and turn them into a floral masterpiece.

He chuckled at how efficient his aunt, yes his aunt Rosa has been able to run their household with great efficiency, poise and professionalism. Her eldest son was now employed by one of our technology businesses and yes it was his voice that was so pronounced today on the conference call.

"Wow, business savvy does run deep in our bloodline. It amazes me how the world views several ethnicities as a negative, and I see how the ingrained wisdom, knowledge, endurance, and stamina of a people have helped build strong and productive global markets. Would someone who has a warped mine filled with prejudice, racism, and supremacy conjure up ways to destroy a viable business just because the owner does not look like them?"

In his mind the answer was yes, because of the years sitting around the board table before and after his father's death, he saw those same actions and ideas too many times. However, it was his father who often brought to light these adverse actions and thoughts to the forefront and did not allow them to taint his business or his business growth and directions.

With his eyes watching the waves as they flowed back and forth against the outline of the Greek terrain, he whispered to no one in particular, "Dad, I am not sure if I have the same savvy and makeup as you. I will need your guidance and directions to help me continue in your giant footsteps. I do not know how I will be able to weather the giant waves that are coming my way. I know my children grew up in a diverse world and do not view others as the old establishment does. I know I can lean on them."

Again he looked down at the package picked it up and flung it against the wall of the room. He was angry, tired, bewildered and upset with his father. Why would he leave such a heavy task to him? He did not know in what direction to take this. Yes he had his beloved Jen who worked in this area on a daily basis, his friend Colby that even with all of the obstacles hurled at him daily, he was able to maintain and grow his father's business, but did he have the same tenacity and strength each of them displayed professionally and personally.

Then there was Danielle, Colby's wife, how certain groups in the state of Massachusetts fought so hard to keep her from being the director and CEO of the children's wing of Memorial Hospital. I have good examples, but do I have the internal strength to combat the darts of evilness, hatred, injustice, lies, etc., of those who would want me to fail once my true identity is revealed.

I love my family and my friend, but I know that I will need more than them, I will need professional help to let me know I am as capable as my father and my other ancestors. I, too, have the bloodline and endurance to warn off adverse words and actions, continue the course of my heritage and show the world that no matter what man tries to do to halter my success, it is ingrained in me and will not dissipate.

Edwin walked over to the place where the package had fallen. He looked at the many pictures that had been dislodged from the package. He was not aware of this one photo, but it was a picture of his mother, his father, his grandfather and he on the island of Maui. In the picture he was about three or four sitting on his father's shoulder and adorned in a superman's costume. He saw it so clearly his hands were extended straight up in the air and each were form into a perfect fist symbolizing strength, tenacity and endurance. Yes, he may have the DNA, but some source will have to help him bring them out.

His mind wandered to the day he met the clinical psychologist, Dr. Shannon McCullers. He had placed her business cards in his case. Once he gets back to the state, his first call will be to Dr. McCullers, not for his business, but for his personal life.

He had at least another hour of reading before he met up with his traveling companions.

The story began to take an interesting twist away from his mother and concentrating more on Tessa. Not until now was he made aware of the number of miscarriages Tessa had experience nor had his father ever shown any signs that she caused each of them.

In his soul, he felt this would be the part of the package where his father would cry out in desperations regarding his extra-marital affair and his treatment of Tessa. No matter how many people confess they don't entirely believe in God and heaven, it is ironic how many of them attempt to clean up their lives right before death visits hoping to be able to see the face of the Lord and enter the heavenly realm and not the hell of damnation. His father and Tessa attended church faithfully and contributed handsomely to the Presbyterian Church, but were they spiritual and true believers in His word. Only my father and Tessa knew the answer to that question.

As Edwin continued to read, he knew his father would clearly provide the reasons why he felt the miscarriages were not induced by nature but by Tessa. His father gave a vivid account of Tessa's relationship with her parents and how her father always considered he was far superior than his wife.

Once he finished his father's account of Tessa's false miscarriages, he moved on to the section of the package where his father revealed was the real reason for Tessa's actions. He smiled for it was Rosa that had given him the proof that Tessa was hiding her true heritage from him.

He looked up from the pages and wondered if Tessa's falsified birth certificates for her and her mother were still in her old room. When he gets back to Charleston he will consult with Rosa, even though she had retired and only came to assist when asked.

From his father's writing it appeared that he also knew the reason why her mother was so thrilled for him to marry her and why her father who was a senior manager in the textile portion of their corporate conglomeration was not so kind to his wife or to Tessa.

Tessa's mother and father were born in a city that no longer exists, Hamburg, South Carolina the same one where my mother was born. It appeared from my father's account there had been a special type of Animal and human breeding done in that city on a farm owned by my great-great-grandfather Adolph that was unknown to the other inhabitants of the city. Since real birth certificates were not recorded until the early 1930s, it was very easy for Tessa to change her and her mother's ethnicity. The original paper of her mother's birth had an R for her ethnicity and Tessa's had been left blank.

This was too much for him to comprehend. How many others are walking among us not really know their true ethnicity? Can there be a large part of the population where their ancestors left out just a small portion of their heritage and DNA composition? It was interesting to finally discover that there had been a population of people born in Hamburg, South Carolina, who had been given a specific ethnicity due to inbreeding of other humans. I wonder what happened to my mother's great-uncles who were told to never return to the farm and find their own niche in life. I may have to do what my father did, find their offspring.

Edwin's head began to hurt and never before had he had one so intense. He needed to find an Aleve, an Advil or something to calm his pulsating temples. They had one more day on the island before returning to Athens to board the plane for home. This had been a trip to remember: the economic disaster in the Greek countries and then learning of his ancestor that he never knew existed.

As he walked toward his room, not only were his temples pulsating more and more, but just in front of him, he saw a mirage of his past ancestors smiling as though life will often uncover situations that have been buried for years, but don't worry, for life will also give you a way to endure, and the smiles on each of their faces were the evidence.

Edwin stopped by the shop in the hotel to buy some Aleve. In order for him to be a more active member of the vacation adventure he needed to get rid of his headache.

As Jennifer entered her hotel suite, she was surprised to see her husband asleep across the bed. He had not taken the time to remove his clothing. Edwin was fully clothed and in a deep sleep. She noticed on the nightstand the package and an opened bottle of Aleve.

Yes, I am sure learning about his mother's heritage and his father's admission about not feeling guilty all those years regarding his mistress must have shocked his system. What was puzzling was in all the years she had been married to this wonderful man, and no matter how many professional and personal situations that had occurred, he always remained calm. He very seldom to her knowledge had suffered headaches due to certain circumstances.

She walked close to the window facing the sea. Looking over the terrain and not speaking to anyone in particular she stated, "I know you did not expect the cleansing of your soul to have this impact on your son. Why would you leave such a difficult task to me to walk my husband through something you should have shared years ago?"

Jennifer decided to let her husband sleep and not disturb him. She walked over to her purse and removed her cell phone. As she began to dial Danielle's number she saw her husband stir. She slipped into the living room section of the suite.

"Hi, Danielle, Edwin is not feeling well this afternoon so we will miss the planned activities for tonight. Tell Colby, I may need to speak to him later on this evening regarding Edwin's condition."

"Sorry to hear that Jen, even though I am a pediatrician, is there a medical reason for his situation and may I provide some medical assistance?"

"Thanks, Danielle, at the moment, I do not feel he needs any medical assistance. He has taken some Aleve, which indicates he may have a headache or some other type of pain."

"Colby and I may stay in and eat in the hotel's restaurant. We have done a lot during this vacation and we may need to rest before we board the plane for home. I'll call you later on this evening. If you need me please call."

"Thanks, Danielle. I will just have room service send us up a light dinner entrée when Edwin awakes. I will call you later."

Jennifer had experienced these types of situations in her practice, but never in her wildest dreams did she expect her knowledge and expertise would possibly impact her own family. This situation will not require her legal knowledge of one's civil rights, but more of one's knowledge in human behavior and psychological effects. She may have to ask her friend who is a clinical psychologist to help her husband work through this newly learned information.

As she turned around, she could almost see how this knowledge had in less than twenty-four hours placed an element of age and stress on her husband's facial features. If she noticed it on his face, she just imagined how it may have affected his internal organs and his mental state. Again she wondered why William never shared this information with his son. He was such an intelligent man when it came to business savvy. Why did he not have the same understanding of human behavior and how keeping secrets could and would affect them.

"Why did you want to cleanse your soul of some of your not so good behavior in written form instead of orally discussing this with Edwin and me before your demise? Now that you have caused confusion and worry in your son, do you really expect me to be the one to subdue his confusion?"

"Hi Jen, were you speaking to me? How long have I been asleep? I can't believe that my body could be so tired."

"I know and I have already informed Danielle and Colby that we will forgo dining out tonight and order room service. You want to talk about your tiredness?"

"Thanks for taking care of that, I just need some me and you time. What is there to talk about? Tiredness is just tiredness."

"I know you understand my reason for asking, did the contents of the package put you on edge or something different? I know you had an important conference meeting so it could be a combination of both situations."

With ager or arrogance in his voice, Edwin looks at Jen.

"I am not on edge just a little disappointed that my father, the man whom I have looked up to all of these years, elected for years not to tell me about my complete heritage. As a person who has sat at the table of some of the biggest business meetings globally to discuss mergers or buyouts, he could not come clean with his own son on his DNA composition."

"Let's discuss your feelings. Maybe William did not believe it would have such an impact on you or he did not want to broach the subject when you were younger and as you became older and involved in the business, he may have either forgot to discuss it with you or felt with your success there was no need discuss it."

"Jen, this is my life and no matter what, I should have been told. Now that you know, are you having second thought about being my wife?"

"You are the same person I fell in love with over thirty years ago and regardless of your lineage, I would still have chosen you for my husband. What makes you think that I would abandon you now?"

"At this moment, I am just confused. How can I possibly discuss this with my family, with my best friend and I bet Aunt Onnie will have a field's day with this news."

"Edwin, the fabric of the land had changed and people of all ethnicities are among the 1 percent of the richest people of the world. Your DNA will not affect your standing in the business world. Many of your colleagues know you and have come to trust you and your business acumen. This information can remain with the family. You do not need to discuss it with the world. Most of the people in the USA and in other countries are not really sure of their ethnic makeup."

"How can I look at my son William with a straight face especially with my behavior toward Krystal? She is a wonderful lady. The ringing in my head from the chatter of some of my colleagues and social media had me to focus more on her ethnicity and not on who she is as a person. I fear the same will happen to me."

"If you feel this strongly maybe we can have a family discussion with my friend Myrtle Goodsome, the clinical psychologist, to work through the anguish and behavior that you are experiencing."

"Who said I was experiencing anguish and certain behaviors? I am just discussing this with you. I do not want to have a session with your friend, Myrtle or any other psychologist. Right now I am hungry. I need to take a shower and change clothes. Call Danielle and let them know we will meet them in the restaurant for dinner."

Jennifer watched her confused and bewildered husband remove his clothes and make his way to the shower. All she wanted to do at that moment was to hold him like a mother would hold her youngest son who is experiencing the valleys and peaks that life sometimes drops on us. I want to kiss him and let him know that the valleys and peaks of life don't last forever and with determination and patience one can rise above the circumstances of most of life's trial and mishaps.

Instead of running toward her husband to show him that he had her support and love, she picked up her cell phone to call Danielle.

At dinner, I found myself walking lightly around egg shells to avoid Edwin from regressing into the Edwin I observed earlier. I kept the conversation light talking about our trip to Greece and the historical sites we had visited. No one at the table seemed to hone in on Edwin's disposition for he was so loquacious that I began to believe that this afternoon was my dream and not his reality.

As we said our good-byes after dinner and agreed to meet for breakfast prior to sailing back to Athens, Edwin put his arm around my shoulders and suggested an evening stroll along the seashore.

Walking along the seashore must have been his way of showing his love and his sorrow for his afternoon demeanor. He pulled me passionately into his arms and began kissing me with all the grandeur he could muster. His hands caressed the middle of my back and his tongue explored places in my mouth I did not know existed. The moon's light reflected a silhouette of a couple so deeply in love that no wave or sea breeze could pull them apart.

As he slowly released my tongue and lips, he looked deeply into my eyes not with confusion but for want of understanding.

He whispered with all the air he could conjure up, "I love you, Jen, and I need you. No matter how I react to the contents of the package, I need your strength to help me through it. Tell me that your love for me is as strong as the day we first met and you will always be there beside me to help me overcome this internal struggle I am experiencing."

Jennifer placed his face between her hands skillfully kissed him on his lips and with a convincing smile said, "You will always be my first and only love. We will work through your internal struggles together. No words on a piece of paper coined by a dying man who wanted to rid his spirit of his human frailties will never become a wedge that separates us. Our love and our bond are stronger than any conscience-clearing document."

As they walked back to the hotel, she knew that she had a task on her hand, but she also knew she was up to this task. William's package would never destroy her love for Edwin or her family. The next Thirty years will be far greater than the last. Yes, she will experience some great challenges, but she had the will, the strength and the tenacity to be victorious through all of them.

Jennifer caught her husband's hand ad began to swing it with the rhythm of their steps. Jennifer smile for this action reminded her of two lovers walking through the journey of their love encounters.

EPILOGUE

E dwin could not remember the flight back to the states for he must have slept or was in dreamland the entire flight. He was happy to be back in Charleston in the office overlooking Charleston Bay. He felt comfortable just sitting watching the ships and sail boats and the beautiful blue sky. This was his calming haven and it has allowed him to concentrate more on business than on his personal circumstances.

Little did he know that the flick of the TV remote would change his entire mood. As he turned on the TV, there in front of him in living color was the account of the murder of nine (9) people in the Emanuel AME Church during their Bible study. Was he dreaming this or was this happening today at the moment where he was wrestling with his DNA makeup and his heritage. Yes it was real and the young man who shot the nine people did so because of his hatred and prejudice for people who did not look like him.

Was this a sign for him to learn how to heal the internal fight he was having with himself? Was it time for him to make contact with Dr. McCullers? Even though he had told Jen he was fine and would learn to live with his interesting found; he was not totally honest with her since he learned of this delicate piece of his heritage.

He slowly opened up the middle drawer of his beautiful Mahogany Desk and removed a business card. He lifted the phone from the cradle, pressed his private line and dialed the number to Dr. Shannon McCullers.

He wondered how she would feel about helping him realize that the blood of another ethnicity flowed through his vein would not diminish who he was as a person or a business man. Should this information change who he is or should the course of his life continue on the same path where he started?

As he heard the click on the other end of the phone, his first reaction was to hang up, but it was too late.

"Good morning, Dr. Shannon McCullers's office, may I help you."

Edwin cleared his throat to eliminate the fear and the unsure in his voice. "Good morning" flowed in a much cheerful voice than he had anticipated. My name is Edwin Langley and I met Dr. Cullers during a Greek Island cruise. I had discussed the possibilities of using her services for my company. If she is available, I would like to personally speak to her."

"I will check with her to see if she is available. Will you hold the line?"

Edwin's hands were shaking and his lips were quivering. He had never felt so uncomfortable. He had begun working in his father's several businesses at the age of twelve and today at the age of fifty-seven, he is feeling nervousness like never before. He heard the click of the phone.

"Good morning, Mr. Langley, it is good hearing from you. I did not expect you to personally make the call. I expected your director of HR. Is there a particular date and time you would like for me to meet with your HR director and their staff?"

Edwin steadied himself so that when he spoke, it did not sound false. In fact when he was making a point to his colleagues or to another business constituent, he often paced the floor and looked out at the Harbor. Yes this is what he should do.

"Good morning, Dr. McCullers, in addition to your services for my company, there is another matter I would like to discuss, but I would prefer to do so in person."

Edwin walked around the office a couple of times and then sat down in his winged back chair. Was this the right move to make? He was not sure if his secret meeting with Dr. Cullers would offend Jennifer, but at this moment he was being selfish. He wanted to make himself feel whole again without depending upon Jennifer. Yes she had said she loved him in spite of the information she had learn from William Sr. package, but was she truthful with him? Again he looked around his office and took in all of the material gains he and his father had accumulated; however, all the wealth in the world could not erase the confusion and the hurt that was growing inside his very essence.

The appointment had been set for 2:00 PM at Dr. Culler's office in the Charleston area. He had wanted to meet at one of her other satellite offices; however, she felt this one would be perfect for their meeting.

During their conversation, Dr. Cullers had asked about the nature of their meeting, but his answer was so evasive, that even Edwin was unsure about his visit.

He picked up the package that was in the center of his executive desk. This handwritten document from his deceased father has shattered his confidence. Was this his father's intention or is he making more of this information than he should?

It is very odd how the hatred and prejudices against people of different ethnicities in the United States had escalated to an all-time high, how many of the police departments in many of the cities had become more aggressive in the brutal attacks against people of different ethnicities and how lady justice and her laws only worked for certain ethnicities.

Then his father sprang the ultimate upon him, his true DNA or bloodline. He wiped a lone tear from his face, a tear of anger and not of sadness. At fifty-seven years old this should not be happening to me. Is there another message my father is trying to send me. I hope Dr. McCullers will help me figure it out and bring healing to my now confused body.

Edwin placed the package in his business laptop case, looked around his office one more time. As he exited his office, his mind thought about what tomorrow's meeting would bring.

ACKNOWLEDGMENTS

I would like to thank my two special friends Shirley Dixon and Martha Clarke for their encouraging words and directions while I was writing this novel.

To my friend Shirley, thank you for giving me the confidence to let my imagination run freely with the telling of the story of the Hamburg, Langley, and Dusett families. Thank you for telling me daily that it was an interesting storyline that would capture the minds and the imaginations of the readers, thus keeping them interesting in the next plot or action. Thank you, Shirley, for believing in my writing abilities and giving me the extra push to get it completed.

I know that I spoke to you daily about my work, and I am thankful for your daily encouraging words.

Martha, you are some special friend, using your exceptional skills in English and language arts to ensure that the content was easy to understand and comprehend and the grammar was on point. I would like to thank you, Martha, for your encouraging words and your thoughts regarding the plot and the theme of this novel. Your red pen was a blessing! Now I know why many in your profession voice how excellent you were in teaching grammar and language arts to your students. You are much needed in the school system, for the teaching of grammar and language arts is a dying skill.

To my adopted daughter, Dr. Danyelle M. Loveless, thank you for allowing me to quiz you regarding some of the medical conditions in the novel. Now you understand why I often asked you specific questions.

Although my parents, C. A. and Lena M. Thomas, are not physically with me, I felt their presence as I penned each part of this novel. Daddy, I thank you so much for passing on your prolific writing skills to me, your baby daughter. You often wrote speeches for your church audiences and your masonic brothers and love poems to Mom. Not only were you a great writer, but you were also an excellent impromptu speaker.

Mom, thank you for all of your teaching and training, especially in the avenue of reading and writing. One of your methods of punishment was to give me time out and a book. This method solidified my interest in reading. It broadened my knowledge of the world and what was outside my immediate environment. After assigning a book, you would often ask me to write down some interesting facts about it, or you would have specific questions related to the book's content. There were always novels by famous Negro authors, books of inspiration, the English classics, Grimm fairy tales, *National Geographic*, children Bible stories, *The World Encyclopedia*, *Reader's Digest* short stories, magazines, etc.

I thank God each and every day for loaning Dad and you to me, because to me you were the best parents in the world.

To my late Aunt Minnie, the teacher and educator in the family, thank you for correcting my grammar, teaching me how to phonetically pronounce words, and making me use the dictionary to learn the meaning of unfamiliar words.

Minnie L. Smith, an elementary teacher in the Barbour County School System. She played an intricate part and significant role in developing my love for all types of books. She would often bring books home from her classroom for me to read. Her obsession with each of my siblings' ability to speak and write correctly has been a foundational force in the penning of this novel. Thank you, Aunt Minnie, for the English and language arts workbooks I used throughout my formative educational years.

During my years of growing up in Eufaula, Alabama, people of my ethnicity were not allowed to get a library card or check a book out of the library. My mother made sure that our family was surrounded with books; therefore, she either bought them or borrowed them from others in the neighborhood. Two special citizens of Eufaula, Alabama, who gave our family reading materials were the owner of the *Eufaula Tribune* and the wife of the president of the textile mill.

Another person who loaned us books and often bought books for us as a birthday, Christmas, or graduation present was a member of our church. This wonderful lady introduced the children at our church and at our school to a plethora of Negro authors. She would often visit the schools and read poetry to the students. I remember her well for she made poetry come alive as she read it to the schoolchildren or during different events at the church.

To this day I still have several novels and poetry books she personally gave to me. This is the reason why I love to read—my dad, my mom, my aunt Minnie, and our special neighbors and friends. Not only did their actions help improve my visual imagination of the world and other inhabitants, but they made me realize that I, too, could become an author.

One of the most phenomenal statements my dad ever said to me was in the year of his one hundredth birthday. As I opened the door to his home, my father was holding a calculus book that must have belonged to one of his six children. After I hugged him and placed the luggage in my room, I came back to where he was sitting and asked him, "Do you understand how to work the problems in that book?"

He looked at me with a big smile on his face and answered, "No, but if I continue to read and study it daily, I know I will understand the contents and how to work the problem." I smiled for it was my father who helped me understand the dynamics of how to work seventh-grade word problems.

To all of my book club members in the states of California, Georgia, Ohio, and Indiana, thank you for accepting me as the editor of your newsletter. I am sure many of you never read the contents, but it gave me great pleasure finding topics to write on, summarizing our monthly meetings, providing inspirational thoughts, and reminding us of our next big event. This task helped me hone my gift from God, and I am glad he used me in this capacity.

Thanks to my nephew Brian Lawrence of Red Lion Graphic Art Company for designing my book cover.